CU00693295

The Grand Alliance

Blood on the Stars XI

Jay Allan

ISBN: 978-1-946451-12-5

Books by Jay Allan

Flames of Rebellion Series
(Published by Harper Voyager)
Flames of Rebellion
Rebellion's Fury

The Crimson Worlds Series
Marines
The Cost of Victory
A Little Rebellion
The First Imperium
The Line Must Hold
To Hell's Heart
The Shadow Legions
Even Legends Die
The Fall

Crimson Worlds Refugees Series
Into the Darkness
Shadows of the Gods
Revenge of the Ancients
Winds of Vengeance
Storm of Vengeance

Crimson Worlds Successors Trilogy
MERCS
The Prisoner of Eldaron
The Black Flag

Crimson Worlds Prequels
Tombstone
Bitter Glory
The Gates of Hell
Red Team Alpha

Join my email list
at www.jayallanbooks.com

List members get publication announcements and special bonuses throughout the year (email addresses are never shared or used for any other purpose). Please feel free to email me with any questions at jayallanwrites@gmail.com. I answer all reader emails

For all things Sci-Fi,
join my interactive Reader Group here:

facebook.com/groups/JayAllanReaders

Follow me on Twitter @jayallanwrites

Follow my blog at www.jayallanwrites.com

www.jayallanbooks.com
www.crimsonworlds.com

Books by Jay Allan

Blood on the Stars Series
Duel in the Dark
Call to Arms
Ruins of Empire
Echoes of Glory
Cauldron of Fire
Dauntless
The White Fleet
Black Dawn
Invasion
Nightfall
The Grand Alliance

Andromeda Chronicles
(Blood on the Stars Adventure Series)
Andromeda Rising

The Far Stars Series
Shadow of Empire
Enemy in the Dark
Funeral Games

Far Stars Legends Series
Blackhawk
The Wolf's Claw

Portal Wars Trilogy
Gehenna Dawn
The Ten Thousand
Homefront

Also by Jay Allan
The Dragon's Banner

Chapter One

1,200,000 Kilometers from CFS Tarsus
Sigma Vegaron System
Year 320 AC

"Gray Wolf Nine, tighten that formation, now! You're Seven's wingman, and that means you keep up and cover his flank." Stanton Hayes was a veteran, at least by the standards of the raiding force currently closing on the Hegemony convoy. That designation was relative these days—a large part of Hayes's claim to elite status was merely the fact that he had graduated the Academy before the White Fleet had returned from its ultimately disastrous mission, bringing with it the Hegemony and a war like none that had come before.

There was more to that than simply the historical notation. Hayes had completed the entire Academy course, and his class had been the last to graduate before the curriculum had been accelerated to feed graduates more quickly into the battle lines.

To the pilots who had survived the last war against the Union, and racked up countless kills in the process, Hayes was a journeyman at best. The fact that his fighter still flew devoid of any of the marks pilots used to track the fighters they'd defeated denied him access to the truly elite rankings of the Confederation's fighter corps.

It wasn't fair, of course. The current war, the war in which he'd made his bones, was without fighter duels, completely absent the massive dogfights that had played such crucial roles in prior conflicts. The Hegemony was a deadly enemy, larger and more advanced than any on the Rim, and its invasion had taken the Confederation to the brink of the abyss. Its capital was occupied, and hundreds of its warships had been destroyed in continued desperate—yet mostly futile—attempts to stop the onslaught.

But the Hegemony didn't have fighters.

That string of defeats had finally ended in the bloody space around Craydon. The Confederation, and its allies from around the threatened Rim, had held against the enemy, and the Hegemony fleet had retreated for the first time since the war began. The enemy still held the capital at Megara, of course, and numerous other vital systems, but the Confederation had managed to hang on to most of the Iron Belt. Those worlds had the production to sustain the war effort, and hope of eventual victory.

For now.

"I'm in tight, Commander. Less than two hundred kilometers." The voice on the comm was high-pitched, tentative. Doug Velet was a sparkling new ensign, as raw as they came. Hayes had struggled to remember the names of all the new pilots cycling through his wing. The newbs, raw and rushed through training to feed the war's butcher bill, died so quickly that it was hard sometimes to memorize their names. Velet's was firmly in his mind, however, because the rookie was the shakiest of the newest batch of baby pilots dumped in his lap.

"Two hundred kilometers? You might as well be back at Craydon, having a snack and waiting for the battle report to come in. If you're not under a hundred kilometers, you ain't a wingman, you got that? Now, tuck in there and hold your formation!" Hayes knew the wingman's role had more or less disappeared in the Hegemony War. Without enemy interceptors to worry about, it just wasn't all that important a tactical element. But the new pilots were half trained, at best, and sloppiness in one area of doctrine spread to another. It was what Hayes knew, what he'd been taught, and he was determined to shape up the unprepared pilots he commanded…before every last one of them managed to get himself killed.

"Yes, Commander…"

Hayes didn't like the sound of Velet's response. It was soft. Shaky. He knew the pilot was well aware of where he should be. He understood how difficult it was to maintain position when your ship was moving at almost one percent of light speed, but going easy on the rookie would be no kind of favor. The enemy might not have interceptors, but they had become increasingly adept at anti-bomber tactics, and their escort cruisers and frigates had developed into war machines deadly to the attacking squadrons.

Velet—and his comrades—had to get one hell of a lot sharper in their Lightning craft than they were now. Or they would all die.

It was that stark, and that simple.

"Listen up, all of you…we're moving into the defensive perimeter. These bastards don't have fighters of their own, but that doesn't mean they won't blast you to atoms if you aren't damned careful." They were likely to blow away a good number of Hayes's ships whether his people were careful or not. But they didn't need to hear *that*.

"Stay tight and keep at those evasive maneuvers. You rely completely on the nav computer, and I'll be back aboard writing 'I'm sorry to inform you' letters to your folks. And I hate writing those damned things!" It was a reminder Hayes had made so often that he couldn't stand hearing himself say it again. It seemed impossible that his pilots didn't know what he wanted them to do…yet he'd watched dozens of them fly right into the thickest enemy fire with nothing but canned AI evasive routines to save them from getting blasted to plasma. The results had been depressingly similar.

More letters to write.

So, he kept at them. It was all he could think to do.

He looked up at his main screen. The scanner readings were getting tighter as his strike force moved closer to their targets. He'd been leading attacks on enemy shipping for over a year, since just after Admiral "Sledgehammer" Winters had led the daring strike on the enemy support fleet at Megara, destroying over ninety percent of the Hegemony fleet's logistics and supply capability. The attack hadn't forced the enemy to withdraw, but it had stolen their massive logistics advantage. They were now dependent on conventional supply lines in a way they hadn't been before, and that had provided the Confederation and its allies with something they'd previously lacked in the war: a weakness to exploit.

The Hegemony command was aware of just how crucial their supply lines had become. The size of the escort contingents attached to the convoys had steadily increased, and with each successive raid the Rim led, their defensive tactics improved.

There was a line of two dozen enemy escorts just ahead of Hayes's incoming bombers, bristling with the latest in Hegemony point defense weaponry. They were organized in a convex line, directly between his wing and the freighters that were his targets. Any attempt to change vectors to avoid the defenders would involve massive thrust, and far too much time. The slower-moving cruisers and frigates would simply adjust their own positions, far more easily than his squadrons could, and position themselves astride any modified approach vector. There was no choice save the obvious—and very unpleasant—one. His wing would go right through the escorts.

Worse, they would take all the Hegemony ships could

throw at them without fighting back. His ships carried the new cluster bombs, which gave them half a dozen shots instead of the single one a torpedo provided, but even that was a limitation on the punch his birds packed. There were over a hundred freighters and tankers lined up beyond the first line of defenders, and it would take every bomb his ships carried, and then some, to cut them down.

Or at least to destroy enough of them to strike a serious blow to the Hegemony war effort. The war had been at a stalemate for over a year, ever since the bloodbath that had gone into the records as the Battle of Craydon. Hayes knew, as he suspected did Admirals Barron and Winters—and every other competent officer in the fleet—that putting a crimp in the enemy's supply chain was crucial to any strategy to gain the upper hand. Only then could they begin pushing the Hegemony out of Confederation space, rather than just stopping their advance.

He watched as the scanners updated, the warning lights along the top of his panel blinking yellow to alert him that he was approaching enemy firing range. He could feel his body tighten, and as much as he tried to take deep, controlled breaths, he found himself gasping raggedly. He was scared. It was something he'd never admit to his pilots, but he'd come far enough along his own personal trail of development to acknowledge it to himself. He was an elite pro, a hardcore veteran to the inexperienced Lightning jocks he was leading into the fight. But he knew, inside, where his deepest thoughts resided, that he was only a middling pilot. Perhaps with the talent to become more, but lacking the serious battle experience needed to match the grim warriors flying under Jake Stockton's command in Craydon.

You may not be one of them, *but what you're doing here is important, too. In some ways, every bit as important…*

His eyes caught the first flashes on his screen, enemy defensive fire coming in. He'd already been deep into evasive maneuvers, but as he saw the incoming fire—and watched the first of his ships vaporized by it—he moved the throttle even more wildly, his ship shaking all around in a desperate attempt to fool the Hegemony targeting computers.

Six minutes.

That was how long it would take his fighters to get past the Hegemony defensive line. Assuming the enemy escorts didn't come about as his squadrons flew by, following the bombers in toward their targets at full thrust. The Hegemony forces had done that in the last raid, a new development in their defensive tactics. It had cost him an extra dozen ships at least, and seriously cut down on the effectiveness of the strike.

He angled his thrust to the side, an abrupt, jerky motion that slid him away from most of the incoming fire. It was half a response to what he was seeing on his screen…and half wild guess, or intuition, depending on how one viewed such things. Two more of his people were gone, victims of fire they hadn't managed to evade as skillfully as he had.

At least the rest of them are putting some effort in…

Watching his people die was a form of personal hell, but there was one good thing to it. Nothing spurred the others to avoid incoming fire like watching their friends and comrades blasted to plasma.

Hayes didn't like placing a value on the deaths of his men and women, or seeking gain from such losses, but if he could lose five to save ten, it was a devil's bargain he would make every time.

Ten fewer letters to write…

* * *

"They're through the forward line, Captain. They'll be in launch range in…four minutes thirty seconds." Bart Tarleton's voice was a deep and powerful bass that almost rattled the looser components on *Tarsus*'s bridge.

"Acknowledged, Commander."

Sonya Eaton sat in the command chair, a perch positioned not quite in the middle of the vessel's irregular-shaped bridge, but close enough. *Tarsus* had begun her life as a freight-carrying ship, and she'd served in that capacity for close to sixty years…until someone high up in Confederation logistics came up with the brilliant idea of converting freighters into something new, inventively dubbed the escort carrier.

It seemed like a joke at first thought, and from the perspective of an officer commanding eight of the slow and fragile ships, a pretty bad one at that. But fighters were the Confederation's—*no,* she reminded herself, *the Grand Alliance's*—greatest strength. The swift attack craft were the only thing the enemy couldn't match, and Sonya knew, as did everyone, that the war would have been lost long before without the desperate and repeated attacks of the wings.

For as long as Confederation history recorded such things, fighters and bombers had been based on battleships, huge vessels, heavily armored and bristling with weapons. Until ten months before, that was, when the first two modified freighters blasted out from the Craydon shipyards and made their way—slowly—to launch a strike on the Hegemony supply line.

Neither of those ships returned, though one, at least, had made it about halfway back before her crew, unable to repair her damaged reactor, had been forced to ditch her. The lessons of that inauspicious beginning had been well used, however, and Eaton had to admit that her eight ships, though slow and with hulls as thin as paper by comparison to real warships, packed some serious punch. Each one had eighteen Lightnings crammed into spaces that had once held cargoes of various kinds, and one hundred and forty-four armed bombers made up a strike force no Hegemony convoy could ignore…even if all but a handful of her pilots were bright green, readier for a few more years of training than for combat.

That didn't matter, of course. Not in this war. The Confederation was fighting for its life, for its very existence, and the enemy culture was so alien that anything short of outright triumph was unthinkable. She regretted sending unprepared pilots to their deaths, but she also knew she'd strap toddlers still sucking their thumbs into those birds, too, if that was the difference between victory and defeat.

Sonya herself wasn't even close to experienced enough for the command she now held. She wore the platinum and gold striped eagle on her shoulders, the insignia of perhaps the least-used rank in the navy. The "fleet captain" designation had been thought up way back during the Second Union War, likely in the dark days before the original Admiral Barron had led the battered Confederation forces to resurgence and victory. Its purpose then had likely been very much the same as it was now…to signify a level of command for an officer promoted far too early to carry even a commodore's single star.

Eaton fit that bill, completely. She'd spent years as an executive officer, serving under Tyler Barron, and later her sister. She'd gotten her own command only a couple years before, and she was the first to admit that she had no place suddenly commanding a fleet of sixteen warships, not to mention an entire strike wing of bombers.

She'd served with distinction, acquitted herself well—even her naturally humble psyche could acknowledge that. But she held her rank for one reason, the single factor that pushed officers up the order of battle more quickly and surely than accomplishment.

Casualties.

There was a vacuum at the top ranks of the Confederation command structure, one that nearly five years of war had created and continued to expand with each gruesome battle. Eaton had been swept up to fill one of those holes and, like many other capable officers, found herself somewhere she shouldn't yet have been—not for years, if ever.

Her eyes were fixed on the main display, on the scrolling figures along the left side, watching as the AI updated the casualty reports. Eight of her Lightnings were gone, and another six were damaged. Two of those were pushing ahead, struggling to complete their attack runs. The other four were frantically trying to make their way back toward the base ships, squeezing out every bit of thrust their battered engines could produce. They were sitting ducks, of course.

She tried not to focus on that, though. Losses were irrelevant, certainly at that moment. Damaged—or destroyed—ships were of no use to the attack, and that was all that mattered. It was cold, almost fiendish to think that way of spacers who had died carrying out her orders, but the war left no room for warmth, or even basic morality. It was a struggle to the death, and there could be no letup, no hesitation to do what had to be done. If the enemy got enough supplies through to Megara, they could hold on to the Confederation's capital…and to the simpering, collaborationist rump Senate. The politicians' cringing proclamations were making their way across the Confederation to worlds that were still resisting the enemy, urging, ordering, haranguing them to lay down their arms and heed the surrender documents the craven politicians had signed.

Never!

Eaton couldn't speak for everyone in the Confederation, but she had a good idea that most of the fleet's personnel, at least, felt the same way she did. No surrender. Not now, not ever. She would fight, her people would fight—and as many of them would die as need be—but they would never yield, never end the battle.

If the Hegemony wanted to win the war, they would have to kill her first…and Tyler Barron and Clint Winters, and the thousands who followed them to battle. The Confederation was battered, but it wasn't beaten yet, not by a long shot.

She watched as Stanton Hayes led his ships into the maw of the enemy's second line, his lead birds launching their cluster bombs as they completed their attack runs.

No, no surrender…not by a long shot…

Chapter Two

"Senator Garrison, I am extremely disappointed in the effectiveness of your proclamations. It seems the Confederation citizens care very little what you and your colleagues have to say…at least outside of the areas our armed forces control." Chronos was wearing his finest military uniform, an almost absurd creation, one he despised for its foolish ostentation. The garment was light gray, almost a shimmering silver, and resplendent with the decorations and badges of rank one might expect from the eighth most perfect human alive. It might have served to bolster ego and morale for one who lacked the quiet confidence Chronos had always possessed, but he found it unnecessary and, quite simply, stupid.

Appearing in full uniform was a rare gesture, and one with a very definite purpose: to remind the politician standing before him that he commanded several million Kriegeri, fierce warriors all, and each one of them ready to follow his every command without question. Even if that order was to gut Garrison like a fish destined for his dinner plate.

Ready? Most of them would be thrilled if I gave that order.

Chronos knew his warriors, most raised from birth for military careers, detested the craven Senators and other Confederation politicians. These men and women crawled before them, and even assisted in the battle against their own soldiers. All to save themselves, and to preserve whatever scraps of their power and privilege they could.

"Are you certain, Master Chronos, that the proclamations were delivered past the lines of the traitors still in arms, and to the people, who love and respect the Senate?" Garrison's voice was a strange combination of fear and defiance, as if his gutlessness was struggling with his need to blame someone else for his own failures.

Chronos was as repelled by Garrison as his soldiers were, probably more so, but practicality was his first order of business, and he was willing to exploit them if they could be useful. He had bought them surprisingly cheaply, with simple promises of physical safety and comfort, plus some farcical pretenses of continued influence and power.

"I am quite certain, Senator, though I need not even consider such distant destinations as other systems. Your declarations have done little to quiet the residual resistance even here on Megara. Where we do not employ force of arms and violent sanctions, the people rise up and oppose us. It would appear you and your colleagues have been wholly unable to deliver on your promises. I wonder now, if I should repudiate the guarantees I provided you."

Chronos found it amusing to watch the politician's warring reactions of terror and indignation. Garrison had enjoyed many years of political power and prestige, and the man was no doubt accustomed to being pandered to and humored, despite the fact that he appeared to have served no useful purpose at all.

"Master Chronos, I…I am…"

"There is no need for argument, Senator. My word is my word—apparently unlike yours." Chronos still was not entirely sure he *would not* change his mind, but for the moment, he did not feel it would serve him to punish the politician. "It is my fault anyway, for failing to investigate your claims. I have bought something that proved to be useless, and will have to exercise more caution next time."

The politician shuffled his feet and looked as though he was about to speak, but Chronos waved his arm. "No, Senator, no more. Leave me. Now." His voice hardened. The sight of the politician—a traitor to his own people and an utter failure at it to boot—was making him sick. He flashed a glance toward one of the Kriegeri standing along the far wall. The soldier moved forward, but the Senator took the hint first, and turned and walked quickly toward the door.

Chronos sighed softly, making an effort to keep it to himself. A Master, especially one as highly ranked as he was, had to maintain a certain image for those around him. He was intelligent, capable, superior in every measurable way from almost every other human being in known space…but he was also aware of his limitations. He had expected a far quicker victory when he had accepted the top command for the invasion, and he had been humbled somewhat by the resistance his forces had met. The easy arrogance of his lofty genetic rating had faded somewhat, and a cautious respect for his adversaries had replaced unfettered confidence.

The Confederation military had impressed him. In spite of his growing frustration at the current stalemate, on some level he admired his counterparts in the enemy command structure…and the rank and file, as well, the men and women who had fought so relentlessly against his own superior forces. They were, in every respect, a worthy enemy.

Which only affirmed the need to make them part of the Hegemony. The vast polity he served was dedicated to the protection and preservation of humanity, and, above all, the prevention of another disaster like the Great Death. A population as large and as capable as that the fleet had found on the Rim simply had to be absorbed, at almost any cost.

His admiration for the enemy fleet and soldiers did not apply, however, to what he'd seen of the Confederation's civilian leadership on Megara. His condemnation was short of universal, of course. There were some politicians who had left the capital, not to flee the planet, but to join up with the soldiers fighting against his invading forces. Ten percent, perhaps, at least at the Senate level. The others were divided into two groups, both of which he casually despised. The ones who had fled before the invasion, left their places in the Senate and run like scared children…they were bad enough. But the ones who remained and sold their souls to him were even worse.

The Confederation and, based on far spottier reports, all of the other Rim nations suffered from the same disease that had destroyed the empire. They were ruled by dishonest leaders, men and women far from the best their populations could provide. The corruption and self-dealing among the ruling class had become a weight, dragging down the society's vitality. It had been the same in the old empire, with aristocrats and bureaucrats indulging in ever more outrageous privileges and spending less and less time addressing the needs of the imperial population. Finally, they were destroyed by their own creations, and over three terrible decades, hundreds of billions had died in an unrestrained orgy of violence and destruction.

He understood how the Hegemony could appear alien in its ways, at least to those on the Rim. And yet he believed, as he always had, in the profound logic behind it. The best and the brightest, the most capable, made decisions—ruling over, and protecting, the multitudes. Ensuring the survival of the race, something that had come close to ending three centuries before.

He was not sure how to deal with the politicians, especially those who clearly lacked the strength and intellect their positions required. Chronos was, almost always at least, a man of his word, but more than once he had thought about repudiating the promises he had given the collaborationist Senators. Was his word given to such creatures really binding?

He suspected he might find out soon enough. He had imagined controlling the—at least somewhat legitimate—Confederation government would be useful in pacifying the armed forces in the field and gaining control of more planets without bloodshed. It had not been.

He had been more hopeful months before, but despite the efforts he had taken to see that the Senate's proclamations reached dozens of Confederation planets, there had been little in the way of wholesale capitulation. A few worlds had obeyed the Senate orders and surrendered. Three, to be exact. The others had either ignored the commands to yield, or they were under the control of the Confederation military, which, to a man, it seemed, were united in their determination to fight the Hegemony to the end.

The war situation was bad enough, though given enough supplies and reinforcements, he was still confident he would be able to resume the offensive and complete the conquest of the Rim. His forces retained technical superiority in most areas, save for small attack craft and the stealth technology the enemy had apparently used to destroy the Logistics Fleet. Even those were deteriorating assets for the Confederation. His escort craft had continued to develop systems and tactics to counter the enemy bombing strikes. The fighters were still dangerous, still a great advantage for the enemy, but less than they had been at the war's outset.

The research teams had been working on the stealth technology as well, with an initial focus on detection methods. They had not completely cracked the code, so to speak, but the next time the Confederation tried to sneak ships into the Olyus system, there was a good chance they were in for a nasty surprise.

No, it was not the tactical situation that had Chronos's insides twisted into knots. It was time that troubled him most, and the realization that he had the bulk of the Hegemony's military power tied down in a war approaching its fifth anniversary, and without a clear end in sight. It would be a year more, at least, before he had built up his bases and supplies in Megara to support a renewed push forward, and even his most optimistic analysis suggested it would be several years more before the Confederation were totally defeated.

He had never been totally convinced the Others were the threat the annals made them out to be…or that they would return at all. He wondered, sometimes, if they even still existed.

But now, with the forces that had been built up over generations to face that very threat committed almost fifty transits and five hundred light-years away from the capital, he found himself worrying ever more about the mysterious enemy…the only force that had ever clearly outmatched the Hegemony.

He had even considered reaching out, sending delegates to negotiate with the Confederation forces. There was no question in his mind there were Master-level individuals directing the fleets fighting against his own, and not the slightest doubt that the Hegemony and the Rim would both be at grave risk if the Others returned. The Rim cultures called the end of the empire the Cataclysm, and they patted themselves on their backs for coming back from that dark age. But it had also become clear to Chronos that their histories knew very little of what had caused that nightmare of human history that the Hegemony had labeled the Great Death. If the Rim dwellers had any real knowledge of what had almost destroyed mankind, perhaps they would think differently about the Hegemony, and the basis for its existence and culture, instead of taking undeserved credit for the survival they owed almost entirely to the remoteness of their location.

No, he realized. *There can be no negotiation, not now.* War had a way of overtaking rationality and logic…and creating hatred in their places. The Confederation had a natural aversion to yielding to an outside power, but now that stubbornness was reinforced by their rage and hatred. Chronos believed utterly that his forces had come to help the Rim, to save them from themselves. They were already on the same course the empire had taken, and he knew where that led. But the Confederation saw only an enemy, one that had killed their people and invaded their worlds. They saw over a million of their Marines dead on Megara, and almost countless others on the worlds so far engulfed in war. Chronos respected his enemy, but he knew there could be no half measures. He had to break them utterly. Only then could they be rebuilt and take their rightful places among the peoples of the Hegemony.

He would see that done, whatever it took. Akella had assured Chronos she was with him, and the supreme leader of the Hegemony had concurred with his assessment that the Hegemony needed the population, resources, and dynamism of the Rim. She had promised reinforcements and supplies…and one other thing.

It had been in development for almost as long as Chronos could remember, and for many years, it had seemed little more than an endless hole, sucking in resources. But Akella's last report had suggested its completion was close at hand. She had not promised to deploy it to the war front, but he suspected she would if it was needed. It was likely to be the force that broke the stalemate and accelerated the conquest of the Rim.

Project Zed.

Chapter Three

"Die, you bastard...die." Stanton Hayes was pulling back hard on his throttle, struggling a bit to clear the hulking freighter right in front of him. He'd almost come in too close, and he suspected if he'd been a second later pulling back—maybe even half a second—he'd have slammed into the target vessel. That wouldn't have been a pretty sight, not at almost 0.01c.

At least it would have taken the freighter out...

Hayes had never had a particularly self-sacrificial attitude, as so many in the fighter corps seemed to possess, but the desperation of the war had preyed on him as it had on all his comrades. Defeat was unthinkable...and yet, despite the previous year's victory at Craydon, it seemed likely enough. Hayes wasn't ready to throw his life away to take down a supply ship—especially not one he'd already hit with half a dozen cluster bombs—but he'd learned never to say never about anything. He'd lost too many friends, watched too many things he'd thought impossible happen. The Confederation's capital had fallen, and it was still occupied by the enemy. As much as he knew that was a fact, on some

18

level, he couldn't quite accept it. Even more astonishing, the Senate had actually surrendered. That didn't mean anything, not materially. Save perhaps that all of them, from Admiral Barron on down, were now renegades and rebels.

He brought his ship around and blasted his thrusters, setting up a return vector toward the fleet. That meant another run past the enemy escorts, and more of his people killed. The cost of war.

He stared at the screens, watching as his scanners updated. His people had paid the price of their inexperience in blood, but they'd taken their revenge on the supply ships. At least two dozen of the big vessels were critically damaged, and eight of those were dead in space. That was millions of tons of Hegemony supplies that wouldn't make it to Megara. Not a battle won, perhaps, nor even the total destruction of the convoy, but still a small gain, one step closer toward the liberation of Megara…and to chasing the Hegemony out of the Rim.

He looked over his formations on the screen. "Formation" was far from an accurate description of the chaotic cluster of dots, each one of them representing a single bomber. Squadron integrity was a thing of the past, and he doubted one in ten of his people was were the flight plan directed them to be. But they'd done their jobs. They'd cut up the convoy pretty well…even if they'd lost almost a fifth of their number in the process.

His eyes settled on one of the dots, and a quick flick of his fingers confirmed his initial thought. Doug Velet had made it, at least this far. Hayes been worried about the rookie. More than worried, really—he'd expected the young pilot to die in the strike. He'd lost a lot of his people, but somehow the thought of one of the greenest making it back gave him something to grasp on to, a refuge from the pain.

There was just one problem. They weren't back yet.

"Gray Wolf Nine, adjust your vector, zero seven two. Now." Velet was heading back on a direct line toward the waiting fleet, but the Hegemony escorts were on the move too, positioning themselves for one last chance to take down the fighters that had so badly damaged their supply ships. There was no reasonable course to avoid the onslaught, but the rookie was heading right into the middle of it.

Velet wasn't the only one making that mistake.

"Attention all squadrons…adjust your courses to come around the starboard side of those enemy escorts. You may all think this fight is over, but no one's back aboard yet…and those ships are still hunting us." The brief euphoria Hayes had felt at the successful completion of the attack run was gone, replaced by the stress of combat. The flight plan had been designed to avoid the escorts on the way back, at least as much as possible, and Captain Eaton had moved the carriers accordingly. But the enemy had been quicker to adjust than expected. Hayes had read the accounts of the war's early battles, had even fought in a few that probably seemed ancient to his rookies. The Hegemony forces had adapted to facing fighters, improving with each passing battle…and now, it seemed, they'd become adept at guessing the squadron tactics they faced.

Hayes had hoped his people would slip back to the landing platforms with minimal casualties, but as he watched the enemy ships moving and did some quick calculations, he realized it was going to be a hard and bloody trip back. The butcher's bill was still running.

"Full evasive maneuvers…all ships. We're not back yet, and I want everyone focused." *There's still time to die here…*

He swung his throttle to the side, adjusting his own vector, trying to stay as far from the approaching escorts as possible. He wasn't going to clear them entirely—whoever was commanding those ships was damned good—but he figured he could avoid the fire of all but the two on the starboard flank.

Maybe three…

"On me. All of you. Follow my maneuvers." It wasn't a textbook tactic, telling his people to copy his actions, but his gut told him it was the best way to get them past the enemy, and back to the landing bays.

His screen lit up, quick flashes indicating incoming enemy fire. It wasn't close enough to be a problem. Yet. At least not for him.

His eyes darted to the side. Thirty or more of his people were heading directly into the primary enemy fire zone. Some of them, perhaps half, were following his orders—but too late—blasting their thrusters in a vain effort to try and follow his vector. The others were just moving blindly forward, into the maw of the enemy.

"On me, everybody. Full thrust, around the starboard end of the enemy line." But he knew it was too late. Anybody following his orders now was as likely to streak along the front of the enemy line, right through the fire zone. He almost rescinded the command, but he stopped himself. Most of his people would still be better off trying to follow him. Perhaps a dozen and a half would not. He felt the urge to order those ships to push directly forward and get through the enemy line as quickly as possible…but he knew it was too late. He would only risk confusing the others. He mourned for those who were about to die, but it was a numbers game. Snapping out orders, confusing his already raw and terrified pilots, would only make things worse.

He leaned back in his seat, struggling a little against the g-forces bearing down as he fired his engines at maximum thrust. Part of him wanted to change course, to fly over to his most vulnerable ships and run the gauntlet with them. But that would serve no purpose…and it was an option his duty denied him. He was one of maybe three pilots in the fleet who could organize and lead the strike force, and everybody else was expendable. It was a gruesome reality and one that made him feel like shit, but it was true, nevertheless.

Nothing was more important than winning the war.

Nothing…and no one.

*   *   *

"The damage assessments are in, Captain. Nine supply vessels destroyed outright, twelve severely damaged, and likely crippled. The AI projects a seventy to ninety percent loss rate on the cargoes on the most heavily damaged vessels."

Eaton just nodded. Her aide's report was complete and accurate, as always…but just then, she was more concerned about her fighter squadrons than Tarleton's account of the tonnage of Hegemony shipping they'd taken out. She knew that was shortsighted, that the only way to win the war—to avoid otherwise inevitable defeat—was to strangle the enemy's logistics, but sending out hordes of unprepared pilots again and again was wearing her down. She told herself it was war. It was her duty. She knew that was true.

But it didn't feel that way. It felt like murder.

She turned toward Tarleton's station to speak, but she remained silent. There was nothing to do, no orders she could give to aid her returning pilots. If she'd led battleships, she would have ordered them forward, closed with the Hegemony escorts and given those vessels something to worry about besides hunting down her fighters. Indeed, she had almost issued the command anyway. But her escort carriers were almost laughably weak in battle, just paper-thin steel hulls, devoid of weaponry save for half a dozen or fewer short-ranged point defense turrets. Her eight escorts were all light frigates, no match for the enemy counterparts, and much less the handful of cruisers out there. All she could do by advancing was get her fleet destroyed…and her orders in that regard were clear.

Bombers were expendable, but her carriers were not. They were junk, hastily repurposed in the shipyards of Craydon and the other Iron Belt worlds, but they carried bombers. And in war, especially a war against the Hegemony, that made them indispensable. The directives she'd received—from none other than Tyler Barron himself—were distressingly clear and detailed. Not only was she to keep her carriers out of range of enemy warships at all times, she was to flee the instant any enemy forces threatened them. Even if it meant abandoning every single bomber.

She turned toward the kill figures, partly to analyze the success of the attack, and partly to distract herself from watching her green pilots struggling to make it back. The strike had gone well, and one look at the size of the supply ships gave her a good idea of the sheer volume of war matériel her people had destroyed. It was inconceivable in terms of the factory output and hours of labor it represented…but it was also less than twenty percent of what the convoy carried. It would hurt the enemy, but they would still get eighty percent of the supplies. They would come that much closer to turning Megara into an impregnable fortress at the center of the Confederation, a logistical center that could support their continuing war efforts.

Even as she winced at the losses her squadrons had taken, she considered launching a second strike. She was no expert on the logistics of war, but she knew twenty percent wasn't enough. The struggle against the enemy supply lines *had* to do better than that. Her pilots would be exhausted on a second attack, their bombers hastily refitted instead of carefully prepped as they had been for the first strike. But she would have done it anyway…if there had been time.

Her authority allowed her to play with the lives of her pilots, but not with the hulls that carried them. She would have just enough time as it was to land her survivors, and then her fleet had to bug out before the enemy escorts could close with her carriers. Allowing the convoy to escape without further damage was bad enough, but losing the ships that allowed future strikes would be disastrous.

"All right everybody"—he turned and looked around *Tarsus*'s cramped bridge—"a successful strike all around." She felt guilty for declaring the mission a success while her pilots were still out there dying, but she'd learned enough about command to understand how crucial morale was, for all of her people. "The enemy will feel the loss of those supplies." *Not enough, though.* "Now, let's get our squadrons back on board. I want all engine crews ready. We're blasting off at full thrust as soon as the last fighter is back in the bays."

And maybe sooner…especially if any of these rookies lag too badly.

The idea of leaving even one of her pilots behind sickened her, but she had her orders. She understood the costs war demanded, and the immense price that would be extracted if there was to be any chance of victory.

* * *

Stanton Hayes sat down hard in the chair. He was exhausted from the mission, sore from hours spent in his Lightning's cramped cockpit—and the g-forces from *Tarsus*'s prolonged acceleration weren't helping any of it. The converted freighter wasn't what anyone would call a fast ship, but she also lacked the modern dampeners that offset the crushing force of acceleration in proper warships.

He wanted to lie down on his bunk, to close his eyes and sleep. But he couldn't. He had a job to do first, and it was one he'd never believed could wait. He felt himself dying a bit more with each mission, at least the part of him that was good for anything but war. Little remained to him that meant anything, save duty, and he took that very seriously. He lived to lead his pilots, in battle and in between engagements. He had to be there for them, to hold up their morale and bolster their courage. And to do what he could for them when they were gone.

He tapped at the keyboard of the small workstation on his desk, but his mind was still on the final moments of the mission. He'd watched from his cockpit, in frozen horror, as the fleet's carriers engaged their thrusters while a third of his bombers were still coming in. He understood, of course, that the safety of the carriers came first. It was something even his half-trained pilots had heard many times in the Academy. Fighters were expendable. Warships were not.

Still, horror scenes had whipped through his head in those terrible moments, images of several dozen of his people left behind. Despite all he knew about doctrine and about the realities of the war, he'd felt a surge of anger and resentment…and he'd deliberately ignored the orders to land, declaring he would come in only when the last of his people had. It had been a foolish display, and one that could have had severe consequences under a commander less restrained than Captain Eaton. But he'd done it…and he knew he would do it again.

And Eaton had looked the other way, as he suspected *she* would do again if need be.

He leaned back and sighed, moving his hand back through his hair and then massaging his temples. His head throbbed, though he couldn't guess what combination of fatigue, stress, and g-forces was responsible.

But he had work to do, work that couldn't wait.

He began tapping on the keyboard, bringing up a blank screen. Then he paused, staring at it, his mind momentarily blank. He'd faced the enemy, endured the terror and stress of battle again and again…but this was the thing he hated most. The task he feared the most.

He shook off the malaise and the fear, and he forced himself to focus. Then he began typing.

It is with the greatest regret I must inform you that your son,

Ensign Douglas Velet, was killed in action fighting against a Hegemony fleet. Doug was a brave pilot and he was beloved and respected by his colleagues…

Chapter Four

Orbital Platform Killian
Planet Craydon, Calvus System
Year 320 AC

"Any improvement, Doctor?" Tyler Barron stood in the hallway of the naval hospital, a sprawling facility that occupied almost a third of Craydon's largest orbital station. There were hundreds of beds, as well as operating theaters, critical care wards, and the like. Mercifully, the vast infirmary was quiet, almost eerily so. A year before, it had been a virtual ruin, blasted almost to bits in the desperate fight to hold Craydon, but still, its beds, corridors, even its gritty, debris-covered floors had been full of the wounded and the dying.

The images remained vivid in Barron's thoughts.

"I'm sorry, sir...Admiral Nguyen suffered a massive stroke. We managed to save his life—barely—but the damage is quite extensive. We can repair much of it with microsurgery, but it will require repeated procedures. Even if everything goes perfectly, he will never fully recover. We may manage to restore some quality of life to him for whatever time he has left, but I can say with absolute certainty that he will never again command the fleet...or return to duty in any capacity, save perhaps a purely ceremonial one."

Barron felt the words like a punch to his gut, though he'd heard them before, and they only matched what he already knew. He wasn't the kind to hide from reality, but the loss of Nguyen inflicted far more on him than pain and sympathy for a friend's ills. It stripped away his last line of defense, the final veneer that had allowed him to at least pretend the overall fleet command wasn't his.

There was no place to hide. Every spacer in the fleet, every man and woman crawling through the guts of a warship, sweating and struggling at their posts in battle, would look to him now. The shade of his grandfather had never weighed more heavily on him, and despite his experience, and the seemingly endless string of battles he'd fought over the past dozen years, he'd never felt so utterly unready for anything as he did just then.

Did you feel this way, Grandfather? Is it like this for all men in times like these? Or am I truly not ready?

"Do what you can for him, Doctor." It was a foolish thing to say, or at least unnecessary. But it was all that came to his mind.

Barron turned and walked down the corridor. He'd intended to visit Nguyen as well as check up on his condition, but the admiral was still in a coma…and Barron just didn't have it in him to look down at the officer, one who'd once been so strong and vital, even at his advanced age. The war had surrounded Barron with death and suffering, but even he had his limits.

"Tyler…any change?" Clint Winters turned the corner just up ahead, and he walked toward Barron.

"I'm afraid not. Unless the doctor—doctors—are all wrong, at the very least, the admiral's career is over." A pause, and an expression that displayed both Barron's pain and his tension. "It's on us now, Clint."

Winters nodded, and then he managed a thin smile. "It's

on *you*, Tyler. We both know it's got to be you. You're senior, and you're a man every spacer wearing the uniform would be proud to follow. Myself included."

Barron managed a jerky nod, but it took him perhaps half a minute to manage his response. His mind raced, trying to think of a way out. But he knew Winters was right, and his colleague's clear willingness to accept the second position had sealed his fate. One of them had to be senior. The fleet could only have one top leader.

And that was him.

He faced perhaps the greatest challenge his people had endured, one even more desperate than that his grandfather had tackled. The parallels were almost eerie, and part of him wanted to shed his uniform and take off to some remote planet, never to be heard from again. But he knew that was impossible. He was a Barron…and, by God, he would behave like one.

"Your support means a lot to me, Clint. You could make a credible claim to the top job, too." At least part of Barron wished his friend had done just that. But he knew it would never happen.

"You're up to it, Tyler. I don't have any doubt. I'll be proud to follow you wherever you lead, and I think every spacer in the fleet will do the same. None of us expected this war, but if we've got to fight it, we're damned lucky to have you to lead us."

Barron pushed back against the emotion, struggling to maintain his cool demeanor. "You were coming here for a reason, I'll bet. Right?" Barron had suddenly realized Winters had been on duty. He wasn't at the hospital to visit Nguyen…and that meant he'd come to find Barron. Something was up. And probably that something was bad.

Winters frowned. "Yes, that's true, Tyler." A pause. "There's been another accident. Orbital facility G-9, the engine parts plant."

"Bad?" Barron already knew the answer. Winters's

expression was like a book.

"Really bad. They're still not sure what happened, but a series of explosions ripped through the facility, and part of the hull was blown out. The latest count is seventy-four dead, but that's likely to rise. The plant is completely shut down right now, and it will be at least two weeks before even partial operation can be restored."

Barron shook his head, but he didn't speak. What was there to say?

"There's no way to be sure it had anything to do with the expedited production schedule."

Barron looked at his friend. "We can keep telling ourselves that, Clint, if it makes you feel better." The last two months had seen a series of industrial accidents, both on the surface and among the orbital production facilities. Every militarily useful factory and plant was working at breakneck speed, as they were on all the other worlds of the Iron Belt. The fight to save Craydon had been a costly one, very costly indeed, and Barron and his comrades had pulled out all the stops, driving the industrial princes of the Iron Belt, and, by extension, their millions of sweating workers, almost at the point of a bayonet. Barron hadn't actually threatened any of them—not yet, at least. But he'd done nothing to calm their fears about reprisals for failing to comply with his demands for ships and matériel.

The two men stood silently for a moment, and then Barron continued. "Have you checked out the data on industrial fatalities and injuries prior to our arrival here? Craydon was no model of responsible workplace procedures, mind you, but we've killed over ten times the previous average…and that doesn't include the thousands who've been injured."

"That's not a fair comparison, Tyler. We've tripled production over the last year. That was bound to cause an increase in accidents."

"We tripled production, but we didn't add many

factories. There just wasn't time. We've increased output by driving everyone—industrial barons, plant managers, workers—to the brink. We killed a lot of those workers, Clint. You know we did."

"And how many spacers have died fighting the Hegemony?"

Barron just nodded. The Confederation was fighting for its life, and the thousands upon thousands who'd died fighting the remorseless Hegemony onslaught were no less dead than a factory worked incinerated in a plant explosion. Winters's logic was flawless. But Barron had been raised from birth to serve in the navy, and duty was always paramount to his sense of place. The navy—and the Marines and other military—were there to protect the civilians. From his point of view, it was a failure on their part to allow the factory workers to end up effectively on the front lines.

Finally, he turned toward his comrade—he'd found a true compatriot in the admiral, and a man he was happy to induct into his tightknit band of true friends. "Assuming we can sustain a cold-blooded view of things, that nothing is more important than victory"—Barron hated that idea, but through the guilt and doubts, it *was* how he felt, absolutely—"let's consider a more practical issue. There's already unrest brewing. On Craydon certainly, and on some of the other worlds, too. And it looks ever worse if you read between the lines on the reports. What do we do when there are riots? Clear the streets with fire? How about when the civilians decide the sacrifices are too much to endure, that freedom isn't worth so much blood?" It was an idea that was anathema to Barron, but he also knew people had a history of undervaluing things like liberty, of trading them away for sometimes empty promises safety or protection.

"We do what we have to do to keep the fight going." Winters's voice was stone cold, and it left no doubt in Barron's mind where his compatriot would stand if they had to make difficult choices. Shooting down mobs, arresting politicians? They seemed unlikely tactics to preserve freedom, and yet yielding to the enemy, becoming slaves to the Hegemony...would any fate be worse than that?

"Maybe we should cut back on production levels, just a bit? If we ease off on the—"

"Tyler, you were there with me, in every one of those battles. We've got raiding forces out there, flying around in those tin cans we call escort carriers. It'll be a miracle if half of them don't suffer critical failures without even taking a hit from the enemy. We're sending out little baby pilots so wet behind the ears, I doubt half of them know which end of a Lightning to point at the enemy. And, despite all of that, we know vast amounts of enemy supplies are still getting through. Even the spotty intelligence we're getting from Megara is clear on one thing: the Hegemony is fortifying the system. If we give them another two or three years, we'll never take it back, not with a thousand battleships. No, we can't slow down...not on anything. We can't wait. We've talked mostly about holding the line at Craydon and the rest of the Iron Belt, but you know as well as I do the giant question we've avoided talking about."

Winters stared right at Barron, his eyes cold, intense. "We have to take Megara back, Tyler...and we have to do it sooner rather than later. In twenty-four months, it will be too late. It will be too strong, and the enemy too reinforced."

Barron felt his stomach clench, and he struggled to hold back the feelings welling up inside him. The idea of going on the offensive was absurd. There was just no way they could pull it off.

But Winters was right. They *had* to do it, and they had to make it work.

Somehow.

* * *

Barron sat quietly at the end of the table, watching the assembled delegates prattling on pointlessly. Each one who spoke seemed to somehow sound even more self-important than the one who'd come before. Barron detested gatherings like this one, but he was the acting commander in chief of the combined fleet—Admiral Nguyen still held the official assignment, pending further action—and that left him little choice but to sit where he was and endure.

The Grand Alliance. It was an impressive name, especially for a group of nations, most of which fielded a wild assortment of obsolete or battle-scarred ships. The Confederation fleet was a shadow of what it had been, no fewer than half its ships gone in the endless series of battles it had fought against the enemy. The Palatian forces had suffered almost as greatly, and for all the courage and honor of Vian Tulus's warriors, their ships had never been a technological match for the Confederation's vessels, much less the Hegemony's.

The contingents from the rest of the Grand Alliance were worse. The Union forces under Admiral Denisov were essentially refugees, considered traitors back on Montmirail. They could expect no support, no supplies, no reinforcements. And the wild assortment of vessels from the Far Rim were even more bizarre, many of them looking almost like museum displays to Barron's sensibilities.

Those primitive hulks saved your ass during the battle last year…

Barron knew just how close the fleet had come to defeat in the fight to defend Craydon. His people had managed to hold long enough for the Hegemony commander—for the first time in the war—to blink, to call off his attacking forces. There was no way to be sure what would have happened if the enemy had been prepared to fight it out to the end, but Barron had a pretty good idea. The margin had been razor thin. He still wondered why the Hegemony leadership had pulled back. For all his relief at finally gaining a victory, he was almost certain the enemy *could* have won the war right at Craydon, albeit at an almost unimaginable cost.

It was the first sign that the enemy could be deterred by losses, and Barron knew that could be a vital bit of information at some point.

"It is essential that each national representative have veto power over any major decisions of this body, particularly on military matters." Gisha Levara was the senior ambassador from the Sapphire Worlds, one of those nations from the Far Rim who'd sent their fleet of rustbuckets to answer the Confederation's call for aid. Barron didn't like thoughts like that about his allies. The Far Rim spacers had fought, and died, much the same as his own always had. But the pomposity of the diplomatic missions from those tiny nations on the edge of human habitation almost defied his comprehension.

And Levara was the worst of the lot.

"The Enlightened One was quite clear on this matter, Chairman Dorsey," Levara pressed.

Barron managed, somehow, to conceal the snort that tried to escape his lips at the mention of the absurd title of the Sapphire Worlds' leader. He felt an instant of pride in his restraint—a pleasant, if fleeting, change from the general disgust in which he'd been wallowing.

"Your Excellency, we have discussed this a number of times…at great length." Victoria Dorsey sat at the head of the table, owing her position to her status as one of the Confederation's representatives, but also to some skilled negotiating that had allowed her to slip past two more senior colleagues who'd stalemated each other with their mutual animosity. Barron usually wasn't one to admire such political maneuverings, but he had to admit to himself that he was damned glad to have Dorsey in that seat rather than either of her two rivals. She seemed to have some sense, even if she was a politician at heart. "The Grand Alliance was formed to counter an enemy that endangers us all. As has been said many times before, the Confederation—and the Alliance—have lost by far the most spacers and ships, and it is Confederation worlds that have been occupied by the Hegemony. All members of the Grand Alliance will be respected, and their views will be taken with grave seriousness. But it is simply not possible to fight this war if any member of this Council can interfere with military affairs alone and at any time."

Barron watched the proceedings continue, and he found himself resisting—barely—the urge to get up and leave the room. He'd heard warnings all his life about "watching the sausage being made," and apart from the fact that he disagreed vehemently with the way government typically functioned, there was little arguing it was unpleasant to see firsthand.

Barron had faced hardship and pain, lost friends and suffered in one terrible battle after another, but that wasn't what threatened his strength the most, wore away at his ability to summon the endurance he needed to continue. He was disillusioned, and he'd begun to wonder just what he was fighting to preserve. He'd seen the Confederation's government in action far too closely, and he'd even been the target of its machinations. There was corruption everywhere, and misuse of power was endemic. The Confederation was the only place on the Rim—and, it appeared now, anyplace mankind still existed—where any level of freedom existed, but now Barron was asking himself far too often just how much truth there was to that easy and fortifying assumption.

What was he fighting for? Freedom? For whom? Certainly not the working classes on the Iron Belt worlds, virtual serfs effectively under the control of the great industrial families. The people? Barron had seen the workings of the Senate entirely too clearly the last few years. He'd watched law and "justice" bartered and sold, seen politicians strive for personal power and little else. Was the "cause" his people fought for, the great reason they struggled and died, largely a lie?

He'd fought off the doubts, told himself the Confederation, for all its faults, was far better than the Union or the petty kingdoms on the Far Rim...not to mention the Hegemony and its rigid structure of genetic rankings. He'd managed to hold the line, maintain enough belief to drive him forward, to do what he had to do and to endure the cost. But staring at the Supreme Council of the Grand Alliance, as they'd augustly named themselves in one of their first official actions, he found himself sorely tested. That didn't even take into account the Provisional Senate, so designated to differentiate it from its counterpart on Megara, which had already officially surrendered the Confederation to the Hegemony.

His eyes moved around the table, settling on Dorsey. The Senator had been absent from Megara when news first broke of the coming Hegemony assault, dealing with a family matter of some sort on her homeworld. That placed her a step above the other Senators—just over half that body's numbers—who'd managed to stream away from the capital as the enemy approached. He saw through their myriad hastily concocted excuses, and detested them for their cowardice. But he'd checked and confirmed that Dorsey's reason for being back on her home world was legitimate.

How do those who fled rank next to the ones still on Megara...the ones who surrendered, and are even now, by all accounts, collaborating with the enemy?

Dorsey was Barron's distant cousin, too, or so he'd confirmed after she'd mentioned the connection to him in her campaign for the chairmanship. He'd been doubtful, and angry too, but then he discovered they did, indeed, share a great-grandfather. It was a tenuous and immaterial link, save for the prestige that surrounded the Barron name—which, of course, Dorsey didn't share. His initial anger had faded quickly. He had decided he needed someone he could believe in, someone he could work with. Politician or not, Victoria Dorsey seemed like the best he could hope for.

There was something else, too. Sympathy? Empathy? He looked around the table, and for a moment he was grateful his place was in the battle line, facing death and battle…and not trying to deal with the laughable assortment of backwater lords and diplomats.

He'd never imagined the hell of war seeming like salvation, but at that moment, that was exactly how he thought of it.

Chapter Five

CFS Tarsus
Osalon System
Year 320 AC

"Captain, my squadrons are severely understrength, no more than sixty percent…and that's assuming I can get a dozen lightly wounded pilots out of sickbay and back in the cockpits in time." Stanton Hayes spoke in a strained voice, his fatigue instantly apparent in his tone and his hunched posture.

"Commander, I realize your people are tired, and that they have suffered heavy losses, but you understand the military situation as well as I do." Sonya Eaton was tired, too, though she did her best to hide it, especially from the commander of her squadrons. She knew what he'd been through, on the strike missions…and on dealing with the aftermath. "The two convoys we've hit were both larger than intelligence reports indicated. The last one by nearly fifty percent. The enemy is getting far more supplies through than the high command projected, in spite of our raiding efforts. That means they're fortifying Megara faster than expected."

"I understand, Captain, but…" Hayes hesitated. Eaton imagined his rationality and his loyalty to his people were waging a war in his head. She knew her strike force commander was no fool. He understood as well as she did the state of the war, and the developments that were likely to come next. But she was also fully aware of the kinds of losses his understrength squadrons would suffer in yet another raid.

It didn't matter, though. The drones she'd sent through the Belton transit point had left no doubt. Yet another convoy had transited into that system, and was even then making its way across, toward the next jump. They would be in Osalon in a matter of hours, and if Eaton's fleet didn't launch an attack, another link in the Hegemony supply fleet would make it all the way to Megara unmolested. There simply wasn't time to get any additional forces there.

"Captain…if the fleet could deploy a few battleships to the raiding operations, or even heavy cruisers…" The pilot looked around with a sour expression at the dull gray space that passed for *Tarsus*'s conference room. "Something that could close with those enemy escorts and give them a fight. They're almost entirely retrofitted with anti-fighter batteries, Captain. Anything with some real punch would make a huge difference, and cut our loss rates by a good chunk."

Eaton didn't answer right away. She didn't think it would help to remind Hayes that in the great calculus of the Confederation's war effort, his people were more expendable than battleships, even than heavy cruisers.

Hell, that's why we've got almost nothing but half-trained rookies out here.

As unprepared as the green pilots were for shipping raids, it paled in comparison to the slaughter that would result if they were thrown into action against Hegemony battle fleets. Jake Stockton had known just what he was doing when he funneled so many new pilots to anti-logistics operations. And she was pretty sure he was painfully aware of how many of them were unlikely to return from their first assignments, despite his efforts to spare them from even more dangerous adversaries.

"Stanton, you know as well as I do what shape the fleet is in. They can't spare cruisers, or even experienced pilots. If—when—the enemy hits Craydon again, Admiral Barron is going to need everything he has, and probably more. It's hard, I know." Her voice choked a little. The dead pilots haunting Hayes were *her* people, too. "But we have our orders…and our duty."

Hayes didn't answer. He just nodded.

"I'm going to give the launch order in fifteen minutes, and you need to be there waiting for your pilots. We've got to hit this convoy as it comes through the transit point. With any luck, you'll get a strike in before their escorts are fully in position. You can do some damage and break off before they hurt you too badly." She said it, but she wasn't sure she believed it.

She wasn't sure Hayes believed it either, but the officer stood up at something like attention and snapped off a reasonably crisp salute.

"We'll do our best for you, Captain."

"I know you will, Commander." Eaton stood up and nodded, and then she watched as Hayes walked out of the room and into the hallway beyond, wondering if he had any idea how deeply those two words had cut at her.

Yes, they're doing their duty, but they're also dying.
For you.

* * *

Stanton Hayes pulled back on the throttle so hard that, for an instant, he thought he'd broken it. His ship was swinging around in a tight arc, the slow overall velocity allowing far sharper vector changes than normal. His squadrons had been formed up in front of the point, almost at a dead stop, waiting for the Hegemony ships to transit through.

He'd sat in his cockpit for over an hour, nursing the

tightness in his gut, hoping his squadrons wouldn't find themselves facing an oncoming wall of escorts. Then the freighters came through, one after another…and he gave the strike command.

His pilots, still green, but toughened somewhat by the missions they'd completed, hit the supply ships hard. Unfettered by the escorts Hayes knew would come through eventually, they'd savaged their targets, and in less than three minutes, four of the big ships were bleeding atmosphere and trailing great clouds of radiation behind their battered hulls.

"Second line, commence your run now!" Hayes stared out at the one-sided fight raging all around, and he managed something that had been in short supply for as long as he could remember: a smile.

He knew there were Hegemony spacers on those ships, that men and women were dying, many of them in agony. On some level, he felt the slightest wave of sympathy. From what he'd heard of the Hegemony and its culture, he doubted many of those operating the enemy ships were there through any real choice of their own. But he drove the feeling away quickly, pushed it into the darkness by the faces of his own dead pilots. They were the enemy, and he would kill as many as he could. They weren't defending their worlds, they were invading the Confederation, killing and enslaving its people. There was no room for empathy, not for the invaders. For them, he had only hatred…and he brought them only death.

He listened as the second group of squadron leaders confirmed, and he glanced down at his scanners, watching the bombers move forward, creeping across the screen as their engines powered them up from almost zero velocity. He felt another touch of relief that his people had caught the enemy without their escorts. His ships would have been cut to ribbons if a line of cruisers and frigates had come through first. The tactic had been based on a review of previous Hegemony transits, but it was still a gamble, and it was paying off.

He angled the throttle again, pushing his vector to align with that of his approaching squadrons. He'd advanced with the first line, but he hadn't made his attack run. He still had six cluster bombs in his bays, and he'd be damned if any of his ships were going back with unexpended ordnance, his own included.

His eyes darted across the screen, pausing for an instant on each enemy contact. The temptation to go at one of the wounded vessels was strong, the lure of watching an enemy ship vaporized as his warheads detonated almost irresistible. But the damaged ships were virtual wrecks already, and the chance anything in their holds was still usable, even if the ships themselves were saved from total destruction, seemed nil. The mission wasn't about the glory of the kill, or even taking out enemy freighters. The primary goal, the only one that really mattered, was to cut down on the supplies reaching Megara, to do everything possible to cut off the Hegemony's deepest advance into Confederation space.

That meant hitting a fresh target.

His eyes narrowed on just that, a blip emerging from the transit point. It was big.

Really big.

Hayes's hands moved over his controls, and he fed the incoming data into the AI. The mass estimates began to steady and close in on a final determination.

He froze as he saw the final number. Over six billion tons. He'd never seen a freighter that size. The ship was truly massive, a hulking monster that almost challenged him to pour bombs into its enormous hull. If the Hegemony had supply ships that size, why hadn't he seen them before?

Then the energy readings began to come in, and the AI identified the vessel's class. Hayes suddenly felt cold.

No…please, no…

* * *

Sonya Eaton watched in horror as the image on her screen sharpened and came into focus. Her mind recoiled, and she struggled to accept the reality of what she was seeing. *It's a freighter, a very large one. It's got to be…*

The thought was soothing, but only for a few passing seconds. Then cold recognition set in. She was staring at a Hegemony battleship. One of the big front line jobs. Even as she came to grips with what was rapidly becoming a foreboding new situation for her fleet, a second contact appeared, just as large and ominous as the first.

"Captain! We've got—"

"I see them, Commander." A cold feeling moved through her body. "Issue recall orders to the strike force. Now!" She glanced down at her side, realizing her hands were clenched tightly into fists.

"Yes, Captain."

Eaton nodded, and then she looked at the main display, and at the range figures. She had a good idea of just how much thrust Hegemony battleships could generate, and her mind was halfway to calculating how long she had to get her fleet out of there, when the AI beat her to it and the numbers flashed onto her workstation screen.

Eighteen minutes, with some margin of safety. Twenty-four if she wanted to risk it.

And "risking it" meant putting every one of her ships in desperate danger.

Eaton had commanded one of the Confederation's battleships in the major engagements of the war. She knew, from up close and personal experience, exactly what those deadly behemoths could do in battle…and she imagined just how quickly their massive weapons would blast the tin cans she called escort carriers to dust. Her eight converted freighters were almost unarmed, and even the light frigates were useless against Hegemony capital ships. Not one of her vessels would get into firing range, not before all sixteen of them were reduced to rapidly cooling clouds of plasma.

Part of her knew she should issue the withdrawal order immediately. But she just couldn't leave her pilots behind to die. Not without giving them a chance to get back.

"Get me Commander Hayes." Even as she snapped out the order, she realized the futility. There were officers who needed close direction, but Stanton Hayes wasn't one of them. She'd already given the order to the squadrons to return to base, and that was all her strike force commander needed. He'd have his people on the way back as quickly as possible.

But would it be fast enough? Perhaps she could push, squeeze a minute or two from the schedule.

"Commander Hayes on your line, Captain."

"Stanton...you know why I'm calling."

"We got the recall. We're on the way back, Captain. We don't have much counter velocity to overcome, which is a help, but I still don't think we can make it back in time. You may have to leave us, Captain. Maybe you should bug out now. You can't lose the carriers...and you've got to report this to fleet command.'"

"To hell with that!" Eaton roared out her response with a determined assurance that surprised even her. Rationally, she knew she couldn't allow her carriers to be caught and destroyed, not even if escape meant leaving every pilot behind to die, Hayes included. But at that moment, the thought of abandoning her strike force was inconceivable. "Just get those birds back, Stanton. I don't care if you burn every reactor to slag...get those ships here as quickly as you can."

"Yes, Captain." She couldn't tell from Stanton's tone if he believed his people had any chance, but he sounded more hopeful than he had a few seconds before. And that was better than nothing.

She turned and looked back at the screen as a third and

fourth enemy battleship took shape.

Come on, Stanton…I know you can do it…

But she didn't know. She was only sure of one thing: Hayes was right. She *had* to get word back to Tyler Barron. The Hegemony wasn't just bringing supplies to Megara.

They had heavy reinforcements moving forward, as well.

Chapter Six

Tyler Barron lay on his back, his eyes wide open, focused on the ceiling above. The light in the room was dim, just the bathroom fixture he'd left on—or Andi had, he wasn't sure—reflecting off the stark white walls of the quarters he'd assigned himself on Platform Killian.

He'd tried to avoid taking a cabin on the station, preferring to spend as much time as possible in his quarters aboard *Dauntless*. The battleship wasn't *his Dauntless*, of course. His beloved vessel had been gone for years now, lost in the fight against the Union. *The war before the war.* She'd died heroically, and her replacement had served well, doing the memory and name of her famous predecessor good service. Barron had come to accept the newer ship, even develop some affection toward it, but he knew it would never be the same. For one thing, she was never really his. Atara Travis commanded the new *Dauntless*, a position she richly deserved and executed flawlessly. Barron was just an admiral flying his flag there.

"Still can't sleep?" It was only half a question, and, considering how wide awake Andi sounded, one with some irony to it as well.

Barron had let himself think she was asleep, but now he wondered how long she'd just been lying there next to him, eyes wide open, probably hoping *he* was getting some rest.

"No…and I can see I'm not the only one." He felt the urge, for about the thousandth time, to suggest that Andi leave the Calvus system, go somewhere safe. But he held silent, for the same reasons he had for over a year.

First, he doubted she would ever leave him again. He knew her well enough to be damned close to certain of that, and while her devotion touched him deeply, he still wished she could be far from the horror of the war.

Second, there was no place safe. If the Confederation lost the war, the rest of the Rim would fall quickly and certainly…and any refuge would soon enough be conquered and occupied, as assuredly as Megara already was.

But it was the third reason that truly held him back. It was simple, and also complex, born of his conflicting feelings for her. He loved Andi Lafarge, and he wanted to protect her, he wanted that with all his being. But she was a veteran in her own right—of combat, of adventure, of struggles as dire as any he had endured. He gave her his affection because he loved her…but his respect came because she had earned it. He just couldn't bring himself to try to guilt her into running away, as he had done once before. It wouldn't be right…and he had some idea of what it would do to her if he somehow managed to heap enough guilt and pressure on her to drive her away.

How she would feel in that kind of reluctant exile, getting news of his death.

"I don't need much sleep. Never have." That was true, he knew, to an extent. Andi had always been able to operate on just a few hours' sleep. But he was guessing she hadn't had those three or four hours that usually sufficed for her in the last week combined, much less on any given night.

"I tell myself that, too…but we both need *some* sleep."

She didn't answer, at least not beyond something that sounded like a playful snort, half executed. If Andi Lafarge was capable of voluntarily showing weakness to anyone, it would be Tyler Barron. But he knew it was still difficult for her, even with him, and he wasn't about to push. His empathy was heartfelt, and based solidly in reality. He was exactly the same…and she had always respected his needs in that way. He could do no less for her.

"What is it, Ty? I know something is getting to you…I mean more than usual. The Council? The protests on the surface?"

"Yes." It was a simple response, and the only accurate one he could give. His mind was consumed with every issue she had just listed, and a number of others, too. His new job, provisional as it still was, carried a lot of extra responsibilities with it, obligations having more to do with fencing with politicians than developing battle tactics to fight the enemy.

To a warrior who'd been to hell and back more than once, *that* was the truest essence of a nightmare.

"You'll handle it all just fine, Ty." She managed to force a thin smile. "I mean, you'll hate every minute of it, especially dealing with the Council, I suspect…but you'll get it all done. I have no doubt you will, and neither should you."

Barron just nodded. Andi's words were the best she could offer, the best anyone could have just then, but he knew there was some performance in what she said, even mild hypocrisy. He'd seen her agonize over things before, been on the other side of the very same exchange, assuring her she could do whatever she had to do. He knew she believed in him, and that she only wanted to support him any way she could…but he was also plagued by self-doubt, by real concern he wouldn't be able to complete the task he'd inherited. That despite his best efforts and all the sacrifices of his people, the Confederation was still likely to lose the war.

He was going to respond, to thank her for her words, or something similar. But then he just leaned over and kissed her on the side of her face. He pulled her closer and held on tightly for a few seconds. He'd have stayed there longer, savoring the warmth of her next to him, but he had work to do.

He always had work to do.

This time, there was something else, too. Barron was tormented by all the things Andi had listed, as he'd been for months…but there was another shadow stalking him. A thought, a conclusion, one still forming, one he'd been resisting for weeks, with dwindling success.

It was born of his analysis, his tactical and strategic ability. The more he'd tried to discredit it, the more sense it made. He knew, somehow, in the deepest part of him, it was what had to be done. There was just one problem.

It terrified him.

Still, he knew he couldn't argue against it anymore, not even with himself. And he suspected Clint Winters would be with him, that his number two had very likely come to the same conclusion already, and probably kept it to himself for reasons similar to Barron's.

They weren't going to win the war standing on the defensive, waiting for the enemy to make the next move. That was a losing strategy, and Barron was more certain of it with each passing day.

They had to bring the war to the enemy.

They had to take back Megara.

* * *

"Now, Samson, you surprise me. I thought we'd become friends as well as co-workers after spending so much time together." Andi Lafarge looked right at Samson Davidoff, and while her tone had been entirely pleasant, the industrialist was clearly tense. She'd enjoyed tormenting him, ever since the day she'd first arrived on Craydon, sent there by Tyler Barron before the Battle of Megara. She knew Barron's intent had been to keep her safe—as safe, at least, as anyone could be with the Confederation teetering on the edge of ruin. But she'd taken the job he'd given her—to get Craydon's factories working at full speed to produce war materials—seriously.

She'd been aggressive when she arrived, figuring a little fear of physical violence might help overcome the entrenched privilege of one of Craydon's wealthiest industrialists. She'd continued because it still seemed to motivate Davidoff and his colleagues more than anything else she'd tried.

And also, because she enjoyed it. The man was an arrogant ass.

"Captain Lafarge, the situation on the planet is rapidly getting out of control. Civil unrest has become a major problem, especially among the factory workers. If you wish us to meet the quotas you have placed on us, we're going to need the military's help. Soon."

Andi Lafarge didn't like Davidoff. Growing up in abject poverty on the streets of an Iron Belt world had hardly predisposed her to kindly relations with industrial oligarchs. Still, perhaps it was nothing more than familiarity, but she'd found that Davidoff had grown on her. She didn't like him, and she doubted she ever would, but she'd learned to tolerate him.

Now, however, she felt a flush of anger. She knew what the magnate wanted. He wanted her to get Tyler Barron to send Marines into the streets of Craydon, and onto the factory floors. She knew the growing dissension was beginning to affect production, and that it wouldn't be long before it started to seriously hamper the war effort. But she knew something of the working conditions and pay levels in Davidoff's factories, as well, and she suspected there were perhaps some ways to address the unrest other than putting the sweating laborers under the guns of Confederation Marines. Her father had been a factory worker, by all accounts, until he'd been tossed out in some dispute with a supervisor, and ultimately killed himself…leaving her mother, pregnant with her, to wander the streets and survive the best she could.

Andi knew she'd probably do what Davidoff wanted if she ran out of alternatives, but it wouldn't be easy for her—and she knew it would be torturous for Tyler to issue the orders. Before she went down that road, she was going to be damned sure Davidoff had exhausted *every* other option. And that included throwing some money around, and investing in improving safety and working conditions. She'd use threats of violence in the factories to save the Confederation, and to give Barron the ships and matériel he needed in the war, but she'd be damned if she was going to do it to save Davidoff's already obscene profit margins.

"I suggest you try some pay raises, Samson, and at least some pretense at trying to improve conditions. I realize it might crimp your profits a bit, and perhaps encourage some bad habits, at least from your perspective. But your nation is fighting for its life, and the spacers and Marines doing that fighting are dying out there, in part to keep your factories, *your* factories, and not the war booty of the Hegemony. If the lawns on the Davidoff estate have to go down to weekly mowings to support the effort, I don't think it will stop Craydon's rotation, do you?"

"Captain Lafarge, you do not understand the intricacies of an operation like the Davidoff…"

"No, Samson, perhaps I don't. But I know I will do everything I can think of before I will send Marines to further intimidate your workforce…and that includes offering your bloated carcass to them in exchange for staying at their jobs. I'm not entirely sure they'd rip you into bloody chunks, but I have noticed that you rarely visit the factory floors, and when you do, you always have a large contingent of guards."

She looked right at the man, trying to stifle the amusement she felt as she watched a giant bead of sweat slip slowly down his forehead. "Do you think those guards will be able to protect you from me, Samson?"

Davidoff looked back at her, unable to hide the fear. Andi's battle against Ricard Lille had been the most difficult struggle of her life, and she'd tried to forget it as much as possible. Which, unsurprisingly, she hadn't been all that successful at.

But that particular nightmare had its upside, for one thing, intimidating the shit out of pompous fools like the one standing in front of her. She still remembered the expression on Davidoff's face when he'd first found out just what she'd done.

He looked a lot like he does now...

"Very well, Captain." Davidoff's voice was a little shaky, but he was holding it together better than she'd expected. *I guess I've toughened him up a little.* "I will do what I can...but if my colleagues and I are to keep our factories operating at this pace much longer, it's going to take all of that *and* the guns of your Marines to keep things going."

Andi didn't respond, partly because it wasn't necessary...and partly because she realized Davidoff was right. The workers had been on twelve-hour shifts, even sixteen hours, for more than a year, and with the rise in workplace accidents, the situation had become ripe for all manner of organizers and rabble rousers on the factory floors. She'd even contributed, inadvertently, by refusing to allow Davidoff and the other magnates to bring in their own security to remove the troublemakers.

It's going to be even worse if you do end up sending Marines in there and start arresting people. When the first Craydon worker dies under a Marine's gunfire...

She'd deal with that when she had to, but there was no

point in worrying about it now. If she stayed on Davidoff, made sure he followed through, just maybe she could postpone the escalation she knew would eventually come.

"Go, Samson. See to all of this as soon as possible." She paused for a few seconds, and then added, "I don't want to have to come find you if you don't, and…listen to me carefully…" She stared at him with eyes as cold as space. "…*you don't want that either*. Do we understand each other?"

Chapter Seven

CFS Tarsus
Osalon System
Year 320 AC

"Captain!"

Bart Tarleton was a calm and controlled officer, not at all prone to outbursts, but he hadn't been able to restrain his tension any longer. His tone wasn't disrespectful, but there was no mistaking the urgency in his voice.

"I know, Commander, I know." Eaton had nothing else to say. She'd already sent most of her fleet toward the transit point, but she'd kept *Tarsus* in position, waiting for the last of her deployed squadrons to return and land. It was foolish, perhaps, and certainly a violation of just about every regulation in the book, but she just couldn't run and leave the pilots to their deaths.

At least not until the absolute last second. Which was rapidly approaching—or already past—depending on just how close you wanted to cut it.

She was relying on confidence, in herself and her crew, a belief that she'd somehow get her flagship through the point before the Hegemony battleships closed to firing range. She'd seen assumptions like that succeed in the battles she'd fought, struggles with Tyler Barron or her sister in command, but this was the first time she'd faced so desperate a situation with no one but herself issuing the orders. Her calculations were based in reality—theoretically, at least, she did have time to make good her escape—but the whole thing relied on an ever-lengthening sequence of things working just right. Her course had to be spot-on, her crew at the top of their game, and, perhaps most concerning, the cantankerous old freighter she called a carrier had to perform impeccably. In her career, she'd dealt with mechanical issues, reactor slowdowns, engine malfunctions from numerous causes and of varying severity. Any one of those, and a dozen other issues, even if quickly repaired, would condemn *Tarsus* and her crew to certain death.

She flipped on her comm unit, reconnecting to Hayes's line. "Stanton...I need your people to push those reactors harder. Seconds count."

"We're pushing as hard as we dare." A pause. "You've got to go now, Captain. We're not going to make it on time."

"Well then, fire up those reactors. Go to one twenty, even one twenty-five. How much worse can the risk be than being left behind and blasted to atoms by Hegemony ships?" She was pretty sure she'd made her point, but there was no time for confusion. "That's an order, Commander. Every bomber to one twenty-five output *now*."

"Yes, Captain."

She turned and watched the display, seeing one by one as the small dots jerked forward, their reactors generating energy at a far higher rate than their design specs called for. As close as the ships were, it wasn't going to make *that* much difference...but even a minute could be the line between life and death. She was cutting things close—probably too close—but she *would* blast the thrusters and leave the pilots behind at some point. She could risk the five hundred seven crew members on *Tarsus*, put them on the line to save their comrades, but she wouldn't condemn them to certain death. At some point, she would cut bait and run.

"Get engineering on the comm, Commander." She flashed a glance over at Tarleton. "I want them ready to get *Tarsus*'s reactors up to one twenty-five as well." She'd fought next to some of the Confederation's most celebrated officers, men and women not afraid to push themselves, and their ships and crews, to the limit. But she'd never witnessed Tyler Barron or Clint Winters or her sister push a ship the size of *Tarsus* up to one hundred twenty-five percent reactor output. Worse, her flagship wasn't a new warship, designed to the highest standards. It was an old freighter, hastily retrofitted to carry fighters. Pushing the old hunk of junk so hard was begging for problems. But it also bought her an extra two minutes, perhaps even two and a half.

She turned back to the display, and her eyes immediately fixed on one of the dots falling behind the others. She almost reached for the comm to call Hayes again, but there was no need. The bomber she was watching had no thrust at all. The push to one twenty had probably burned out its reactor, there was no other answer. It was better than a total meltdown, or the destruction of the ship in a thermonuclear blast, at least in theory. But in the current circumstances, it was just as deadly. Dying from radiation poisoning, being incinerated in an atomic blast, or getting shot by pursuing Hegemony ships…in the end, it didn't matter much which shadow of death won the day. The result was the same.

"Captain, engineering acknowledges, but advises heavily against pushing the systems to that level."

"Noted." She leaned back and let out a deep breath. She'd risked her ship, her crew, herself, to try to save her pilots. She'd known it was a gamble all along, and it was far too late to prevaricate.

"One twenty-five on the reactor on my command…"

* * *

"Dammit!" Stanton Hayes saw another of his ships vanish from his screen, and he knew all too well just what that meant. Two of his birds had been vaporized by reactor explosions and, perhaps a worse fate, two more were lagging behind. Those pilots were sitting at their now useless controls, still breathing and watching their scanners. But he knew they were as dead as the two who'd disintegrated with their ships.

His own Lightning was shaking wildly, and he could feel heat behind him, the overloaded reactor overwhelming the shielding as it poured a huge flow of energy into the straining engines. He'd used the power first to increase his bird's acceleration, but now he was decelerating just as hard. He was close to *Tarsus*, so close now that he couldn't afford an instant's loss of even a fraction of that power. If he couldn't decelerate in time, he'd zip right by the carrier, and if he was sure of one thing, it was that there would be no time to come about and try again.

He felt a little lightheaded, but whether that was fear and fatigue—or radiation leaking through the shields and ravaging his body, he wasn't sure. He'd know if the nausea hit him, of course, but so far, his stomach was quiet, save of course for the tight feeling of barely restrained terror. He'd been concerned for his pilots, for *Tarsus* and her crew. Such commendable tenets of command leadership carried with them a more selfish benefit. It took his focus from himself, from the not inconsiderable likelihood that his life would now be measured in minutes, if not seconds.

He let his eyes move, noting the large circles on the edge of the display. Two Hegemony battleships were chasing the fleeing remnants of his wing. Ten of the huge vessels had transited in total, along with several escorts and other ships, but the two chasing him were more than enough to take out every fighter he had, plus *Tarsus* and, if they hadn't already made good their escapes by now, every vessel in Captain Eaton's fleet.

None of the almost dozen and a half pilots still following him back had faced Hegemony capital ships in battle. He was the only one who'd flown a Lightning into the maw of one of those giants, planted a plasma torpedo into the vast hull and then flown away, traveling back past the ship's defense grid on a wild ride to his mother ship. He knew just what those ships could do, and at what almost inconceivable ranges they could fire.

And they were damned close.

Damned close.

But so was *Tarsus*, finally.

"All right, let's get in approach formation. We're going to land in range order."

Almost range order. Hayes was the closest, but he was landing last. There was no negotiating that, though he wasn't sure what he'd do if Captain Eaton gave him a direct order.

"Blackwing Seven, you're first. Then Banshee Four." He'd considered trying to organize the landings by squadrons, but his formations were a hopeless morass.

He watched as his pilots, not quite rookies anymore, but still pretty wet behind the ears for so desperate of a landing operation, adjusted their vectors and came about to approach *Tarsus*. The first ship went in, decelerating all the way...and then slid right into the bay.

Perfect!

Then another, and another. The first six ships landed in textbook form.

Seven came in too quickly. Hayes could see it, and he grabbed the comm, shouting his commands in an almost brutal tone. "Red Streak Eight, pull up...now! You're coming in too fast. Break off and come around again." The orders blurted out almost on instinct, a mercy of sorts, since he knew the order was almost certainly a death sentence for the pilot. There would be no time for second approaches, and he knew that well. But he just couldn't take a chance on one hard landing closing the bay. That would kill nine of his people instead of one.

He watched as the pilot obeyed his command, and the tiny dot changed vector and whipped past *Tarsus*'s hull. He wondered if the pilot knew he'd been sacrificed, if he'd made the course change knowing it meant his own death. Or if he'd just reflexively followed orders.

Then he wondered which would be worse.

The rest of his ships came in, a few of them sloppy in their approaches, but they all managed to land. As the last two made their final approaches, he brought his own ship around. He took one last look at the final remaining dot floating near *Tarsus*, Red Streak Eight. He sighed, and he fought back a feeling of guilt at the prospect of his own survival while he stared for a few fleeting seconds at his doomed comrade.

Then he locked in his final approach course, and slipped into the landing bay.

He'd made it. But Sonya Eaton had waited a long time for his people to land.

Very possibly too long. His people were back in the bay, but they were far from safe.

He sat back in his now still bomber and sucked in a deep breath, trying to take a guess at the odds that he and everyone on *Tarsus* were as dead as Red Streak Eight. *Carlin,* he thought. *If a man has to die, you can at least remember him by his real name.*

No matter how many times he tried to calculate those odds, he came up with the same thing.

Right around fifty-fifty.

* * *

"They're firing, Captain." Tarleton's tone was controlled, if a little less rigidly than was usually the case. The Hegemony ships were still pretty far back, at best in a gray area that just *might* be within firing range. Eaton knew her aide was well aware the odds of a hit at that distance were very low, but getting shot at, especially by something of *that* size, was disconcerting to say the least.

She'd never met anybody, herself included, who didn't feel *something* run up their spines at the sight of those immense Hegemony vessels.

"They're still too far out, Commander. They're just working out their frustrations because they know they're not going to catch us." It was a reply to Tarleton, but it was mostly directed at her bridge officers. They were all clearly scared, their eyes riveted to the display and their controls. Fear had already done its job, and more terror could only do further harm. Being on edge was a good thing. Hopelessness, however, was something entirely difficult.

And there was no cause for it. Eaton was far from *sure* they'd make it out, but they had a damned good chance.

Tarsus was shaking hard, and Eaton could hear the strain in the old ship's bones. It seemed like every structural support was screeching, about to snap and crush a section of the hull, killing large numbers of the crew in the process. And she didn't dare imagine what was happening down in engineering, what kind of hell her people were enduring to keep the tortured power plant going.

There was a large white circle on the display, and it was getting closer. The Hegemony ships could follow her through the point, of course, but she doubted they would. They were at least an hour behind at their current velocity, with no scouting of what lay in the system beyond and with no idea what course changes she might execute after the jump. She doubted the enemy would chase after *Tarsus* once it left the Osalon system.

She tried to ignore the flashes on the display, the almost constant fire from the pursuing battleships. They were still at extreme range, and even if they managed to score a hit, it would be at massively reduced power. But *Tarsus* was an old ship and poorly protected, and Eaton was driving her so hard, the vessel was on the verge of coming apart by itself. It wouldn't take much of a hit to put an end to the escape attempt.

She looked down and realized she was gripping the sides of her chair. Her hands were clenched tightly, her fingers almost stark white as the blood was forced out of them. *Tarsus* was only two minutes from the jump, an insignificant time that somehow seemed to be stretching out to eternity.

She could almost feel each second pass, and as she sat in the center of the carrier's small bridge, there was hardly a word spoken. She'd done all she could, issued every command possible. There was nothing for her bridge crew to do but wait.

Down in the lower levels, she knew her engineers were working feverishly. She felt sympathy for them, for the burdens and work she'd placed on them. *At least they have something to do, save discovering just how long one hundred twenty seconds can be…*

The enemy fire was heavier now. They were still at very long range, but they were out of the gray area. *Tarsus*'s evasive maneuvers were making the ship as difficult a target as possible, but every second brought the enemy battleships closer, and increased the chance of *Tarsus* taking a hit.

One hit is all it will take. The ship's power grid is beyond maxed out, and she'd an old tub. Even when she was new, she wasn't made from the stuff to face Hegemony rail guns…

She watched, taking her eyes from the countdown clock and focusing them instead on the enemy ships. They were closer now, but the range was still long.

She was counting softly to herself, down from the twenty-eight seconds the clock had displayed when she'd looked away. She was down to twelve.

A flash on the screen caught her eyes, and for an instant, she felt as though she'd been punched in the gut. She'd almost expected to feel her ship rock hard from the impact of the shot, but there was nothing. Nothing save the sweat pouring down her back.

That was close.

She looked down at her workstation, at the AI report coming through. The shot had passed within four hundred meters of the ship. In terms of space combat, things didn't get much closer than that.

She could feel her heart pounding, even as her resumed countdown went from eight to seven…to six…

She could almost feel the ship shaking hard, hear the sickening sound of internal explosions, of savaged steel girders giving out. But it was all in her head.

Tarsus's luck held out. Her luck held out.

The ship slid into the center of the transit point, and slipped from normal space into the strange and poorly understood dimension that allowed nearly instantaneous interstellar travel. She normally felt a little queasy during transits, but the strange sensations that gave her stomach flops felt like nothing this time more profoundly than they did relief.

Her people had made it out.

Now, it was time to get back to Craydon…and to let Admiral Barron know the enemy was moving serious reinforcements forward to Megara.

Chapter Eight

Hegemony Supreme Headquarters
Megara, Olyus III
Year of Renewal 265 (320 AC)

The massive docking bay was brightly lit, and Kriegeri soldiers stood along both sides of the wide and carpeted walkway, resplendent in their dress uniforms, their weapons held at their sides with parade ground perfection. The Hegemony's soldier-class focused mostly on combat training, but they were more than capable of putting on a display of martial brilliance when welcoming a VIP.

Chronos stood at the front of the open path between the two groups of soldiers, staring at the still-closed hatch of the cutter. He wore his dress uniform as well, his chest covered in medals and decorations, many of which he acknowledged—to himself at least—had been won by his rank and placement, and not by heroism in the field. He did, however, have a few that were genuine, and he drew pride from the fact that, among the ten individual who formed the supreme ruling council of the Hegemony, he had by far the most military experience.

Which is why you are here, stuck in this morass, while rivals back home no doubt question your inability to crush "primitive barbarians."

He continued to stare at the shuttle.

The reception was indeed suitable for a VIP, and the primary occupant of the shuttle fit that bill, perhaps more than any living human being.

He watched as the hatch slid open. Two soldiers came out, dressed in a familiar red livery. Then, a woman's head appeared, and an instant later, she stepped into the bay. She was dressed simply, as she usually was, and she looked almost out of place among the finery on display.

Almost…because despite the simple tunic and pants she wore, there was a gravity to her presence. Akella was not only the supreme leader of the Hegemony…she was the most genetically perfect human being in all known space.

Chronos walked forward to greet her, his head awash with conflicting thoughts. She was his superior, of course, and he acted with the respect her position demanded. But he had personal feelings at work too, longstanding affection, something he was pretty sure she returned, at least to an extent. Resentment, too, however, at Akella's decision to mate with Number Two, which had crushed—or at least delayed—a pairing Chronos had coveted himself.

It was all logical enough, and Hegemony culture discouraged mixing emotions with decisions such as mating…but he still found the whole thing unpleasant. It was one reason he had accepted the military command. He had expected to push the unwelcome hurt from his psyche, to focus solely on subjects more fitting his own station, but watching her debark, he realized it was still there. Reduced perhaps by time apart, but far from gone.

"Number One, I am very pleased to see you. Welcome to Megara." They were not actually *on* Megara yet, only on one of the rebuilt orbital stations, but Chronos included the Confederation capital in his greeting anyway. Its capture was one of the few true accomplishments of the war. In every other way, the effort was behind where he—and everyone else—had thought it would be.

"Chronos, my old friend. I am pleased beyond words to

see you. It has been far too long." Her voice was soft, friendly. Akella was never one to speak or act in an officious way, despite her lofty station, but Chronos found his feelings renewing themselves in her presence.

"I could, of course, give you a tour of the station. It is but one of those we have begun to rebuild as part of the fortification effort." Such forced nonsense was the kind of waste of time Akella usually detested, but he'd felt it necessary to offer anyway. Whether it was simply out of rote, or because the building program was another of the few true successes of the campaign, he was not entirely sure.

"I would enjoy that very much…but, perhaps we should get down to the surface as quickly as possible. We have much to discuss, and I fear I cannot stay long this far from the capital."

Chronos nodded. "Of course, Number One. If you would follow me, I have a shuttle waiting to take us to the ground."

Akella smiled, and she took a few steps forward, her guards moving almost in lockstep. She paused and turned toward the leader of the detachment. "Hectoron, I do not believe I will need an escort here. I will be quite safe with Number Eight and his people. You and your troopers can see that my baggage is transported to the surface."

The guard hesitated, just a few seconds, clearly not happy with Akella's decision, but even more obviously unwilling to challenge her. "Yes, Number One. As you command." The officer turned, with another brief but noticeable hitch, and then he snapped out orders to the guards. They formed up into a column and marched back toward the cutter.

Akella turned back toward Chronos. "Let us go, my friend. I would speak with you at length…and as soon as possible."

*   *   *

"You have done well, my friend. Truly. I mean that." There was kindness in Akella's words, something Chronos had not expected, at least not when discussing the war.

"My thanks, Number One, but you must have expected the conflict to be far closer to its end by now, if not entirely over." A pause. Chronos had never had the politician's way of approaching things like some of his peers. He was usually brutally honest, and he saw no reason to lie to Akella. She was no fool, not in any way, and she was perfectly aware he, and everyone else, had expected the war to move more quickly.

"I did, of course. And I know that you did as well, when we first made the decision to invade. Very possibly, had we had a clearer view of what we would face, we might have chosen a different strategy…yet, it is our destiny to guide and protect all humanity, wherever it exists. So, perhaps we had no real choice after all." She looked at him intently for a moment. "And we are alone here, so let's make a deal. You do not 'Number One' me, and I will not 'Number Eight' you."

Chronos smiled. "That would be my pleasure, Akella. We have been friends for a long time. Very long." Aside from his affections, more or less hidden at the moment, Akella had always been a friend, and one of the few people he really trusted. He doubted he would have accepted command of the invasion if anyone else had been in the top position.

"Anyway, as I was saying, I believe it is reasonable to note that no one anticipated the fierceness and capability of the Rim dwellers. Certainly, many now seem to recall expressing such concerns, but the view of such things is always clearer when looking back, and neither of us has ever had much taste for placing that kind of spin on the facts."

"No, we never have. And we are not going to start now." He was gratified by her words. He had already known, of course, that the Rim nations, and especially the

Confederation, had proven to be far stronger than expected—their small attack craft especially had been an endless problem—but he felt relieved hearing the same thing from her. He needed her continued support to maintain his position, but it was more than that. Chronos did not enjoy feeling like a fool, and he damned sure did not want Akella seeing him as one. Intelligence and strong genetics only went so far in overcoming human insecurities, and as much as Chronos tried to ignore what others thought and said, it was not always easy.

"That is one reason I made this trip, Chronos. I wanted to assure you that you still have my unflinching support. Our purpose is to unite mankind, and once these Rim dwellers are absorbed into the Hegemony, their surprising industry and fighting spirit will be enormous assets. Given some time, the Hegemony will be stronger than it has ever been, readier to face any enemy. Even the Others."

Chronos nodded. "That is my view as well." He had generally been less concerned about the Others than Akella, though he had to admit, thoughts of the mysterious enemy had been heavier on him in recent months. "And I will do everything possible to end this conflict as quickly as possible." He hesitated, feeling a bit uncomfortable. "Perhaps we might consider altering our terms somewhat to make them more palatable. Many of their leaders have proven to be quite weak and easily bought with mere promises of continued comfort and the veneer of sustained political power." Another pause. "Others have been considerably more…intransigent."

Akella sat for a moment, silent and thoughtful. "That is difficult. Our sacred duty is to unite all men and women, to guide the race forward…and to prevent another nightmare like the Great Death. Perhaps we could offer a slower schedule for true absorption, or something of the sort…yet, from your reports, it does not seem likely that what little concession we can offer would be acceptable to the diehard elements of the enemy military. We cannot abandon our efforts on the Rim, not after all we have lost already…and, not ever, unless we are to fail in the most central tenet of our purpose."

Chronos was nodding as she spoke. "You are right, of course. It is regrettable that we must destroy so much of what appears to be the strongest segment of the Rim's population. The warriors we face would be of tremendous value as part of our own forces. But they will never yield, not until we have battered them almost to obliteration."

"Then there is nothing to do but continue our present course."

"And Project Zed?"

Akella took a deep breath and exhaled, but she did not reply, not right away. Finally, she said, "I do not know, Chronos. It does appear that Project Zed will be completed very soon…but with so much of the fleet deployed on the Rim, I am reluctant to commit Zed as well. It is a very powerful weapon, and does much to bolster our home defenses while so many of our ships are tied down here."

Chronos wanted to argue, but he knew she was right. As useful as Zed would be on the Rim front, he believed he could win without it. "Very well. I understand your decision…and I believe we can prevail."

She looked back at him and managed a faint smile. "I came here to assure you of my support, Chronos, but also for another reason." She hesitated, and looked over at him with a tentative expression on her face. "The fact that I have only one child at my age has become an outright scandal back home. The council has all but demanded that I begin another pregnancy as quickly as possible. My protestations of waiting until the war is over have become less effective as the realization sets in that the conflict will be longer than expected." She looked at Chronos intently, with perhaps a touch of emotion evident in her expression. "I know you are quite occupied with your command responsibilities, but

I would mate with you, if you are still willing."

Chronos was stunned, not so much at the idea as the timing. Seeing her had reignited his old feelings, but the demands of the war had long since driven away any expectations he might have had over a future mating.

"Now?" It was not much of a response, but it was all he had.

"I know the timing is far from ideal, but if the war is likely to go on for several more years…I just cannot wait any longer, my old friend. I have delayed this far too long as it is." She paused for a few seconds. "I could have chosen a mate back on the capital…perhaps I should have, considering the weight of your current responsibilities." She looked at him, her expression revealing a vulnerability she almost never showed. "But I would have you…if you are willing."

Chronos was older than Akella, and he already had five children, so it was not as pressing a matter for him to mate again. It would also be an odd distraction while he was deeply involved in running the war, but certainly a pleasurable one.

He wondered if Akella had allowed other factors to affect her decision besides genetics. Emotion perhaps, or even a desire to prove to him he still had her full support? A pregnancy seemed an extreme way to show confidence in a comrade, but he had no trouble believing the pressure for her to mate again had become unbearable. A Hegemony woman of her extremely high genetic rating was expected to have at least four children, and preferably six or seven. Akella still had a number of years of likely fertility remaining, but she was going to have enough trouble reaching that minimum number of four. That was unprecedented for a Number One. It was enough even, potentially, to undermine her authority.

Genetic ratings were just about the final word in rankings in the Hegemony, but a Number One who willfully refused the sacred obligation to reproduce might even face accusations of treason.

"Of course, Akella…it would be my honor to pair with you." It was something he had wanted for a long time, and he regretted that now that it had come, it was hard to feel the joy through all the stress bearing down on him.

At least he no longer feared he had lost Akella's support.

Chapter Nine

Grand Alliance Headquarters
Planet Craydon, Calvus System
Year 320 AC

"They're not going to like it, Tyler. You know that, right?"

Barron listened to Clint Winters's words. The admiral was standing right next to him, but he didn't turn, didn't look over at his friend. He was focused, and determined, and while he knew Winters was right, the cold truth was, he didn't give a damn if the Council liked it or not. They were going to give him the approval he wanted…or else…

"I don't really care if they like it, Clint, but they're *going* to approve it." Barron wasn't sure if his words were coming out as those of a man supremely confident, or one who was about to lose his shit, but perhaps the most troubling thing was, he didn't really care. The Council could go along with him based on cold analysis, or because they were more scared of their crazy admiral than they were of the enemy. Barron would take it however he could get it.

Winters just nodded, something Barron barely caught out of the corner of his eye. He could feel his comrade's tension, and he understood. Winters was no less wired. The two agreed on the right strategy for continuing the war, and if Winters was still worried about the Council, he understood it. But Barron had finally stopped fighting against himself, and he'd accepted what he knew was necessary. Sonya Eaton's report had been the last straw. If the enemy was able to bring reinforcements forward in the strength she had witnessed, there was no gain in waiting. Time was the enemy, not an ally. The Hegemony would grow stronger faster than his forces could, and that didn't even consider the fact that the invaders were a single entity, and the Grand Alliance consisted of almost a dozen squabbling allies. How long could a monstrosity like that hold together, especially if there was no action, if the men and women waiting just the other side of the door in front of him began to imagine the threat was receding, the enemy's energy spent?

Or worse, if the Hegemony began offering a separate peace to some of them. That wouldn't work with Vian Tulus, but he suspected a good enough deal could strip any of the Confederation's other allies away in an instant.

Barron's plan was dangerous, he knew that. It risked faster defeat if it failed. The forces of the Grand Alliance would never recover from a second loss at Megara. But it also offered the only real prospect of victory in the end. If everything—his life, the fleet, the future of the Confederation—had come down to a choice between one final roll of the dice with some chance of success, or a long, slow slide into defeat and ruin, he was ready to see it done.

Still, Winters was right. The politicians and diplomats were going to fight tooth and nail. They were on Craydon themselves, and they would resist anything that weakened the provisional capital's defenses. He didn't have the slightest doubt the diplomats would look to themselves first.

So be it. They were gutless vermin as far as he was concerned, something he believed even more after he'd watched the Senate on Megara surrender after so many courageous and dedicated warriors were killed in four years of war. Tyler Barron had never shied away from a fight. He wasn't about to start.

He turned toward Winters and gave his friend a quick nod. "You heard Sonya Eaton's report, Clint. You know we can't keep up with that level of reinforcement or production. We don't have any choice, none that offers any hope." Then he strode forward without waiting for an answer, trying against his own nature to force every bit of Barron familial pride and haughtiness into each step. He was the pure warrior, resplendent in his dress uniform, with every decoration and badge of service he possessed on display.

"Admiral Barron, Admiral Winters, please enter and take your seats. You requested this special session, so let us dispense with unneeded procedure and begin." Victoria Dorsey was standing at the head of the table, opposite Barron's chair. She had clearly been waiting for the two officers to arrive, and she at least looked interested in what they had to say. The rest of the delegates, sitting along the two sides of the table, were more of a mixed bag. They wore various expressions, ranging from curiosity, to what Barron guessed was smoldering resentment at being summoned on short notice.

He didn't care, and he wasn't in the mood for diplomatic dance steps just then. He wondered if Dorsey had sensed the tension, or if she'd simply chosen to expedite things of her own accord. She was a politician at heart, heavy with traits and attributes he detested, but she had something most of her brethren seemed to lack. Common sense. It was just possible his distant cousin could be an ally of sorts, at least on the Council.

"Thank you, Senator. I will waste no one's time prattling on about nonsense." Barron had made some efforts to speak the language of the diplomats in previous sessions, but not this time.

"I have analyzed the situation intently, extrapolated all possible courses forward. We have done what could be done to bolster Craydon's defenses, as well as those of the other Iron Belt worlds, and we have accelerated production of new fleet units. To this moment, our strategy has been correct, and we have achieved all we likely could have."

He stared out at the group. Most of them were looking at him with a range of attentiveness, though a few seemed to lack any interest at all. Barron took no offense. He barely noticed them. However little they cared what he thought, he doubted any of them could challenge his own disregard for their opinions.

"We must now, however, pursue a different strategy. New intelligence and scouting reports confirm the enemy continues to move reinforcements forward…in numbers that greatly exceed our previous estimates. We grow stronger with each passing month, but the enemy gains even more than we do. We are not catching up as we hoped to do. We are falling farther behind. That must stop immediately."

"Admiral Barron, I am sure we all appreciate your analysis, however it is my understanding—from your prior presentations—that we are already doing everything that can be done to build ships and fortifications. Were you incorrect then? Are there additional avenues we can pursue to increase production?"

Barron suppressed his anger at the quasi interruption. *Gisha Levara. Of course…*

The ambassador from the Sapphire Worlds had been nothing but trouble, almost from the second she, and her ridiculously large entourage, had arrived at Craydon. Her staff, and her constant presumption and interference, was greatly out of scale to strength of the military contingent her Far Rim nation had contributed. Barron wanted to reach down and flip the table over in rage, but he managed to control himself. He wasn't completely sure if it was due to effective anger management, or the realization that he'd look like a fool trying to flip over a table that had to weigh at least a thousand kilograms.

"Ambassador Levara…" The name came out with an edge in his tone, and he paused for an instant and continued more calmly. "…I am not proposing changes to our production schedules or anything of the sort." He glanced around the table. He figured Andrei Denisov would be with him. The Union admiral had been forced to wear two hats—warrior and ambassador—since the Union, still not officially part of the Grand Alliance, hadn't sent any diplomatic personnel.

The two men had been old enemies, but they'd gotten past that and managed to adapt to their new roles as allies. They'd always respected each other, even when they were on opposite sides, and Barron suspected Denisov would understand as well as he did what they had to do.

"Then, if I may ask, Admiral, what was important enough to summon us all here on such short…"

"Silence!" Barron slammed his hand down on the table. He hesitated, just a second. He wasn't about to show the Council any weakness, though he was upset with himself for losing his temper.

He expected a wave of outraged challenges for his brusque manner, but the room was utterly silent. Even Levara sat, stone still, a blank expression on her face. Barron had no doubt half of those present, at least, were imagining ways to put him in his place, or they would be when the shock wore off. But the display of unrestrained rage from so celebrated a warrior had unleashed a force even more powerful than pomposity and pride.

Fear.

"Listen to me, all of you." Barron had come close to apologizing, but he couldn't force the words out of his mouth. "We must act. Every day that passes reduces whatever chance we have of winning this conflict. And it will take time to prepare. I estimate it will be impossible to move in less than three months…and certainly, no sooner than two."

"Move? I'm afraid you've lost me, Admiral. What, exactly, are you proposing we do?" Barron had expected Levara to interject herself into the discussion again, but the voice was Dorsey's. He flashed a glance down the table, and his eyes connected with the Confederation Senator for an instant. He wasn't sure, but he guessed she had spoken in an effort to beat Levara to it. Whether that was because she truly wanted to hear what he intended, or if she was simply trying to keep Barron and the Sapphire Worlds representative from any further conflict, he didn't know.

"Yes, Chairman Dorsey. Move. As soon as the fleet can be prepared, and proper plans and logistics put into place, we must move out."

"Out?" This time, Levara had spoken too quickly to stop. "You mean send the fleet away from Craydon?" Her tone suggested Barron had just proposed leaping off a kilometer-tall building or something equally insane. "That's absurd."

Barron felt the anger welling up inside him again, and he tried to block it. But he'd come to despise the ambassador, and the best he could manage was to temper his reply.

Slightly.

"Ambassador, it is not only *not* absurd, it is essential."

"Admiral…if we allow the fleet to leave this system, Craydon will be defenseless." It was Dorsey again. Despite the moderate tone she'd managed to maintain in the Council's proceedings, Barron could tell she was also shocked by what he had said.

"Chairman, Craydon is far from defenseless. The system's fortresses, minefields, and laser platforms are all substantially stronger than they were during the first attack." Which, Barron knew, was a very relative assessment. There wasn't a facility in the system that was more than half-finished.

"Yes, Admiral, but even the bolstered fortifications are far too weak to repel an enemy assault without the fleet. If you withdraw the ships…"

"Who said anything about withdrawing the ships?" Barron felt his resolve hardening, even as another glance around the table told him there was no way he'd get a majority to approve his plan. "I can assure you all there will be no enemy attack on Craydon, not once the plan is underway."

"Then, with all due respect, what exactly are you proposing, Admiral?"

"I am proposing, Chairman and Council members, that the fleet set out from Craydon and proceed to Megara…and once there, that we launch an all-out attack to retake the capital."

The room was silent for perhaps fifteen seconds. Then, it erupted.

"That is preposterous!"

"Inconceivable."

"Are you insane, Admiral?"

Barron stood for a minute, allowing the diplomats to shout out their reactions. He ignored it all. There was probably something he cared about less than some Far Rim politician's thoughts on military tactics, but at that moment, he couldn't think of it. Vian Tulus would be with him, he was certain of that. Even if the Imperator hadn't been his blood brother, no Palatian would be against taking the war to the enemy.

Denisov had remained silent, but the look on his face suggested he, too, agreed. Two votes wouldn't be nearly enough, of course, and even if Dorsey went his way, he could see the proposal was going to be voted down, at least after it was shouted down.

There was no point even waiting for the vote.

"There is no choice. What I demand"—there was no more use for words like "propose"—"is the only alternative that offers even a hope of victory."

"Admiral, if you attack Megara and lose, there will be no hope at all of holding Craydon."

"No, there will not be." Barron looked at the Council member, a Confederation Senator named Carruthers, his memory told him with reasonable certainty. "But if we do nothing, there is no hope at all. We cannot catch the enemy in technology, nor outproduce them, at least not in the time we'll have. If we stay here, we might buy another year or two, but when the Hegemony comes, they will come to finish things. Our best chance is to seize the initiative *now*."

"Our best chance? And what might that chance be, Admiral?"

Barron paused, but just for an instant. "One in three, I'd say." It was a lie. He figured it was more like one in five. But that was still better than nothing.

"One in three?" The room broke out in a wild debate again, if debate was the right word for screaming and yelling among a group of people, almost all of whom agreed with each other.

Barron waited for a moment, and then he tried to outshout the Council members. But they were beyond convincing. It was fear more than anything, at least that was what Barron believed, and his disgust became more than he could control. He thought, for a few seconds, about calling for Marines, disbanding the council and making himself what he'd always feared. A military dictator.

He told himself he wasn't sure the Marines would obey such an order, but he realized the true danger was that he was all too aware that they would, and that almost every Confederation naval officer would follow him. That left no restraint save his own principles, and they were strained to the very edge.

He might have done it, too, sacrificed all he believed in, save for one fact. He needed the *entire* fleet, all the contingents from all the member nations, if he was to have any chance of victory. If he'd just been dealing with his Confederation officers and spacers, he might have done something different. That was a thought that would nag at him the rest of his days. But he knew he'd never get all the contingents to rise up with him in what they could only see as mutiny.

There was only one more thing to do.

He reached up to his collar and tightened his fingers around the four platinum stars there...and he tore them from the jacket. He looked down the table, and he tossed the insignia.

"If you're determined to lose this war, you can do it without me." His voice was caustic. "I resign my commission."

He turned around, ignoring the shouts...and the pleas to stay and remain, to discuss the situation. The time for discussion was over. Tyler Barron would risk his life, and give it up if need be, to strike a blow for victory. But he'd be damned if he would fight and sweat and bleed to hold Craydon for an extra year or two, especially for a pack of pompous fools.

To hell with them. To hell with them all...

Chapter Ten

AS Invictus
Orbiting Craydon
Calvus System
Alliance Year 71 AC (320 AC)

"We have to increase production levels, Cilian. Significantly." Vian Tulus sat in his plush office off *Invictus*'s bridge, reviewing the latest reports from Palatia. The Alliance had never matched the Confederation, either in technology or industrial efficiency, but Tulus had made significant efforts to close that gap, even sending Confed production managers to review and improve procedures. That had been a moderate success, though many of the changes had been difficult for the Alliance upper classes to accept, especially those that allowed more independence and greater advancement for the millions of subjugated Pleb workers who manned Palatia's factories. Such thoughts had come hard to Tulus as well, raised as he was in a culture dedicated to military might and still scarred by memories of a century of subjugation that were slipping slowly from living memory.

"The last two years have shown fourteen percent annual increases, your Supremacy. I acknowledge the desperate need, but I'm not sure it is reasonable to expect much more so quickly." Cilian Globus was the Alliance's Commander Maximus—the highest military rank, save that of the Imperator himself.

"There is truth to your analysis, my friend, save for one thing. Reason has little to do with the current situation. If the Hegemony prevails, if the Confederation falls, you know as well as I do, we will be next…and the rest of the Rim as well." Tulus prided himself on his logic and realism, but it was still difficult for a Palatian warrior to admit an inability to defeat an enemy.

"Perhaps if you were to return to Palatia. Surely, the word of the Imperator will push even our factory workers to excel."

Tulus shook his head. "No, my friend. The fleet is here, in such strength and concentration as never before in our history. The battle is here. My place is to lead the warriors of Palatia." He paused. "Besides, Cilian, we both know the Plebs in the factories are not the same as our warrior classes, nor, to be frank, as interested in the words of the Imperator. They are the conquered, old friend, and it was hubris to allow ourselves to believe they have become accustomed to their servitude. I am a product of the Palatian warrior creed, as are you, but now I see that we made a terrible mistake in allowing pursuits such as engineering and manufacturing to be deemed dishonorable to our own people. The best of each generation has long gone on to military careers, leaving not just labor to the conquered, but also engineering and research. We are not ancient warriors carrying spears. Our technology and production are our strength as much as our courage. I fear we have developed a system with a fatal weakness. I can inspire our warriors with my words, no doubt, but there is likely little I can do to drive the workers in the factories."

Globus was silent for a short while, clearly considering what he'd heard. Tulus was sure of his conclusions, but he also knew much of it would be virtual heresy to most Palatians.

"There is no doubt, your Supremacy, that the production of war materials is vitally important to fighting a modern conflict." A pause. "And I begin to see your point about the Plebs. Perhaps we *should* have offered them a way to rise from their positions through excellence in their work. That may indeed have been wiser...but we came from whence we did, and our past has forged our ways. We cannot go back and change the past...nor can we radically change our society. Not instantly. Not without inciting massive unrest among our warrior class."

Tulus stared at his friend. Globus had once been a Palatian firebrand, as he himself had. Both of them had changed enormously, and despite the vestiges of old prejudices that still pulled at both of them, they had come to see, and agree, on which perceived strengths of Palatian culture were actually weaknesses. But they were two men, both of lofty rank with considerable freedom of action and thought...and it had taken *them* years. Following on that path would be harder for lower-ranked warriors. Globus was right. Any structural changes to Palatian culture would take years, probably decades to implement, whether it was modifying the opinions of the ruling class, or convincing the long-subjugated workers that promises of better futures were legitimate.

Right now, you don't have years. None of us on the Rim have years left, not unless we can win this war...

He was sure he was correct, that the Palatians needed to change their ways...but, oddly, given that the time constraints removed that as a current possibility, he realized his best option was almost the exact opposite.

If encouragement and rewards couldn't push the workers to produce more quickly, perhaps fear would. But it had to be fear delivered from trusted hands, from someone Tulus could be sure wouldn't get carried away, or worse, enjoy it.

There was only one choice that met those criteria.

"I cannot leave, old friend. The warriors would not take that well on the eve of battle. However, perhaps you can go in my stead, carry back my words. I know you wish to stay as well, but as much as your warrior's heart craves to be in the coming fight, I believe you can better serve your people by returning home. When you return, you will issue proclamations, tie rations to increased production goals, and position soldiers in every production facility. Disciplined veterans who will not be easily provoked. If we are tied to the ways of our fathers and grandfathers, let us pursue them with a vigor even they could not have imagined."

Tulus couldn't quite believe the words coming from his own mouth. He'd come to think of himself as an agent for change, as the Imperator who would lead his people from their grim warrior's ways. Now, he was reversing everything he'd come to believe...but he knew he didn't have any choice. The legions of Plebs sweating in Palatian factories would see no improvement as slaves of the Hegemony. He *would* bring them the chance at a better future. But first, they had to win the war.

And he would do anything he had to do to gain that crucial victory.

"Your Supremacy, I can't..." Tulus could see the torment on Globus's face. He understood how difficult it would be for his second-in-command to leave the fleet, to possibly miss the next battle, whenever it came. But he could see, also, that Globus understood he *needed* to go. Because the Imperator ordered it, of course, but also because it was necessary, because no one lesser in rank and prestige could see it done.

"Very well, your Supremacy. I will go. I will carry back your words. How much leeway do I have? What am I authorized to do?"

Tulus stared at his friend, his eyes dead, cold, a signal he detested what they were about to do. But he spoke coolly and with utter certainty. "You may do whatever you think is necessary, Cilian. You have all my own authority." He paused ominously. "Do whatever you have to do. There is no time now for restraint, or for mercy. There is only victory or defeat."

*   *   *

"You look magnificent, my boy…no, no longer a boy, but a man. And the model of a Palatian warrior, from head to toe." Tulus stood up from his desk as the young officer stepped inside his office. Warder Rigellus wore a spotless black uniform, meticulously pressed, as though a wrinkle wouldn't dare interfere with its perfection. Warder was a sub-commander, newly graduated from the Academy, and without any combat experience. But he had one trait that set him apart from the thousands of other new warriors streaming to the battle zone.

He was Katrine Rigellus's son.

Warder had been young, still a child, when his mother died commanding the first *Invictus* in its epic battle against Tyler Barron's *Dauntless*. Tulus had been no more than a peer and casual acquaintance to the elder Rigelli, but he remembered Kat well, nevertheless. Few who'd met her had walked away without a favorable impression, and in many ways she had been the model Palatian. She'd even somehow escaped the blot that usually accompanied dying in defeat, and after a few mixed feelings circulated in the first years after her death, she'd transitioned into a tragic hero in the collective mind of her people.

Tulus certainly respected her, and after fighting alongside the Confederation, he had come to understand just what she'd been up against. Palatian pride too often turned to Palatian arrogance, and her defeat in battle against Barron had likely done more to strengthen her people than any of her prior victories.

"It is an honor, your Supremacy, to be granted an audience." Warder nodded solemnly, and there was nothing but sincerity in his tone.

Tulus returned the nod then walked across the room and extended his hand. Warder hesitated for an instant, and then reached out in surprise, grasping Tulus's arm in the traditional Palatian handshake.

"It is well called for, young Rigellus. Your scores at the Academy were outstanding. Your mother would have been proud beyond words to see you graduate first in your class."

Warder nodded again, holding his head bowed for several seconds. "Your Supremacy is far too kind. Simply being in your presence is an honor and a privilege."

Tulus wondered how much of Warder's conduct was genuine humility, and how much careful self-control. It was certainly true that not every newly-graduated officer received an audience with the Imperator, but Warder was not just any rookie officer. His mother was a hero of the Alliance and, even at his young age, he was the patriarch of one of the oldest and proudest Palatian houses. He and his sister, herself two years past the Ordeal and entering the Academy in the fall, were the only survivors of their noble family, the sole two still-living Rigelli. They were also the adopted wards of the last Imperator, the great Tarkus Vennius, who had stepped in after their mother's death to supervise their care and educations.

An audience was the least Tulus could grant.

There was more than just respect for a noble house at play, however. He may not have known the younger Rigelli very well, but he knew how close Tarkus Vennius had been to Katrine, and to her children. Tulus felt he owed it to the man he'd replaced to continue to look out for them.

He'd considered trying to get Warder posted somewhere away from the front lines, but fully ninety-five percent of the fleet was committed to the war effort, and Tulus had decided he couldn't strip the boy of his honor in an effort to protect him. So he'd done the next best thing, and seen that Warder was posted to the flagship. To *Invictus*, the namesake of his mother's fateful last vessel.

Invictus wasn't a safe place to be—against the Hegemony, there was no such thing—but at least he would be able to keep an eye on the young Rigelli, and perhaps protect him from the kind of unrestrained heroics that got so many officers killed in their first years of service.

"I look forward to seeing you in action, Warder. As you know, this ship is named for your mother's old command." Tulus had become somewhat accustomed to Confederation behavior patterns, and he felt an instant's hesitation at bringing up such a topic. But Palatians didn't approach death the way their allies did, and with the sadness and loss, there was honor and pride. "I felt it only right that you should begin your service here…and, I must confess, I look forward to serving closely with you." That was a lie. The idea of getting Kat Rigellus's son killed in his first battle was horrifying to him. Perhaps he'd been around the Confeds for too long, but he'd lost the ability to see the death of so promising a young warrior as glorious or steeped with pride.

It cut against all he'd been raised to believe, but he sincerely hoped he would be able to keep the officer alive…and he longed to see if the young Rigellus would grow in ability and wisdom to match his famous mother.

If any of us live that long…

Chapter Eleven

Orbital Platform Killian
Planet Craydon, Calvus System
Year 320 AC

"What the hell happened to you?" Tyler Barron looked up in surprise as Clint Winters strode into the room, his boots snapping loudly on the metal floor. Winters's shirt was rumpled, the front of his collar a mass of torn fibers, much like Barron's own.

"I resigned…just like you did. I don't know what you're planning, but you can count me in." Winters's voice was raw, edgy. He'd had at least an hour to get a grip on himself since the council meeting—it had taken at least that long to get a shuttle back to Platform Killian—but he hadn't cooled down much in that time.

Barron wasn't sure how he felt about what Winters told him. He'd been wondering if he'd been right to do what he'd done, and he knew, on some level, he'd only found the strength to resign knowing Winters was there to take his place. Without either of them to command the fleets, there was no way to know what would happen next. The Confederation had never been in worse trouble, and for all Barron's disputes with the council, there was no way he could abandon his spacers, not now. But he couldn't let a pack of appointed bureaucrats control military decisions either, not when the future of the Rim was on the line, and their primary focus was on protecting their own miserable hides.

He'd never imagined Winters would resign, too. *Though perhaps I should have…*

What have I started?

"I wasn't planning anything, Clint." Barron was torn. He'd worn the rebel's hat before, in a fashion, but at least then there had been some reasonable doubt about the legitimacy of the government he opposed. He didn't care much for the rump Senate, or for the self-styled Council of the Grand Alliance, but there wasn't much doubt they were the genuine authorities, at least the closest thing that still existed. "I just lost my temper."

Winters looked back at Barron, his expression a cross between amusement and panic. "I figured you were planning some kind of move. After all, if we let those glorified paper pushers run the show, we're as good as dead anyway…or Hegemony slaves, at least."

Barron found himself nodding, a subconscious reaction to Winters's words. His comrade was right, and he knew it. He'd always taken his oaths seriously, but now he wondered. Was his duty to mindlessly follow orders? Or to save the Confederation…assuming he even could?

He'd never wished his grandfather could give him council more than he did then. He was uncertain, hesitating, his usual firmness and decisiveness eluding him.

The Confederation spacers would follow him, he was fairly sure of that, especially with Winters at his side. But what about the others? He didn't doubt Vian Tulus would line up behind his standard, whatever flag he raised. His blood brother would no doubt congratulate him on "clearing out the parasites and time wasters," or something to that effect. What about the rest? Denisov and his Union spacers were already in a precarious situation, and while he believed the Union admiral would join him, he wasn't sure if his new ally had enough control over his own fleet to endure the chaos an outright mutiny would cause.

The contingents from the Far Rim were even greater wildcards. He'd been stunned at Sara Eaton's success in bringing so many ships back with her, even uniting sworn enemies in the relief fleet that had saved the day a year before. But would those Far Rim potentates and petty dictators side with a rebel general as easily as they would with the Confederation government?

He turned back toward Winters, about to say something, though he wasn't sure exactly what…but the hatch to the room opened suddenly, and Gary Holsten walked in. The head of Confederation Intelligence, and frequent manipulator of affairs, had a wide smile on his face.

"You did it, Ty." He walked right up to Barron and slapped his hand against the officer's shoulder.

"I did what?" Barron was completely confused.

"Your bluff—yours and Clint's. You scared the shit out of them. They panicked after both of you left. It was a wild scene, and a considerable shouting match, at least for a while. But then Vian Tulus stood up and declared the Palatians would withdraw from the Grand Alliance unless *you* were in command of the fleet. They caved almost instantly. They issued a proclamation calling you both back to your posts…and granting you full authority on matters of strategy. The Grand Alliance council doesn't have authority over Confederation policy, of course, but the rump Senate is voting on the measure right now. It's just a formality. The Senators are as scared of losing the fleet as you are. I'm not sure whether it's fear of facing the Hegemony without you, or of you rebelling and rallying the fleet behind you, but, either way, it worked. That was ballsy, guys, even by my standards. How did you work up the confidence to put it to them like that?"

Barron glanced over at Winters, and then back to

Holsten. He felt a brief urge to play the role, to accept the congratulations on his bold and daring tactic...but he'd never lied to Holsten before, and he wasn't going to start. "I got pissed off, Gary." He paused and shook his head. "I'd like to claim I had some grand strategy, but I just lost my temper...and I figured Clint could take my place. I had no idea he was going to follow my lead. And while I can't say I'm surprised at what Vian Tulus did, it wasn't something we'd discussed."

Holsten looked surprised, something very rare for the magnate and longtime spy. "I'll be damned. I thought for sure it was a set up." He laughed, a short, sudden burst of grim amusement. "We struggle endlessly to do what we can, but sometimes, despite our best efforts, things come down to dumb luck. If we manage to win this war, they'll say the turning point was now. They'll credit our strategy, the courage of our spacers, the mettle of our leaders." He looked over at Winters and then back to Barron. "But there won't be one history book that says, 'things turned around when Tyler Barron lost his temper and stomped out of the room!'"

* * *

"Are you sure about this, Tyler?" Atara Travis was standing in the corridor outside the large conference room. Clint Winters was waiting inside, with Andrei Denisov, Vian Tulus, and all the commanders of the Far Rim contingents. It was a council of war, called because Tyler Barron had decided the time had come to plan the liberation of Megara.

Now, his closest comrade was putting him to one final test, a last chance to decide if the massive—and deadly dangerous—invasion was truly something on which he wanted to wager the future of the Rim.

"It will be costly, Atara, I know that. And dangerous. We could lose, perhaps we're even more likely to lose than to win. But what chance do we have if we stay here? The analysis was bad enough before, but Sonya Eaton's report only made it that much worse. Our defense last year held Craydon and the Iron Belt, and Clint's raid on the enemy supply fleet bought us a year's respite, maybe even another one if we stay put. What will happen after that? Will we win this war sitting here, hiding behind fortifications waiting for the enemy to attack? What if they don't come right at us? What if they ignore Craydon, and start invading the rest of the Confederation? How many worlds besides Craydon have defenses that can hold off even a moderate Hegemony attack? One, two? None?"

Travis was nodding in agreement. Barron wasn't surprised she'd asked him if he was sure—she'd been his aide and sounding board in one way or another for almost fifteen years—but he considered it a sure bet she agreed with the strategy one hundred percent. Barron wasn't one to yield the initiative if he could avoid it, but Travis was even more averse to anything that even seemed like backing down. She was the image of the polished and capable officer now, but he never forgot where she'd come from. She'd fought her way up from the streets and forced her way into the Academy, sustained by a relentless drive and a chip on her shoulder the size of a concrete block.

"You're right, of course, Ty. I just want you to be sure. I'll follow you into anything, you know that."

"We can't win sitting here, and we can't let them build up their strength. All our old defensive lines, the fortresses intended to ward off Union invasions, they're backwaters in this war. The enemy is already into the soft underbelly of the Confederation, and we don't have the strength to defend in more than one or two places." He paused. "Those are my tactical justifications, and I stand by them...but there's more to it than that."

Barron paused, but he didn't alter his gaze. His eyes bored into hers, and he felt the certainty of his decision strengthening him. "We've been retreating this entire war, and now we're sitting here, hiding behind fortresses. I'm tired of running, Atara. I'm tired of hiding. They've fought this war when and where they've wanted to, and we've done nothing but allow them to do just that." Another pause, and when he continued, his voice was deep, his tone dark. "We're through running. We're through hiding. We're taking the initiative now. We may lose. Every one of us may die…but by God, we're going to do it on our own terms, and we're going to fight a battle that at least offers us the chance of meaningful victory."

Barron had been uneasy, uncertain, but now he was filled with resolve. He could almost feel his grandfather in the room with him, and he was sure the old man would have been with him completely. He was far from sure of success, and his dark view of the future remained, but he also felt as though a load had been lifted from him. He would do his best; his people would do theirs…and that was all anyone could offer. They would win or lose now, but there would be no more running, no more hiding.

He held his stare on Travis. "Let's go, Atara. Let's get this thing moving. It's time to show the Hegemony just how we fight on the Rim."

*   *   *

"How are we going to get word to Bryan Rogan?" Winters's voice was tentative, and it was clear from his tone that he was far from sure the Marine general they'd left behind on Megara was still alive, or that any of his forces remained under arms over a year after the Hegemony invasion.

Andi Lafarge was standing outside the door. She'd been on her way in, but now, she paused and listened. She'd known about the war council, and she'd almost crashed the session from the start. She wasn't bashful, not by any means, but she also realized none of her qualifications—

smuggler, adventurer, hastily-commissioned captain, renowned killer of Ricard Lille, lover and companion to Tyler Barron—rated admittance to such a gathering. She'd probably have come anyway—she knew most of the major players herself—but she suspected the pompous fools from the Far Rim might take some offense. Barron was having enough trouble with those troublesome lordlings, and she hadn't wanted to make it worse.

So, she'd floated around the vicinity of the conference room, and she'd headed there as soon as she saw that the meeting had broken up. As far as she could tell, only Clint Winters and Gary Holsten remained with Barron, and she knew neither of them would have a problem with her presence. But now, she held back.

"If Bryan's still in the field…" There was little doubt in Barron's tone that his words meant, "if Bryan is still alive." "…he'll have a comm monitoring the priority channel, looking for any word from us. We're going to have to send some kind of ship to Megara, and without satellite receivers to relay the signal, that ship's going to have to get into orbit to transmit, or damned close to it."

"The stealth generators?" That was Holsten's voice, sounding far from confident. "Do we know how much progress the enemy has made on penetrating the stealth fields?"

Andi hadn't heard anything specific about the Hegemony developing countermeasures to detect ships protected by the fields, but it made sense. They'd suffered a terrible setback from Winters's raid, and there wasn't much doubt coming up with some way to overcome the stealth systems would have been a top priority. Especially since they didn't realize the fleet only had a few of them left, and no real ability to build more, at least in the short term.

"It's only been a little over a year, and they've been devoting a lot of resources to fortifying Megara and the other worlds they've taken. No doubt they're working on it, but there's a good chance they haven't come up with anything yet. Or, at least, nothing perfect. A single ship, taking a roundabout course, and being damned careful, should have a good chance of getting through."

"Especially a ship like *Hermes*." Andi almost lunged through the door as she spoke. Barron looked up, surprised.

"Andi…no, that's not what I…"

"You need a ship to get word through to the Marines on Megara." She left out any doubt that there still *were* any Marines on Megara. She had the same concerns as everyone present, but certainty of any kind was in short supply. "There isn't a ship in the fleet faster than *Hermes*. Better still, she's already got a stealth unit installed, and it's been well-tested."

Barron looked back, and for an instant, a look of unrestrained horror replaced his cool, non-committal expression. "Andi, we haven't even decided for certain to send anyone. We don't have any reliable information on the Marines' status."

Andi felt a touch of amusement at Barron's scrambling, but it quickly gave way to something more complex. She loved Tyler Barron, and she knew the amount of stress bearing down on him. The idea of sending her on such a dangerous mission—she knew how difficult it would be for him, and part of her wanted to back down, to spare him that pain. But she was who she was, and she knew she couldn't change that. She wasn't an admiral, she couldn't command fleets. She wasn't a scientist developing new weapons, or even a spy like Gary Holsten, gathering what information was available and striving to hold the whole thing together. This war was *everyone's* war, and she knew well the chance that Tyler Barron would die before the conflict was over. She *had* to do her part. Perhaps if she could succeed, she could increase the odds of victory. Maybe even give Barron a better chance to survive.

And she wouldn't back down on that, no matter what.

"Yet, you are planning to send someone. Who is more qualified than me? Your Academy education didn't teach you how to evade detection and capture from naval ships, did it? I was dodging navy cruisers with my hold full of old tech before I ever met you, my dear Admiral." She paused, her eyes darting quickly around the table. "You know I'm the best choice for this job...all of you do. There isn't much I can do to help in a fleet action, but I can damned well get this done. Whatever message you want to get to Bryan Rogan, I'll see it delivered...whatever it takes."

Chapter Twelve

Hegemony Supreme Headquarters
Megara, Olyus III
Year of Renewal 265 (320 AC)

"I believe we will be in a position to launch a renewed assault on the Confederation stronghold at planet Craydon in approximately eight months, perhaps six if we cut corners. The convoy and reinforcements you advised me of will certainly accelerate our timetable. But…" Chronos hesitated. He had always been comfortable with Akella, and certainly now, with their pairing efforts underway, they were closer than ever, but he was still uncertain whether she would agree with his new strategic thinking.

"But?" She looked back at him, her expression professional, businesslike. Hegemony culture separated sexual liaisons, either for recreation or for reproductive purposes, from strong influence on personal feelings. Chronos knew Akella was an old friend, and a member of the Council who shared his views on many things, but he had no illusions that their attempts to conceive a child would automatically compel her to endorse his desired change of plans.

"I have an alternate strategy, one I now regret we did not pursue earlier."

"Please…enlighten me."

"My original thought was for a lightning strike, a fast and direct blow at their capital. That effort was successful, from a purely military point of view, though it was clearly disappointing in terms of its effects on ending the war. Even with the Confederation Senate compelled to surrender to our forces, there has been very little effect on the enemy position at Craydon or, for that matter, on most of their other worlds. They remain intractably opposed to absorption into the Hegemony."

"That does seem to be the case." Akella paused. "I also expected more gain from taking their capital. Clearly, we underestimated the Rim dwellers. In many ways, occupying Megara has just created extended logistics and a host of other problems."

"Yes, we are of like mind. But perhaps we can find an answer in mathematics."

Akella looked back, a confused expression on her face. "Mathematics?"

"Yes. The enemy has fortified Craydon, and they have made it the center of their defense. It is one of their most productive worlds, and well-located, too. They can send relief to six other systems in their so-called 'Iron Belt,' with less than a three-day transit time." Chronos reached down and picked up a large tablet displaying a long-range star map. "Attacking them there is charging right at their greatest strength. There are advantages to that, of course, and a complete victory there would almost certainly lead to a swift ending of the war."

"But you do not want to invade Craydon again?"

"No, I no longer believe that is our best alternative. Such an assault would, as I noted, could certainly end the war…but the cost of the victory, against the enemy's massed fleet, the planet's partially-rebuilt fortifications, and, worst of all perhaps, thousands and thousands of the small attack craft, would be enormous. We would trade matériel and lives for time, for a chance to end the war in one stroke. But such thinking also led us to Megara. Perhaps we are wrong, perhaps they will not fight to the end at Craydon. What if they withdraw, move their fleet to another Iron Belt system? They would be weakened, certainly, but our chance for a quick victory lies not in taking Craydon itself, but in destroying their fleet. We assume they will stand and fight to the end. But they didn't do that at Megara."

"You believe they will retreat if we attack Craydon? Perhaps that is reason to do so immediately rather than waiting."

Chronos hesitated for a few seconds before answering Akella. "Yes, that is something I considered. But, first, I may be wrong. If we invade with what we can send forth right now, and they stand and fight, we could lose. I would still give us the edge, but perhaps something on the order of sixty percent, perhaps sixty-five. That is not a gamble I am willing to take with the fleet, not this far from home, not with so much of our strength deployed to this war."

Akella nodded her agreement.

"Also, the chance that they will retreat instead of fight increases with our strength. In eight months, we will be in a position to deploy considerably more hulls to an attack, which increases the chance that the enemy will run rather than fight. But even then, the capture of Craydon without the effective destruction of the enemy fleet is only an incremental gain, one more productive world removed from their control, but not a crippling defeat."

Chronos paused, looking silently across the table toward Akella. "Perhaps there is a better way. What if we launched a series of campaigns against other worlds of the Confederation? Iron Belt manufacturing powerhouses located beyond supporting distance from Craydon, for example, or key resource worlds farther out. Transit point nexii, cutting their logistical and supply routes? Our analysis of the captured enemy databases suggests that the Craydon system, while unquestionably an industrial powerhouse, is self-sufficient neither in food nor raw materials. It is a more complex plan, almost certain to take considerably longer. But if we can cut off their support, the stronghold they have built at Craydon will wither on the vine…"

"There is certainly some wisdom in that approach, but have you planned this meticulously, Chronos? How certain are you that you can eventually compel them to surrender?"

Chronos took a deep breath. "I have underestimated this enemy, and I do not wish to do so again. Their military forces have considerable fighting spirit, and they are very tolerant of losses. But I am thinking more in terms of incremental reductions in their overall production and logistics. We might even compel the enemy to split up their forces in a doomed attempt to protect dozens of worlds at once. Perhaps we can win this war without another titanic battle that would cost us huge numbers of ships."

Akella sat for a moment, a thoughtful look on her face. "There is merit to what you suggest, Chronos. I must return to the capital as soon as the…matter…between us is complete. Do you believe you can complete your analysis and campaign plan in that time? I would review it with you and approve it before I depart."

Chronos nodded, completely aware of what Akella was offering. A mere blanket authorization to make decisions at the front would leave the consequences solely on him. By reviewing and approving the final plan—assuming she did approve it—she would be adding her name to his, sharing the victory, or the defeat, with him.

"I will see it done, Akella, if I must work around the clock to do it."

*   *   *

"It was a pretty good haul, Bryan…and we managed to get in and out almost without trouble."

Bryan Rogan looked up at the officer who'd just climbed through the meter-high entrance to the hole in the ground that served as his main headquarters. Dan Prentice's uniform, already more a pile of rags than a proper set of combat fatigues, was freshly torn in at least three places, and blood trickled slowly from a gash on the side of his neck. It was pretty clear to Rogan that his second-in-command was taking considerable liberty with the term, "without trouble."

"That's good news, Dan." Rogan shook his head when the officer, even taller than his own one hundred ninety centimeters, tried to perform some facsimile of standing upright and at attention. He waved his arm, and then he shoved an old crate across the floor, what passed for a chair in front line reality of the command post. "Sit, before you fall down. There's no point in formalities. We're not Marines anymore, not really. We were resistance fighters for a while, at least, but now, we're what? A pack of fools, hiding in holes in the ground while the enemy tightens its hold on the planet?"

"That's a pretty grim assessment, Bryan." Prentice's words challenged Rogan's point of view, but the weariness on his face suggested considerable agreement. "We're still in the field, still in arms."

"Are we?" Rogan laughed slightly, a gesture rooted far more firmly in bitterness than humor. "What did you bring back from this last raid? Rations, blankets, maybe a few doses of antibiotics or antivirals? Not exactly the kind of stuff we can use to fight off the Kriegeri when they find us." Rogan's Marines, what was left of his almost-obliterated defense force, had retreated to the Catacombs, the commonly-used name for the ruins of pre-Cataclysmic Megara. The almost endless tunnels and underground chambers had been picked clean of artifacts and old tech— almost entirely, at least—but the spaces themselves were ideal for hiding surviving fighters. The ancient, high-tech materials provided excellent protection from scanners and other surveillance devices.

"Anything that keeps us alive keeps the fight going." There was real defiance in Prentice's tone, though he was having as much trouble as Rogan in hiding his growing sense of doom and utter defeat.

"You're right, of course, Dan." Rogan turned and looked at the opposite wall, no more than three meters from where he sat. A makeshift desk, or table—he wasn't sure how to label it—sat against the eerily smooth white wall. It was covered with items: tablets, a small generator…and a comm unit, placed in the corner, all by itself. "Did you find any batteries?"

Prentice hesitated, and then he shook his head.

Rogan looked back at the comm unit. It was the only link his people had, not to anything tangible, but to the hope of relief. The device was set on the Prime Channel, a military frequency. If—*when*, he forced into his mind—the fleet returned to liberate Megara, he would hear it first on that comm unit. His people had alternated between periods of relative warmth and comfort, courtesy of the ancient materials that hid their fires and heaters from detection, and stretches of time when they didn't have fuel, or even firewood. But, whatever happened, Rogan was determined to ensure that the comm unit was fully operational at all times. He wasn't sure he really expected any communication to come…but he had to at least believe it was possible. Even Marines needed something to keep them going, driving forward each day through the growing hopelessness.

"We're down to two spare power cells for the comm." He paused, looking as uncomfortable, he suspected, as he felt. "We're going to have to hit some place we can get some extras…even if it's just a few for the comm." Rogan had allowed his people to run heating units and build fires, but he'd drawn the line at any sort of real energy generation. He trusted the old tech walls and ceilings, to a point. But that didn't extend to running any kind of power plant or reactor, even if his people could have found one and gotten it working. It was just too much of a risk, and he refused to lose sight of the fact that his people were alive—the few who still were—by virtue of the fact that he'd managed to keep them hidden.

Prentice looked back, clearly trying to hide a frown. "Do you really think we're going to hear anything on that comm?"

Rogan looked back at his number two. "I have to believe it, Dan." Rogan was, by nature, a no-nonsense Marine, not one to indulge in pointless hopes or groundless optimism. He wasn't as sure as he'd made it seem that they would hear anything on the comm. But he was sure of one thing, without the slightest doubt.

He would never surrender.

*   *   *

"Commander Raketh, welcome to Megara. Your trip was satisfactory, I trust." Chronos stood outside next to the just-landed shuttle, watching as the rest of Raketh's party debarked. Under normal circumstances, he would have never come to the landing pad to welcome a Master as lowly ranked as Ninety-Six. Low, of course, only by comparison to his own Number Eight. In the Hegemony as a whole, Raketh was one of the highest elites, a first century Master accustomed to being in command wherever he went.

He'll adapt on that account…

"Master Chronos, it is a great honor. I certainly did not expect you be among those in my reception party."

But you did expect a reception party…

Chronos held back a frown. He believed completely in the Hegemony's system of identifying the most genetically perfect humans and elevating them to positions of authority, but he'd long found it frustrating how many of his peers, even the most intelligent, highly rated ones, became distracted with pointless pomp and privilege. Chronos had never had any trouble asserting his own authority, but he despised ceremony and useless puffery. It was a trait he shared with Akella, though, of course, with her position as Number One, she was subjected to an even greater barrage of it all than he was.

"I wanted to speak with you as soon as possible, Raketh. Your work on Dannith is to be commended. By all accounts, the base there is operating quite efficiently."

"Thank you, Number Eight. Your words are a great reward."

Chronos didn't like Raketh, though he had to acknowledge that the Master rated Ninety-Six was intelligent and competent as well as pompous and irritating. And he had nothing to gain by abrasive behavior, and everything from encouraging a comfortable rapport with his subordinate. Dannith would play a significant role in his planned series of offensives, and he wanted to make sure Raketh was fully briefed and understood exactly what would be expected of him.

"I trust Master Carmetia and her prisoner accompanied you, as I...requested." Chronos was trying hard to sound accommodating, holding back harder-edged terms like "order" or "command." The conflict was at a crucial stage, and he needed the best everyone had to give him, not a war effort hampered by rivalries and personal grudges.

"Yes, Number Eight. They remain on my flagship, though I can send for them any time you wish."

"Then do so." The words were a little sharper than he'd intended, but he was annoyed. *Why the hell do you think I ordered them to come if I didn't want to see them?*

"At once, Number Eight." Raketh turned and snapped off a command to one of his attendants. Chronos held back a frown at the number of personal aides who had followed Raketh out of the shuttle. It was an amusing comparison, not only to his own, almost solitary way of moving about, but also to Akella's. The Hegemony's supreme ruler had exited her shuttle only with a pair of guards…and she had sent them away as quickly as she could.

"Come, Raketh. Let us go to my office. We have much to discuss. I would hear all you can tell me about Dannith and any reports of nearby systems you may have to share." He had seen all the regular reports, of course, but now he was going to grill Dannith's commander for all the details he could get. He wanted to know everything he could.

He needed to know if the rest of the Confederation was as undefended as it appeared to be.

Chapter Thirteen

Orbital Platform Killian
Planet Craydon, Calvus System
Year 320 AC

"Admiral Barron...Admiral Denisov is here, and he wishes to speak with you."

Barron was staring at the figures on his screen so intently, he heard the aide's words, but it was a good ten seconds before their meaning registered. *Denisov? Here to see me?*

"Show him in, Commander." The words were almost automatic. He'd likely have made himself available to any of his senior officers—though he might have tried to dodge one or two of the pompous fools from the Far Rim—but Denisov was the last person he expected to show up unannounced.

Barron and the Union general had gotten over their mutual dislike and suspicions, to a point at least, but they were far from comfortable together, and Barron doubted they'd ever become real friends. There was too large a gulf between them, too much blood spilled in the war they'd fought against each other.

He stood up and began walking around the desk, just as the door slid open, and the aide escorted Denisov inside.

The Union admiral was walking under his own power with a cane, but his face was haggard, and it was clear the exertion was draining. The assassination attempt on Denisov, the work of a Sector Nine killer, had come a hair's breadth from success, and his doctors had only saved him by replacing his heart with an artificial one. That kind of procedure was well-advanced in the Confederation, but Union medicine lagged, as did most of its technology. Barron had intended to arrange for Denisov to have a replacement implant in one of Craydon's hospitals, but the recovery time for a procedure like that was months…and he hadn't dared to leave the Union contingent without its commander for so long.

After the war. It's the least we can do to repay him for bringing his ships to our aid.

Barron wasn't quite to the point where he liked Denisov, but there was definitely some respect developing. And that, he figured, was a start.

"Will there be anything else, Admiral?"

"That will be all, Commander." Barron hesitated a few seconds, as the aide turned and left the room. Then he extended his hand. "I am glad to see you, Admiral Denisov." In truth, he wouldn't have gone right to *glad*. "How can I help you?"

Denisov grasped Barron's hand reasonably firmly, likely the best he could manage, the cane wobbling a bit in the other hand as the two men held each other's grip for at least five seconds. Then, the Union officer replied, "Thank you for seeing me on such short notice, Admiral. I apologize for not contacting your office and arranging something in advance, but I've…well, I've been thinking, and…"

"Go ahead, Admiral…" Barron gestured toward one of the chairs. "Please have a seat…and, by all means, tell me what you're thinking. There is nothing you can't discuss with me, certainly nothing of military significance."

"Thank you, Admiral." Denisov sat down, unable to hide

all of the relief he felt. "Well, it is simply this. I have become concerned about the fleet—*my* fleet—and the morale status of my spacers."

"We're all under great stress, Admiral. Morale is a problem for all of us…though I can see how, in some ways, it is more challenging for your personnel."

"I maintain a high level of support among the spacers, Admiral, but obviously, there is resentment as well, and some are beginning to voice outright opposition. It's more than the fact that we are—were—enemies, Admiral, and now we fight together. I believe they all understand the threat the Hegemony represents to all of us, and they have fought alongside your spacers without significant problems." He paused. "But they are all branded traitors back home. They have friends, families…and, I'm not sure how much you know about Sector Nine and its practices, but their taking action against family members and loved ones is definitely a concern."

"I know enough about Sector Nine, Admiral." He knew more than he wanted to know, and he had his own list of resentments against the Union intelligence agency. "But what can be done about that? If your people go back—apart from the threat of Hegemony conquest—they will more than likely face arrest for treason, will they not? Even if they are not all executed, the senior officers almost certainly will be, and I can't imagine the rest would get away with less than long prison sentences. I assume Union detention facilities are as bad as I've heard."

"They're worse. And, of course, the fleet can't return. I wouldn't consider withdrawing the forces from the Grand Alliance. The Hegemony is a threat to all of us. I am merely suggesting that perhaps it is time for someone to return, to try and make the case for what we have done. To see if Gaston Villieneuve can be convinced of the true danger. Perhaps the Union can be brought into the war in total, as a unified nation, and not a renegade fleet without supply and crewed by increasingly demoralized refugees."

Barron sat down in his own chair as he listened. He was silent for a moment after Denisov had finished. The admiral had made sense, in a theoretical kind of way, but from what he'd heard of Gaston Villieneuve, convincing the homicidal psychopath of anything was going to be difficult.

And damned dangerous for whoever went.

"Do you really think that's possible, Admiral? Certainly, you know more of Mr. Villieneuve than I, but from what I've heard…" Barron let his words trail off.

"Likely, Admiral, what you have heard is but the half of it. And I suspect he has only become worse since the death of Ricard Lille. The assassin was his only true friend, the one person he ever trusted, or at least as close as he could come."

Barron didn't say anything. The mention of Lille just made him think of Andi, and the fact that she was leaving in a few days. He'd tried to convince her not to go, but he couldn't argue against her qualifications for the mission…and, in the end, he hadn't had it in him to try to order her to stay.

"Nevertheless," Denisov continued, "I believe I must try."

"You?" Barron's mind had wandered to Andi, but now it was back on Denisov with razor focus. "You can't mean you're suggesting that you go yourself."

"Of course. It's too dangerous to send anyone else…and I believe I can make the very best case for…"

"You can't." A pause. "Andrei, Villieneuve is as likely to have you executed on sight as he is to listen to the first word out of your mouth. You didn't just defect, you took damned near the whole Union fleet with you. He must be beside himself. He already tried to have you killed once. Do you want to finish the job for him?"

"Of course, I understand the risks…but I led my people here, and I have a duty to them."

"You have a duty to remain here with them, to go into battle with them. Would you leave them here to fight without you, to face the Hegemony forces without their leader?"

Or worse, to decide to pull out once you're gone?

"I don't want to leave them, but I don't know who else could go. I wouldn't send one of my officers to answer for what I've done, or to pay the price for their loyalty to me."

Barron's mind was racing. He couldn't order Denisov to stay. The Union contingent's position in the Alliance hierarchy was still a very gray area, and Denisov was both an officer in the Grand Alliance's military structure and a member of the Council. Barron understood the admiral's concerns. In Denisov's position, he too would want to go, to try to negotiate some way that his spacers could return home when the war was over. But he simply couldn't let it happen.

"Perhaps we can come to another solution, Admiral. No one can replace you here. Your spacers followed *you* into this war, not orders from the high command. We have no idea if they would even follow anyone else, and they deserve to have you with them. But perhaps there is someone else we can send to Montmirail."

"I can't order any of my officers to return, Admiral. It's too dangerous."

"What about an ambassador?"

Denisov looked back, somewhat confused. "An ambassador?"

"Yes. Perhaps Gary Holsten can supply one of his people, one with significant knowledge of Union affairs, and experience in diplomacy. We could...*persuade*...the Council to appoint the emissary as a representative of the Grand Alliance, with full diplomatic privileges. There is no guarantee, of course, that Villieneuve will respect such credentials, but I think it's a far better idea than sending an officer whose grizzly death the maniac has probably been fantasizing about for more than a year. Don't you?"

Denisov looked down at the floor for a moment before returning his gaze to Barron. "I don't like sending others to take risks in my place, Admiral."

Barron almost smiled. "We're like animals that way. It's probably the hardest thing to do. But tell me, Andrei— when was the last time you got to do something because you *wanted* to?"

*   *   *

"Admiral Barron, allow me to introduce you to Alexander Kerevsky. Alex is an old friend, and an ally in some…difficult…situations. He's a rare breed, a man who has genuine experience both in diplomacy and espionage." Gary Holsten turned and gestured toward the man standing at his side. "He also knew your grandfather, I believe."

"I think 'knew' is a bit of an overstatement. The admiral—your grandfather—was lecturing at the Academy during my first year. This was shortly before the Third Union war, and he left to return to active duty during my second year." There was a pause, and an uncomfortable silence. The elder Barron had died in that conflict, and it was clear Kerevsky was concerned he'd touched on an unpleasant topic. "I am Alexander Kerevsky, Admiral Barron. It is a great pleasure to finally meet you. Your reputation has, of course, preceded you." The diplomat, agent, whatever he was, extended his hand.

Barron reached out and shook with the visitor. "It is my pleasure as well, Ambassador Kerevsky." The "ambassador" part wasn't formal, not yet at least, but Barron had no doubt, after the showdown with Clint Winters and himself, the Council wasn't going to make an issue out of the totally rational idea of sending an emissary to the Union. "It is always a pleasure to meet someone who knew my grandfather. I'm afraid my memories of him are those of a child, more concerned with fishing and hiking in the woods than with his military tactics and his wisdom. Perhaps when this is all over, we can find time to sit and talk about him in some detail."

"I would greatly enjoy that, Admiral."

"As would I." Barron turned toward Holsten before he continued. "I am sure Gary has given you the details, but I want to be sure you understand the risks. Gaston Villieneuve is unpredictable, and he is capable of doing almost anything. By all accounts, he is now the uncontested dictator of the Union, and the loss of so much of his fleet to Andrei Denisov's defection *has* to have him in a volatile state."

"You're trying to tell me he's as likely to clap me in irons or have me shot—or worse—the instant I debark. Yes, Gary was quite clear about that, though I daresay I understood that from the instant he told me about the mission."

"And you're still willing to go?"

"Of course, Admiral." Kerevsky looked back at Barron for a few seconds. "It's a rational decision, I think. First, Gaston Villieneuve, while unpredictable, is clearly an intelligent and capable man. Somehow, he managed to survive the turmoil after the last Union war, something no one else on the Presidium managed to do. He turned a desperate and dangerous situation around, and ended up more powerful than he was before. So, as brutal as he can be, he is clearly capable of adapting to reality. He tried to join with the Hegemony against us—also a move that made sense from his perspective—but they rebuffed him and tried to destroy his fleet. He knows that is no longer a viable course to pursue, and he must be equally aware that if the Hegemony defeats us, the Union will stand no chance."

Barron looked back, wanting to say something, but not sure exactly what. Kerevsky's points were valid, logical, clear...but Barron despised Villieneuve, and he had trouble imagining the Union leader as anything but a crazed psychopath.

"Second, even if I am wrong, even if Villieneuve is not as rational as I imagine…do I risk any more than your spacers do? This is the most desperate fight the Confederation—the entire Rim—has every faced. Even as we sit here, the Confederation's capital is occupied by an enemy, for the first time in its history. Megara didn't even fall during the Cataclysm, and yet now it is controlled by the Hegemony. Is there risk in this mission? Certainly. I would be a fool to say otherwise. But if we can bring the Union in as a true member of the Grand Alliance, the benefits will far outweigh the dangers. Admiral Denisov may have brought a large number of ships, but there are more still in the Union, and while their industry doesn't match ours, it is far from insubstantial. Never forget, the Union is almost twice the size of the Confederation. Can we afford to forgo the chance to add that strength to our forces? A few diplomats enduring some level of danger seems like a small price to pay." He paused, and then forced a smile, one Barron took as a bit of gallows humor. "It's a good bet, don't you think?"

Barron was impressed with the diplomat, though he shouldn't be surprised. He'd known Gary Holsten would find someone up to the job, and the ambassador seemed to have the good sense and intellect the mission required, and definitely the courage to take whatever risks were necessary.

"Very well, Ambassador. You may choose anyone you wish to bring along. I can assign you Marines for personal protection, but…"

"But there is little point. What would a dozen Marines, or even a thousand, do to protect me on Montmirail? No, I daresay you will have more vital uses for your warriors, Admiral. I would request one of the Torch transports, as it seems time is short, and the sooner I can get there, the better. But besides a skeleton crew to fly the ship, I will take only my own small staff. I believe there is a significant chance of success…but clearly there is danger as well, and I see no need to risk anyone non-essential."

Barron was silent for a moment. Then he said, "I will send word to have a Torch prepared for you immediately. You can leave whenever you are ready. Good luck, Ambassador." He reached out and grasped Kerevsky's hand again. "Take care…and make it back as soon as you can, so we can have that talk about my grandfather."

Chapter Fourteen

Orbital Platform Killian
Planet Craydon, Calvus System
Year 320 AC

"Captain Eaton, *Tarsus* has been fully serviced, along with the rest of your ships. Your fighter squadrons have been reinforced back to full strength, and you are cleared to depart at any time."

Eaton listened to the maintenance supervisor intently, perhaps wincing slightly at the mention of the fighter squadrons. She'd lost a lot of her pilots on the last series of raiding missions, something that stood out all the more since her ships hadn't closed to combat range themselves, and she'd only lost two other spacers, both to accidents.

However, the "cleared to depart" bit really caught her by surprise. She didn't have any orders yet, and with the preparations for the fleet's attack on Megara, she'd just assumed her ships would be integrated into the main force structure.

"Sonya…" She recognized the voice immediately, but she was still startled when Admiral Barron walked out of the corridor right around the corner. She was about to reply, when Admiral Winters followed right behind.

She snapped to attention. "Admiral…and Admiral."

"At ease, Sonya…I think we'll leave formalities to the Council," Barron said. "For now, we would like to have a word with you."

"Of course, sir." She was confused, the surprise far from having worn off, but she was curious, too.

"You know that we're preparing to retake Megara."

"Yes, sir, of course." She'd been surprised to be included in the small group of officers who'd been let in on the secret. It had been hard to think of anything else. Success might mean a real turning point in the war…and failure would almost certainly lead to final defeat.

"There's no easy way to put this. I've known you for some time, and I respect and admire you…" Barron's words made her feel good…save for the unspoken "but" she could feel coming. "…but your task force will not be part of the attack."

"Yes, of course, sir. Whatever you decide." She tried to hide her disappointment, but Barron's own expression told her she'd fallen well short.

"Sonya, this is no lack of confidence in you, I can assure you of that. There is no fight where I wouldn't want you at my side. But I need you somewhere else."

"Yes, Admiral, certainly." She believed Barron. Despite the disappointment still hanging in her thoughts, she rationally knew Barron *did* believe in her. Whatever reason he had for excluding her task force from the invasion, it had nothing to do with a lack of confidence. Barron had long been her biggest supporter. He'd advanced her up the chain at an almost blinding pace, and she was the first to acknowledge she had no real place commanding sixteen ships. But, still, the thought of not being part of what could be the decisive battle, the long-awaited effort to reverse the course of the war…it was difficult to accept.

"I know this is hard, Sonya, believe me…no one understands that as well as I do. But we have to do everything we can to keep the planned attack secret from the enemy…until the last possible moment. We've had to pull ships away from the supply raids to reinforce the main combat units, but if we stop hitting their cargo shipments entirely, they may see that as a red flag and know something is going on. If they decide we're planning some kind of operation, it could cost us our surprise."

"You want me to go back to the cargo raids?" She understood the logic, but the idea of blasting a handful of freighters while her comrades were fighting to retake the capital was a bitter pill to swallow.

"Yes…partly. I want you to go for several reasons. First, your raids have been by far the most successful. We've pulled a lot of ships back, and I'm counting on you to disguise that fact, to hit them as hard and as often as possible, so they don't notice they're dealing with fewer attack forces."

Sonya nodded. She understood, and despite her lingering disappointment, she was glad to hear Barron express his satisfaction with her operational results. She knew her task group had the highest kill rate of all the raiding forces, but it was still nice to hear.

"We can manage that, Admiral. We were hesitant before to hit them too hard. Forcing them to more heavily escort their convoys would have been a short-term gain, but it could have just about shut us down, as well."

"Well, now, anything you can get them to send after you is that much less we'll face at Megara. That will be helpful, especially if they detach more anti-fighter escorts…" Barron paused. Eaton knew he was very aware of what increased enemy escort strength would do to her green pilots. "It will be hard on you and your people, but your ships will probably do more good drawing off enemy warships than they would in the battle itself. At Megara, you can only fight in one place, but if you draw enemy strength off into three or four convoys, you'll really help our fighter strikes in the main battle. You know as well as I do, getting Jake

Stockton's wings through the escort lines and to the enemy battleships is the key to victory."

"Yes, sir...I know. And I'll do my best to give them a reason to send more ships to garrison the supply lines."

"I know you will." Barron hesitated for a few seconds. Eaton could see there was something else, something he was reluctant to say.

"Sir?"

"Sonya, I know we've been choosing spots to hit the convoys, systems fairly far out from Megara. We wanted to hit them where they were most vulnerable, and where they couldn't expect reinforcements from nearby systems. That was successful for the most part, but now I'd like you to target the systems close to Olyus, no more than three jumps from Megara. You're likely to run into increased levels of enemy patrols there, and you'll have to be nimble...and keep your mother ships the hell way from any transit points on the direct route to Megara. I know it's dangerous, and it's likely to make your job a lot more difficult...and costly. But I'm banking on the fact that you'll be able to get some decent intel on what they've got coming up. Our scouting patrols at the top end of their supply chain, near Dannith, have run into a lot more resistance in adjacent systems. We're pretty much looking into a black hole as far as what reinforcements they've got coming up the line. Maybe you can get us a last-minute look...and shout out a warning about anything we're not expecting to find in Megara. Supplies are one thing, but if they've got a whole pack of battleships we're not expecting, I need to know."

"Of course, Admiral." She still wished she was moving out with the fleet, but now she understood why Barron wanted *her* on the enemy supply lines...and just how much he was counting on her. Jake Stockton's people had flown scouting runs to the Olyus system and gathered what intel they could on what was already at Megara. Those efforts had been few and focused—too much activity would have risked letting on about the planned attack—but it was all Barron had to go on, and he had no way of knowing what reserves might be coming forward. At least until she was able to warn him of any unexpected enemy units.

"I'm giving you two of the Torches, Sonya. They're the fastest things we've got—and these are just about the last ones still uncommitted. If you discover anything you think I need to know, send one immediately. We'll leave coded signal buoys on the approach to Craydon once the fleet leaves. When you send someone back, give them the priority codes so they can figure out where to find us. Even if we're about to transit into Olyus, it's never too late for me to have the latest intel. Understood?"

"Yes, Admiral. Understood." A pause. "When do you want me to leave, sir?" She knew the answer, even as the words slipped past her lips.

"As soon as possible. Your ships are ready to go. Do you think you can have your people in place by 0600 tomorrow?"

It was tight timing, and it didn't leave a lot of time to prepare, much less to give her people a chance to say their goodbyes. But duty came first. "Yes, Admiral. I'll make sure the task group is ready to depart at 0600." She was already scheduling her time in her head, trying to cram three days of tasks into a few hours. She wouldn't sleep, that was a dead certainty, but there was one thing apart from duty she was determined to do before she left…see her sister. Sara was an admiral, and there was little question she'd play a key part in the attack on Megara. Sonya knew her own mission carried greatly increased risks, and she couldn't even imagine just how deadly and dangerous the assault on the capital would be. She didn't want to think about the chances she and her sister would never see each other again…but she was damned sure going to find at least a few minutes before her group left.

It might be the last time.

* * *

"Did you get a chance to see your family, Bart?" Sonya Eaton was standing in the elevator car next to her aide. The task group was about to depart, and both of their places were on the bridge.

"I just have a nephew on Craydon, Captain. He's a freshly-commissioned ensign assigned to Platform Killian. The rest of my family is out on Warwinden…thankfully."

Sonya nodded, glad for her exec that most of his loved ones were out of harm's way, at least for the time being. Of course, no one was safe in this war, not really. If the fleet lost at Megara, or if the enemy took Craydon, it was as good as over. It might take the Hegemony a few years to mop up, but no one was going to stop them then. "Your nephew, he's not a…pilot, is he?" Eaton didn't know the life expectancy of raw Lightning jocks, but she had an exact count of how many had died under her command.

"No, thankfully. He's an engineer."

Sonya nodded again. An engineer assigned to the largest base orbiting Craydon. That was about the safest posting a new officer could have in the current situation, at least until the enemy came back to Craydon. Engineering seemed like less of a combat-oriented position than many others, regardless of posting, but that was often a misconception, one clear to anyone who'd seen technicians burned to death trying to get engines and reactors restarted or poisoned by intense radioactivity. There were no safe spots on a combat vessel. None.

"There are rumors that the fleet is planning something big." Tarleton looked around as he spoke, though they were still alone in the elevator. "I guess we're out of it…whatever it is?"

Sonya wanted to tell Tarleton. The ongoing preparations around Craydon were obvious to anyone who was conscious, but the fleet's target was still a secret, and the general assumption was that there was intel suggesting the enemy was coming back to Craydon. She appreciated that Barron had included her in his confidence, and she wasn't going to betray that trust. As much as she didn't like keeping secrets from Tarleton, she just shook her head. "Something, I guess, Bart…maybe they have some intel on enemy movements or plans. Or maybe Admiral Barron just has a bad feeling." She wasn't sure how convincing she'd been, but the doors slid open and rescued her from further discussion. *Tarsus*'s bridge lacked the sprawling enormity of a battleship's control center but, with flight operations crammed there instead of in a separate area, there were a good dozen officers there. Too many for Tarleton to continue the conversation, even in careful whispers.

"Welcome back, all of you." Eaton stood next to her chair and addressed the bridge crew. She planned to speak to the entire fleet once her ships were underway, but there wasn't time just then. "I know all of your leaves were cut short, and you were rushed back here with almost no notice. Admiral Barron needs us back out there on the enemy supply lines, as quickly as possible, and we're going to do our part. We're going to be upping the intensity of our operations on this run, doing some things differently than we have before. All I can say is, if we do our part, and trust that our comrades in the main fleet will do theirs, one of these days we can all go home and see our loved ones again."

She wasn't sure how convincing she'd managed to be. It took one hell of a leap of faith to imagine not only the Confederation keeping the fight going, but actual victory and peace. In truth, she didn't believe it, not really. She'd spent less than an hour with her sister before she had to get back to *Tarsus*, and she'd fought the feeling that she'd never see Sara again the whole time. She'd barely gotten away, back out into the corridor, before the tears came.

Sonya was a warrior, through and through. She would

never give up…but there was a limit to anyone's endurance. She didn't know where her limit was, but she didn't doubt she'd find it.

If she lived long enough.

"Let's go…Commander Tarleton, all ships are to break docking and prepare to engage engines."

Chapter Fifteen

Hall of the People
Liberte City
Planet Montmirail, Ghassara IV
Union Year 224 (320 AC)

"These reports are entirely unsatisfactory, Minister Ciara. Utterly useless!" Gaston Villieneuve was raging, as he'd done so often in the near year and a half since Andrei Denisov had defected with almost two thirds of the fleet. Villieneuve was angry with himself, certainly. He'd appointed Denisov because the officer had displayed extraordinary skill in battle, something his political creatures had rarely been able to match. And Denisov had seemed "by the book" all the way, a creature of the fleet, and sworn to duty. He appeared to be an unlikely perpetrator of a coup attempt, and he had never shown any signs of disloyalty to the Union.

Until he made off with the fleet.

In fairness, Denisov didn't seem to be seeking gain from what he'd done, and he'd only fled after the Hegemony had launched a surprise attack that came very close to obliterating his command. In the few moments when he managed to think objectively about the situation, Villieneuve knew Denisov had taken the only route he could have. Had the renegade admiral made his way around the Union's periphery and back to Montmirail by the indirect course, he would have forgiven the admiral, at least once his initial anger faded. He might even have decorated the gifted officer for pulling the fleet out of a trap that seemed almost certain to see it utterly destroyed.

But he hadn't come back. By all accounts, he'd headed straight into the Confederation, and made common cause with the Union's most hated enemy. Villieneuve always expected treachery, and he trusted almost no one—no, exactly no one, since Ricard Lille had been killed—but Denisov's action had taken him utterly by surprise. He'd suspected bribery at first, or some kind of payoff from the Confeds, but then he'd come to realize Denisov had done what he believed he had to do. The Hegemony was a dire threat to the entire Rim, and the career naval officer, in his political naivety, had taken it on himself to arrange some kind of pact with the Confeds.

Villieneuve saw the logic behind it, to an extent, but the fool hadn't even considered bargaining positions or concessions. As dangerous as the Hegemony was, the Confeds were the most threatened. Even if Villieneuve might have considered some kind of cooperation, he would have gotten more for it than the "thank yous" that were almost certainly all Denisov had obtained.

Ciara was staring down at the small cluster of tablets on the desk in front of her. She was maintaining her composure, more or less, which was impressive considering Villieneuve could have had her dragged out of the room and shot—or something much, much worse—on a whim. As ruthless as Villieneuve had been, he'd always maintained a calm, professional approach to things. He would use torture when he had to, murder when it served…but never out of sadism, only to attain his goals.

That had changed with Lille's death. The Sector Nine assassin—and Ciara's mentor—had been Villieneuve's only real friend for decades. Villieneuve had never expressed the slightest show of grief at his friend's loss, at least not that he'd allowed anyone else to see, but the flow of blood surrounding his rants had turned into a torrent.

"First Citizen, I appreciate the need for the most detailed intelligence, but the location of the primary standoff between the Confederation—excuse me, Grand Alliance—forces and the Hegemony fleet is along a narrow band running between the Olyus and Calvus systems. The Confeds are dug in on Craydon, and the Hegemony at Megara. As far as we can tell, there have been no significant military operations conducted in over a year. It is a stalemate, sir. One in a location almost impossible for our spy ships to reach."

Villieneuve turned and glared at the newly-appointed Minister. He'd chosen her because she was one of Lille's protégés. It was a desperate—perhaps futile—attempt to replace his lost comrade. But there was something about Ciara that the others—three that had preceded her in rapid succession—lacked.

Guts.

Ciara had shown proper respect when speaking with him, but she hadn't cowered like a pathetic fool. That was not the way to handle him. Lille had always known that.

Perhaps Ciara does as well, or will learn it in time.

"So, what do you propose, Minister? We can't simply wait here, hoping that Admiral Denisov deigns to bring the fleet back when he's done with it. Or, that he doesn't, depending on his intentions." Villieneuve suspected that if Denisov returned, the admiral would make a play for power. It was impossible for him to imagine any other course of action. But he allowed for the possibility that the admiral was as wide-eyed and naïve as he appeared to be, that he just might bring the fleet back and throw himself on Villieneuve's mercy.

That would be a grisly day if it ever happened. Denisov

might have made an understandable decision, but it was treason, and the admiral—and every officer of high enough station to have opposed him—would pay the price when he finally got his hands on them.

Which he would…one day. Things always came around.

"I'm not sure this is something you've considered, First Citizen, but perhaps we could contact the Confederation government—or this Grand Alliance they seemed to have formed. We need information, but why continue to send spy vessels to their doom trying to sneak around Confed and Hegemony fleet units? Why not send a ship openly, and declare our desire to join the fight?"

Villieneuve sat back in his chair, the tension draining away from his arms and his fists unclenching. "A deception…disguised out in the open." He paused for perhaps another half minute. Then: "Brilliant!" He shook his head. "Nothing but useless, grasping fools all around…not one suggested such a course. You're right, Minister. You're the first person I've had here who came up with something that would have made Ricard proud."

"Thank you, First Citizen."

Villieneuve's mind flashed back to encounters with Lille, strategy sessions the two had shared. Lille had manipulated him a few times, he knew that, but for the most part, he'd been an accomplice with the courage to stand up to him. Villieneuve had almost despaired of finding someone to take his lost friend's place…but now, he had some hope.

"Go, Minister Ciara. Take your idea and craft it…and return here at noon tomorrow with a full operational plan. Our proposal must be well thought out. It is essential the Confeds believe we are sincere in our desire to join them."

"Yes, First Citizen."

"And, remember…we cannot materially interfere with the Confederation's operations against the Hegemony. Andrei Denisov must pay for his treason, but we have to be careful with that. Perhaps we can make contact one of his

chief subordinates, someone we can count on to break away
and return home with the fleet…at the right moment, of
course. If we are fortunate, the Confeds and their allies will
rid us of the Hegemony…and be left battered and prostrate
from their efforts, open for us to reassert our place as the
dominant power on the Rim. A complete conquest seems
unlikely, but if we can get the fleet back, we just may be able
to demand concessions, and gain some crucial border
systems."

"Understood, First Citizen."

*   *   *

Gaston Villieneuve was insane.

Ciara sat at her desk, alone. She'd cleared the room of
her chattering aides and assistants with a feigned temper
tantrum. News of her apparent favor with the First Citizen
had spread rapidly and made her somewhat of a figure to be
feared, even more than she had been before. No one rose as
high in Sector Nine—*the People's Protectorate*, she reminded
herself—as she had without shedding some blood. All those
gathered around her, seeking to ride her coattails, knew that
well.

She had always kept her wits, though, and she'd only
resorted to outright brutality when it was necessary. As
she'd always heard was Gaston Villieneuve's way.

Or, at least, had been.

The man she'd come to know the past few months was
out of control at best, and, at the worst, batshit crazy.
Villieneuve had been through a lot the last few years—the
loss of the war, the deaths of the rest of the Presidium, the
rebellion and the establishment of a new government.
Villieneuve had handled himself masterfully way during that
difficult period. His presentation of himself as a man of the
people, and his astonishing success in pulling it off,
hardened her view of him as a political mastermind. And

confirmed her belief in the stupidity of the masses.

She'd watched as he'd shamelessly insinuated himself as the leader of the revolution, buying credibility with the sacrifice of many of his old colleagues. Then he'd slammed down the hammer and mercilessly taken total control, eliminating anyone who posed a conceivable threat. Villieneuve had somehow come through the near-collapse of the Union and emerged even stronger and more powerful than he'd been before.

That was an achievement.

But now she wondered if there had been a cost to what he'd done, if the stress and exhaustion of all he'd been through had cost him some part of his rationality.

Or perhaps it had been the loss of his only friend that had pushed him over the edge.

She glanced down at her desk, at the stack of tablets and the large pile of data chips. She'd been reading the scouting reports since she'd left Villieneuve's office, and while the data was patchy, it told her one thing without question.

There was a chance the Confederation and its allies could lose the war.

No, not a chance…perhaps a probability.

They'd been driven back constantly since the invasion. Finally they'd managed to stand at Craydon, to win, if the pyrrhic nightmare described in the reports could be called a victory.

Ciara had spent her entire career working against the Confederation. Before that, in the slums of Vertiare, she'd listened to endless propaganda on the vid about the enemy. *The Confederation is to blame* was the message on repeat as she waited for her factory-worker father to come home. He was usually so tired he could barely eat a meager dinner and tuck her and her brother into bed.

She had no love for the Union's longtime enemy, and more, she had her own heavy resentment for the loss of her little brother. He had been a distinguished spacer, and he'd fallen in the last war, a victim of the Confederation's butcher, Tyler Barron. But she understood a greater threat when she saw one.

Villieneuve was right. If the Confeds managed to barely defeat the Hegemony, the Union would be in a position of relative power—for a short time, at least. But that seemed like a poor bet and, perhaps worse, a victorious Confederation would recover quickly, and exact vengeance for whatever blackmailed concessions Villieneuve managed to extract in the shorter term.

Ciara wished the Union could defeat the Confederation and dominate the entire Rim, but that was unrealistic for the next ten or twenty years. *If* the Hegemony could be defeated, and *if* the Union could complete its recovery and rebuild its military, maybe one day it could challenge the Confeds again. But for now, she agreed with Denisov. The Union *had* to work with the other Rim nations. The Hegemony had to be driven back…and open cooperation would buy the goodwill of the trusting Confeds. The naïve fools just might drop their guard in the future, once the war was over. The time for thinking of advantage, of vengeance would come…but it was not now.

She had handled Villieneuve as well as could be expected. She was gaining, not trust perhaps, but some level of familiarity. She had to get him to see what she saw—what everyone who'd seen the report saw.

It would be dangerous. She couldn't count on him to listen to reason, however solid the evidence. Even suggesting anything but her stated plan of deception could be dangerous. One tiny slip could undo all she'd done.

She would be careful. She would undertake her proposed course of action, and she would wait for the right moment to try to persuade Villieneuve.

Or she would kill him. Before he discovered her true intentions and killed her.

She was a manipulator, as he was, willing to use almost

any measures to attain her goals. But she was something else, something Villieneuve might have been before he'd lost the better part of his sanity.

She was a patriot.

And she wouldn't let the Union fall if she could help it. Not to the deadly enemy from coreward in the galaxy, not to the Confeds, the longtime enemy, and not to a First Citizen who could no longer face reality.

Chapter Sixteen

Orbital Platform Killian
Planet Craydon, Calvus System
Year 320 AC

"We need all the firepower we can get. We've got—what, two dozen of the new primary units available? I understand they're Confederation technology, and highly classified...but there isn't going to be any Confederation if we don't win this war." Tyler Barron understood all the reasons for holding the leading-edge weaponry from the Confederation's allies. But he knew what he would face in Megara. He was far from sure his people even had a chance, but he was damned certain they needed everything they could get. To hell with the future balance of power on the Rim. All he cared about now was victory.

Survival.

"Tyler, I understand where you're coming from, but you can't possibly be suggesting we hand over enhanced primary batteries to..." Winters looked around. There was no one present save for trusted Confederation officers, but he clearly wanted to be sure. "...crazed barbarians from the Far Rim. If it's even possible to cram the things in those buckets they call ships."

Barron almost responded immediately, but Anya Fritz

beat him to it.

"It's not," the engineer said bluntly. "Most of their tech would have been museum quality in your grandfather's day. They don't have the power generation capacity to support even standard primaries, and they certainly don't have the transmission infrastructure."

Barron still believed the only thing that mattered was winning the war, but Fritz's cold engineering report brought him back to reality. Winters was right, too. The Far Rim potentates weren't the exactly the most trustworthy allies.

"Fine, if not the Far Rim dwellers, then…"

"What, the Union? You can't be serious." Winters's voice was getting louder, his tension pouring out. "You can't possibly trust them enough for that. I'll consider us lucky if we can get through this war without them turning on us. If you give them enhanced primaries, we'll be facing fleets of battleships with them a few years later."

"No…you're right. Maybe Denisov…" He was teetering on the edge of trusting the Union admiral, but there were thousands of spacers on those ships, and most likely some Sector Nine agents he hadn't rooted out. "Clint, we're never going to win this war if we can't trust our allies." It wasn't an appeal to trust the Union. It was a lament about a lack of options.

Winters's response pounded the point home. "We're just going have to judge each situation as it comes. We may decide we trust Denisov well enough. He's a man of his word, I'll buy that. But he has a duty, too, beyond his promises to us. And putting primaries into Union hulls? All it will take is one of those getting back to Montmirail, and…"

"That won't work either, so the political debate is pointless." Fritz again, just as certain as she'd been a moment before. "I mean, it's probably *possible*, but it would take a massive retrofit, and the addition of some higher-powered reactors, so you'd be giving them *that* technology as well. The primaries are spinal mount weapons, so installing them in *any* existing ship is going to require some serious jury-rigging, and tearing the thing half apart. A Union ship? A year. Maybe. More likely, eighteen months."

"Which we don't have." Fritz's argument wasn't the same as the one Winters had pursued, but the admiral jumped on it anyway.

"So…anything?" Barron was looking over at Fritz.

"Maybe the newest Alliance ships. There's already some Confederation tech in those, thanks to our treaties signed during and since the civil war. Nothing on the extreme cutting edge, but probably good enough. They're big ships, too, with highly rationalized designs—a huge difference from the twisted jumbles of circuits and power lines that used to dominate their fleet." She paused, clearly thinking for a few seconds. "I'd say a year to retrofit under normal circumstances, but if you really want the bottom line, we might be able to do it on a *couple ships* in two months, maybe even six weeks." She hesitated again. "That's breakneck speed, Captain, with thousands of workers conscripted to get it done. And I can practically guarantee accidents. It will be a miracle if we don't lose a dozen workers per ship, and it could be a whole lot more. The amount of vacuum work alone is incredibly dangerous."

"We might be able to make that work." Barron was thinking about the time factor. He barely heard her comments on the dangers involved. The part of him that focused on that warning tried to gain his attention, but he slapped it away almost subconsciously. Tyler Barron wasn't an unfeeling monster, but he'd seen thousands upon thousands killed in the war so far, with nothing to show for their sacrifices. He'd mourn any workers and techs lost in the retrofits, no more or no less than he did the spacers he would certainly be sending to their deaths.

He wasn't sure if his forces could win at Megara, but victory or defeat, if there was one certainty he didn't doubt for an instant, it was that, either way, the losses would be almost beyond count.

"Before you make any decisions, Admiral, let me be clear." Fritz's personality was relentless, her drive almost unstoppable. It was that, as much as her knowledge and intellect, that made her such a wizard at her job. But now, Barron could hear the doubt in her tone, the hesitation. "That means a full-scale effort, redirecting *thousands* of workers, as I said—and I mean highly skilled workers. That will hit some of the other production operations hard. And there are no guarantees. We could as easily end up with several battleships sitting in spacedock, disabled. You'd actually have less firepower, and still be out the production of all those workers." She paused. "There are a hundred problems that could come up, issues I'm not even thinking about now, like difficulties in meshing systems and tech, trouble matching Confederation and Palatian conduits."

"Do you *think* you can do it, Fritzie? If I put you in charge of the operation with unlimited authority to direct *any* resources you need to the project? Say, four ships total?" Barron was thinking of the four newest Palatian vessels, *Invictus* and her three sister ships. They were powerful warships, useful in the battle line, but their range disadvantage against the Hegemony railguns had severely impaired their ability to bring their own powerful broadsides into the fight.

"I think so, Admiral…" Fritz was clearly still uncomfortable. "I want to be blunt, sir…I can't make any promises. We could just as easily knock those ships out of the OB for half a year as get the primaries functioning in time for the attack."

"But you *think* you can do it?"

There was a long silence. Then: "Yes, sir…I think I can."

"Then do it. I'll need to get Vian Tulus's okay first, but I don't think he's going to turn down the chance of getting weapons that can engage the enemy at almost double his current range."

"What about the Senate, Ty?" Winters sounded concerned, though only slightly.

"What about them?" Despite his feigned innocence, Barron knew exactly what his comrade was saying. He was about to give sensitive Confederation technology to a foreign power, and blood brother or not, there was no question he *should* get Senate approval before he even brought it up with Tulus.

He couldn't imagine the Senate agreeing without weeks of furious back and forth. That would have been a crucial stumbling block. If he'd given a shit.

The Senate had granted him broad military authority, and even expanded it after his resignation stunt. He knew what they would do if he raised the issue beforehand. They would argue and debate, and talk endlessly…and then they would do what he asked, because they had no choice. Because he was completely ready to throw his admiral's insignia at them again.

He didn't have the time to waste on that kind of foolishness, or frankly, the stomach for it either.

"Don't you think we should get their approval?" Winters asked again, as halfhearted as before.

"Probably. But, honestly, I don't give a shit what they have to say about it…and perhaps we're better off not even bringing it up. If we do and they say 'no,' we'll have to outright disobey them, or threaten them. Again. A little gray area can be a good thing, don't you think?"

Winters sat for a few seconds, thinking. Then he smiled. "I'm okay with that."

Barron was glad to hear his comrade's words. Though he hadn't been overly concerned that an admiral called "the Sledgehammer" was going to be overly concerned with political protocol and the sensitive egos of Senators.

"Okay, Fritzie…I'll talk to Vian right now. You should

be good to go officially in a couple hours, so start figuring what you need now. I mean it, Fritzie. If you need half a dozen magnates to march around the spacedock in their underwear, I'll send the Marines to go get them. Your only priority besides getting the batteries installed and working is time. Get them ready for the invasion, whatever it takes."

"I appreciate the support, Admiral…" A rare smile slipped onto her lips. "Though, I think I'll pass on that kind offer, amusing as it would likely be."

Barron returned the smile, for a few seconds. Then his grim expression clamped down again. "We're not taking any shit from anybody down there, Fritzie. When I say, 'whatever it takes,' I mean just that…so keep that in mind. And if any of those industrial titans or local politicians gives you a problem, you tell them they'd better get the hell out of there before I wander along."

It was the kind of thing people said but didn't really mean. But this time, Barron was dead serious. "If they interfere with your work, I'll have them shot on sight…or, more likely, I'll shoot the bastards myself."

* * *

"Jake, come in. Pour yourself a drink." Barron gestured toward the small bar set up in the corner of the room. He'd never been much of a drinker himself, but he kept a few high-quality liquors on a table in the corner. He was trying to see as many of his senior officers as possible to discuss the coming attack, and he figured, with the firestorm they were about to head into, if they wanted a damned drink to make their orders go down easier, he'd see that they had one.

"No thank you, Admiral. I don't think I'll be drinking for some time."

Barron looked at Stockton, standing straight, his face a mask of grim focus. Barron remembered the wild young pilot he'd found on *Dauntless* when he'd first arrived to take command. Jake Stockton had always been a gifted pilot—and the terror of the battleship's poker games—but he'd become far more than that. He was a leader now, in every sense of the word—and a damned good one. Barron had seen the razor-sharp weapon standing in front of him forged from that young Lightning jock by pain and war and suffering.

"Sit, Jake." Barron gestured toward the large sofa where he sat. He'd taken some of his meetings in his office on Station Killian, but Stockton was posted to *Dauntless* anyway, and it was a good excuse to get away from the insanity churning all around the orbital platform.

Dauntless's crew was used to his presence, and they were protective of him, and of his privacy. He could get some quiet on the battleship, some peace. He'd been issuing orders and having pep talks with hundreds of officers, but Stockton was an old friend, a link to happier times, when he was a freshly promoted ship commander, and almost a decade and a half of unrelenting bloodshed was still a dark and unknown future.

Stockton nodded, and he sat down about half a meter from Barron.

"Jake, I wanted to have a talk with you about what we're planning." His eyes caught the gleaming stars on the pilot's collar. It was still hard to believe Stockton, that half-crazed lieutenant and squadron commander, had become an admiral. Barron had pushed the promotion through himself, of course, and he was only sorry there was nothing else he could do to recognize just what Stockton had done to keep the Confederation in the war. There had never been an admiral in the fighter corps before, not one who stepped out from behind a desk and led missions personally...but then the Confederation had never fielded strike forces of thousands of fighters, either. Command of so vast a force was an admiral's billet, and it was unthinkable that anyone else wearing the uniform could lead those wings better than Stockton.

"Yes, Admiral, of course." Stockton was on the select list of officers who'd been informed of just what it was the fleet was preparing to do. The rest knew something was up, of course. The upsurge in activity around the base stations and the fleet couldn't be completely disguised. Some no doubt suspected the truth, though from the gossip and rumors he'd heard, Barron knew the most common guess was there was intelligence warning that the enemy was coming back to Craydon sometime soon. A distant second-place assumption was that the fleet was falling back again, abandoning the Iron Belt system.

Only the hardiest of souls—or the crazy ones—had dared to speak of a return to Megara, of the fleet truly taking the offensive for the first time in the war.

Which, of course, was just what Barron intended to do.

"Jake, you know what a difficult fight this is going to be…and no one knows better than you what a crucial part your people will play in any victory." The new weapons systems, and the increased ranges of the enhanced primaries, would make the fleet's capital ships a larger factor than they'd been in earlier battles, but there was no question in Barron's mind—and he was sure Stockton's—that the bombers would again bear more than their share of the load.

"Yes, Admiral…of course." Stockton's youthful sense of invulnerability had given way to a darker relentlessness, but despite age and fatigue, he remained an unstoppable force. "We'll be ready to do what you need us to do."

Barron nodded, feeling a touch of guilt. The attack on Megara was likely to be the worst fight yet, the casualties almost beyond what he could force himself to imagine. And Stockton's people would pay the worst price.

"Jake…I've been thinking, and I'd like your opinion."

Barron sat silently for a moment, and Stockton replied, "Yes, sir, of course."

"I'm considering stripping the Craydon defenses, assigning every squadron we can into the fleet...anywhere we can cram them in. It will leave this system extremely vulnerable...and it will cut both ways on your strike force. You'll have more wings, perhaps considerably more if we're creative about loading up the bays...but the cost will come in turnaround times during the battle. It's one thing to pack a couple extra squadrons into a battleship's bays, we've done that before. It's entirely another to refit and relaunch all those ships under combat conditions."

"I think we can manage that, Admiral. It will take some planning, but we should be able to get the wings on some kind of rolling schedule that reduces the effects of overloaded bays and flight crews. I can't promise we won't have some problems, but in my book, we'll be better off having more ships in the fight. Besides, how much of a concern is the defense of Craydon? Megara's not a long journey, and it's unlikely some kind of enemy attack will strike while we're moving on the capital. Even if the enemy hit Craydon, with the fleet gone, will an extra thousand fighters really make a difference? We both know these new stations are at best half-finished, and none of them have fully-operational defense grids."

Stockton hesitated again and looked right at Barron. "Besides, sir...this is something of an all-in bet, isn't it? If we win at Megara, the enemy will be forced back. The war probably won't be over, but we'll be in better shape for sure. And, if we lose, if this attack fails...we're finished anyway, aren't we? We might hold out another year, maybe two...at least if they don't pursue us right out of Megara as we retreat. So, why cut down on any power we can put into this push?"

Barron was nodding, but he remained silent for a few seconds, a bit surprised at the accuracy of Stockton's analysis. Barron had known all along he was betting the Confederation on the operation, but hearing the pilot's no-

nonsense analysis gave him a moment's pause. Not doubt, not really—he'd already decided on the course of action—but certainly a reminder of what was at stake.

"The Craydon squadrons are packed with rookies, Jake…and maxing our strike force means bringing all the available escort carriers with the fleet. We've used them against supply lines, but in a straight-up battle? I doubt it would take long for a Hegemony cruiser—or even an escort—to blast one to atoms. That's not only the loss of the ships and their crews, but it only makes a bigger mess with managing the strike force refits."

"I wouldn't worry about that, Admiral. Stara Sinclair can manage it all. She'll find berths for the squadrons from destroyed carriers, and…" A moment of silence. "…well, sir, we both know a lot fewer ships will be coming back to refit than the number that took off."

The two men were silent for perhaps thirty seconds. Then Stockton repeated, softly, "A lot fewer."

Chapter Seventeen

Umbilical C14, CFS Hermes Docking Connection
Platform Killian
Planet Craydon, Calvus System
Year 320 AC

Andi walked—stumbled was a more accurate description—
reaching out to steady herself on the shifting walls of the
umbilical. The flexible docking tube connected *Hermes* to
Station Killian, allowing her crew to report for duty without
getting in the way of the larger supply link about ten decks
below.

She made her way forward, and finally poked her head
through into the ship's open airlock. She lurched forward,
pushing one leg through and holding on until she felt the
hard metal deck beneath her boot. Then she climbed the
rest of the way into the confined space, moving completely
inside. The airlock was large enough for three or four
people, but Andi was alone. She was the last to board
Hermes before its departure, and as soon as she closed the
airlock's outer doors, the umbilical would detach, and her
ship would be ready to depart.

She paused for a moment, and then she tapped the
controls, and the outer door slid shut. The umbilical was
fully pressurized, but procedure still called for full safety

protocols, and that meant sealing off the ship before opening the inner door. There was no need to wait for pressurization, though, and perhaps a second after the outer door clicked firmly shut, the inner one opened.

Andi stepped out and into one of *Hermes* lower corridors. She'd intended to take one of the ship's small shuttles to dock after *Hermes* had pulled away from the station, but there was some kind of problem with the bay or the launch control…or something. The report she'd gotten had been unacceptably vague, and she was damned sure going to have a talk with her bridge crew about that. She was on edge about the mission to begin with, and she'd had to race down and get through the umbilical before *Hermes* detached from the station. She'd been late because of her protracted goodbyes with Tyler, and while she knew that being late because of last moments with a loved one was a privilege her officer and spacers lacked, leaving him hadn't put her in a very good mood to begin with. Having to rush down, with barely enough time to see that her baggage was loaded, had her in a frame of mind that could only be described as caustic.

She'd insisted on going on the mission, of course, above Tyler's protests, and she still believed it was the right choice, that she was the one with the best chance of pulling the mission off. But she was far from sure she could do it and, if she was being honest with herself, she was just flat out scared. Since she'd killed Ricard Lille, she'd developed some kind of reputation for supernatural courage or invincibility…or something of the sort.

If they only knew how scared I was fighting Lille…

She walked down the corridor, heading for the flight deck. Her boots cracked loudly on the polished floor as her purposeful stride took her quickly to her destination. She didn't know how some still-unclear malfunction on the landing bay had escaped the final pre-mission inspections, but she was damned sure going to find out, and when she did…

She stopped dead in the corridor, just short of the entrance to the bay. There was a man standing in front of the door…and there was a big smile on his face.

"Vig," she almost shouted, rushing forward and throwing her arms around her old number two. She was thrilled at first—she hadn't seen any of her old crew in almost six months—but then confusion set in.

"What are you doing here, Vig? We've got to leave now. You have to get back to the stations." She turned and looked behind her, back in the direction of the umbilical. "I have to stop the…"

"I'm staying, Andi. There's no need to stop the debarkation."

She turned around, surprised again, and now a bit angry. "No, you're not, Vig. This is *dangerous*. I don't want you to…"

The door behind him slid open and three more familiar figures stepped out into the corridor. "We're all going with you, Andi." It was a woman's voice, a familiar one.

Andi was stunned, and her eyes watered as she saw Rina Strand, Lex Righter, and a towering giant who was partially obstructed by the bulkhead and his position behind the others, but who could only be Dolph Messer.

She didn't understand what her old crew was doing on *Hermes*, but she knew one thing. They couldn't go with her, not into the hell that awaited her ship and its desperate mission. Vig Merrick had sat at her side on *Pegasus* for years, they all had. She wasn't about to put them in danger again.

"I'm thrilled to see you all, and touched that you came…but you've got to go, all of you, right now. I'll see if the umbilical is still…"

"I'm afraid that's impossible, Captain Lafarge." Merrick was still smiling. "We've got orders, admiral's orders that supersede your own, I'm afraid. We're official

Confederation officers now, you see." Merrick held up a small box, opening it in front of her. It contained the bars of a Confederation commander, and as she looked behind Merrick, she saw that the others had similar boxes.

"I don't understand…"

"Admiral Barron didn't want you going on this mission alone…well, not exactly alone, but you know what I mean. I think he'd have come with you himself if that had been even remotely possible…but he must have figured we're the next best thing."

"Look, all of you…if Tyler convinced you to come on this mission, you can forget about that…"

"He didn't convince us of anything, Andi. He just told us what you're doing…and we practically held him hostage until he signed the commissions and transfer orders. We faced enough shit together, Andi, that I wouldn't expect you to think we'd let you do this without us."

"But, you…" She wanted to argue, to convince them to stay behind. But even as she resisted, she felt a sort of relief. She was nervous, and scared…and there was no question the sight of her people standing there bolstered her spirits. Finally, she gave in to the inevitable.

"You guys are too much…I just don't know what to say."

"And that says it all, Andi. Not that any of us need words after all we've faced together."

She moved forward and hugged each of them in turn. She was still reaching up, trying to properly embrace Dolph, when she stepped back and paused. "Wait, what are you guys all doing down here by the shuttle bay? I thought flight ops was down." She looked through the still open door, but she couldn't see more than a meter or two in.

"That was a little bit of a deception, Andi, but don't hold the crew too responsible. We brought something with us. Not sure if we'll need her or not, but she's certainly carried her weight in the past." A pause. "We had to ditch both of

Hermes's normal shuttles, though, to make room."

Andi couldn't believe what she was imagining, and she pushed past them all and stepped into the bay itself.

There she was, in the place of the two gleaming new shuttles, a gray, battle-scarred hull as recognizable to her as her own reflection.

Pegasus.

* * *

"She's gone."

Tyler Barron was standing on *Dauntless*'s observation deck, staring out into the dark void. It was the height of pointlessness, of course. Even when the scanners had shown *Hermes* was still in the system, he hadn't had the slightest prayer of seeing even a glint of sunlight off her hull. Still, he'd come to *Dauntless* just to "watch," and he'd made up half a dozen excuses that looked good in the file, but that no one who really knew him believed for a second.

Certainly not the woman standing next to him.

"She'll make it, Tyler. She's the toughest woman I've ever known...and I *mean* that."

Barron could hear in her tone that the statement was an honest one. And when Atara Travis called somebody tough, it *meant* something.

"I know, Atara, but this mission...If that stealth unit fails, or if they've figured out a way to penetrate the field, she won't get a light second into the system before they're on her."

"Anya Fritz inspected that system like nothing I've ever seen before, Tyler. I think it's the only thing she's done except work on the primary battery installations in over a week now...and that includes sleeping and eating. I don't know what's keeping her up. But the stealth unit will work."

Barron nodded, and even managed a smile. Atara was trying to help, and he pretended not to notice how she'd completely ignored the greater danger, that the Hegemony had developed a way to thwart the stealth unit. There was no answer to that. It was a massive danger, without question, likely the greatest one Andi would face on her mission. And there was no way to know, not until *Hermes* jumped into the Olyus system…and was discovered or not.

"You've just got to trust her, Tyler, in her abilities. She's incredibly capable. Even if she runs into trouble, I'd never bet against her."

Barron knew Atara was doing her best to take his mind off Andi, but watching her leave, the vanguard of the fleet's coming attack, had been the hardest thing he'd ever had to do. He'd spent as much time with her as possible, and they'd parted well, if such a thing was possible. But his fear for her hurt like an open wound, and he knew he had to find the strength to push it aside, to stop thinking about her.

The fleet was relying on him, tens of thousands of spacers looking to him as their leader…and they deserved all he could give them. They deserved the efforts of an admiral forged from steel, not a wounded man, riddled with fear and worry.

"Well, Atara, whatever I believe, it doesn't matter now. She's gone, and we've got work to do." Barron did feel better for sending Vig Merrick and Andi's other crew members—at least the ones he'd been able to find in time—with her. They were devoted, and they would do anything they could to help her, to see that she came back. That would have to be enough.

He had his own work to do, his own desperate, dangerous mission, and he suspected she was as worried about him as he was about her.

Maybe someday we'll get past our battles, all the desperate fights. Maybe we'll both survive, and endure until we can share peace.

It was a pleasant thought, and it gave him a moment's joy…but he didn't believe it, not really.

* * *

"So, now you all know just what all the preparation is for." Jake Stockton looked out at the other four officers in the room with him, waiting for the shock to slip from their faces.

So far it hadn't.

"If we lose…" Dirk Timmons was the first to speak, though he still looked stunned as any of the others. That didn't stop him from coming right to the heart of the matter. "…even if we retreat, we'll never get enough out to hold Craydon. The casualties will be staggering, win or lose."

"That means we can't lose." Stockton's words were strangely matter-of-fact, even to his own perception. He'd always been bold, and often cocky, but his words in that room were nothing but the absolute truth.

They *couldn't* lose. Not unless they wanted to end up dead…or Hegemony slaves.

"The wings are all at full strength, at least…though I'd be happier if we had more veterans in the ranks." Olya Federov was sitting next to Stockton, and she turned and looked at him as she spoke. Dirk Timmons had known Stockton the longest—the two had been Academy rivals—but Federov had served the most time with fleet's strike commander, ever since she'd reported for duty on the old *Dauntless*, six days before the battleship had welcomed its new commander, Captain Tyler Barron. She was his closest friend in the wings, and she had been for years, ever since Kyle Jamison had been killed. She was one of his tenuous links to the past, one of the few that remained in the cockpit, and he'd come to rely on her more and more.

"More than full strength, Olya." Stockton could see confused looks slipping onto the faces of the four officers staring at him. "I spoke with Admiral Barron, and we decided…we're going to assign as many of the Craydon squadrons to the fleet as we can cram into the bays."

"But with a strike force the size of the fleet's, is it even possible to overload the bays and keep things functioning?" Alicia Covington was one of the two new members of Stockton's inner circle. She'd come from Clint Winters's fleet that had fought to defend Dannith from the initial invasion. That gave her claim to considerable experience fighting the enemy, but Stockton and Federov had fought the Hegemony in that power's own space, as part of the White Fleet that had made first contact. If there were real veterans in the war, it was the pilots and spacers from that ill-fated expedition, however many were still alive.

Stockton guessed that number would be lower than he wanted to hear. Which was probably why he'd never looked it up.

"We had *Dauntless*'s bays double loaded when we first got to the Union front in the last war, and *Intrepid* was even more packed full of strays from damaged and destroyed battleships. We managed."

"Yes, Admiral…for a short while, with two ships. This fleet is the biggest concentration of force ever assembled on the Rim, and, I don't think any of us need to be reminded, we've got a dozen kinds of fighters, from different nations, all with varying tech, capabilities, and doctrine. Can we really handle more disorder and confusion?" Covington paused, and then she added the other thing they were all thinking. "All to get another thousand rookies, ninety percent of whom haven't faced a Hegemony ship?"

Stockton took a deep breath and held it for a few seconds before exhaling. "Alicia…all of you, there's no easy way to put this, so I'm just going to say it. This battle is vital. We *can't* lose it. If we were facing interceptors, if our wings had to get through dogfights to close, maybe those green pilots would be more hindrance than help. But we need to deliver as much ordnance as possible. We need as many torpedoes and cluster bombs hitting those Hegemony battleships as we can manage, and the more squadrons we have, the better chance that more weapons will get through."

"Regardless of loss rates?" Johannes Trent had been silent, but now he spoke up. Despite his choice of words, there was no condemnation in his tone, not even disagreement.

"Yes, Johannes. To be brutally blunt, casualty rates are not our primary concern. Not in this fight. We need to hit those enemy ships, take out so many they can't stand the pain. So, they retreat, and leave Megara to us before our entire fleet is destroyed. If we don't succeed, even more will be killed, and they will die for nothing."

The room was silent. Stockton was sure none of them liked the idea, that they were all concerned about taking rookie pilots into a maelstrom the rookies weren't ready to endure. But he was equally certain they all agreed with him.

There was no choice.

Stockton thought about all the pilots in the freshly-built hangars on the orbital stations. Many of them were still full of piss and vinegar, as he and so many of his colleagues had been, more years ago than he cared to count. Part of him knew it was wrong to throw them into the fight that was coming.

No…lead, not "throw." You'll be with them…

And what the hell are you going to do with so many? You may keep a few out of trouble, but in the end, that's a rounding error. You're going to take them to Olyus, send them at the enemy forces defending Megara…and hundreds of them are going to die.

He knew what all the new pilots were. There was a term, an ancient one he barely understood. But it seemed dead on in this case.

Cannon fodder.

Chapter Eighteen

Orbital Platform Killian
Planet Craydon, Calvus System
Year 320 AC

Tyler Barron stood in the bay, his eyes fixed on the shuttle. He'd always admired the sleekness of the Palatian designs. Their warships couldn't match those of the Confederation in power, but their small craft were a treat for the eyes.

The ship had just landed, and steam floated in the air behind its still-hot engines. Under normal circumstances, Barron would have been waiting in the reception area instead of out in the main bay…or, more likely, given the rank he was still getting used to, whoever wanted to see him would come to his office.

But the occupant of that shuttle wasn't just anyone, it was the Imperator of the Palatian Alliance. A head of state, and a person of sufficient importance to rate every show of respect Barron could muster.

Even though the two were the closest of friends.

Getting clearance to commence work on the Palatian battleships had been as simple as a two-minute talk over the comm and, while Barron intended to make some time to see his blood brother face to face before the fleet set out, he hadn't expected it so soon.

Barron had been reviewing the work in progress on the orbital shipyards, something he—and probably Anya Fritz as well—knew was a cover for checking up on his engineer's efforts to install enhanced primaries on the four largest Palatian battleships. If she didn't finish on time, he was not only going to lose four very powerful vessels, but he was going to have a very unhappy Imperator on his hands, blood brother or no.

The work was still on schedule, though, which made him wonder why Tulus had asked to see him immediately. Vian Tulus was his friend and comrade in arms, but he was also the Palatian ruler, and the commander-in-chief of the fleet's second strongest contingent. Barron would have gone to Tulus, but the Palatian flagship was in a state of partial disassembly, and the Imperator had been staying on the surface of Craydon. Vian Tulus had been spending much of his time being wined and dined by dignitaries and ambassadors and, Barron was sure, hating every minute of it.

Better him than me…

But it explained Tulus's decision to come to Barron.

Barron would have stood with Tulus against any danger or enemy in the galaxy…but he wasn't above pushing his friend into the line of fire of the politicians and the chattering hangers-on. He wasn't proud of it, but dealing with pompous, self-aggrandizing fools was his weakness, and it was a miracle he'd managed to control himself, more or less, in his many encounters with such creatures.

Barron watched as the hatch on the shuttle opened, and a guard climbed out. The Palatian dress uniforms had always made Barron a little jealous. They were crisp and elegant, but also sleek and fairly simple in overall design, unlike the over the top foppery so common in those of the other powers, the Confederation included. Barron was grateful for the short notice that had given him an excuse to forgo his own fancy garb—most of all the ludicrous hat that, in one form or another, had plagued the Confederation's officers for almost fifty years.

Tulus climbed out of the ship right after the guard. Barron smiled as he watched, wondering how many heads of state would have stepped out of the ship without honor guards and all sorts of useless pomp and ceremony. Tulus was from a culture steeped in its own ways and formalities, but he'd swept many of the more foolish ones away in his years as Imperator and, with his own prepossessing manner, he set the example for others as well. Barron's knowledge was purely anecdotal, of course, but he'd noticed considerably less overt ceremony around the senior Palatian officers since Tulus had ascended and taken the scepter. His memories of his time serving in the Palatian Civil War offered somewhat of a stark contrast, and he could see just how much difference Tulus had made in a few years.

"My brother, it is good to see you again." Tulus walked across the deck, directly toward Barron, gesturing for the guard, who'd been trying to stay ahead of him, to step aside. "This is my blood brother, Commander. I have no need of your protection in his presence."

The guard looked uncomfortable, but the word of the Imperator was law. He slowed his pace and allowed Tulus to walk the rest of the way toward Barron, though he remained close enough to intervene in the event some unforeseen threat developed.

"Your Supremacy, I am honored, as always, at your visit." Technically, a Confederation officer was not obliged to use the Palatian honorific, but Barron often did when greeting Tulus. The Palatian was a close friend, a comrade, and a trusted ally. Perhaps more relevant, Barron, though a Confederation citizen by birth and a loyal career naval officer, had held a strange dual status since the blood brother ceremony with the Imperator. Tulus had granted him a wide array of privileges, including lordships and estates on Palatia. By all accounts, it was the first time such had been done for an outworlder.

"And I am honored to see you, Admiral, commander of the fleet…and my brother." Tulus stepped forward and embraced Barron. "Though, I daresay you remember my name, so perhaps we can dispense with the 'your Supremacys and the 'Fleet Admirals.'"

"Very well, Vian." Barron smiled and stepped back. "But brother or no, you didn't come here for no reason…so what can I do for you?"

"Ah…no nonsense, to the point. How refreshing after putting up with the Far Rim dignitaries down on the planet. I have proven through experimentation that pomposity has little correlation with the power one represents. I could hear my ancestors laughing at me as I treated with arrogant fools from tiny principalities of three systems. I realize my people must embrace a new way forward. Still, I understand the old ways…it was easy to think of such pretentious upstarts as prey, and tempting to subjugate them and see them dragged out of the room in chains rather than listen to them prattle on endlessly."

Barron held his smile and nodded. Such talk from a Confederation officer or politician would have been strongly criticized, but Barron was well-versed in Palatian culture. They had a rigid set of honor and military ideals forged by ancestors who had spent over a century in bitter bondage, enslaved by one of their neighboring worlds. It was an ignominious shame they had taken out on the systems around them for more than half a century.

Besides, the image of arrogant politicians and diplomats being dragged around in chains held a certain appeal to Barron.

"So, my friend…what brings you here?" Ideally, Barron would have taken Tulus to his office and waited for his ally to disclose the purpose of his visit, but neither one of them had time to waste, not before the fleet was scheduled to depart.

Tulus turned and nodded to a pair of guards who had followed him out of the shuttle. They snapped back perfect salutes, and then one of them turned toward the open hatch and said something Barron couldn't make out. A few seconds later, another officer emerged.

The young man stood tall and proud, looking much like the hundreds of Palatian officers Barron had fought alongside...and against. But as he came closer, Barron's eyes fixed on his face, and he felt a strange familiarity. It was hazy, and he wasn't sure what it was...but he felt almost as though he'd seen the officer before.

"Fleet Admiral Tyler Barron, commander of the Fleet of the Grand Alliance...I present to you my new aide, Sub-Commander Warder Rigellus."

Barron heard the surname, and it echoed in his mind like the ring of a massive bell, unleashing old memories.

"It is my pleasure, Sub-Commander." His response was crisp, but his voice was soft, almost distracted. He stared at his new acquaintance's eyes, and in them, he saw back almost fifteen years.

"The honor is mine, Admiral." There was nothing but respect in the Palatian's voice, and Barron wondered if that was genuine, or if the young officer was a master at disguising hatred. He hadn't consciously accepted the realization, not yet, but deep in his mind, he knew who Warder was, even before Tulus told him.

"Warder is the son of Katrine Rigellus, Tyler. He is recently graduated from the Academy, and he will be serving as my aide in the coming campaign." A pause. "I wanted to introduce you before the fleet set out."

Barron was silent for a moment, his mind racing back through the years. He struggled for what to say to the young man standing before him. *I knew your mother...I killed her?* That didn't seem quite right.

He knew he wasn't being fair. The battle between *Dauntless* and *Invictus* had been a titanic struggle, but it had taken place in Confederation space, and Kat Rigellus had led her ship there.

And you didn't killed her. She killed herself.

It had been the dark side of Palatian honor in practice. Katrine Rigellus had been unable to accept defeat, to compel herself to surrender or return to Palatia in disgrace. Barron had thought of her then only as an enemy, if an honorable one he admired in some ways. But now he realized the true tragedy of her decision. If she'd surrendered, she and her survivors would have almost certainly been repatriated, and she would be there to see her son wearing the uniform she had worn for so long. She would be standing with Barron and Tulus and all the others, ready to fight to the end, to defend the Rim at all costs.

"If there is ever anything I can do for you, Sub-Commander Rigellus, you need only ask. I am available to you…always." It was all he could think to say. The Palatians, as a race, had mostly cast aside the hatred they had once had for him as the enemy, and they had come to embrace him as an ally, and as a warrior worthy of their respect. But he didn't know if that extended to Kat's son.

He wondered how he would feel, being introduced to the man who'd defeated his mother, who was responsible for her death, even if he hadn't done the actual deed.

"You do me great honor, Admiral." The Palatian bowed his head solemnly, looking completely sincere as he did.

Barron understood why Tulus had wanted to see him, and why the Palatian Imperator had come to him. The middle of a battle was no time for such revelations, and if Warder Rigellus was to serve as the Imperator's aide, he would be in the center of things when the fighting started.

Barron could see Tulus's eyes moving between the two of them, clearly trying to read their feelings, their reactions to each other.

He didn't say anything, but there was one thought in his mind, overruling all of his concerns.

I will do all I can to help this young man, Vian. For you, of course, but even more, because I owe it to his mother.

But he knew he'd have to keep an eye open as well, at least until he could be sure Warder Rigellus wasn't harboring any vendettas. He was a Palatian after all, and from a family rich in military tradition.

Barron resisted the urge to shake his head. He hoped fervently that Warder would accept him, and forgo any attempts at vengeance for his mother. Still, despite his best efforts, he couldn't banish the images of the young man lurking in a corridor, knife in hand.

Nothing in Warder's demeanor fed his concerns, but doubts floated deep in his own mind, charged with his own inability to answer a single question.

What would Barron himself do if the roles had been reversed, if the Palatian had killed *his* mother, or his grandfather?

Please, please…don't make me kill another Rigellus…

Chapter Nineteen

Grand Hotel
Troyus City
Megara, Olyus III
Year of Renewal 265 (320 AC)

"That is extraordinary news, Akella. My joy is without bounds." Chronos stood in the large room he used as a parlor. He had had his choice, of course, from the mansions of the politicians who had fled Megara before the conquest—or, for that matter, those of the ones who had remained. He had little compunction about evicting one of the Confederation's former political leaders, who, he had come to realize, were far from the finest of their people. But he had decided it was smarter to centralize the residences of his top personnel and, as a result, his people had occupied the luxury hotels that dotted the central zone of the capital city. The Grand had been the plushest of them all, and he had claimed the top floor for his own residence. It was large and opulent, but quite a bit smaller than one of his stature might have demanded…and even more so once the Hegemony's Number One had essentially taken up residence with him.

"I, too, am pleased, my old friend. It is right that we coupled, that we mix our genes. I wait with great anticipation to see the intellect and abilities of the child we conceived."

Chronos felt a flash of jealousy. He had long wished to mate with Akella. Not out of the clinging desires for lasting monogamous relationships that seemed so prevalent in the Confederation. But it had somewhat wounded his pride that a friend as close as she was had initially chosen another to pair with, and not him. She should not have to wait for their child—they should have mated long ago.

He scolded himself for such thoughts during a joyous moment. Petty jealousies and strife resulting from such things had been a factor in the empire's fall. Hegemony Masters, especially those ranked as highly as Chronos, were supposed to be above such things, their intellects the drivers of their decisions, and not envy and lust.

Akella was Number One, and that meant *she* was the proper initiator of all mating pairings. Hegemony custom, and even law, was clear on that. The higher rated parent was the prime mover, both in initiating the mating, and in the raising of the resulting child.

Which was just as well, since it was beginning to look like Chronos would be stuck out on the Rim for years.

"All is well?" Akella was as healthy and physically fit as a woman could be, but it was a natural enough question.

"Yes, as far as can be determined. It is still quite early, and I will remain here several more weeks before I depart."

"It saddens me that I will be unable to assist you during your pregnancy. It is likely I will not even be back on the capital for the birth." Chronos was sure he would be stuck in the war zone longer than that, and he wondered how old his new son or daughter would be before he saw or held his progeny.

"That cannot be helped, sadly. But you are here fighting for the Hegemony of the future, the one we will bequeath to our child. With fortune, the war will be won in a reasonable time, and you will return, along with the fleet."

"Yes…with fortune." Chronos had believed that completely…once. But he had begun to wonder just how long it would take to subjugate the entire Rim. Every plan from the outset had been based upon inflicting enough defeats on the enemy to break their morale. The strategy worked very well with the civil authorities on planets like Ulion, and even with the national Senate on Megara. But the surrenders of these groups had done little to reduce the ferocity of the Confederation fleet and its allies, or even the troops on the ground on the conquered planets.

He pushed the doubts from his mind. It was a moment for celebration. There would be more than enough time for worry and for war.

*   *   *

Bryan Rogan moved through the swamp, pushing aside the tall grasses that blocked his way. He was chest high in the murky water, and, save for the pistol holstered in a belt hanging around his neck, his weapons were zipped up in the waterproof sack slung over his shoulder.

The mission was a foolish one, at least in some ways. His forces had been ravaged—in any real sense, destroyed. He'd stopped counting Marine losses at one million, and he had no real idea at all of the losses of the other troopers and security forces that had refused the Senate's order to surrender and flocked to his tattered banner. It was more than he could bear, and the combined number, aside from being almost impossible to fully grasp, would serve no useful purpose. It was all best ignored. If, by some miracle, he survived the doomed resistance effort on Megara, he was sure the ghosts would still be there, waiting for him in the darkness of sleep.

"About two more kilometers, General. The relay is just to the north of our target coordinates, and about half a kilometer south is Wesland. It's a small town, no real tactical significance save for two ground transit lines that intersect there. The intel we could get suggests we can probably score at least some basic supplies there. Food, almost certainly, and maybe some other things." Dan Prentice was right next to Rogan. The second-in-command of the Megara defenses—almost certainly an outdated title since virtually the entire planet was occupied by Hegemony forces—had long argued to keep Rogan back at the command post. But he'd given that up a few months earlier. Rogan wasn't sure if he'd just gotten tired of being rebuffed, or it he'd decided the force remaining in the field was so small, it was no longer of sufficient urgency to keep the commander someplace safer.

Or perhaps it was simply the realization that no place on Megara was safer.

"Okay…we're a long way from Troyus here, and I don't expect there will be much of a garrison at the relay…or at the town, for that matter." Rogan knew his sole advantage—if any factor affecting his beleaguered and defeated force could be so described—was the distance to the enemy's home worlds. Every soldier they deployed, every armored vehicle, had to be transported over an almost unimaginable distance. The Hegemony had landed a sufficient force to crush his Marines in open battle, but they hadn't been able to fully garrison every remote point of military significance. That, more than anything, had kept the remnants of his force in action, picking and choosing secondary and tertiary targets.

He didn't fool himself into thinking his people were severely crimping the enemy's takeover of the planet or their overall war effort, but as long as his people retained the ability to hit the enemy, they were a force in being.

He trudged forward, feeling some gratitude when the ground rose a bit, and more of his body emerged from the brackish water. He was still walking through knee deep swamp, but that was a big improvement, one enhanced by the gradual firming of the ground beneath his feet.

He turned and looked behind him. He had about three hundred of his people with him, more than ten percent of his remaining strength, and perhaps closer to twenty. He'd scattered his people over a large area, sending them mostly to various underground ruins of pre-Cataclysmic Megara. It was just about the only place they could hide. The Hegemony scanners were too effective for them to remain undetected anywhere else. He did get periodic reports from some of the outposts, but the best he could calculate was a range of two to three thousand, in varying—but all poor— states of readiness. A sad remnant of the massive force that had taken the field against the invaders.

"Dan, you take the demo teams up to the relay. I don't expect there's much there in the way of deployed guards, a squad at most." That was a guess, of course, and he knew the enemy OB didn't include "squads," but his gut told him there'd be maybe ten Kriegeri positioned around the relay, and to a Confederation officer, that was a squad.

"Yes, General." Rogan had become more casual in his mode of address recently, but that was a far easier thing to do from the top down. Prentice still addressed Rogan as "General," at least most of the time.

"Take a full platoon with you, though. No sense taking chances." Rogan didn't think he'd need over two hundred-fifty Marines to take Wesland and raid its warehouses, but his forces had deteriorated to the most primitive of all supply and transit resources…the arms and backs of his people. He'd brought most of them not to fight, but to carry back whatever they were able to find and secure.

"Yes, sir. Good luck, Bryan. We'll meet you right back here in…two hours?"

"Two hours it is, Dan. Hopefully we'll find something worth eating down there." The Marine force wasn't out of supplies, not exactly. But the crates of hard and stale biscuit weren't the most appetizing thing to eat, and even those meager rations would only last another week, maybe two if they really stretched things. Rogan had no idea what shape the other outposts were in—he'd avoided unnecessary contact. Every time he sent someone in or out, he risked detection. He'd take that chance to gather food or conduct a raid, but not to gain himself data he couldn't use anyway. He'd put good officers in charge of each group, and he trusted them to do all that could be done to keep their people alive.

He turned and snapped out a series of orders to officers standing around him. Then he took one last glance at his exec moving off, gathering his own command around him.

The Marines were battered, tired, hungry...but they were still fighting.

And, as far as Bryan Rogan was concerned, as long as his people—any of his people—were still in the field, weapons in hand, Megara wasn't conquered.

No, sir...not while a single Marine stands in opposition to the invaders.

* * *

"Master Carmetia, Colonel Blanth...welcome to Megara." Chronos stood up from behind his desk, and walked around toward the man and woman as they entered. It was a bit over the top in terms of hospitality. Carmetia was a Master, but her rating was far below Chrono's own...and Blanth was a prisoner of war.

Chronos had been surprised when he had received the reports of the attack on Hegemony headquarters on Dannith, and on the death toll, which had included a Master named Develia, the military governor of the planet. He had been even more surprised to discover that Carmetia, Develia's immediate superior, had not had Blanth put to death immediately. He had almost ordered the execution himself, but he had held back. Defeating the Confederation was going to take more than brutality, and though Blanth's alleged actions during the fight certainly warranted death, he had thought perhaps mercy could reap some gains as well.

He did not really expect the Marine to willingly betray his people...but there were multiple ways to accomplish a goal, and as he looked out at the two new arrivals, he decided Carmetia had been right.

The Marine was more useful alive than dead.

"It is an honor, Master Chronos." Carmetia bowed her head in respect. Blanth said nothing. He showed no overt signs of defiance, but neither did he exhibit any respect.

"I am pleased to see that your wounds have healed, Colonel." Carmetia had submitted a full report of the attack on the Dannith headquarters, including a mention that Blanth had been critically injured...and that she had not only spared him summary execution, but ordered his wounds treated.

Blanth nodded, an acknowledgement of Cronos's words, but he still remained silent.

"My apologies, Master Chronos. Colonel Blanth does not understand who you are."

Chronos smiled thinly. "I daresay, if he did, he would hurl himself across the room in an effort to kill me. Though perhaps we can get past such things, Colonel. You oppose our presence here, I understand that...yet, you have been treated humanely, even after you attempted to intervene in the attack on the Dannith headquarters. We are not friends—indeed, we are still enemies, but perhaps we can be civilized ones. You may oppose our purpose on the Rim, but we do share some goals. To reduce the losses among your people, for one. You must have noticed our forces have not engaged in wholesale orbital bombardments, or the widespread use of high-yield weaponry. We are here not to destroy your people, but to protect them. I do not expect you to believe that, but perhaps you will work with me to reduce suffering among your people."

Blanth shifted his feet back and forth, clearly looking uncomfortable. Chronos knew he had maneuvered the Marine, put him in an impossible situation. There was no realistic way he could offer resistance, not in his current situation. But could he refuse to help his own people, to save lives?

And if he doesn't realize in doing so, he is helping to find and eliminate the last of his comrades, so much the better...

Chapter Twenty

Shuttle Bay
Orbital Platform Killian
Planet Craydon, Calvus System
Year 320 AC

"Tyler, wait…I'm coming with you." Gary Holsten came running across the gray deck of the shuttle bay, followed by an aide carrying two large bags.

Barron had been walking toward the shuttle, but as soon as he heard Holsten's words, he stopped abruptly and turned around.

"Gary…"

"I want to come with you, Tyler." Holsten came to a stop about a meter from the admiral. "We both know what this fight represents. I may not be of much help, but I know enough to stay out of the way."

Barron exhaled slowly, struggling to keep the breath from turning into a sigh. "Gary…you know I'd love to have you with us. You're an asset in any situation." Barron had a long history with the intelligence chief, and he still believed Holsten's role in arranging Van Striker's appointment as fleet admiral had saved the Confederation from defeat early in the Union War. He'd never gotten all the details of that affair, but he'd long been convinced Holsten had taken some considerable chances.

Gary Holsten wasn't a combat spacer or a Marine, but the man was no coward…and he was a fit comrade to have along for any battle.

Save for one problem.

"If you come along, who is going to stay on top of production and ensure the defenses remain at the ready?" Barron wasn't sure how important all that was, especially since he'd drained the partially-operational fortresses of three-quarters of their fighters. If the enemy came to Craydon again, the defense would crumble almost at once. There was little doubt of that.

But if the attack on Megara was successful, the fleet was certainly going to need supplies and replacements to sustain its effort to drive the Hegemony back into the Badlands.

"We also need you to keep a watch on the Senate, and on the Grand Alliance council." Gary Holsten was one of the few people Barron really trusted to deal with the politicians, mostly because the spymaster detested them with the same intensity Barron himself did. He wasn't overly concerned about the minor mischief that might go on in the fleet's absence, but he hadn't forgotten that the Senate on Megara had approved formal surrender documents, caving in almost immediately to the Hegemony occupiers. Those edicts had been mostly ignored, but Barron wasn't about to risk another group of Senators and diplomats losing heart and undercutting the fleet's efforts.

Holsten stood where he was, looking back at Barron. It was clear he hated the idea, that the last thing he wanted was to stay behind and babysit the Senate. But it was just as obvious he agreed with Barron. He knew he had to remain.

"I just hate sending you off again, and staying here. I was never a soldier, Tyler, you know that, but I know how important this fight is…and I feel a real pull to be with you all."

"I would be honored to have you at my side, Gary…but

without you here, we could lose everything we're fighting to defend." Barron paused, then he turned toward Atara Travis, who was standing right behind him. "Atara, issued a fleet level command. I am placing Gary Holsten in command of the Craydon defenses, with the temporary and provisional rank of admiral. All spacers, base personnel, and Marines are to obey his orders as though they were mine."

Atara nodded. "I will send it out as soon as we get to *Dauntless*. I'll make sure the Senate and the Council both get copies." That was Atara being comprehensive, Barron knew, but it was also her taking the chance to send a jab toward the politicians.

Holsten looked on, the surprise in his face obvious. For most of their time working together, Holsten had been the more powerful of the two, but Confederation Intelligence had been largely unable to penetrate Hegemony security, and consequently, Holsten's importance had diminished. He was still intelligence chief, and one of the wealthiest men in the Confederation, but Barron's power and prestige had risen so high, he'd been able to bend the Senate and the Council to his will with no more than a threat to resign.

"I will stay." The disappointment was clear in his voice, but also a spark of gratitude. Barron didn't doubt Holsten would have found a way to do whatever he decided needed to be done anyway...but now he could simply issue an order and dispense with the cloak and dagger for once.

He looked up at Barron. "Go, Tyler. You know what has to be done. Don't worry about things here. Just retake Megara...and send those Hegemony sons of bitches heading back where they came from."

* * *

"I'm still worried about the escort carriers, Clint. We're all at risk, of course, but sending crews forward in a bunch of tin cans seems like...murder. You know as well as I do, a couple hits could take one out, and I'm not talking about railgun hits. Hegemony cruisers will cut them to ribbons, and even most of the escorts." Barron had been of two minds on the escort carriers since they'd first been suggested. He'd take any extra fighters he could get in a fight against Hegemony forces, and the ability to project the attack craft into small actions without detaching battleships from the main fleet had vastly expanded the anti-shipping operations against the enemy supply lines. But he dreaded what would happen to the ships in a pitched battle. He imagined not just a heavy casualty rate, but quite possibly losing them all.

"Tyler, I understand your concerns. They're all valid. But what about this conflict, the situation and the odds we face is ideal? It's not a question about the risk the crews are taking. The question is can the fleet win the battle…because if it doesn't, you know how bad our losses will be, in battleships and cruisers as well as the small carriers. Even whatever ships get out will just face the enemy again, in increasingly hopeless efforts to stop their advance. You're my friend and my commander, and I'd follow you into hell if you led me there, but you've got to cut yourself some slack on this. You've got to accept the fact that losses don't matter, not now. Only victory does. If we win, and if we can go on from there to save the Confederation, believe me, there will be more than enough time to torment yourself over everything you did in the war. And if not…what difference does it make?"

Barron felt the urge to argue, but he knew Winters was right. They were both exhausted, but Winters seemed to have adapted better than he had to the likely costs of the commitment to retake Megara. Maybe it was a look at the inner strength that gave Winters his nickname, or perhaps it was the relative solace of the number two position. Whatever the effect, though, "the Sledgehammer" seemed coldly focused, and ready for the fight.

Barron, on the other hand, felt edgy. He was dedicated to completing the operation no matter what, but he was also troubled by one aspect after another. He knew it was a combination of factors affecting him—worry over Andi, the stress of the top command, the realization that failure in the next days would likely lead to total defeat.

The Barron admirals will be a pair of bookends, one who saved the Confederation…and the other, who lost it…

The elevator doors opened, and the two men stepped out onto *Dauntless*'s bridge. Winters flew his flag from *Constitution*, as he had for years. The battleship was a relatively new vessel, and it had been refit and upgraded with every new system available, including enhanced primaries. It was about thirty thousand kilometers away, holding position with the fleet's Second Division, waiting for the admiral to shuttle over and step onto the bridge.

But Winters had something to do first. He'd come to *Dauntless* to stand by Barron as the commander in chief addressed the fleet. They wanted to let the spacers waiting to depart see and hear their two commanders, side by side.

Barron walked toward his chair, snapping off a few routine commands as he took his position. He didn't sit. He would make this speech standing, Clint Winters at his side.

He glanced over at the tiny sphere on the ceiling, the camera that would transmit a visual feed along with the audio. Barron was introverted by nature, and he hated the idea of his image as well as his voice being transmitted to tens of thousands of spacers. But they were all at their posts, almost certainly afraid, and they deserved to hear from their commander before they set out on what would be, for many of them at least, their final journey.

"Everything is ready when you are, Admiral." Atara was about a meter from her workstation, looking over at the two admirals standing on her bridge.

"Let's go, Atara…let's get this over with."

Travis turned and gestured toward one of the bridge

officers. A few seconds later, she looked back toward Barron and said, "You're live, sir."

Barron took a deep breath. "Spacers of the fleet, warriors of the Grand Alliance, this is Admiral Tyler Barron. I am here with Admiral Winters, as the fleet prepares to set forth on its great mission. For those of you from the Confederation, we go to liberate our capital, the world that founded our nation more than a century ago as it emerged from the darkness of the Cataclysm. For the rest of you, we go to fight a climactic battle, one conceived to break the momentum of the enemy's advance…and to begin the crusade that will save the Rim.

"Make no mistake, any of you. When we reach Megara, you will be fighting for your families, your loved ones, and your nations. You will be fighting for your homes. For if we fail, if we are defeated, the Rim will almost certainly fall…and we will lose our ways of life, our beliefs, all we hold dear."

Barron's voice was loud and strong. As always, he wasn't sure where the strength came from, but despite his trepidations, he'd always managed to give his spacers the support they needed.

"Admiral Winters and I will be with you, in the main battle line, fighting the enemy. The entire fleet will be together, driving forward, with a relentlessness that can come only from the righteousness of our cause. Stay with me, spacers, fight at my side…and we will drive the enemy back where they came from. We will chase them from the Rim, now and forever!"

Barron turned and gestured toward Winters. "With an officer like the Sledgehammer at my side, and veteran spacers like all of you, I have no doubt of our victory…none!" Barron hated lying to his spacers, but sharing the trepidation he truly felt would have made for one hell of a bad speech.

"Come with me now…to Megara and to victory!"

Barron couldn't see or hear the other spacers of the fleet, but he couldn't ignore the cacophony on *Dauntless*'s bridge. Every officer was on his or her feet, shouting and applauding. If the other ships of the fleet were anything like the flagship, his people were ready.

He just hoped he could lead them to victory, that he had the skill they believed he had.

He had decided to throw the dice, to make one great gamble and trade a long, slow decline for one last chance at victory.

Now, it was time to see it through.

Chapter Twenty-One

Bridge
CFS Hermes
Megara, Olyus III
Year 320 AC

"We're through…" Vig Merrick sat at the sole spare workstation on *Hermes*'s small bridge. Andi had been concerned her regular naval crew would resent the presence of her comrades from *Pegasus*, but she'd been pleasantly surprised to see that wasn't the case at all. She'd had a hard time acknowledging the reputation that had built up around her, especially since her battle with Ricard Lille. The notoriety of defeating the deadliest Sector Nine assassin had only increased interest in the rest of her past, and the vast wealth she and her companions had earned exploring the Badlands for lost technology made them folk heroes of a sort.

Her people on *Hermes* had treated her almost as a celebrity from day one, but it hadn't taken long to realize that same respect extended to Vig and the other veterans from *Pegasus*. She'd disliked the almost fawning attention at first, but now she was grateful. It had been much easier to integrate her people into *Hermes*'s operations…and she'd come to realize not only how much she'd missed her old friends, but how much better she felt having them around her. She regretted leading them into danger, but Barron had been right in what he'd done. Having Vig on the bridge and Lex Righter down in engineering could only increase the chances of success…and that was more important than anything or anyone. If she failed, the fleet would face far greater odds when it arrived, and the chance of the Rim escaping enslavement would drop significantly.

She was edgy—no, she was scared—but she was glad she'd insisted on taking the job. If she could help the fleet succeed, reduce the danger Tyler was charging into even a little bit, it was worth any risk.

"Keep your eyes on those scanners, Vig." The ship's scanning suite hadn't even rebooted from the jump, but Andi wasn't going to waste any time. The stealth unit was operating at full power, and it had run so far without a hitch. But that wouldn't mean a damn if the Hegemony was able to penetrate the protective field around the ship.

"I'm watching, Andi." Vig had been making every effort to maintain a calm, focused demeanor, but now that they were in the Olyus system she could hear the tension slipping into his tone. Her people—both the old *Pegasus* crew and her Confed navy regulars on *Hermes*—were courageous and capable, but there was nothing they could do just then but hope the Hegemony forces hadn't yet developed a way to detect cloaked ships.

Andi caught herself holding her breath, and she inhaled a deep lungful of fresh air, at least as fresh as recycled spacecraft atmosphere ever got. Her hands were on the armrests of the chair, gripping tightly, and her eyes were glued to the display.

Nothing. *No, wait…*

There was some suspicious movement. Two ships, small escorts. They had just started to change course. It was hard to tell what their final vector mods would look like, but they were definitely altering their headings in the direction of the transit point.

Andi's eyes darted around. The sensors were fully active now—though she didn't dare engage the active scanners. There were satellites positioned around the point, as expected, scanners and warning systems. Even if the stealth unit was keeping *Hermes* hidden, it was possible those units had picked up energy readings from the transit itself.

Her mind raced, considering half a dozen options. She could stay where she was...but if the enemy was alerted enough to do a thorough and comprehensive scan of the area, she might be better off risking a bit of thrust and putting some distance behind her...

"Vig, have the engine room prepare for five percent thrust...and not a bit more." The more she considered, the more certain she was that she had to get *Hermes* away from the transit point. It was the place the enemy was most likely to look for her, and besides, she hadn't come to Olyus to hang around the outer system. She had to get to Megara anyway, probably into orbit, if she was going to have any chance of getting the message through to Bryan Rogan.

Getting out after that was another matter entirely. But she'd worry about that later.

"Engine room reports ready for five percent thrust, Andi."

"Course 102.340.065..." It wasn't right toward Megara. That, too, would be suspicious. If the enemy scans revealed anything at all at the transit point, the route directly toward Megara would be the first to receive intense scrutiny. "...five percent on engines...now."

Andi leaned back in her chair, and then she realized she was holding her breath again. She exhaled hard and turned toward the display. The two Hegemony escorts were definitely heading toward the point...and that meant the enemy had picked up *something*. But there wasn't any reaction to *Hermes*'s engines and course change.

Not yet, at least…

* * *

"No further reliable scanning data, Commander. We have a sequence of intermittent energy trails, but they're very faint. The AI assigns a seventy-one percent probability to natural causes, most likely small cosmic energy conglomerations or the inadvertent transit of larger than normal concentrations of granular matter."

Tiergan stared straight ahead, his gaze fixed on *Garara*'s main display. Tiergan was a first generation Kriegeri. The Hegemony had come to his world when he was a young boy. His people, their society still shattered and divided by the horror the Hegemony called the Great Death, and its aftermath of war and suffering, had been almost unable to resist. He remembered his father fighting in the streets as the defenders were gunned down by the relentless Kriegeri soldiers.

"The entire squadron is to execute a vector change. We're going to sweep the area around the transit point." Tiergan didn't know if some kind of Rim force had slipped past the scanners at the transit point, but he was damned well going to find out. Seventy percent was shit. It left far too great a chance the scanning contact had not been a natural phenomenon.

The enemy had sent scouting forces through over the past year, more than one of them using the stealth devices that had enabled the disastrous attack on the supply fleet over a year before. Tiergan's ships had received a full scanner upgrade since that disaster, and two follow-up software updates. The changes hadn't completely eliminated the threat of the enemy stealth units, but it had vastly increased discoverability, especially under a skilled commander attentive to small clues and transient readings.

Tiergan might have seemed an odd specimen to show

such devotion to serving the Masters. He had hated the Hegemony, at first. His father had survived the fighting against the initial invasions, and after a period of captivity following the final capitulation, he'd been released. He'd remained defiant, speaking of rebellion and driving the invaders off the planet…until Tiergan's mother's pleading for him to stop endangering the family had finally had an effect. But Tiergan had seen the restraint in the Hegemony's release of those who had fought against its forces, his father included. He'd witnessed far more brutal conduct among the armies of his world's pre-invasion nations—mass slaughters and vast concentration camps, genocide and virtual enslavement of defeated populations—following the planet's various wars.

The hatred of the Hegemony faded, first in Tiergan, already softening from his observations, and further subjected to considerable pro-Hegemony teachings in the hastily revised and restarted education programs. But eventually, his parents came to accept the new reality as well. They had all felt patriotic feelings for their world, or at least the nation that had governed their part of it, but there was little argument, from their perspective, that things had changed for the better.

There had been frequent famines in the years before the Hegemony arrived, and plagues and other calamities. But ever since the invasion, Tiergan and his family—and the rest of those on the planet—had enjoyed enough to eat, and widely distributed medicines had already begin to improve living standards and lifespans. Communications systems, transit, even entertainment, had all improved dramatically. The Hegemony had taken from his people whatever had once passed for freedom…but it also brought prosperity of a sort, at least to the lowered expectations of people who'd known only constant wars and frequent starvation a generation earlier.

The genetic testing had begun soon after the end of

hostilities, though it had taken some years to complete the absorption of the population into the Hegemonic system. The majority of the planet's residents were classed as Arbeiter, workers, much as they had been before…but Tiergan had scored high on physical attributes and also on mathematics. He was categorized as Red Kriegeri…and destined for service with the Hegemony's navy.

Whether Arbeiter or Kriegeri—or, especially, the few who attained Master status—the people of his world were almost all objectively better off under the Hegemony then they had been before.

All save the Defekts.

The bacteriological and nuclear combat of the Great Death had not spared his world, and many of its people carried DNA scarred and damaged by the nightmare. They had fared poorly prior to the invasion, subject to poverty and various forms of discrimination…but under the Hegemony, they were no longer even considered people. They were damaged in the eyes of the Masters, their reproduction a danger to the human race as a whole, save in highly controlled circumstances to produce expendable workers. The Masters ruled the Hegemony utterly, but the Arbeiter and Kriegeri had rights of a sort, or at least protections. The Defekts had none.

They were used for dangerous labors, mining radioactive materials and the like, and they were expended without hesitation. Tiergan had never been comfortable with that aspect of Hegemonic rule, but as the years had passed, and his career in the navy had taken him far from home, he'd largely left such concerns behind. He'd found excellence in himself, in his success in the navy…and he'd become loyal to the Masters, a rigid, unquestioning faith in the Hegemony's mission to reunite, and protect, humanity. In the end, he'd seen tens, even hundreds of billions of people better off than they'd been on their own fractured, violent worlds before absorption.

"We're approaching the transit point, Commander."

Tiergan refocused his attention on the display. "Send all readings to my workstation." He looked down at his smaller screen, his eyes moving from one energy trail to the next. Some of them were clearly natural, but there were others, too…and he just wasn't sure…

* * *

"Nudge the thrust level up, Vig. Go to twenty percent. Let's keep this angle for another hour, and then we'll swing around and adjust to bring us more on a line toward Megara." Andi had been watching the display for hours, her eyes moving from one enemy contact to the next. None of them seemed to be coming toward *Hermes* yet, but she was sure now the enemy had picked up some kind of contact near the transit point.

That means they're searching for us…

Andi wasn't one to underestimate her opponents, and after the devastating attack on their supply fleet just over a year earlier, she didn't think they were going to ignore *any* signs of an incursion into the system.

"We're at twenty percent, Andi. Still on our previous course."

She was doing everything she could think to do, trying to keep as low a profile as possible. But she *had* to get to Megara, and she had a time limit as well. Her mission was to get word to Bryan Rogan in time for his Marines—assuming the general and any of his people were still alive—to disrupt the enemy as much as possible before the invasion force arrived. She'd been skeptical at first, not just about prospects for Rogan's survival, but also just what his almost certainly battered and degraded forces could do to help the invasion. Then, Barron had confided in her, told her his reasoning for getting word to Rogan.

The Hegemony forces were powerful, their capabilities

immense. But just over a year wasn't a long time to rebuild the destroyed orbital platforms and networks that protected a world like Megara. Barron was betting that the Hegemony command structure was based largely on the planet, that most of the enemy's effort had gone into rebuilding weaponry and fortresses, and not orbital command facilities. If so, damaging ground communications facilities at just the right moment might badly disrupt the defensive command and control. It would require pinpoint timing, not the least of which meant Barron getting the fleet in position at just the right moment. She didn't doubt he would be in place, but that would mean nothing unless she had managed to reach Megara. And Rogan's people somehow managed to take out the facilities exactly on time.

"Bring us up to thirty percent, Vig…and let's shave a bit off that angle, come in a bit more on a direct line." She felt her insides tense. The more energy she poured into the engines, the closer to a straight line to Megara she came…the more she increased the risk.

But her people had a job to do, and a schedule to keep. And that came first.

If we can pull this off, it might save thousands of spacers.
It might save Tyler…

Chapter Twenty-Two

Sandrine Ciara sat in her office, still stunned at the news. She'd been working around the clock, trying to manipulate Villieneuve, at least as much as she dared, and cautiously searching for potential allies...in case she had to make a move. She didn't *want* to oppose Villieneuve. She'd been loyal to him for a long time, and, even more, if she was being blunt and honest with herself, because the First Citizen's enemies had a way of ending up dead. Gaston Villieneuve had left a trail of corpses behind in his thirty-five year rise to power, and she didn't intend to see her name added to that list.

She wondered what Ricard Lille would have done if he'd survived. She had learned her trade under Lille, and later emulated his operational style. She'd become a cold-blooded killer, cast from the mold Lille had created, and she'd always asked herself what her mentor would have done when she faced a difficult problem.

She suspected the current situation would have been an especially troubling one for Lille. The assassin had been

Gaston Villieneuve's only real friend—and Villieneuve had been his. But Lille had never allowed emotions to interfere with his judgment, nor things like loyalty to stop him from doing what had to be done. Would he have betrayed Villieneuve, moved against him?

Almost certainly, she believed, the answer was no...or at least it would have been until recently. But Ciara had replayed her recent meetings with Villieneuve over and over in her head, and she'd come to one hard and fast conclusion, one that seemed more certain with each replay. One she doubted even Lille could have ignored.

Gaston Villieneuve was insane.

The First Citizen had always seemed that way, at least to the standards of people weighed down by conventional morality. He was a monster, of course, as all people who attained such levels of power were, in one way or another. But the Villieneuve who had built Sector Nine into the most capable security and intelligence force on the Rim had been coldly focused, rational. While he'd never hesitated to do what was necessary, he'd been far less sadistic than others who'd held his position before him. He'd always been just as content to attain his goals without bloodshed whenever that was possible. Murder, terror, torture...they were always in his toolbox, but he'd never seemed to derive any pleasure or satisfaction from their employ.

But the combination of the Hegemony invasion of the Rim, Denisov's mutiny, and Lille's death had broken him. He'd become intensely cruel, almost unhinged, and his paranoia had run amok. The sadism he'd long lacked had taken hold with a vengeance, and he'd sent subordinates to the cellars of Sector Nine headquarters for the slightest perceived offenses or failures. Sometimes, it took no more than the misfortune of crossing his path when he was in a particularly bad mood.

There was no way to know what he would do next, but the likelihood that he would be able to steer the Union through the grave threats swirling all around it was nil. He *had* to be removed…and the sooner the better.

But how?

She'd spent the last year and a half dancing around Villieneuve, managing to stay on his good side, increasing his trust in her. She'd been motivated by her own ambitions, by her perception of the likeliest route to advancement. But now, she was thinking of the Union itself. As single-minded as she'd been about her own career and power, she was, at heart, a patriot. She served the Union, and no less so for her expectation to accrue power and rewards in return for her loyalty. And she detested the Confederation. Her earliest memories of the longtime enemy were of hatred and fear.

But if the Rim didn't unite to face the enemy, there wouldn't be a Union or a Confederation. Gaston Villieneuve's inaction was almost certainly killing the Union.

She'd tried a hundred times to devise a plan, a way to communicate with the Confederation, or with Denisov, but crazy or not, Villieneuve was no fool, and he was watching *everything*.

The door to her office opened up, and two armed guards walked in, her assistant shuffling up behind them.

"I'm sorry, Minister, but they wouldn't wait."

"That's fine, Stoke…you may return to your work."

The aide turned and left, still looking very uncomfortable…but Ciara wasn't unduly concerned. Villieneuve had taken to sending armed guards to fetch those he wanted to see, something she figured was part of his twisted mind's plan to keep everybody around him on edge. It had worked on her, once or twice, but once she'd figured it out, she had adjusted. It seemed easier to use the comm, but she didn't think complaining about it would be useful…or wise.

"The First Citizen wishes to see me?"

"Yes, Minister. There is a ship approaching Montmirail, and he would consult with you at once."

Her first thought was the Hegemony. She'd lived in a state of near panic for months after Denisov's defection, sure the fleet that had attacked him would assault Montmirail. But the Hegemony forces simply withdrew...probably, she'd realized later, to reinforce the invasion of the Confederation.

Which, she acknowledged with some shame, was currently the premier power on the Rim.

She stood up, feeling a little weakness in her legs. If the Hegemony was back...

"What ship?" It was all she could think to ask.

"It is a Confederation ship, Minister, broadcasting ambassadorial credentials."

She felt a wave of relief almost immediately...followed by a another of tense anticipation.

A Confederation ambassador...there must be some way to use this...

Assuming Villieneuve doesn't have the ambassador shot on sight...

* * *

Alexander Kerevsky bowed his head, drawing on all his diplomatic experience to show the utmost respect to a man he utterly despised. Kerevsky wasn't the typical diplomat, imprisoned within rigid protocols and devoted to a masquerade of pointless fakery. He'd spent as much time in his role with Confederation Intelligence as he had in the Diplomatic Corps, and he knew ambassadors were mostly full of shit...and heads of state *almost always* were. He hadn't come to Montmirail to spend months or years debating the finery of treaties and agreements that would almost certainly be breached once they were no longer convenient, by the Union at least, if not also by the Confederation.

No, he'd come to scare the shit out of Gaston Villieneuve, and he didn't need anything to do that but legitimate details on the battles and scanning reports on the Hegemony warships.

He was also there to discern the actual state of the Union and its government, and to try to communicate the desperation of the Rim's situation. In other words, to convince Gaston Villieneuve that, if the Hegemony wasn't stopped in the Confederation, they would eventually come to Montmirail...and his bloody reign would end in the lancing beams of Hegemony warships and the stomping boots of Kriegeri soldiers.

Villieneuve was a tyrant, a cold-blooded killer, a man who would—and had—done almost anything to get what he wanted. But he wasn't a fool. At least, he never had been.

Kerevsky's first order of business would be to find out if that was still the case.

"Ambassador Kerevsky...welcome to Montmirail. It has been far too long since we have had an envoy from our friends in the Confederation." Villieneuve turned to the side and gestured toward a woman standing next to him. "Allow me to introduce Minister Sandrine Ciara, one of my key advisors."

"Minister." Kerevsky bowed his head again, and as he straightened, his eyes caught Ciara's. There was something there. She was trying to communicate to him, somehow. He was sure of it.

Was there dissension between Villieneuve and his minister? Some kind of disagreement?

"It is my pleasure, Ambassador Kerevsky." Ciara nodded slightly as she spoke.

Villieneuve sat down, and then he gestured for Kerevsky to do the same. Ciara stood for a moment, sitting only after both Villieneuve and the Confederation ambassador had.

"So, Ambassador...I presume you come here on matters related to your recent war."

"Yes, First Citizen, I do...though I daresay it is the Rim's war and not just our own."

"That is still a matter of opinion. I must, of course, wonder if the Confederation has made appropriate efforts to maintain the peace. From the data I possess, this Hegemony is quite advanced technologically. They would make a very attractive trading partner, and a strong ally. I ask this with no disrespect intended, but who was the initial aggressor in this conflict? Did not your White Fleet invade the Hegemony's space?"

Kerevsky sat calmly. Villieneuve was trying to provoke him, but he wasn't going to allow himself to be so easily manipulated. "I would characterize events in somewhat of a different manner. The White Fleet inadvertently visited a world the Hegemony claimed as its own, but that was purely accidental. As you know, almost no one on the Rim suspected human populations still existed so deep beyond the Badlands, much less such a vast interstellar polity. As soon as Hegemony vessels appeared, Admiral Barron attempted to communicate, offering to withdraw at once...but his efforts were rebuffed, and his fleet attacked."

Villieneuve sat with a vague smile on his face. "I do not doubt your integrity, Ambassador, but surely you know well that different eyes see things in various ways. For example, were we to discuss the causes leading to the last war between our nations, I am willing to wager our points of view would vary enormously. You would, no doubt, see us as the aggressors, while I would point out that the Confederation's policy of strangling my people economically was the primary cause. I suspect little would be gained from the exercise of exchanging such thoughts."

"No doubt that is so, First Citizen...but regardless of intent, there can be little doubt the Hegemony have invaded the Rim in massive force, and pushed aside every attempt to stop them."

"Correction, Ambassador...they have invaded the Confederation. Yet, you are presumably here to urge me to commit the Union to your struggle."

"Most of the Rim nations fight at our sides, First Citizen. They see this as a struggle to preserve the Rim's freedom." Kerevsky wasn't sure how hard he should push. He'd never met Villieneuve, but he'd always heard the man was cool and deliberative. There was something unsettling in his eyes, though, a glassy, glittering look. Still, he didn't have time to waste, and that meant pressing forward. "Also, I believe the Hegemony forces attacked your own fleet approximately eighteen months ago, did they not?"

Villieneuve's smile vanished, replaced by a scowl. "What you refer to was brought on by the traitor Denisov and his unauthorized aggressive movement against the Hegemony. They responded to his foolish actions, yes...but you will note that while they have seized numerous Confederation systems—including your capital, I might add—they have not invaded the Union, nor seized a single world from us." A pause. "But you should know all of this, Ambassador. The criminal and his traitorous followers have allied themselves with you already, have they not?" Villieneuve was silent for a few seconds, staring directly at Kerevsky. "Of course, any alliance between our nations to combat the—as you put it—'dire threat to the Rim,' would be subject to your turning the traitor over to us at once."

Kerevsky had expected Villieneuve to be difficult, but he'd hoped to defer discussion of the Union fleet serving at the front. It was a difficult situation to say the least, and one that defied easy solutions. Turning Denisov over to Sector Nine was out of the question, of course, even if it had been possible to sacrifice the admiral and maintain the loyalty of his fleet.

That's what makes us different from the Union...

But Kerevsky was uncomfortable at how long his thoughts had paused on the idea of surrendering Denisov. The Confederation's survival, the whole Rim's, depended on defeating the Hegemony.

How different would it be? Denisov could die in combat with far less gain...

He clamped down on the thoughts, extinguishing them like a fire, with waves of self-loathing in the place of water.

"That, of course, would be one of many subjects to discuss." Kerevsky might not be a diplomat at his core, but he'd picked up a few skills of the trade in his journey. Vagueness and procrastination included.

"I'm afraid it will have to be the first topic of discussion, Ambassador. I couldn't even begin to discuss a possible treaty with a power harboring the vilest traitor in Union history."

Kerevsky was scrambling, trying to come up with something to say, some way to dance around the issue...but Villieneuve saved him, for the moment, at least.

"But where are my manners, Ambassador. You have had a long journey, and you must be tired." He looked toward Ciara. "The Minister here will see that you and your staff are assigned appropriate quarters. We will begin serious discussions after you have enjoyed some of our hospitality."

Kerevsky almost said he wasn't tired, that time was of the essence, but he stopped himself. It was pointless. Villieneuve wasn't ready to conduct talks. Whether he wanted time to confer with his advisors, or to spy on Kerevsky and his people, the ambassador didn't know. He even gave about a fifteen percent chance that the "hospitality" he was headed for was a subterranean Sector Nine cell somewhere. But that was the chance he'd taken when he accepted the mission.

They were better odds than the spacers at the front faced.

"Come with me, Ambassador. We will see to your lodgings...and I will order food prepared for you and your aides." Ciara's voice was stone cold, not a hint of anything but obedience to Villieneuve's orders.

But the look was still there in her eye...barely detectable, but *there*. He was sure of it.

"Thank you, First Citizen, for your kind hospitality. I look forward to our first session of talks."

But he was looking forward even more to what Ciara had to say once they were alone.

Chapter Twenty-Three

Bridge
CFS Hermes
Megara, Olyus III
Year 320 AC

"There's definitely something going on, Andi." Vig's tone wasn't panicky, but there was an edge to it. "I wouldn't say they've put out a full-scale alert, but they're definitely looking for something. For us."

Andi just nodded. She'd been sure almost since *Hermes* had transited into the Olyus system. She wasn't sure how much of that was keen analysis of the data and how much the grim pessimism she'd applied to most of the things in her life, but she'd been watching every ship movement *Hermes*'s passive scans could track. Many of them were normal enough, the standard traffic around a fleet and base the size of the one at Megara, but she'd pegged at least forty she thought looked suspicious. She knew the old saying, about the signs that predicted fifty of the past ten disasters. She knew the Hegemony fleet didn't have *that* many ships chasing *Hermes*. If they'd launched that kind of search effort, it would be obvious.

But she was certain *some* of those ships were looking for her, at least looking for *something*.

"Let's stay on our current course…for now." *Hermes* was cruising toward Megara, her engines shut down. Andi had held off the urge to increase her ship's speed…the more she accelerated on the way, the more she'd have to decelerate, when she got close to Megara, deep within the maximum danger zone for detection and interception. She'd been holding back the contents of her stomach for almost two days, now…and the last thing she wanted was to blast the engines at full right before she reached her target.

She glanced over at the display again, a quick check of *Hermes*'s position relative to Megara. Everything was on target, exactly where it should be, but she was still nervous, and she shifted around in her chair, telegraphing her edginess and fear rather more directly to her people than she'd have liked.

Her thoughts drifted back to Tyler. *The fleet will be on the way by now.*

Her crew didn't know just how tight their operational window was. They didn't need to know, but little else had occupied Andi's thoughts for the past two days. She was determined to do what she'd been sent to do, and she'd reviewed every aspect of the operation at least a hundred times.

"Vig, while we're coasting along…I want the comm units checked out, and I mean thoroughly. Tell Lex I want him to make damned sure the system is ready, and the codes are in place." Andi didn't elaborate. She didn't need to share with her crew the certainty she felt that if *Hermes* reached Megara orbit, her people would have only moments, perhaps seconds, to complete their mission. Then they'd be on the run, trying to escape before the Hegemony forces could secure a hard lock on their position from the transmission.

Or, they'd be dead.

"Yes, Andi." A few seconds later. "Lex advises he's already checked out the comm units…but he'll do it again."

Andi's mouth had been open, a knee-jerk intent to

respond to the first part of Vig's report, though her friend had addressed what she was going to say before she had the chance.

Righter was the best engineer Andi had ever known, save only for Anya Fritz, who was outright superhuman. She knew she should count on his ability, and relax in the near-certainty, at least, that if she could get *Hermes* in position, the comm unit would be ready.

But Andi never relaxed about anything…and something told her this wasn't the time to start.

*   *   *

Where the hell are you? And who are you? Why have you come here?

Tiergan stared at his screen with a withering intensity. He had lines running in various directions, projected courses for…what? He didn't know. It was possible he was still chasing a ghost. He'd reported his contact, and his suspicions, and fleet command had responded by adding two other squadrons to his own. There were more than twenty ships now looking for whatever he'd seen, though as the hours had passed and turned into days, he was sure his fellow officers were losing faith in his suspicions.

He'd come close to losing it a few times, but when it came right down to it, he was certain there was something out there. It didn't make sense. It couldn't be a large force, nothing that could seriously threaten the inner defenses. No substantial fleet could have gotten through the scanner net at the transit point, not even if every ship had been equipped with one of the enemy's stealth units. He'd have picked up energy displacements, shielding leakages…*something*.

"*Ysintl* and *Herinth* are to alter the vectors to 320.089.101 and increase thrust to fifty percent. I want both on active scanners at full power." That would tell whoever was out there he was looking for them, but it didn't matter.

Whoever is out there is no fool. He or she already knows we're looking…

Garara was at the center of a formation of escorts deployed over trillions of cubic kilometers of space. Tiergan had held a number of his ships near the transit point for a long while, too long, he'd finally decided. Whatever he'd detected—if it *was* anything, and he believed it was—had long since moved in-system.

He glanced over at the Megara defenses. His search area had been moving closer to the Confederation's former capital, an inevitable tightening of the search zone. That was a gamble, but he simply couldn't look through the entire system. He was already combing a vast volume of space, and it would have required hundreds of ships to search the whole system thoroughly. Fleet command had taken his report seriously enough to assign him increased resources to investigate, but not enough for that.

Wait…

He was staring at the screen, at the course projections and estimates he'd superimposed over the scanner readings. He'd seen something, then again. It was an intermittent contact…very intermittent.

But it was directly on one of the roundabout courses he'd plotted for a vessel approaching Megara.

It was far from conclusive—so far, he hadn't even bothered to report it—but he was completely convinced now. There *was* something out there.

And it was heading toward Megara.

He reached out, his hands almost flying over the controls, cutting out the other course data and directing all scanning resources along the chosen line. It was a hunch as much as factual analysis, but he was going to go with it.

He was sure he was tracking *something*…and its course suggested strongly its destination was Megara.

"Course change…*Utara, Ghoslan, Overon*. And us. Bring us in for a roundabout approach to Megara. We're going to overshoot by three hundred thousand kilometers, and then we're going to come back in from the sun side. Full thrust, all ships."

He'd found what he was looking for—or at least he'd gotten a trace of it. Now he had to be careful. If he made it too obvious, his target might abort or change course. He would have moved in immediately, but he had a general vector, not a precise location. He didn't know where the ship was…but he was pretty sure he knew where it was going.

And he was going to make damned certain he was waiting for it when it did.

*   *   *

"We're ready to make a final approach to Megara, Andi."

"Hold current course and velocity for now, Vig." Andi was still staring at the screen, as she'd been doing almost nonstop for eighteen hours. Her eyes burned, and her back ached…she was feeling sluggish from the stims she'd taken. But she hadn't moved from her perch on the bridge for more than five minutes at a time in over two days.

She'd pegged two groups of Hegemony ships. One, she was pretty sure, was some kind of freight convoy carrying something vital. It was inbound to Megara, decelerating hard. It was possible those ships had detected her, but they could have plotted a much less obvious course than the one they were taking if they were concerned about an enemy ship lurking somewhere nearby.

That was what troubled her about the other group of ships. They had been moving in the general direction of Megara, but then they'd zipped past the planet, coming within two hundred thousand kilometers, but showing no signs of angling in to establish orbit.

That could have been normal enough—the system's second planet had a few mining and scientific outposts on it.

It was possible the Hegemony was utilizing those for some purpose, that the ships heading in-system were bound for there.

But she didn't buy it. And, as she watched, she only became more convinced. The course was all wrong for a voyage to Olyus II, or anywhere else in the system.

Whoever is commanding those ships…he suspects we're here…

Her eyes narrowed as she tracked the line the enemy ships had taken so far. They were coming right for Megara…and then they branched off.

Trying to throw us off?

There was no way of knowing. One instant, she was sure, and the next, she was convinced she was being paranoid. No one was sure *Hermes* was there…or there would be a general alert in progress. There were at least three hundred warships near enough to Megara to respond, and so far, save for the ones she was watching, none had made any suspicious moves.

"Vig…I want you to listen to me. We're going to be very precise. When I give the word, we're going to move into orbit as quickly as possible…full thrust when necessary. We've got to make sure the transmission hits all of the surface, and that means nearly a full orbit. We have no idea where Rogan or any surviving Marines are. I figure we need to make it just over three-fourths of the way around." Her fingers were moving over her workstation, calculating the exact numbers. 76.9 percent. "I want all weapons ready, and I want engines prepared for an emergency blast out of orbit as soon as we're done."

"Understood, Andi." Her friend sounded nervous. She didn't blame him.

He should be flat out terrified. And he probably is…

Andi figured she had a decent chance of making the transmission, even of hitting every part of the surface with it. Getting away after was something else entirely. They had a chance, of course. If her life had taught her anything, it was never to give up. But that chance felt like it was becoming more and more remote as her eyes moved over the screen.

I think the technical term is "piss poor"…

The transmission would be like a signal flare, and whoever was searching for them was clearly no fool.

"Now, Vig!" She reached out, an instinctive move when expecting a high thrust maneuver, but *Hermes* was a new ship, outfitted with the latest in dampening technology. She felt an instant of pressure, and a few hard jerks, but nothing more, save for a moderate feeling of increased weight. The display confirmed that *Hermes's* engines were blasting at almost 50g, but it felt like no more than 1.5g to her.

The stealth units were supposed to hide her ship at any level of energy output, but that assumed pre-raid Hegemony tech. She'd have bet her last credit the enemy had made at least *some* kind of progress on tracking cloaked ships…and she was practically waving a torch to anything that could get even partially through the field.

She hadn't planned such a bold move so close to Megara, but if those other ships were on to her anyway, then time had become her biggest problem.

"We're entering orbit in twenty seconds, Andi."

She was still staring at the screen. *If those ships* are *on to us, we'll know in a few seconds.*

They would have to adjust to match her sudden change in vector and thrust, and that would turn her suspicions to fact.

"Fifteen seconds…"

She stared, watching, waiting…but still nothing.

"Ten seconds…"

Her eyes burned, but she held them fixed, barely blinking as she waited for the move she knew would come. Only it hadn't. *Was I wrong?*

"Five seconds…"

The doubts poured into of her mind, recriminations

against herself, for allowing her paranoia to direct her actions. If she'd blasted her engines at full for no reason, she might have given *Hermes* away for no reason.

"Entering orbit…"

Then she saw it. First, one of the ships. Then the rest of them, in succession. They were blasting their engines at what had to be at least nearly full thrust. She had been right, after all…and her last-minute maneuver had bought her some time.

Assuming half the fortresses in Megara orbit didn't pick up our approach…

"Vig, commence transmission as soon as we're in orbit…full power to the comm!"

Chapter Twenty-Four

CFS Tarsus
Inner Kuiper Belt
Venga System
Year 320 AC

"Launch all squadrons!" Sonya Eaton sat on *Tarsus*'s bridge, not even trying to hide the sweat pouring down the sides of her face or the stark, glassy look in her eyes. She was stretched almost to the limit, fighting back both fear and the recriminations her own mind inflicted on her. She'd issued the orders almost without thought of the consequences...but she hadn't had any choice, and as crazy as it seemed, she knew her people were where they had to be.

She'd hesitated to scout for enemy units only one system from Venga, the blue-white star the planet Ulion orbited. Ulion was one of the Confederation's seven Core worlds...and the first to fall to the Hegemony. She'd spent most of the last year hitting convoys en route to Ulion...but she'd never dared to venture as close as one system away. The main enemy fleet was at Megara, but there were very likely more than enough forces at Ulion to obliterate her forces.

Then she got the scanner readings. She'd caught an

enemy convoy in-system. Not just in-system, but well on the way to the Venga transit point.

She'd launched an attack immediately, sending her bomber squadrons in with orders to hit the freighters hard. Then, the *rest* of the convoy had emerged from behind one of the system's gas giants.

Twenty battleships. An awesomely powerful force...and she knew immediately she was seeing more than a supply convoy. Her scanners were clear about that. She was seeing reinforcements bound for Megara.

Ships that would arrive just as Barron's fleet was attacking.

It was a force vastly stronger than her own, one she couldn't hope to defeat, or stop.

But *just maybe* she could delay it. A day, even a few hours, might make the difference.

She'd redirected her fighters toward the battleships, and her rookie pilots got their first taste of fighting enemy capital ships. The battleship hulls were nothing like the unarmored skins of the freighters, and while her squadrons scored an impressive number of hits, they fell short of taking down even one of the battleships. They did cause damage, however, enough to materially slow two of the giant vessels. Staring at the scanning reports, she realized what her people had to do.

The enemy wouldn't know the fleet was attacking Megara, not yet...so there would be no urgency. If she could slow enough ships, maybe the others would drop back to maintain the formation until the damaged vessels could conduct repairs. That just might work. At least until word of Barron's assault arrived.

Would it be enough time to make a difference? She didn't know. Her best guess was, it would be close. But it was all her people could do, and she'd committed to it, then and there. Even though it almost certainly meant following the enemy into Venga...and exposing her people to whatever forces the Hegemony had stationed at Ulion.

It wasn't quite as insane as it sounded. Both of the transit points, the one leading into Venga and the one leading out and toward Olyus, were deep in the outer system, far beyond the orbit of the eleventh planet. It would take time for anything stationed at Olyus to respond…and if the Hegemony convoy continued on its course to Megara, the running battle would likely have moved on before Ulion-based assets could arrive.

And if the Hegemony ships altered course, if they moved in-system toward any relief forces…she would have completed her mission, prevented the enemy reinforcements from reaching Megara in time to intervene in the battle.

"All ships report squadrons launched, Captain." Tarleton sat at his station, resolute as always. She knew he understood the risks she was taking, and why she was taking them, but he hadn't let on to any of it.

She'd violated orders in telling Tarleton what the fleet was doing, and why their raiding force had been sent out ahead of schedule and in such a hurry. It was a court martial offense, perhaps even treason to a literal view, but she'd come to trust Tarleton, and, honestly, she didn't think he'd rat her out if they tied him to a rack.

She needed one friend on this mission. Two, actually. She'd also told Hayes. Tarleton was a close comrade, someone else who understood what the fleet had to do and why…and just how far she would go, how many risks she would take to slow the enemy convoy.

And Hayes? She'd told him because she couldn't see any other way he would lead his pilots into the nightmare she was about to put them through.

* * *

"Let's go…all squadrons. I know most of you haven't faced

enemy warships before, save for the escorts with the convoys. Well, now you know what Hegemony battleships look like, and you're going to find out how damned tough it is to hurt them." Hayes's tone was defiant, and he spoke as a man who'd battled against the Hegemony's biggest and strongest battleships, but the truth was, he'd only seen them on the distance on his scanner, and he'd never flown his ship against anything bigger than a cruiser.

"I know it's tempting to choose one of those monsters and see if we can blast the thing to dust...but that's not what our comrades need us to do. We've got to slow these bastards down, and that means doing some engine damage to at least six or seven of them."

Eaton had filled Hayes in on her plan. Whatever they did, they *had* to slow those things down. Hayes was one of the few in Eaton's fleet who knew what was about to happen at Megara...and twenty more battleships would almost certainly shatter a plan that was already balanced on a razor's edge. Barron's fleet needed his squadrons to keep those ships occupied, at least for a day or two. He and his people *had* to slow the enemy reinforcements down, keep them away from Megara until the battle there was won.

The only problem with that was, he was far from sure it was possible.

He ran his hand over the comm controls, sending out a pulse on the datanet. "Everybody, listen up. I just sent you six contacts. They should be highlighted on your screens now. Those are the ships we're going to hit...and the only ones. I don't want to see even one of you going after another battleship—or a freighter or an escort. We've *got* to stop those six battleships. If we can hit them hard enough, the rest of the convoy may have to slow to regroup." They didn't have to, of course, but that was Captain Eaton's bet. Hayes figured it was a good one, and he couldn't think of any other option.

He was tense as he listened to the chatter on the comm.

He knew his pilots wouldn't understand the true urgency of their mission, why they were throwing themselves at a line of massive battleships instead of picking off freighters as they'd done before.

He almost blurted it out, told them why he was about to lead them against the Hegemony killing machines again and again, without pause, without rest. They deserved to know. But he'd been sworn to silence, and he couldn't betray Captain Eaton's confidence. Even more importantly, as good as Confederation encryption was, he couldn't be sure the enemy hadn't broken the codes. The last thing he intended to do was risk alerting the Hegemony about Barron's impending attack on Megara...to betray the secrecy of an operation he wasn't even supposed to know about.

He nodded as the acknowledgements came in, a little late but reasonably sharp, nevertheless. He'd expected at least one or two green squadron leaders—almost half his people were newly assigned since the last mission—to question the orders, but none of them did. He wondered if it had been the grimness of his tone, or simply the fact that even his rookies understood the true stakes they were fighting for.

Or didn't understand just what they were heading into.

It didn't matter. They'd know well enough soon...and however many of them died in the first assault, it wouldn't change a thing. He'd lead the survivors out again, as soon as their ships were refit. And again.

As long as necessary. As long as any of them were still alive.

"Let's go, on me...straight through those escorts, and on to the battleships. Let's show these bastards just what Lightning bombers can do!"

* * *

"We've got preliminary casualty reports from the fighter wing, Captain."

Eaton had known the numbers would be ugly, even before the edge in Tarleton's tone told her just how bad they were. But she had a mission to do, no matter what the costs, and exact loss figures weren't going to do a damned thing to help her get through it.

"Not now, Commander." She watched as the cluster of dots moved forward toward the enemy battleships. The escorts had taken their toll, as always, but Hayes's formations were still in decent shape. The attack vector against the battleships was clearly a surprise to the enemy. It didn't take a deep analysis to determine the Hegemony defenders had expected the assault to hit the convoy's supply ships.

That's a benefit we'll only get one time. Once Hayes and his people hit the battleships, the enemy will know just what to expect from the second wave.

And the third wave, and the fourth…as many as it took.

"Fleet order, Commander…all ships, prepare to execute nav plan Sigma-4." The fighters wouldn't bear the entire risk, not on this mission. Eaton had needed to figure a way to do enough damage to the battleships…and however she'd tried to come at it, the end result was always the same.

She needed to get more bombing runs in…and that meant the rest of her ships had to come closer to the enemy that they had before.

Dangerously close.

"All ships report ready, Commander."

She stared at the display. When she gave the command, her sixteen ships would blast their engines at full thrust, rapidly cutting the angle of their vector, and bringing them right in front of the enemy's advance. Then they would swing around again, allowing Hayes's bombers to blast into their attack runs at high velocity, and continue on without requiring massive course chances to meet up with the carriers on the other side of the Hegemony formation. It was daring, dangerous...but it would shave almost two hours from the bombing wing's turnaround time. And that just might be the margin between success and failure.

She watched as a line appeared on the display, the projected course for her fleet, and she took a deep breath as she saw the closest point to the Hegemony convoy's line of approach. She hoped to race across before the leading enemy escorts came within firing range, but she knew it was going to be close.

It was a risk, but no graver than those her pilots were taking...or anyone in the fleet.

The fleet will be on the way to Megara by now. Everything we've got left. One last push.

She wished she was with the invasion force, commanding a battleship under Admiral Barron as she had before...but even where she was, she felt like part of the grand assault. If she could keep these new Hegemony battleships out of the fight, her people would contribute more to victory than they ever could have done in the ranks at Megara.

She was scared...for herself, for her people, and for the fleet heading to the titanic struggle about to engulf the Olyus system.

But there was something else, too. Excitement. A grim satisfaction that the fleet was no longer on the defensive, waiting for the enemy to come. Win or lose, Admiral Barron was bringing the war to the enemy. If they were successful, the battle just might be the turning point of the war.

And if they failed, well, Eaton would rather die on the attack, throwing everything she had into a last lunge for victory than hiding and waiting for inevitable doom and defeat. She was pretty sure Barron and most of her colleagues felt the same way.

"Commander Tarleton, all ships...execute Sigma-4."

Chapter Twenty-Five

Marine One HQ
Ninety Kilometers South of Troyus City
Megara, Olyus III
Year 320 AC

"General Rogan! General Rogan!" The sergeant raced through the dark and damp corridor, shouting wildly as he did. The non-com had been a hardcore veteran even before the fighting on Megara, and he'd fought and survived a battle that had turned to an extermination, one which had claimed better than ninety-nine percent of his comrades. The man was as tough as they came. Which was why Bryan Rogan couldn't understand the almost panicked shouting.

"What is it, Sergeant?" Rogan had been on his sleep period, which mostly meant lying on his lumpy cot, thinking about the plight of his Marines and trying to devise plans—any plans—that would allow him to damage the occupation forces without getting the rest of his people killed.

The major difference between sleep periods and the time he spent ostensibly on duty was that he usually closed his eyes when he was lying wide awake on the cot.

"We're getting a message, sir…"

"A message? From one of the other strongholds?" His people were supposed to be on strict radio silence. They owed the fact that they hadn't been found mostly to imperial old tech materials that shielded them from the enemy's scanning attempts…and the fact that they just weren't important enough for the Hegemony forces to make the effort to fully eradicate them.

"No, General…the Priority comm unit!"

Rogan had been sitting up on the cot, staring at the sergeant, but when the Marine's words hit him, he felt his stomach shrink to about a tenth its normal size, and he leapt to his feet.

"The Priority line?"

"Yes, sir!"

Rogan lunged through the door and raced down the corridor, heading toward the communications station. He'd stopped in every day to check on the unit's status, risked lives to secure batteries and other components to keep the comm unit active, and assigned someone to monitor the thing every minute of every day, despite his declining numbers.

But he'd never really expected to really get a message.

Is it possible? Is the fleet back?

Even as the thoughts poured into his head, he rebelled against them, an instinctive reaction that told him just how little hope had truly remained to him. But when he stumbled into the comm room, he could hear it himself.

Voices weren't always recognizable on communiques. Signal quality, transmission distance, and a hundred other things could affect replay quality. But Bryan Rogan knew Tyler Barron's voice in an instant.

"Replay from the start, Lieutenant."

"Yes, sir." The officer seated at the unit turned and moved his hands over the controls. The Marine was clearly excited, and he blurted out, "They're coming, General. They're really coming."

Rogan stood behind the comm officer, but he didn't respond. Instead, he listened as Tyler Barron's words blared from the speakers.

"Bryan...I am sending this communique in the solemn belief that, despite the impossible situation in which you were left, you found a way to survive, to endure, if not to maintain the fight. If you are there, if any of your people remain fit for action, it is time. We are coming back...back to retake Megara, and you know we need every advantage we can get. The enemy can't have repaired the orbital net, not in full. The ground stations around Troyus City *must* be relaying critical command and control orders to the orbital stations, and by relay, to the fleet." There was a pause, several seconds, and Rogan could hear Barron taking a breath.

"Bryan, we need you now—*I* need you now. You have to disrupt the enemy command and control any way you can. I don't know what forces you have left, what ordnance or equipment...but you have to find some way to take out those transmission units."

Rogan could feel something inside. Fear, yes, and tension...but something else far stronger. He felt purpose again. His mind was already racing, planning. If he had a week, perhaps two, maybe he could...

"Thirty-six hours, Bryan. If *Hermes* delivered this message on schedule, the fleet will be coming through the transit point in thirty-six hours. That's how long you've got."

The final words were a gut punch, but only for a few seconds. Rogan didn't care how long he had...he would find a way.

He would get it done.

"Sergeant...get everybody assembled at once. I want all officers here right now. Everyone else is to prep and be ready to go in two hours. Full combat gear...or the closest they can come. We've got an operation, a real operation. Finally, one that will make a real difference."

"Yes, General." There was a tone in the sergeant's reply, something Rogan hadn't heard in far too long. Pride. He knew he'd be leading his people into danger, that, in all probability, most or all of them would die.

But he knew something else, too…and that was more important.

Their days as rats scurrying around in tunnels were over.

They were Marines again.

*   *   *

"We've sent the message, Andi…full orbital coverage." Vig was nervous, that was clear, and Andi was, too. Exactly how much the stealth generator was able to hide them remained a question mark, but one that didn't matter all that much just then. Not as long as *Hermes* was blasting out a high-powered comm signal with half the output of the ship's reactor behind it.

"Any incoming contacts?" It was a pointless question. Her eyes had been as riveted to the display as anyone else's. But anything was better just then than silence. Especially since she was determined to complete a second orbital pass before breaking out and making a run for it. She hadn't come all this way, put her people in grave danger, to fail to get the message through. If Bryan Rogan—or any Marine who'd inherited his command—was still down there, she was damned sure going to get the communique to him.

"They've picked us up, Andi…I don't think there's much doubt about that. Looks like we got a little lucky. They don't have anything too close to our position, at least in terms of ships in orbit. Their response is a little lackluster, too. My bet is, someone in their command structure is going to hear about this before all is said and done." He paused, and his voice took on a darker tone. "Those escorts are still coming on, though. Six minutes out, and they're adjusting the vectors, coming at us dead on now. Whoever's commanding those knows his shit."

Andi nodded, and then she sighed softly. They were

lucky the orbital command had been slow to react…and all the more so, because whoever was in command of those escorts had been on to *Hermes* for hours, lacking only an exact location to launch an attack. There was a strange satisfaction in realizing that gifted officers were sometimes ignored in more services than the Confederation navy.

"Keep transmitting for three more minutes…then I'm going to want all power to the engines. We're going to blast out of orbit at full strength…and I mean *full*. I want all safeties cut. Every watt the reactors produce is to go into those engines, understood?" That wasn't going to help the stealth unit hide *Hermes*, of course, but she needed distance first. Planetary orbit was too constricted an area. There was no way her ship could hide there, not for very long. She needed more space, more empty, trackless void, if she was going to keep her ship hidden…and that meant she had to run like hell first.

As fast as the Hegemony escorts were, *Hermes* was faster…especially with her reactor and engines on full overload.

She glanced down at her workstation, her eyes fixing on the small screen. She'd hoped, for an instant, she'd get some kind of acknowledgement from Rogan that would tell her the mission, the dangers…and, very possibly, her death and those of her people…had not been for nothing. But, of course, there was nothing. It was beyond unlikely that Rogan, wherever he was, had sufficient power to drive a signal to orbit…and, even if he did, it would be unforgivably foolish, telegraphing his location to the enemy forces on the ground.

She would have to rely on belief…and somehow, in seeming opposition to her very nature, she did just that.

"One minute, Andi…"

"Everybody…strap in. Prepare for emergency maneuvers." She reached down, tapped at the controls, putting her on shipwide comm. "All personnel, strap in or go to the most secure location possible. We're breaking out of orbit in thirty seconds, and it's going to be a rough ride."

She turned halfway toward Vig's station, when she saw a series of flashes on her screen. She knew immediately what was happening…one of the enemy orbital stations was coming into its firing arc.

No…two of them.

She was out of time. The transmissions she'd gotten off already would have to be good enough.

"Break orbit…now! Full thrust!"

Vig turned to his station and moved his hands over the controls. Every wall and deck and bulkhead on *Hermes* shook and rattled. The ship's reactor was pouring energy into the engine circuits, and Andi felt as though a wall of stone had slammed into her body. *Hermes* had the most modern dampeners in service in any ship, but she could see the thrust readings from the corner of her eye…70g…80g…90g…and even her vessel's compensation systems were overloaded at those levels.

Those g-forces would have killed every man and woman in the crew in an instant, but the dampeners reduced the effect enough. Her people were uncomfortable as hell, maybe with a few broken bones or nasty bruises, but they weren't piles of strawberry jam.

Still, despite the discomfort, she felt relief. *Hermes* was breaking orbit, making a run for it, and none of her pursuers would be able to match the acceleration driving her ship.

At least for as long as it lasts.

She knew the reactor and the engines wouldn't hold out under the current level of abuse…but she didn't need forever.

Give me four more minutes…

She was taking it on faith she could get her ship far enough from Megara, that the stealth unit would still function, that the enemy would search fruitlessly…at least until Rogan's people distracted them, and Tyler and the fleet arrived.

She'd almost managed it...and then *Hermes* shook hard.

She didn't know whether something had malfunctioned, or if her ship had taken a hit. And she wasn't sure it mattered.

The cruiser shuddered hard, and suddenly, the crushing pressure was gone. Completely gone.

Hermes was in freefall. No thrust at all.

She looked down at the screen. Her readings showed the stealth unit still functioning, but without the engines, her ship was stuck on a straight-line course. A first-year Academy cadet could triangulate and narrow down *Hermes*'s location...and that assumed the damage wasn't affecting the stealth field in some way the status monitors weren't detecting.

That's what you get for believing in anything...

She felt a wave of disappointment, even fear...but at least she'd completed her mission. Escaping, getting back afterwards...that had always been optional.

*   *   *

"Send these nav orders...and I'll personally shoot the commander who doesn't have his ship in position on time." *Garara*'s commander had been hunched over his workstation, staring at every bit of incoming scanner data, trying to get a fix on the enemy whose presence was no longer a theory. He'd already been almost certain the enemy ship he sought was in Megara orbit...and then moments later, he got reports of an unidentified comm signal.

It made perfect sense. The ship he sought had come to deliver some kind of message. Whether it was directed at the resistance force, or at the population at large, he didn't know. And he didn't care. That wasn't his problem.

The ship itself was.

He'd tracked the vessel, chased it, and if his superiors had been more willing to listen, he might have intercepted it before it reached Megara. That was all in the past, though. Only one thing still mattered to him.

That ship wasn't getting away. Not if he could help it.

He heard the whine of *Garara*'s engines blasting hard, his ship following the nav orders he'd just issued. His first instinct had been to head into Megara orbit himself, moving right to the source of the transmission...but then he changed his mind.

Whoever was in that ship knew what they were doing. They were clearly there to send a communique of some kind, but they would also know a signal that strong was like a beacon pointing to the vessel.

Which means that ship will pull out of orbit as soon as the message is finished.

But where would they go? And, could he track it?

"Commander, the transmission has terminated."

"Full scanners...all ships. Concentrate on the source of the transmission and all points within ten thousand kilometers." It was time. The enemy would be breaking orbit, making a run for somewhere they could hide.

Tiergan stared at the screen, looking for signs of movement, detection of mass, energy trails...anything at all.

He saw the orbital platform open fire. A dozen shots, at least...and then a wave of energy erupted, less than fifty kilometers from the transmission location.

A hit?

There was nothing else it could be. The orbital platform had fired a barrage in the direction of the transmission signal...and it had hit something.

The station's fire continued, but there were no additional hits, at least none he could detect. But there *was* something, a faint trail, so light he couldn't be sure it was real.

But he *knew*, somehow, that it was.

His hands raced across his workstation, zooming in on

what he thought was a trail of particles from the fleeing ship. If that wasn't a trail left behind by the enemy ship, if the vessel was still in orbit, or heading off in another direction, he was going to lose it entirely, but he was ready to bet he was right.

It was the best thing he had to go on. He flipped a control, sending the nav data he'd just completed to the comm station. "Quinquaron…I want these coordinates transmitted to all ships at once…and to fleet command." He was far from sure command would pay him any more heed than it had before, though he suspected the sudden realization that some unidentified ship had managed to get all the way to Megara orbit unchecked might make a difference.

But he didn't need fleet command. He could only guess at the size and power of the mystery ship, but he was sure he had enough firepower to handle it himself.

He just needed to find it.

"Forward batteries…prepare to open fire." He was refining his targeting data, plotting a firing solution based on his best guess of the enemy's location. The trail was fading. He wasn't sure if the enemy had repaired whatever damage was causing the leak, or if clearing the gravitational pull of Megara had cut the stress on the ship enough to staunch the flow of charged particles. Whatever it was, he was running out of time. He didn't know exactly where the enemy ship was, not with the kind of accuracy reliable fire locks required. He just had to bombard the general area and hope for the best.

He pressed a series of buttons, sending the targeting data down to fire control. Then he looked up, eyes fixed on the forward display.

"Open fire."

Chapter Twenty-Six

Hall of the People
Liberte City
Planet Montmirail, Ghassara IV
Union Year 224 (320 AC)

"I'm sorry, Minister…but I just cannot have this discussion with you." Kerevsky stood up, a jerky and abrupt move that communicated his discomfort even more than his tone had. "If you will excuse me…"

"Please, Ambassador…sit." Sandrine Ciara looked across the small table that sat between her chair and the sofa where the Confederation ambassador had been sitting until a few seconds before. "I will endeavor to keep my speech a bit more…circumspect." She knew she'd pushed too hard, too fast. But Kerevsky's report on the situation at the front—as redacted and massaged as she was sure it had to be—had scared the hell out of her. She'd come to believe the Hegemony *was* a deadly threat to the whole Rim, and she was convinced she had to find a way to get the Union involved—beyond Denisov's already committed fleet. She'd left the last meeting in Villieneuve's office trying hard not to shake visibly, or let on that her tunic was pasted to her back by sweat. She wasn't sure if it was the data on the Hegemony forces that terrified her the most, or

Villieneuve's apparent lack of concern.

Kerevsky had painted a picture of near doom and defeat, and his descriptions of the enemy forces and their capabilities had left no doubt in her mind that they would sweep through any forces defending the Union as though they weren't there. Any chance to defeat the enemy, to send them retreating back out of the Rim, would be on the current front at Craydon or Megara, and it would take everything the Rim had. If the Union didn't send what help it could, and the enemy crushed the Confederation, she and Villieneuve would have signed the death warrant for their people.

Kerevsky's report had removed any lingering doubts she had about Villieneuve as well. She was scared to death by what she'd heard, and Kerevsky had obviously been shaken just in the telling...but Villieneuve was calm and cold, unmoved by anything that was said or seen. He'd met with her after Kerevsky had returned to his quarters, and she'd sat there, sure he would see the need to cooperate with the Confederation and the other Rim powers, at least temporarily. But she'd been stunned to learn he'd discounted almost everything the ambassador had said. Kerevsky had brought evidence—scanning reports, video, endless analysis...but none of it had gotten anywhere with Villieneuve.

She'd nursed a fear for some time, thought about it in the dark of sleepless nights, wondered helplessly what she could do about it...but only at the moment had she been utterly certain.

Villieneuve was crazy...and that insanity was going to destroy the Union, and possibly the entire Rim. She *had* to get rid of him...and there was only one way to do that.

But how? He was defended around the clock. His protectors had watchers...and the watchers had watchers. Gaston Villieneuve had always been paranoid, suspicious of anyone and anything, and the loss of his sanity had only taken things to another level. No one was allowed near him with weapons, save his closest and most loyal guards. His food was thoroughly scanned before he touched it, the ventilation leading to his office and residence were closed systems, guarded constantly.

How could she kill him? How could she take steps to aid the fight against the Hegemony? She needed an ally, one she could trust. One who wouldn't have incentives to betray her to Villieneuve. No matter how much she thought about it, how many options she reviewed, she'd only come up with one name.

Alexander Kerevsky. The only man on Montmirail who wasn't beholden to Villieneuve, or too scared of the First Citizen to even consider a move against him.

She looked up at the Confed, trying to seem genuinely sorry. Still, for a few seconds, she thought he was going to leave. If he went to Villieneuve, she was as good as dead…which meant she couldn't let him go. Her hand dropped, almost imperceptibly, to the small pistol she'd stashed under the seat cushion.

She didn't want to kill Kerevsky…the consequences would be devastating, not the least to any prospect of bringing Union forces into the war. But she didn't want to end up staring down at the blood drain in a Sector Nine cell, either, and that was about the best she could hope for if Kerevsky shared the topic of their discussion with Villieneuve.

Then she saw it. The slightest relaxation in Kerevsky's posture. Her Sector Nine career had been a constant exercise in watching people, reading them, manipulating them. She knew immediately that the ambassador was going to remain. At least for the moment.

"Minister Ciara, I understand the…*difficulties* you may face here. Certainly, from my point of view, I consider certain aspects of the Union state to be…problematic, though your perspective on such things no doubt differs from my own. But even if I agreed with you about what had to be done—and I am not saying I do—I have no authorization from my government to do anything save negotiate with the legitimate Union authorities."

"I understand, Ambassador." She paused. "Just to be clear, before we continue, I can assure you this room is secure. I have it swept regularly, and there are no recording devices of any kind." *That was a useless thing to say. Why would he believe you?*

It was, however, true. She didn't even have the AI recording the discussion, for her own use. It would have been far too risky.

"Again, Minister Ciara…there is nothing I can say here that I couldn't say in session with the First Citizen. I am here only to advise you of the gravity of the threat we all face…not to interfere with any aspect of your government."

"Do you want Union assistance in this war, Ambassador…beyond Admiral Denisov's fleet, which must be rapidly deteriorating without access to Union parts and equipment?" It was a blunt question, one that cut right to the heart of the matter. She knew the Confeds wanted Union aid, needed it…it was time to find out just how badly.

"Yes, Minister, of course. I have been clear about that, and candid about the current state of the war. It is in your interests as well to see the Hegemony driven back through the Badlands. You know this, Minister, I know you do."

"Yes, Ambassador…I do. And if it were my decision, you would have the Union as an ally. Let us be honest with each other. I have no love for the Confederation…but I recognize the grave danger that plagues us all." She paused, and decided not to say what she'd been about to say.

Then, she did it anyway.

"Gaston Villieneuve has lost his mind, Ambassador Kerevsky. That is not my propaganda, it is not a negotiating tool. It is a fact. You saw him, you heard his words. Not only is he not going to agree to aid your people...it is entirely possible he will refuse to allow you to leave. He treats you with full diplomatic honors now, but you have not seen his behavior of late. He is dangerously erratic. He is as likely to order you dragged out of his office in chains as host a luncheon in your honor. You are placing the success of your mission, perhaps the survival of your Confederation, on the whims of a madman." Her insides were twisted into knots. She'd gone much, much farther than she'd planned to, and she'd put herself in grave danger doing it. If Kerevsky told Villieneuve a fraction of what she'd just said, she was finished...and likely not in a fast or pleasant way. But there was no choice. Beneath her own lust for power and self-serving manipulation, she was loyal to the Union...and she didn't want to see it destroyed, its people reduced to slaves of the Hegemony.

Some things were worth risking everything for.

"Minister, I understand what you're telling me, I truly do. But I simply have neither the authority or the means to interfere materially in Union internal affairs." He was silent for a moment, and his eyes darted back and forth, almost certainly a subconscious reaction to the danger of what they were discussing. "I can promise you I will say nothing of what has been said here, and I trust that you will conduct yourself as I am sure you always have, like a realist and a patriot."

Ciara watched as Kerevsky stood up, slowly, very slowly. Was he giving her some kind of signal? Were his words a message, an unspoken expression of support for bold action, if not a promise of actual help?

Or am I just seeing what I want to see?

Her hand moved back under her, toward the gun. Letting Kerevsky go would a wild gamble, though disposing of his body and explaining his absence was far from without its own danger.

"I am quite tired, Minister. If you will excuse me, I will

return to my quarters and rest."

The ambassador didn't look tired at all. His eyes were wide open and bright, and they were locked on her own. *Another message?*

Her fingers moved along the hard edge of the pistol's grip. She was almost certain Kerevsky was unarmed. He hadn't been allowed to bring any weapons from his ship, and she was an expert at spotting such things. She'd turned off the recording devices in the room, but not the weapons detector, and that, too, had confirmed that Kerevsky had nothing.

She was an expert shot with the pistol. She could drop the Confed in an instant. He'd be dead before he knew what was happening.

But she didn't move. She just sat, her hand frozen, just touching the weapon but doing no more. Finally, she said, "I understand, Ambassador. Please, have a restful sleep." Slowly, reluctantly, her hand moved away from the pistol. It wasn't trust…Ciara didn't trust anyone. But she was going to bet on Kerevsky. There was more to the Confed than simply a diplomat in love with his own voice. Something deeper, something harder.

He almost reminded her of herself, or one of Sector Nine's top operatives.

Of course! He's Confederation Intelligence. That makes perfect sense.

It also meant that, whatever he'd told her, at some point, he probably *would* do more than simply negotiate. If he was a spy, Gary Holsten had sent him, and though the head of Confederation Intelligence had always been her enemy, she'd never thought him a fool. He wouldn't have sent an operative, not unless there were more at play than a diplomatic mission.

She was still uncertain, and the deadly seriousness of making a move against Villieneuve terrified her to her core. But she was closer to working up the courage to try it.

To be a true patriot.

She watched as Kerevsky left, and one more thought crept into her mind.

Whatever you do…make sure of one thing. Don't survive a failed attempt.

She'd seen the worst Gaston Villieneuve could do, and being gunned down by guards was a blissful escape by comparison.

Chapter Twenty-Seven

Bridge
CFS Hermes
Olyus System
Year 320 AC

Dammit! Whoever is commanding those ships knows what the hell he's doing…

Andi Lafarge was hunched forward on *Hermes*'s bridge, her body damp with sweat, her heartbeat thundering in her ears. She'd managed to pull her ship far enough from Megara, and her people had repaired the damage from the orbital station's hit. But then the ships that had chased her across the system came swarming in…too damned close for her taste.

That hit from the orbital station…there have been some kind of leak, or an energy release. Something those ships picked up and used to track us.

It couldn't have been much. *Hermes*'s own scanners hadn't picked up anything. *But we're stuck on passive scans…and those bastards have been pounding away on active units at full strength.*

Whatever the enemy ships had detected, it was enough for them to direct a barrage all around her ship's position…and to hit the fleeing vessel three times. She was mad at herself, angry that she'd missed the danger. There was no way she could have known the enemy had detected some kind of trace energy leak as *Hermes* broke orbit—but that made no difference.

She'd managed to get away from the attackers, to change course enough to pull her out of the main search zone of the pursuing enemy ships. Then she'd cut the power outputs, and made like a hole in space. That had worked for almost two days…forty-one endless, painful, agonizing hours, broken down into minutes and seconds, and every one of them spent waiting to see if the enemy picked up on something. All it would take was some chunk of steel that had broken free from the damaged hull, or even a tiny cloud of particles. Anything that might put the pursuers back on her trail.

She'd done all she could. Her people would either survive now or not, and if they didn't, as far as she was concerned, it was her fault.

The only advantage was, if they died, she'd die too. There was a mercy of sorts in that, but it was shadowed by the grief she knew it would bring Tyler. She knew the stress he lived under, the weight he carried every day. She wondered if she should have allowed her pride to rule her, to demand that she execute the mission. She'd only done what she thought was right, but she realized she'd added more burdens onto Barron's hunched shoulders.

She felt anger, too, resentment. Not at anyone in particular, but at the universe itself. At the dark turn of fortune that put some capable, relentless Hegemony officer on her tail. She suspected her pursuer—very likely to become her killer—was someone she could respect in different circumstances, someone very much like her in many ways. But right now, whoever was in the lead enemy ship was her deadly enemy. She had to find a way to evade him—or destroy him. That was all she could think about.

Because she was Andromeda Lafarge, and no matter how grave the situation, she never gave up.

"Lex, what's the latest on the reactor?" She was leaning over the comm. She had *Hermes*'s engines shut down, and her reactor operating at minimal power, just enough for life support and to run the stealth unit. That was a bit of good luck, at least…the continued functionality of the unit. If that failed—*when* it failed if Lex couldn't reverse the damage done to the reactor—they were finished. It wouldn't even take long, not with the number of enemy escorts flying all around, looking for her ship.

"No change. Those last two hits were close to critical. I can't fix it, not with what we've got on board. The best I've been able to manage is a patch job…and that won't hold. The reactor is failing, Andi. I've done all I can do to keep it going, but I'm going to lose that battle…and soon."

Andi heard the words, and she knew better than to question them. Not when they came from Lex Righter. Her longtime friend had struggled with his personal issues, certainly—drugs and alcohol among them—but he'd been clean for years now, and even when he hadn't been, he'd never been anything but an expert engineer…and one hundred percent straight with her. He'd saved her ass on *Pegasus* more than once, and if he told her *Hermes*'s reactor was going to fail, then she took it as undeniable fact.

She had to do *something*. She thought about firing at the enemy, luring them closer and then launching a surprise attack…but she realized immediately that wasn't an option. Besides being hopelessly outnumbered, *Hermes* had been built for speed, not combat power. The small, sleek cruiser's weapons were few, and light. As Andi had put it more than once, in various levels of jest, they could boil a pot of water. Maybe.

Besides, engaging in combat hardly seemed plausible with a failing reactor. Things were bad enough on minimal power, but firing the weapons was as likely to knock the thing out immediately as score a hit. And when the reactor failed, her people were finished.

She felt the urge to argue with Righter, insist that he find some way to fix the thing. But asking for the impossible was a fool's game. *Hermes* was going to lose power. Nothing was going to change that. She needed a plan, a way to survive, to save her people. And she needed it soon.

She was running out of time.

*   *   *

"Professor Carlson, I can't thank you enough for coming with us. Your guidance has been invaluable." Bryan Rogan was standing against the strange—almost eerily intact—wall of the ancient transport tube, looking right at the archeologist. He'd given his Marines a ten-minute rest, and while they leaned against the walls and ate their meager rations, he'd taken the opportunity to express his gratitude yet again.

"I am glad I was able to help, General."

Most of Megara's population came from prosperous government classes. Rogan had always been hesitant about labeling such types as "soft," though the Senate's craven surrender had done little to bolster his restraint. The Marines had stood firm, unsurprisingly, through defeat and hardship and death…and the other defense forces had acquitted themselves well, too. But there were few partisans or rebels out there. The population as a whole had proven to be quite passive and easily conquered.

Which made the standouts—like Carlson—so extraordinary. The longtime head of Troyus City's Museum of the Empire had come walking into Rogan's headquarters one day, early in the defensive effort, when battles were still raging across the planet's surface. He'd brought an almost complete knowledge of all the old imperial ruins on Megara, the remnants of cities, transit tubes, and various other installations, many of them buried deep under the sand and dirt of modern Megara.

Almost all of them were physically intact, capable of supporting and—thanks to the anti-scanner effects of the ancient metals and hyper-plastics from which they'd been constructed—hiding the Marines. More amazingly, Carlson had told Rogan he'd wiped the museum databases clean before he'd left, eliminating as much as he could of any roadmaps the enemy could use to search the old ruins.

He looked at the professor for a few seconds, suddenly realizing the extent of the change in the academic who had come more than a year before to aid his people. Carlson had been brave, but soft. A quarter kilometer's run had him gasping for breath. A full kilometer nearly put him in the infirmary. He'd been overweight and out of shape.

Now, he was lean, hard. Standing opposite Rogan in his borrowed Marine fatigues, he looked almost like any of Rogan's people, save for the silver hair hanging down from under his helmet. The Marines had adopted him in appreciation for the aid he'd given them, and now, a little over a year later, he looked the part.

Carlson had saved his Marines, Rogan was sure of that...at least the tattered remnant that had survived the fighting on the surface. And now, he was leading them back to Troyus City. If Rogan had understood the directions correctly, they would come within a kilometer of the main surface to orbit transmission tower.

His primary target. The one he had to destroy, *somehow*, if he was going to help Admiral Barron and the fleet. It had seemed an impossible task, but once again, Carlson's help had produced a near-miracle.

Rogan was worn, exhausted, his body sore from the wounds he'd suffered that had only partially healed. But news that the fleet was on the way had reinvigorated him. He realized that, even as he had continued his obstinate resistance, he'd never really believed the fleet would return. Defeatism was a dangerous and devious force, capable of working its way into even the most defiant minds, lying below the surface and festering, sapping away at one's strength until nothing remained. The Marine was angry with himself for succumbing to it on any level. It wasn't the Marine way.

It wasn't *his* way.

But getting to the comm center was only part of the problem. His people had targeted secondary installations for almost a year now. Those were places they could steal supplies and continue to be a thorn in the enemy's side. But the main comm station would be defended.

Heavily defended.

He didn't know how many of his people would die assaulting the installation, but he was pretty sure this would be their final operation. Whatever number survived, they would be scattered, hunted, low on equipment and ammunition.

But if they succeeded, if they took down the transmission station, they would help the fleet. They would strike a blow to help drive the enemy from Megara.

"All right, Marines…I hope that little vacation reenergized you, because we've got six hours of marching before we get another." Rogan knew he was pushing his people hard, especially after all they'd been through over the past year and a half. But they had a schedule to keep…and if they were going to knock out the enemy's command and control communications before Barron and the fleet arrived, they had no time to waste.

No time at all.

* * *

"Widen the search zone…expand the distance between ships by ten thousand kilometers." Tiergan was frustrated. He'd truly believed he'd had the enemy, that they were at his mercy.

But whoever is commanding that ship is formidable…

At least he had more resources. Once the shock of the still—at least as far as he knew—encrypted communique wore off, fleet command had sent him another four squadrons of escorts and frigates. He had sixty-two ships now, all under his command, searching for any signs of the rogue enemy ship.

Any signs at all.

He was sure he'd scored two hits in the initial barrage, perhaps even three or four. But then the target just disappeared. He'd reacted immediately, sent his ships along every escape route he'd been able to foresee…but they had found nothing.

It was as though the enemy had simply vanished.

"All units acknowledge, Commander. Search grid increased in scope."

"Very well." Tiergan sat bolt upright in his chair, looking out at *Garara*'s bridge crew. His people were capable, well-trained, and loyal to the Hegemony. But they lacked *something*. Tiergan felt a call, like that of a predator on the trail of his prey. His people were different. They followed orders without question, did their jobs with a commendable level of competency. But they lacked a killer instinct.

Tiergan had rarely given much thought to the Hegemony's rigid system. He was a Red Kriegeri, as were all his people on *Garara*. That designation, born of the series of examinations known as the Test, had destined him for a naval career. There had never been any choice, not for any of them. In the Hegemony, one's genetic rating—and perceived capabilities resulting from that analysis—determined one's place in society. If the testing showed you were best suited to work in a factory, that would be your life. If your inherent capabilities suggested a military career, you were branded Kriegeri and sent to training. No choice, not whether to join the army or navy, nor even what branch. A recruit's genes made all the choices.

Now, sitting, waiting almost helplessly for any readings, any clues he could use, his mind wandered into places he'd never before allowed it to go. How did the Confederation, with its chaotic society, produce such extraordinary warriors?

The Hegemony was perfectly ordered, every one of its people deployed in accordance with their aptitude and capabilities. Was that system, that he'd always accepted as perfect, missing something? Did a Confederation officer, one who'd scrambled hard, fought and clawed up to a level beyond what a genetic rating might have allowed, possess some unique abilities? A toughness, a tenacity, that the Kriegeri, locked in a defined range of available ranks and responsibility levels, didn't have?

"Commander...*Yorigoth* is transmitting scanner results, a possible contact..."

Tiergan snapped back to focus. "On my screen...now!"

He didn't have time for the thoughts that had invaded his mind, not just then. He had a job to do, and if Hegemony dogma had held him from commanding a force the size of the one circumstance had just placed in his hands, that didn't mean he couldn't handle the sixty plus vessels under his control. He had more ships than he'd ever imagined commanding, and he was going to do whatever it took to succeed.

To find that Confederation vessel, and its captain.

"Set a course toward the scanner readings...take us there at full thrust."

Chapter Twenty-Eight

CFS Dauntless
Approaching Olyus Transit Point
Covath System

The Second Battle of Megara – "Prelude to Hell"

"Twenty minutes to vanguard transit, Admiral. Projected *Dauntless* entry into the point, thirty-six minutes." Atara Travis spoke softly, calmly, though Barron could hear the effort it was taking for her to sound that way. No one in the fleet was calm. They were heading into what very likely would be the bloodiest battle any of them had yet fought. Defeat would almost certainly mean the loss of the war, so Barron had no intention of breaking off or issuing a retreat order, regardless of what happened. Once his ships jumped into the Olyus system, they were committed. This fight would be to the end.

"Very well, Captain." He glanced over at Atara's station, gave her a quick wink. It was little enough for an exchange between two old friends as close as they were, but it was all either of them had time for.

He held his gaze for just a few seconds, waiting for the return gesture he knew she'd have for him. A small nod of her head...he knew it when he saw it. The interchange had been nothing anyone else would have noticed, but between the two of them it was a wish for good fortune, a sharing of strength…and if fate decreed it as such, a farewell between a brother and sister in arms, and in life.

Barron's eyes moved toward the massive 3D display in the center of *Dauntless*'s bridge, struck for a few seconds by the size of the grand armada he led. The fleet included ships from more than a dozen nations, though the core of it remained his own veteran Confederation spacers and the grim warriors of Palatia, led forward by no less than their Imperator himself. It was nearly all the strength the Rim could muster, save only for the Union forces beyond those in Andrei Denisov's fleet, and those of the principalities out on the Periphery, on the far side of Union space.

All the strength we can muster…and yet, very possibly not enough. Barron was again stunned at the immense size and power of the Hegemony, and at just how wrong presumed facts had been about the supposed dead space lying beyond the Badlands. *We thought ourselves unique, the only survivors of the Cataclysm. Now, we pay the price for that hubris.*

He almost turned toward Atara again, but he stopped himself. Despite her odd position, ship's captain and admiral's aide, she'd done a remarkable job of handling all her responsibilities. Barron knew she was checking on *Dauntless*'s status, preparing her battleship for the coming fight. He might be the fleet admiral, but that didn't mean he couldn't connect his own comm channels.

"Jake…"

"Yes, Admiral."

Barron was struck again by how much had changed in Stockton's tone. The brash, cocky young officer he'd known, who had sometimes pushed him to the limits of his tolerance, was gone forever. Stockton had been battered by war and loss and forged into perhaps the greatest killing machine that had ever existed…or at least the most dangerous to Hegemony warships. The fleet carried 5,842 fighter-bombers with it, and every one of them was under Stockton's command. They were the complements of every battleship and escort carrier the nations of the Grand Alliance possessed, reinforced with squadrons stripped from Craydon's fixed defenses and crammed into overloaded bays. There were deadly aces, and green rookies who'd never flown their ships outside an Academy exercise...and all manner of pilots in between.

Barron didn't dare let himself imagine how many of them would die in the coming fight, even if the attack on Megara was successful.

"I want your people ready to launch as soon as we transit. If the enemy is deployed back from the point, we'll hold your wings in the bays, and get you farther in-system, but if they're going to defend the point, we'll need your people out there and going at their forward battleships as quickly as possible."

"Understood, Admiral. *Dauntless* is somewhat back in the transit order, but Alicia Covington in in *Warspite*, almost at the head of the first battleship column. With your permission, I will give her authorization to launch all available squadrons if she detects enemy capital ships in range of the point."

"Yes, Jake...definitely. Do that. Captain Covington isn't easily unnerved. She won't launch unless there's reason to...and if there are enemy ships waiting for us, she'll hit them that much sooner, and you can get the rest of your people out in support as the balance of the fleet transits."

Barron didn't like flying right into Olyus without any real intel on the enemy fleet dispositions, but he'd decided it wasn't worth the risk to send scouts, or even drones through before the fleet. The enemy would have the point's terminus surrounded with scanners and detection gear, and even with if he sent through ships with the last of the stealth units, he couldn't be sure they would make it undetected.

But you sent Andi through...

There had been pickets positioned in the system, of course, watching for anything approaching Olyus, but Barron had sent fast attack cruisers through first. The Hegemony ships had been badly positioned, too deep in the system to escape and bring back the alert…at least he was pretty sure his people had gotten them all in time.

With any luck, his fleet's entry into Olyus would take the Hegemony forces by surprise…and then it would be a toe to toe slugging match, a brutal and vicious fight to the end.

"Jake…one more thing, old friend. Good luck to you."

"Thank you, sir. And to you as well…to all of us."

Barron nodded his head.

To all of us…

* * *

"Good luck, everybody, and remember, all blasts are to be synchronized. We're…" Rogan looked at the chronometer on his wrist. "…exactly fifty-five minutes from the designated time. That doesn't leave any room for delay." Rogan had deliberately left the timing tight. It didn't leave room for error or unforeseen problems, but too much time could have been even worse. His Marines just *might* be able to take the enemy by surprise, and take possession of the targets…but there was no way they could hold them, not once the Kriegeri realized what was going on. The enemy forces sent to retake the positions would outnumber his people at least twenty to one.

But, if his people came through, if they were able to execute the operation according to plan, there would be no positions left to retake.

"Understood, General."

"Yes, sir…and good luck to you as well."

"We'll see it done, General."

Rogan listened as his senior officers responded. He had six groups moving out. He was leading the largest, the strike force that would hit the main comm center. The other five would target power stations, and auxiliary communications facilities. If the whole thing went as planned, the Hegemony leadership on the ground would be cut off from the orbital stations, and by extension, from the massive fleet in the system. They would restore at least some of their communication reasonably quickly, he knew, so if the fleet had fallen off schedule, his Marines' efforts would be wasted.

It was a gamble in other ways, too. The total effect of the raid would depend largely on which Hegemony commanders were on the ground, and which ones happened to be with the fleet or at one of the fortresses. Rogan couldn't know for sure, but his best guess was, Hegemony operations would be badly disrupted for at least half a day, and perhaps longer.

But whatever happened, however much good the attack did…it was all his people could do. He didn't know if any of them would escape, and for how long any who did would manage to hide could hold out. Some of them might make it back to the ancient tubes, or the ruins…but he was almost certain the days of his force as an operating formation would end in less than an hour.

"Professor…I suggest you go back to the tubes and get to someplace where you can return to the city and try to slip back into the population…or at least go back to the main base. There is food there, and supplies. You can probably stay there for…"

"No, General. I'm no Marine, but I made my choice. I rallied to your side and did what I could, as a Megaran, and as a patriot. I'm afraid I'm well past the time I could slip back into my old life without discovery…and I have no desire to return to the base without the rest of you. I'm not a fighter, as your people are, General, but after a year with all of you, I think I can at least stay out of the way."

Rogan considered arguing, insisting Carlson go back. But

the professor was right. He'd made his choice, and he'd served Megara—and the Marines—well. He had a right to his place with them, and Bryan Rogan wouldn't take it from him.

"Very well, Professor. But stay close to me, okay?"

Carlson nodded. "Thank you, sir."

"And, Professor…you are a fighter, more than you know. I have seen many, and none I've known would hesitate to accept you at their sides. You're a Marine, too, in your heart, one of us through the hardships of the last year, and one of us right now."

Carlson nodded, clearly affected by Rogan's words. He turned, stopping halfway to say, "I will be waiting over there with the others, General." Then he walked away, leaving Rogan with his second in command.

"I wish we could go in together, Dan…but I need you to take out that secondary station. If the raids on the power units fail, we'll still have knocked out most of their comm capacity, at least for a while. But if the backups survive, they'll just cut back to the most important command traffic…and we'll have lost most of our gains."

"Understood, General." A pause. "I know how important this is, Bryan. You worry about the main facility. I'll take out the secondary…whatever I have to do."

Rogan extended his hand. "I know you will, Dan."

Prentice reached out and the two men shook. It was a gesture of good will, a wish from each for fortune to smile on the other.

And, if need be, it was a goodbye, between two friends who both knew they were likely never to meet again.

* * *

"We've got a drone emerging from the point, Admiral."

Barron's eyes darted to the display. He'd held back any scouting efforts before the fleet began transiting for fear of alerting the enemy sooner than he had to. But of course, that was no impediment to the units that had already emerged in Olyus sending back reports.

Barron hadn't expressly ordered any such communiques, mostly because he didn't want the commanders of his lead ships distracted. They would likely face at least some kind of fight just after transit, and he wanted them focused totally on the tactical situation.

But the appearance of the drone suggested there was something the advanced guard's commander thought was important.

And that advanced guard was under Admiral Sara Eaton, Barron's longtime comrade. The two had fought many battles together, and anything Eaton wanted to tell him, he knew he needed to hear.

"Admiral, the drone reports that the enemy had a division of battleships positioned in defense of the transit point. Admiral Eaton's battle line is under fire from the enemy railguns, but she has launched all bombers, and they will be hitting the enemy capital ships any moment."

Barron nodded. It wasn't far from what he'd expected, but the thoughts of Eaton and her battleships getting torn to scrap by Hegemony railguns before the main battle had even begun was hard to endure.

At least she's got the enhanced primaries...that should be a surprise to those bastards. They probably think they're out of range...

Barron was troubled by the viciousness of his thoughts, the primal way his mind celebrated at the thought of Hegemony ships being hit by the heavy guns, Hegemony spacers killed by the unexpected fire. But it only lasted a few seconds. He didn't care anymore. He was what he was, and his job was to destroy the enemy. That meant killing their people.

As many as he could. Any way he could.

"Admiral, we're getting a new comm signal from the transit point...the Volzen point." Barron heard the words, but it took an instant to settle in. The Volzen point wasn't on the line back to Craydon. It led out toward Ulion and beyond, to Dannith and the Badlands.

There was only one force operating there, at least only one close enough to send a message.

"I want that communique on my headset, Atara...the instant it's decoded." The message had to be from Captain Eaton...the other Eaton, Sonya. The one he'd sent out to harass enemy shipping, and to distract the enemy from any expectations of the assault he was launching even then.

But none of that called for a report, and that meant something was wrong. Barron took anything either Eaton sister told him with deadly seriousness.

"On your line, Admiral." Atara gestured toward Barron as she spoke, and an instant later, Sonya Eaton's voice poured into his ears.

"We have encountered an enemy convoy, Admiral, one accompanied by a significant contingent of warships." Barron felt his heartrate soar. What was "significant"? "I have attached as detailed an OB as I've been able to assemble, sir, but in short, there are twenty battleships, all of the larger classes, along with cruisers and escorts." Barron heard the words, and even as he did, his hopes faded. Those ships would be coming in behind his fleet once it had all transited into Olyus. It was a disaster, just about as devastating a development as possible...and he didn't know what to do about it. Could he even call back the advance guard?

No...there's no way. They've launched fighters already. It would take them too long.

He shook his head. *No, we can't stop...the way is forward.*

"My forces have engaged the enemy forces, Admiral. We have launched several raids, and I have managed to keep my ships ahead of the enemy. As I send this, we are in the Venga system, and I am about to launch another bomber strike. We have managed to damage several battleships, and we will keep attacking in an effort to slow down the convoy, to hold them back until the battle at Megara is won."

My God…she's attacking twenty battleships with her eight tin cans and as many escorts.

No, seven escorts. She sent one here with her report.

It was insane, an impossible mission, one that would likely cost Eaton and every spacer serving her their lives.

And it was just what she'd expect from Eaton…from either Eaton.

"Atara…the fleet is to decrease segments between jumps. Our timetable just got tighter. We need to get this fleet through, and we need to hit the enemy. Hard and fast."

Chapter Twenty-Nine

Bridge
CFS Hermes
Olyus System
Year 320 AC

The Second Battle of Megara – "Up now, and to arms!"

"I don't know, Andi. I'm just not sure I can pull it off. It's pretty dicey, and if anything goes wrong, we'll be wide open." Lex Righter sounded more than tense. The engineer was clearly on the edge.

Anyone sane is on the edge right now…

Hermes's reactor was still functioning, barely. It had almost failed twice, both times salvaged by Righter's engineering skills, literally with seconds to spare. Whoever was commanding the ships hunting *Hermes* was no joke. It was a skilled and capable officer out there, and as stubborn as they came. That much was clear, and Andi knew the life expectancy of her people would be measured in minutes from the instant the reactor failed, and the stealth unit went down.

"Lex, old friend…I know it's a long shot. I know I'm asking a lot of you, but there's no other way. Not unless you can keep *Hermes*'s reactor operating for at least three more days." Andi had been watching the ships emerge into the system for the past ten minutes or so. She didn't have a lot of data coming in from the passive scans, not at such extensive range, but she could see enough. The fleet had arrived. But, even if she allowed herself the optimism of hoping for victory, the fight would almost certainly last for days. And if the stealth unit failed before the enemy was defeated and driven out of the system, that meant almost instant death for her people.

"Three days? That's not even possible. I'd bet we've got four hours, Andi, maybe six...twelve would be a damned miracle. Honestly, I'm surprised we've been able to keep the thing running this long."

"Then do what I say, Lex. What damned difference does it make if the thing goes now or in six hours? What do you think is going to change in that time?"

There was a long silence on the comm unit.

"Lex...you know I believe in you. I always have...but now I'm counting on you to hold it together, and to give me the best you've got." She'd always tried to give her engineer a little extra support in tense moments. While she had faith in him, the last thing she needed was him losing it on her just then. He wasn't likely to find a drink or a hit of something down in *Hermes*'s engineering section, but she needed him sharp. She needed every bit of skill he had, and a good helping of luck thrown in. She had a plan, one she thought just might work.

Just *might* save her people.

But it all relied on Righter, and any slip up, however small or seemingly insignificant, would be fatal. She needed him at his best, which was a lot to ask, since she doubted any of her people were at peak efficiency just then. They'd been hunted relentlessly for days, and she imagined few of them had any real hope of escaping. The emergence of the fleet had briefly boosted morale, but she didn't expect it to last.

"Lex! I need you now. You have to focus, and you have to get this done, somehow. If you won't do it for *Hermes* or for the Confederation or for yourself…do it for me. Years ago, I pulled your sorry ass off the floor in a Spacer's District dive, and I helped you make something of yourself. I know you can do this." Her voice was raw, the hard edge designed to slice through her friend's fear and self-doubt.

There was a silence, and though it felt long to her, she guessed it was only a few seconds. "Okay, Andi…I'll try. But I can't promise anything…I'm really not sure I can do it."

"Just do your best, Lex."

And if that's not good enough, we all die…

* * *

"All wings, maintain formation, on my vector." Jake Stockton was back in the cockpit of his Lightning. Where he belonged.

Where it sometimes felt he'd been born.

The Confederation had seen many aces in its history, grim and deadly pilots who'd blazed trails to glory. More often than not, they had all eventually met their matches in combat, or at least lost their good fortune in one fateful battle. But Stockton had developed a reputation as unbeatable, indestructible. He knew it was nonsense and he'd resisted it at first, but as the war against the Hegemony continued, he'd become more inclined to use it, to drive the fear from his pilots.

In his own mind, however, he'd held firmly to a clear distinction between legend and fact. He was a skilled pilot, perhaps, with a reasonable claim to being the best in the fleet. But he'd almost met his match more than once, and his ego, while not immune to a bit of puffery here and there, had never clouded his realization that luck had saved him more than once.

Against Jovi Grachus, certainly. The Alliance ace had been as good as he was, or damned close…and that had been flying an Alliance fighter that was two decades behind his Lightning in technology. If they'd met on equal terms…he was far from sure he'd be there, leading the countless squadrons forming up, or still launching as battleships emerged from the transit point.

Maybe she would be here, remembering the day she'd killed me.

It was pointless to think that way, he knew that well enough. She was dead, and he was there, more than five thousand pilots looking to him for leadership, and some— the rookies especially—nearly worshipping him as a deity. They followed him as though he led them to paradise and not, far more likely, to a lonely death in the frozen reaches of space.

His eyes moved to his scanners, watching as the returning fighters from the advance guard moved onto the screen. He saw Alicia Covington's ship, and he breathed a sigh of relief. He hadn't known Covington all that well before she'd become one of the unofficial group he dubbed his Four Horsemen, but he'd come to respect her skill and courage. If the Confederation managed to retake Megara, he was sure she would play her part in that victory.

As we all will.

It was no more than fact. If all of his people didn't do their part, there would be no victory in Olyus, no reclamation of Megara. There would only be defeat, certain and final.

His hand tightened around the throttle, and he gradually increased his thrust, giving his still-forming wings a chance to match his maneuver. His eyes were still on the screen, his initial excitement at seeing Covington's ship dulled by the thinness of the waves behind her. Stockton didn't have numbers yet, the retiring squadrons weren't all close enough for that kind of data, but his experience gave him an estimate he knew would at least be close.

Covington had perhaps eighty percent of her ships left in formation. Not all of the missing ships were lost, of course. Some were likely cripples, falling behind the main formation as they limped back to their mother ships...and with a massive wave of newly arrived fighters coming on and stopping cold any enemy pursuit, they'd have a good chance of making it back.

But he knew a lot of the missing pilots were dead. Dead or floating in space, kept alive for a while by survival gear, desperately hoping their comrades would push the enemy back quickly enough for the retrieval boats to come and get them.

Before they froze or suffocated.

Covington's people had done all he could have expected of them, and now it was time for him to follow up on what she'd started...and to finish the battleships of the forward Hegemony formation. They were damaged, battered...and Stockton had no intention of allowing any of them to escape.

Not one.

"Warrior...blast your wings forward, full thrust, around the starboard side of the enemy formation. I want you on their line of retreat, at least 250,000 kilometers behind. We'll hit them from the front. You and your people pick off any survivors who run." He paused, and he could feel the anger and bitterness he felt toward the enemy growing, turning his tone caustic. "None of them escape...do you understand me? Not one of them."

"I understand you, Raptor. Consider it done." Dirk Timmons's reply was, if anything, colder and more malevolent. "Warrior" Timmons was the one pilot in the Confederation's entire order of battle who could challenge Stockton's skill, and that made him the natural go to for the most important jobs.

Like making sure not a single battleship escaped to join the main enemy fleet.

I do, old friend, I do. That's why I'm sending you…

* * *

Barron stood in front of his chair on *Dauntless*'s bridge, rigid like a statue, watching the battle unfolding in the 3D immensity of the flagship's main display. The fleet was still shaking down into formation, ships pouring through the transit point. Sara Eaton's advance guard had ten ships in an intense firefight with eight Hegemony dreadnoughts. Her battle line was formed up around her flagship, *Renown*, sparkling new from Craydon's own shipyards.

Well, it *had* been sparkling, before Eaton had transited and gone toe to toe with the Hegemony line. Eaton had already lost two ships, and her remaining hulls were battered, some with gaping wounds.

The fight had clearly been vicious, possibly even a straight up match, which had to be a surprise to the enemy. The enhanced primaries were living up to expectations, at least from the four ships that still seemed to have operational main batteries. The days of immense Hegemony range advantages were past, at least when the newest Confederation ships—and the four biggest from the Alliance—were in the fight.

Covington's bombers, spent now and heading back to their launch platforms, had exacted their price as well. Only three Hegemony vessels appeared to have railguns still firing. Barron's eyes moved along the row of red spheres, and then he looked toward his own workstation, as the AI scrolled damage assessments.

Barron realized immediately that the enemy positioning had favored his forces, to an extent. The forward enemy division had claimed a price against the advance guard, but it had also given his oncoming formations the chance to overwhelm it, to destroy those ships before meaningful support could make it across the system.

He wondered if it had been hubris, the expectation that the battleships' railguns would cut down any transiting ships before they could close and engage. That was a strategy that might have made sense...before the fleet had been upgraded with enhanced primaries.

Barron had wondered if the increased risk of malfunction, or even critical systems failure was too high a price to pay for the longer-ranged batteries, but now he had no doubt. He'd been right to insist the upgrades be installed in every ship that could take them. There would be failures, certainly, perhaps even some that cost him ships...and crews. But he had no doubt which way the scales would drop in the end.

He could hear the whine of the battleship's primaries charging, much louder than it had been before. He'd given the order for the battleships of the fleet's first wave, the ones with enhanced batteries, to open fire when ready. He'd almost ordered the primaries charged before the ships jumped, but the enhanced weapons were dangerously overpowered as it was...to risk carrying that kind of load through the transit point seemed downright insane.

Now, he sat and waited, and tried to keep himself from watching the small display tracking *Dauntless*'s charging status. He'd promised himself he would leave the running of the flagship itself to Atara. She was *Dauntless*'s captain now, and that was that.

His job was commanding the fleet, and however strange that seemed, however much his mind struggled to grasp how that had come to be, he knew what he had to do. He'd never had any choice about who he was, who he would be. He'd been destined for the navy since the day he'd been born, and every path in his life had led to the command he now held, the position that had once been his grandfather's.

His father hadn't lived to reach such lofty heights, but despite the many dangers he'd faced, Tyler *had* survived. He'd survived to do his duty, to lead his spacers to victory.

Or to defeat and death.

He felt his hands tighten, forming two fists at his side, as determination surged through him. He felt almost as though his grandfather was there on *Dauntless*'s bridge, giving him strength, keeping his focus where it had to be.

No…not defeat. We are not going to lose this battle…or this war. I will do what has to be done, Grandfather, as you once did. We will prevail.

Even as he felt the raw defiance strengthening him, he heard the louder, higher pitched sound…*Dauntless*'s primaries firing.

The fight was on.

He turned, and he looked around the bridge, at the officers tensely hunched over their workstations. They were focused, dedicated. He was proud of them all…and determined that they would make it through to enjoy the fruits of peace.

But, at that moment, he had only one thought screaming in his mind.

Up now, and to arms.

Chapter Thirty

CFS Tarsus
Inner Kuiper Belt
Venga System
Year 320 AC

"Stanton, I don't care what it takes…you've got to get your people back on board faster." Sonya Eaton understood the ramifications of what she was saying. She knew pushing the Lightnings so far beyond their standard specs, especially with mostly inexperienced pilots at the controls, was dangerous, that it would likely result in more lost ships…more of her people dead.

But she also knew she had no choice. There were no good options. She'd managed to keep her ships between the Hegemony convoy and the transit point leading toward Olyus…somehow. Stanton's relentless attacks had been no small part of that…but even her slow-moving escort carriers were positioned so they could make the jump, and get to the last system between the enemy battleships and Megara.

But there was no time to waste. None.

Her fleet *had* to get through the point before those battleships were in range to fire. Before the running fight was finished, she'd have to close with her ships, and it would take everything her force had if they were going to slow the enemy enough to hold them back while Barron and the main fleet fought their desperate battle at Megara. But it was too soon now, far too soon, to risk her launch platforms, or the frigates that gave her the only real ship-to-ship combat potential she had.

If she handled things just right, if she made the jump and got her ships in position, she just *might* get two more bomber strikes in before she had to close with the rest of her fleet. The more damage the enemy battleships took from the fighter attacks, the better chance the rest of her ships had of doing some damage to the leviathans before being blasted to bits themselves. The future wasn't looking very bright, not for any of her people, but they had a job to do. She knew what that was…and she was going to see it done.

"Captain…I'm pushing them as far as I dare. If I drive them any harder…I could lose half the wing."

"And if you don't, you'll all be stuck here when the carriers transit." Eaton understood Hayes's reluctance, but she didn't have time for it, and her impatience was on display in her raw tone. "How many of your people do you think can pull off a transit point jump in a Lightning? And if I don't send the carriers through in twenty minutes at most, you're not going to have any place at all to land…on this side or the other side of the point. So, stop arguing with me, and just get it done!"

She turned abruptly toward Bart Tarleton's station. "Commander…I need precise calculations on just how long we can stay here and still make it through the point in time."

"Yes, Captain." The officer turned, and his hands moved over the keyboard and controls. Eaton had a good idea of the timing—she'd been thinking about it almost nonstop for an hour—but she wanted an exact figure. She couldn't risk letting the enemy into range of her ships, not before the bombers had a chance to soften up those battleships a little more…or until she was out of chances to launch new strikes and had nothing left to lose.

Except her ships and their crews…which she'd more or less accepted were doomed. The fight wasn't about survival, not for most of her people…it was about dying for something, rather than for nothing.

"Nineteen minutes, Captain. That's with a ten percent safety margin. Just under twenty-one without."

She looked back at the display, her mind running the same calculations over and over again. It was going to be close, damned close, even if Hayes pushed his people to their absolute limits…and that "safety factor" of two minutes mostly had to do with the lack of exact data on Hegemony weapons ranges. If she waited past nineteen, she risked being fired upon.

She felt a shiver at the thought of what a single railgun hit would do to one of her lightly-armored escort carriers. Even a glancing blow would obliterate any vessel in her fleet. She knew she should leave at nineteen on the dot, but the thought of leaving bombers behind weighed heavily on her. Twenty-one…that was cutting it too close.

"We're transiting in twenty minutes, Commander. I want all ships ready to go, reactors at full and engines ready." She paused for a few seconds. "All landing bays will close thirty seconds before transit. Any bombers not landed by then…" She didn't finish.

She didn't have to. Everybody knew.

*   *   *

"Keep those engines at full power, all of you. We're almost out of time." Hayes had done all he could to drive his terrified pilots on their desperate race to catch up with the carriers. Every ship in the formation was flying without any safeties, their reactors and engines all operating well past the redline. That was difficult enough for an experienced pilot, but Hayes's squadrons were full of rookies.

They were doing better than he'd dared to expect, better than anyone had likely hoped…but there had still been losses. Two ships had been destroyed outright, their rectors overloading. One had gone critical, and the fighter had disappeared in a massive burst of thermonuclear fury. The other had simply killed its pilot with a massive radiation leak, at least a thousand times the lethal level.

Both of those had gone quickly, at least. The ones digging at Hayes, driving his growing urge to bring his ship about and fly back toward the approaching enemy, were the six ships whose engines had simply failed under the strain. Three of them were completely offline, the fighters zipping in a straight line at unchangeable velocities. The other three were operating at severely reduced thrust levels.

All six of them were as good as dead. He'd hoped one of the degraded but still functional Lightnings might make it in time, but its thrust had dropped off since the initial malfunction, and there was no way it was going to make it before the fleet transited…or even before the pursuing enemy ships caught it, and blasted it to dust.

"Have those approach plans ready. You've got your landing sequences, and the bays are ready and waiting." The ships at the head of the formation were coming in as he spoke, the first ones beginning to land. He had his squadrons coming in a tight order, which was another risk for the makeshift bays of the escort carriers and his rookie pilots. He'd been hesitant to move things at such a breakneck pace, especially since the converted freighters had neither the equipment nor the flight crews of a proper battleship's landing bays. But there was no time to spare, and perhaps not enough even to get all his people back.

He watched his screen as the first ships went in. He held his breath as the first wave landed, and then the second. The escort carriers had only a single bay each, and that meant one bomber losing it could shut an entire ship down. The escort units were poorly outfitted in every way—armor, damage control, fire suppression. A bad enough fighter crash in the bay could cripple one of the ships outright.

But no one crashed. His rookies were performing well, and he felt pride in watching them. No one lost it on the final approach, no one hesitated or threw off the landing sequence. Better than half his ships were in when his eyes caught the timer on his screen.

One minute…the carriers would be moving out in one minute. The fighters could continue to land while the carriers engaged their engines, but that was a step up in difficulty. All he could do was hope his people continued to perform, that they found it in themselves to do what they had to do.

There was another problem. His mind raced, factoring in the landings on the accelerating carriers. Even if his pilots executed perfectly, if they didn't lose a beat…they still weren't all going to make it.

He almost hit the comm, one last effort to convince Captain Eaton to wait…but then he saw the Hegemony battleships looming from behind, far too close for comfort. If anything, he realized, Eaton had waited too long. She *had* to send her carriers through the point, and now.

He'd just have to do what he could with the twenty or so ships that would be left behind. He'd read about fighters making transits, he even knew a few pilots who'd done it. Admiral Stockton had successfully completed countless such trips. But he also knew they were difficult and dangerous…and that many capable pilots had died attempting such jumps.

None of that really mattered. He wasn't going to get all his people landed before the carriers transited, and that meant he had two choices. Stay and fight, twenty fighters with empty bomb bays against the entire Hegemony fleet.

Or plunge into the transit point after the carriers…and find some way to make it through, and bring his people along with him.

*Those are two shitty alternatives...*but there was no real choice to be made.

He tapped his throttle, sliding his ship out of the course directly toward the carriers, and on a line to the transit point. There were eighteen birds behind him. He was willing to bet the ones in front could make it before the carriers jumped.

He leaned down and activated the comm unit, setting the channel to the three squadrons behind him. "Okay, Hawkwinds, Skyflyers, Battlecats...let me give it to you straight. We're not going to make it to the carriers, not before they transit...so I want everybody tight on me. Stay close, and follow the nav directions I send you. Whatever you do, keep your shit together. You panic and you're going to die. It's that simple." He paused and took a deep breath. "We're going right through the point, and we're going to land on the carriers on the other side."

Now...just don't panic yourself...

* * *

"We're picking up energy readings from the transit point, Captain." Tarleton's voice was guarded, but Eaton could sense the hope in it. She understood, but she wasn't sure she shared his feelings, or at least that she should let herself dare to.

She hadn't had a choice. As guilty as she felt about leaving Hayes and the last of his pilots behind, there had been no other way. The Hegemony battleships would have obliterated her small, weak vessels in a matter of minutes...and she couldn't allow that. Whatever happened, however many losses her people took, she *had* to keep her fleet in being.

She had to delay the enemy convoy, keep those battleships away from Megara until the battle there over.

She looked at the display. Tarleton was right. Energy readings, weak ones. *Just what a small group of fighters might give off.*

Or a hundred natural phenomena.

Transit points were poorly understood, and anything from heavier-than-normal cosmic rays to clumps of dust could mimic the signs of ships transiting.

Eaton didn't really think she was looking at an asteroid or something else of that sort in the tube. She suspected, as did Tarleton, that the energy readings were, in fact, caused by Hayes and his people.

Her real fear was how many of them would emerge, how many would survive the transit.

Pilots could get lost in the strange alternative space between points, or they could succumb to various effects in their poorly-shielded fighters. It was possible none of them would emerge, energy readings or not. Or ships could come ripping out of the point, flying on unchanging courses, their dead pilots transfixed at the controls.

Her mind raced, imagining every disaster possible and preparing to endure the blame for all of it. None of her people would place the fault on her, of course, and neither would Hayes or any of his pilots who survived. Only one person would hold her totally, inescapably responsible.

Herself.

As she wrestled with herself, trying to hold back the doubts, a contact appeared on the scanner. Even before the AI confirmed it, she knew.

It was a Lightning.

And a few seconds later, another one came streaking through, and then another.

She watched as ships burst out of the eerie darkness of the point, counting them softly under her breath until she realized they had all made it.

She felt a wave of excitement, but it was stunted, held back. Ships emerging didn't mean her pilots had made it.

More than one unshielded ship had come out of a transit point with its crew dead, ghost ships emerging back into normal space.

She waited, her eyes on the display, hoping. She found herself holding her breath, and she forced an exhale and sucked in a fresh lungful of air. Then, the comm crackled.

She snapped her head around, staring over at Tarleton's station. Her tactical officer was wearing his headset, and for an agonizing few seconds, he sat there completely still, his face unreadable, like stone.

Then she saw a smile forming, and she felt hope.

"They're through, Captain...all of them." His words, especially the last three, took a moment to fully sink in.

A wave of relief washed through her, and she slapped her hand down on the armrest of his chair. *All of them! Remember to talk to Admiral Barron when we get back—Stanton Hayes deserves a medal or a promotion.*

But first things first. She had to get her ships away from that point, and get them set up to hit the enemy as they came through. A good hard strike at the transiting battleships was just the thing to slow that convoy down.

And to buy Tyler Barron the time he needed.

Chapter Thirty-One

CFS Hermes
Olyus System
Year 320 AC

The Second Battle of Megara – "To hell now…and if we're lucky, back again"

Yes!

Barron hunched forward, staring coldly at the display, tense as he always was in battle. He'd heard the sound of the primaries firing again, and then he saw the AI's representation of the shot, an electric blue streak of light…and then a glowing halo around the closest Hegemony battleship. A hit.

The range was still long, and Barron had ordered the fleet's ships to cut thrust and remain in place. He had twenty Confederation battleships, all armed with the longer-ranged primaries. Positioned alongside that force stood Vian Tulus's four upgraded vessels. Anya Fritz had gotten the work done on all of them, and now they took their place, in the only spot Barron expected Palatians to be.

The front of the formation.

The long-range duel had been light in terms of damage—both taken and inflicted. Targeting was difficult at such distances, and the vast majority of shots had gone far wide of the targets. Barron didn't like wasting time…but he had two thousand bombers inbound against the battered Hegemony ships, and he saw no reason to put his battleships at any greater risk than they were already exposed to, at least not before the squadrons hit.

Stockton's squadrons would do the job…and by the time they had completed their strike, the rest of the fleet would be in the system, the fleet's massive transit operation complete. That meant over two thousand more bombers.

Barron moved his finger across his workstation, adjusting the perspective on the main display. He zoomed in on the area around the Hegemony battleships, just as two-thirds of Stockton's squadrons were making the final approach. The rest of them had veered off, something that had confused Barron, for just a moment. Then he'd figured out the cold-blooded tactic his strike force commander was employing. The "missing" bombers had moved around the enemy flank…and positioned themselves along the prospective line of retreat. Stockton intended to destroy every one of the forward enemy battleships, and not let even one escape to join the rest of the enemy fleet in-system, around Megara.

The enemy had been careless in their deployments, and they'd left a significant force exposed. Now, they would pay for that mistake.

Barron knew destroying a handful of battleships was only the start of the fight, and that even a total victory in this initial struggle would only marginally affect the outcome of the overall combat. His ships were still too far out for precise readings, but he was sure, damned sure, there were a hundred Hegemony battleships out there, and maybe more.

For all his fire, and his grim determination, he just wasn't sure his fleet was strong enough to defeat the enemy's monster warships. And they had the platforms and fortresses as well, even if those were, as he suspected, only partially completed.

Still, this was a first step, and he intended to watch Stockton's wings move in and tear apart the line of enemy battleships and their few surviving escorts. Covington's people had hit them hard…and now Stockton was going to finish the job.

Then his eye caught something else…something unexpected.

Enemy ships, deep in the system, not far from Megara. They were flying wildly…as though they were searching for something.

But what?

There was nothing else there, save for fifty or sixty Hegemony ships, mostly escort-size.

And then, suddenly, there was something.

A new contact, one that hadn't been there an instant before.

He watched as the enemy ships all reacted, blasting thrusters and trying to bring themselves around to close on the new contact. Barron knew the AI was chewing on the data, analyzing the details coming in, but for once, his own human mind, a billion times slower by normal standards, beat the ship's main computer with the ID. He heard it as if he'd said it, as though some part of himself had shouted it out, inaudible to the officers all around, but almost deafening to him.

And then the AI labeled the small circle, the tiny but sharply rendered letters clearly visible.

Hermes.

* * *

"Come on, Lex…get that thing reconnected." Andi stood in the bowels of *Hermes*, her eyes fixed on the strange apparatus, hastily removed from its place in the engineering station and thrown on a large palette. She looked behind it to the large cable, the conduit that had kept the stealth unit connected to the power coming from *Hermes*'s dying reactor. Somehow, her people had managed to move the stealth unit, fragile, cantankerous, power-hungry thing that it was, without a break in coverage.

Until just a moment before, when she'd ordered the cable disconnected.

"I'm on it, Andi...but I told you, this is going to be tight. This reactor is a lot smaller, and the generator eats a lot of power." Righter paused, verbally only—his hands hadn't stopped moving for an instant. "It might not work at all."

"Just do it, Lex." Andi knew damned well it might not work. It was a desperate plan, very desperate...but it was the only way she could think of to try to save her people.

Some of them, at least.

Hermes shook hard, and she reached out, grabbing onto a handhold attached to the bulkhead to stabilize herself. She'd known the enemy ships that had been pursuing her would waste no time once *Hermes* popped up on their scanners...but that had been *quick*.

Part of her felt as though she should be on the bridge, but there was no point to that. She'd cleared the control center of all her people, as well as every other nonessential section. The AI had her nav program, a wild and random series of vector changes designed with one purpose in mind. To buy a little more time before *Hermes*'s hunters overwhelmed her, and delivered the final blow.

Her ship was doomed, and her people were out of options...save one. A crazy, almost insane idea, and one that would fail if a dozen steps didn't all go off exactly as planned.

But it offered one thing that fighting, running, or any other option didn't.

Hope. And a chance of saving her crew.

* * *

Stockton whipped his ship around, blasting his engines at
full to adjust his course to the desired attack vector. He'd
come about in a wider arc than he'd originally planned, to
avoid a cluster of surviving enemy escorts that had formed
up in a last-ditch effort to protect the Hegemony
battleships. It was a valid tactic, one he would probably have
tried if he'd been in his adversary's shoes. He'd ordered the
waves of attacking bombers to branch into two streams,
blasting their engines hard as the wave parted and passed by
the escorts, like water flowing around a large rock
outcropping. It didn't protect his people from all of the
defensive fire—and the escorts would still be there when his
forces pulled back—but it had dramatically cut down on
loss rates during the approach.

And that was more bombs and torpedoes heading for
those battered and dying battleships. His two thousand
fighters had more than enough force to wipe out their
targets, but Stockton had seen many times just how tough
the Hegemony battlewagons were, and he wasn't taking any
chances.

He'd given his final speech to the attack wings, and he'd
kept it to the point. He hadn't held anything back, hadn't
sugar-coated anything for his people. They deserved better
than that. They'd earned honesty.

He'd said, simply, "To hell now…and if we're lucky,
back again."

The thunderous response on the comm had left him
confident his words had found their mark.

He'd already picked out a target for himself, a huge,
hulking monster that was leaving a trail of refrozen fluids
and vapors behind it as it struggled to accelerate along the
enemy line of retreat. It was definitely one of the railgun-
armed monsters that had so decimated the Confederation
forces in the battles of the war. One quick look at the close-

range scans told Stockton the ship's big guns were offline, if not already blasted and fused into useless globs of rehardened metal.

Still, a battleship that size was a danger to any ship in the fleet, and it would be until it was put down. He looked at his weapons console. His ship packed six cluster bombs…and he intended to plant the entire spread into the target. That meant coming in close, and as battered as the ship appeared to be, he could see that there were still point defense batteries firing.

"Watch these ships, all of you…even if they look like wrecks. They're immense, and they've got multiple reactors and hundreds of turrets. It only takes one shot to turn you into a depressing letter to your family. Stay the hell away from those guns!"

He checked the range. Under ten thousand kilometers, and a pair of quick flashes on his screen warned him to heed his own advice. The defensive fire was heavy, worse than he'd expected, and he let his hand move around on the throttle, allowing his intuition to direct the evasive fire as much as his reasoned intellect.

He flipped a switch on the board, initiating final arming for the bombs…and then another, opening the small bay doors.

Five thousand kilometers.

He stared straight ahead as his ship raced forward. He was still blasting his thrusters at different angles, small pulses along various vectors, just enough to confuse the enemy targeting systems as he made his final run.

But then he stopped…and came straight on. It was the most dangerous part of the attack, those two or three seconds, but it was the only way he could aim his bombs with the precision he needed.

One…

He was counting off in his head, fully aware it wouldn't take long for the enemy tactical systems to adjust their targeting and blow him to bits.

Two…

He ached to launch and then to pull out of the deadly dive toward he Hegemony ship. But years of discipline kept his veteran's hand steady, unmoving. Just another second…

Three…

His finger tightened, and his Lightning shook, six times in rapid succession, as each bomb blasted out of the bay and headed toward the looming bulk of the enemy ship. Stockton watched, for half a second maybe, and he was sure the warheads were going to hit.

Then he pulled back hard on the throttle, and angled it to port…wondering if he'd been on time, or it he and his ship were going to follow the bombs in.

He was sweating, and his heart was pounding, and he held his breath for an instant…until he saw the blackness of empty space ahead of him, where only the dull gray of the Hegemony ship's hull had been less than a second before.

One glance at his scanner confirmed it. He had made it. He'd cleared the enemy by less than a kilometer…much closer than he'd intended to come.

That quick look at the screen told him something else, too.

All six bombs had hit…and over a hundred of his ships were coming in behind him, following his course, and planting their own warheads into the guts of the doomed battleship.

*   *   *

"Vig…get that system running, now! We're almost out of time." Andi pushed her way back through the overcrowded corridor, to where Lex Righter was still working on the stealth unit.

"I'm on it, Andi." Vig's voice sounded distant, partially blotted out by the nervous chatter of *Hermes*'s crew, pressed together like sardines, terrified…and most of them forced to wait and see what happened, with no control at all over events. It wasn't a comfortable way to be, but it was their only chance to survive.

Andi understood, but just then, she wished they'd shut up, as she'd told them to do at least three times.

"Well, Lex?" she snapped as she rushed back to the small space where her engineer was working on the stealth generator, his hands shaking. "We're out of time, old friend…it's your best shot now or nothing." Andi's voice seemed devoid of the fear that seemed to possess everyone else. It was a gift she'd always had, an ability to hide emotions, to push them aside when she had to clear her mind.

For the record, however much control she managed to exert, she was scared shitless. And she was just as happy no one else knew that.

"I don't know if this is going to work, Andi. If I had another hour…"

Hermes shook hard again, and the sounds of distant explosions rumbled down the corridor.

"You don't have another thirty seconds, Lex…just do it!" Her voice was loud, rumbling, a command that practically defied its recipient to disobey.

She watched as he connected the conduit, plugging in the cable that would feed power into the unit…and then *Hermes* rocked again, twice in rapid succession, and she could hear the sounds of structural supports snapping, and of whole sections of the dying vessel blasting open to the vacuum of space.

* * *

Barron watched the screen, absolutely certain the AI's—and his—analysis was correct, that the blip on his screen was, in fact, *Hermes*. He watched as the ships surrounding it fired, pounding the small cruiser, hitting it at least a dozen times.

He felt an urgent need to rush to the ship's aid, to save Andi…somehow. But *Dauntless* was six light hours from *Hermes*'s position, barely close enough to watch the small ship's death struggle. There was no way—none—to intervene.

He could hear reports snapping back and forth around the bridge, mostly damage assessments on the Hegemony battleships. From the sound of things, Stockton's attack was going well. Two enemy ships had been destroyed outright, and the rest of the forward line was being torn apart hit by hit.

But Barron couldn't take his eyes off *Hermes.*

He'd worried about Andi since the moment she'd left, but he'd tried to convince himself she would still be alive when the fleet arrived. His grim nature had clashed with his faith in the woman he loved, and it had been difficult to maintain any level of hope.

Then he'd seen *Hermes* on the scanner…and he'd realized she was still alive.

At least for that moment.

He watched as ship after ship moved in on *Hermes,* bracketing the vessel with fire. He held his breath, waiting, hoping to see the blip disappear again, for Andi's crew—for Lex Righter—to get the stealth unit back online and for them all to escape.

But the symbol stayed where it was, even as more and more vessels joined the attack. Barron could hardly draw a breath without physically forcing himself. He knew what he was watching, but somehow, he just couldn't make himself believe it. It couldn't be happening. Not this way. He hadn't come all this way to find *Hermes,* to discover Andi was still alive, only to watch her die with his own eyes, helpless to do anything about it.

He knew he had a fleet to command, thousands of spacers relying on him. The fate of an entire war and even the future of the Rim were riding on him…but for those seconds, he was transfixed in absolute, uncontrollable horror.

Then he saw the icon that represented *Hermes* vanish from the screen. For an instant, he told himself the ship had slipped back into stealth mode, but the energy scans coming in left no doubt.

Hermes had been destroyed.

Barron sat there, stone still for a moment, feeling as though the slightest movement would send the contents of his stomach spewing out onto the bridge floor. He could feel part of himself dying inside, the loss more than he could bear.

It seemed impossible…and yet he'd seen it with his own eyes. She was gone. Andi Lafarge was dead.

The grief was almost unbearable, but he clamped down on it with an unrestrained ferocity. He had no time for personal mourning. He was a Barron, and duty called. He had never failed it before, and he wouldn't now.

Forward…to victory.

And to something else he needed, like oxygen itself, something he craved uncontrollably from the deepest, darkest part of his soul.

Vengeance.

Chapter Thirty-Two

Outskirts of Troyus City
Megara, Olyus III
Year 320 AC

**The Battle of Megara – For the Confederation…for
Admiral Barron**

The assault rifle felt good in his hands. Even under the
shadow of danger—if not certain death—Rogan was glad to
be in action again, to be striking at something truly
important, fighting a fight that really *mattered*.

He fired a burst of three shots. His people were going
all-in on the series of attacks underway around the capital,
giving everything they had left—in both matériel and spirit.
But they were still low on ammunition, and he'd reminded
his people, and himself, half a dozen times to take their
shots carefully.

The Kriegeri were not to be underestimated. Rogan had
faced many enemies, Union Foudre Rouge, Alliance
stormtroopers…but he'd never seen anything quite like the
Hegemony's deadly foot soldiers. Bred for combat,
enhanced with implanted exos, they were like some kind of
nightmare come alive.

Marines didn't easily admit they had met their match, and

Rogan hadn't quite gotten to the point where he could acknowledge the genetically selected soldiers were *better* than his people. But it had been a long time since he'd been able to convince himself they weren't at least equals.

Equals with unlimited ordnance, and massive reserves probably on the way…

The Kriegeri were only one of Rogan's enemies. Time was another. He was already past the scheduled transit time for the fleet…which meant, unless something had changed, Barron's ships were already entering the system. Every minute the enemy command structure had to respond ate away at the effectiveness of the operation. Perhaps even more important was the certainly that overwhelming Kriegeri reserves could appear at any time…*would* appear.

He glanced down at the chronometer. Eighteen minutes left. He was leading the main attack, and he was well behind schedule. The enemy forces at the comm center were stronger than he'd hoped they would be, and they were clearly from a crack unit. He'd envisioned taking the garrison by surprise and getting the munitions team to work almost immediately, but he was still trying to get past the defensive perimeter.

He'd lost at least twenty Marines in the fighting, and maybe more. The equipment remaining to the Marines was limited and badly battered, and effective battlefield comm exceeded Rogan's resources. He was lucky to maintain contact with his individual platoon leaders, most of whom were close enough to their people to pass on orders by shouting out the commands.

He could feel the taste of defeat growing, bitter in his mouth. Prentice and the others were hitting the backup stations and secondary targets…but none of it would mean a thing if the main facility remained operational.

He'd tried to make a textbook assault, to leapfrog forward, keeping his people in cover as often as he could, but now he realized there was no room for caution anymore. His Marines would either take the comm center in the next ten minutes, fifteen max…or they never would.

"All leaders, listen up…we're running out of time. We've got to go in and take that damned thing, and we've got to do it now! Countdown from my mark…thirty seconds, and then we launch a full-frontal charge. Use your ammo however you need to. We either get in now, or we don't, and there's no reason to die with any rounds left." He paused and took a deep breath. "Mark."

He popped out the almost spent clip in his weapon, feeling a tinge at wasting the five rounds that remained in the rifle's magazine. But he pushed the thought aside. Halfway across the open field between his position and the building was not the place to stop and reload.

Twenty seconds…

He could feel his heart pounding in his chest, and he brushed his hands along his jacket, wiping the sweat from them. He'd been a Marine all his adult life, served in combat often…but he'd never felt death breathing on him as it was just then.

Ten seconds…

Images of that career passed through his thoughts, and they stopped on one time in particular, the years he'd spent commanding *Dauntless*'s—the original *Dauntless*'s—Marine contingent. Shipboard service was less prestigious than other commands, at least some said it was, and Rogan was glad for the experience he had leading forces in the field.

But his happiest memories were of his time serving under then-captain Barron, a man he loved and respected. A man he would die for…and maybe in very few moments.

Time…

"Let's go," he shouted into the comm, and then he dashed out from behind the wall he'd been using as cover, and he raced toward the comm center.

For the Confederation…for Admiral Barron…

* * *

"Number One...and Number Eight...it is an honor to have you here..." The Hegemony officer was a Megaron, and a Master, unused to obsequious behavior...but standing before two of the ten highest rated humans in known space was a bit much for him to handle calmly.

"Get to the point, Megaron." Chronos was irritable. The reports coming in from the outer system were a shock. *Perhaps this is a diversion? For what? Where else could they look to hurt us?*

"The lead division of battleships positioned within range of the jump point has...has been badly defeated, Commander. Half the vessels have been destroyed, and the others are attempting to disengage, but..."

"But? If you stammer and stutter like a fool one more time, Megaron, I will see your next assignment is digging ore alongside the Defekts on Calor Inferni II."

"Yes, Commander. We are also receiving reports of enemy activity to the southeast of the city."

"Ground action?" Chronos scowled. He knew there were still some holdouts from the planetary defense forces, but they had long been driven away from the city proper. And whatever was entering the system, they were a long way from landing ground forces.

What could make them take this kind of risk? And how could they have coordinated with whatever remnants of the defense forces were hiding somewhere?

Suddenly, he understood. The unidentified ship that had managed to sneak all the way to Megara to deliver a—not yet decoded—message. The enemy fleet transiting into the system. Sudden action by the hidden partisan forces? All coordinated?

"This is a full attack..."

"Commander?" Chronos ignored the megaron.

His eyes darted toward Akella, who had remained silent,

watching. She was brilliant, and as capable as anyone he had ever known, but she lacked his military experience, and, for the moment, she appeared content to allow him to handle things.

"Where are the ground actions, Megaron...exactly?" Chronos moved toward the large display in the center of the room. He moved his fingers over the controls, bringing up a map of Troyus City and its environs. "Show me."

The officer stepped forward and reached out, pointing to three different locations. "These are all we have verifications for, Commander...though there are unconfirmed reports from several other locations.

"Where?" Perhaps half a second later: "Well, man...move it. We do not have time to waste."

"Here...and here." The officer pointed to two more areas. "And, we just received a report from here as well." His hand moved a few centimeters on the glowing flat screen.

Chronos stared at the locations, poking at the controls, bringing up symbols of all vital facilities around the city. For a few seconds, his eyes darted around...and then he knew.

"Communications...they are after our ground to orbital comm." He looked up. "Megaron, I want all garrison units activated at once. Dispatch assault teams to every threatened location...and send additional forces to surround the main comm center." Chronos could hear the urgency in his own voice as he spoke, but it was not close to what he was feeling inside. The enemy had sent a small ship, equipped with one of the confounded stealth units, to get a message to their remaining ground forces. And the threat they posed was very real.

They told them when to hit our comm...and that means this is a full-scale assault.

"Go, Megaron...now! There is no time to waste."

The enemy's gambit made sense. It was brilliant. The orbital stations were only partly rebuilt, and most crucial command functions remained on the ground.

They want to cut us off…

Chronos's mind raced. That would create a massive disruption in the defensive efforts…but it would not last long. *They have to realize we would restore sporadic contact quickly, and close to full comm in half a day at most.*

They are going to make the most of it…that means they will be coming on hard and fast.

Chronos had not expected *any* enemy attack on Megara, but he had always assumed, if it came, it would be exceedingly complex, a carefully choreographed advance, making use of the enemy's intimate knowledge of the system to provide cover for their ships.

But if they are banking taking advantage of us losing our comm, they will not waste that kind of time.

A desperate frontal assault? Was it possible, with the enemy's range disadvantage? *They have always kept their heavy units back, tried to strike as often and as deeply as they could with their small strike craft.*

Our entire defense network was set up to meet just that kind of attack.

Chronos could feel his tension growing. Had the enemy taken him completely by surprise? If the fleet was facing a direct attack, he had to revise the standing orders.

He turned, looking across the room, his eyes focusing on a tall man in a crisp uniform. "Illius…" He gestured for the officer to come over to where he was standing. Illius was also a megaron, and a Master, but he was a far more competent officer than the one who'd just made the report. And he needed someone he could trust to do what he had in mind.

"Commander!" Illius stepped up and snapped to attention…and even as he did, a distant rumble echoed through the headquarters, followed by another.

Chronos spun around, and he felt a sudden coldness inside.

Was he too late?

*　*　*

"Move it…now. We're out of time." Bryan Rogan stood amid the wreckage in the main control room of the Hegemony communications center. The place was a wreck, littered with debris, spent ammunition…and the bodies of at least three dozen combatants, split pretty evenly between the two sides.

"Ten more minutes, General." The three Marines hunched over the explosives were working feverishly, their faces glistening with sweat. They were doing all they could, but Rogan knew it wasn't enough.

"We don't have ten minutes, Lieutenant. I'm not even sure we've got five. Can you hear that?" He remained silent for a few seconds, listening to the sounds of gunfire…seeming to get closer with each passing instant. "You heard the explosions…we already missed the synchronization deadline. And the enemy knows exactly what we're trying to do. They'll send every trooper they've got here…they probably already have." Rogan had no idea how many of the people he'd set up to defend the perimeter remained, but his gut told him it wasn't many. There were hundreds of Kriegeri moving on the comm center, maybe even thousands. It was over…or it would be in just a few minutes. All that remained was to see how it ended.

"We're working as quickly as possible, General. This is a chaotic mix of parts, sir…we'll be lucky if we can get the whole thing to arm at once. We've got four different kinds of explosives in here."

"You've got two minutes, Lieutenant. Take any longer, and it won't matter worth a damn." Rogan wondered what to do if the setup wasn't ready in time. Was there any way to detonate it all manually? He didn't relish the thought of staying behind, blowing himself to bits along with the comm center, but he'd do it if he had to. He'd only be sacrificing whatever chance he had of escaping, which, from the sounds of combat getting closer and closer, probably wasn't all that much.

He moved over to the door, holding his rifle up. There was fighting just outside the building, and if the Kriegeri got inside—*when* they got inside—he was the last line of defense. Him alone. He'd already sent everybody else down to bolster the defenses.

He turned and looked back at the three Marines, and then down the steps leading to the entrance. The fighting was just beyond the barricade door at the bottom, but at least it was still *outside* and not in the building. That was a respite he knew wouldn't last.

"We're ready, General." The lieutenant was walking across the room, a small device in his hand.

"The timer was shot...we couldn't be sure it would work, so we rigged this detonator switch. I can blow the thing once we're out of the building. The range is at least three hundred meters...which is still close, but if I can grab some kind of cover..."

Rogan grabbed the remote. "Everything is set?" He looked down at the detonator. "Just press the button?"

"Yes, sir...but..."

"No 'buts,' Lieutenant. Get your people and let's get the hell out of here." He turned and waited at the top of the stairs until the others were right behind him. Then he ran down, stopping at the bottom and waving for the three Marines behind him to move toward the back of the building. He reached down and grabbed his comm unit, holding it up to his mouth.

"All Marines...break off. Get the hell out, any way you can, and find someplace to hide. Fortune go with you all."

He clasped the comm back on his belt, and he followed the three Marines out through the rear exit of the building. The enemy had practically surrounded the facility, but the fire seemed lighter as he ran out into the open space beyond.

He felt exposed, naked, with no place to hide from the fire—and, he realized almost immediately, no decent cover from the coming explosion either.

At least not within two hundred meters, which was where he was going to trigger the bomb. The lieutenant had said three hundred, but Rogan wasn't going to take any chances. A damaged battery, some kind of interference…a million things could go wrong, and shaving a hundred meters could only increase the chance of success.

He raced across the field, his finger on the detonator, ready to press the button with his last breath if he got hit. But the bullets whipping by missing him, and a quick glance behind gave him an estimate of how far he'd come.

Just about two hundred meters. He sucked down a deep breath, and then he pressed the button, crouching down and lunging forward as he did.

There was a delay, barely an instant, and Rogan thought the bomb hadn't worked.

Then he heard the blast, almost deafening, and the shock wave caught him in the back and lifted him from the ground, throwing him down hard at least thirty meters from where he'd been.

His instincts told him to get up, to keep running and find a place to hide. But he couldn't move. A wave of pain struck him, and he realized he was injured, though he couldn't get a real feeling on where or how bad it was.

He was lying on his back, and he could see a plume of fire and smoke where the building had been. Even as his vision blurred and he felt his consciousness slipping away, he managed a tiny, crooked smile.

His Marines had done their duty. They had taken down the enemy communications.

He hadn't failed Admiral Barron.

Chapter Thirty-Three

CFS Dauntless
Olyus System
Year 320 AC

The Second Battle of Megara – "Vengeance, the blood of my enemies…all I have left"

"All ships, full thrust." Barron's voice was utterly cold, not a shred of emotion detectable in a word that came from his mouth. He'd shut down his emotions. It was the only way to keep Andi out of his mind, to stop from replaying the moment *Hermes* had vanished from the display. There was nothing left for him anymore, nothing he cared about, save victory.

The blood of my enemies…it's all I have left.

He'd been a professional warrior his entire adult life, but now he was a killer, more like some demon of the deepest darks than a soldier. He'd been hesitant to lead the fleet forward, to commit to a direct frontal assault against all the Hegemony could field against him, but now he welcomed it. He ached for it. He wanted those ships to come, to engage his forces. He needed it.

He needed to kill Hegemony spacers, as many as he could.

"All ships acknowledge, Admiral. The fleet is moving in-system." Atara spoke softly, calmly. Barron knew his friend understood what he was feeling, or at least that she came as close to it as anyone could. He was glad she was there, and he could feel her support, but part of him wished he could fight the battle alone, that he could claim sole credit for every drop of Hegemony blood that was spilled.

Barron watched with bloodthirsty excitement as the last ship of the Hegemony first line vanished in the maelstrom of thermonuclear fury. Stockton's attack had finished off all but two of the battleships, and Dirk Timmons and his wings had been waiting for those. It almost seemed too easy, watching it all. It would have been, save for the casualty reports coming in. They weren't as bad as he'd feared, as they had been in so many other fights against the Hegemony, but they were substantial, nevertheless.

The battle had just begun, and there would be vast bloodletting before it was done.

"Admiral Stockton is to bring his wings back to refuel and rearm." There was time to turn the bombers around and get them back out before the fleet closed to firing range, but there wasn't time to waste. Barron's ships weren't fencing with the enemy this time, dodging in and out of asteroid fields and dust clouds. They were coming straight on, led by the line of battleships armed with the new primaries.

And that line would be preceded by another bomber strike, the largest in known history—every Lightning in the fleet this time, backed up by the Palatian Strikers, Union Typhoons, and the bewildering array of bizarre and dated attack craft from the Far Rim. Over five thousand ships in all, led by the greatest fighter pilot in the Confederation.

Barron didn't know if it would be enough, and he still couldn't tell if Bryan Rogan had managed to interdict the Hegemony's command comm, but he was sure of one thing.

No one who fought this battle on either side would ever forget it.

At least those who lived to tell about it.

*   *   *

"Lex, I don't want you more than a meter from this reactor, do you hear me? I know the connection's a jury-rigged mess, but you made it work. Now, keep it working." Andi was standing just outside the engineering space, leaning in as she spoke. The corridor outside was jammed full. Andi had crammed every survivor from *Hermes* aboard *Pegasus*, and Lex had managed to connect the smaller ship's power source to the stealth unit. Then, Andi and Vig had cut the landing connection and opened the bay doors. They'd managed to get *Pegasus* out into space using only the positioning jets, and Lex had gotten the stealth unit operational. All just as *Hermes* was blasted to bits by at least a dozen attackers.

She'd conceived the plan and almost discounted it. The timing had to be perfect, and everything had to go exactly right. Her view of the universe left her entirely unprepared to believe that so many things could happen in just the right way, one after the other.

But one part of her nature was stronger still than the grim pessimism. The only other choice had been simply to give up. And that was unthinkable.

The best she could tell, the enemy had not detected *Pegasus*. They were altering their vectors, pulling back after the destruction of *Hermes*, apparently convinced they had finally tracked and destroyed their target.

Everything had worked, *so far* at least. But she was going to have to divert some power to beefing up the life support systems—there were a lot more people on *Pegasus* than she'd ever had before—and she needed to deploy some thrust, get the ship on a vector away from the enemy, back toward the approaching fleet.

One thing at a time…

She squeezed past the spacers jammed in the corridor. They were standing, pressed tightly against each other, and the crowd stretched back to the cargo hold, which was also full of *Hermes*'s crew. She'd gotten everybody out, at least everyone who'd still been alive. She'd lost more than twenty of her crew in the fighting, most of those after she'd dropped the stealth field.

There hadn't been any choice with that. *Hermes*'s reactor had been dying, and at best, it would have held out a few more hours. She and Lex had managed to cart the stealth unit down the corridors of the doomed cruiser, to the bay and into *Pegasus* herself…before cutting the long—and amazingly still functioning—cable that led back to *Hermes*'s reactor. Reconnecting to her old ship's power grid had been difficult, and a wild race against time, but one Lex had managed to complete.

He'd done it faster than she'd had a right to hope, but even that time had been sufficient for the enemy to surround *Hermes* and blast the already damaged ship to plasma. Even that had served a purpose, an indispensable one. The surest way to evade someone trying to kill you is to convince them you're already dead. If the maneuver, including *Pegasus*'s exit from the bay, had truly gone off as well as she dared hope it had, the Hegemony ships wouldn't be looking for her and her people any longer.

As far as they—and anyone who'd been watching—were concerned, she was dead. They all were dead…and in that lay their hopes for survival.

She had every reason to believe the plan would work, and the Hegemony fleet in Olyus had a lot more to worry about than chasing one small ship. *Pegasus* was limited to passive scans, and even those at minimal power, but something the size of the Confederation—no, she reminded herself, the Grand Alliance—fleet was hard to miss.

She made her way forward to the bridge, slipping through the door and breathing a sigh of relief at the—relatively—open space of the ship's small control room. The one thing she'd never called *Pegasus*'s bridge was roomy, at least until that very moment.

She sat in her chair and stared down at the screen, watching the ships of the fleet push forward from the transit point, their course taking them directly toward the—more haphazardly organized—Hegemony force.

She knew Barron hadn't wanted to let her go, and she'd almost stayed back, out of love for him. But she had to be who she was, and sitting on the sidelines wasn't her way. Besides, there would be no future if they didn't win this fight. Hopefully, she'd played a part in that, and what she'd done would contribute to the victory they all needed.

Now it was her turn to sit and worry. About herself and her people, of course, who were still far from safe, but mostly about Tyler and the others she cared about, every one of them now on those warships moving inexorably toward their destinies.

Her eyes caught one symbol, a battleship, and she guessed—with a reasonable feeling of certainty from its position in the line—that it was *Dauntless*. She looked for a few seconds, her eyes moist. It was her turn to sit and watch…and worry about him.

"You can do this, my love. You can win this fight. I know you can." Her words were soft, under her breath, for her alone, and she tried hard to believe them. Barron was the best naval commander she'd ever seen, that she'd ever heard of, but she was far from sure the battle was winnable.

If it is, Tyler will find a way…

She didn't dare let herself imagine the two of them having a future together, after war and strife and so much death.

But then she did anyway, at least for a few seconds.

* * *

"You are a damned fool, Megaron, and you are relieved as of this moment." Chronos was angry, his rage searing hot. He held most of it back, trying to maintain his usual controlled demeanor, but some of the fury leaked out anyway.

He watched as the officer's face displayed his own anger. The Megaron was a high-ranking officer, and a Hegemony Master. He was unaccustomed to being spoken to the way Chronos just had, but the supreme commander of the invasion, and Number Eight in the Hegemony, did not give a shit what that idiot thought. As far as Chronos was concerned, the man was lucky he had not grabbed a pistol and put a pair of bullets in his head right there in the control center.

The officer turned, clearly—and wisely—deciding there was no gain in arguing with one as highly ranked as Chronos.

Good decision, you useless…

Chronos forced his mind from rage to analysis. He had a considerable problem, and even if his forces still held the clear advantage, he had to do something immediately.

His first thought was to rush to the spaceport, to take a shuttle up to the flagship and take direct command himself. He almost did that, going so far as to begin moving toward the hatch leading out of the control center. But he stopped himself when his eyes found Akella's. Number One, the Hegemony's supreme leader, and the woman carrying his unborn child…was standing right there, in the center of things.

In a location that cannot be any lower on the enemy's priority list than the comm center…

He had to get her someplace safe, or better yet, get her off of Megara, and on her way back to the Hegemony. She had been scheduled to leave just a few days later, but now the enemy forces were blocking the primary route back to Dannith.

He was not sure what to do about any of that, but he knew the fleet needed direction, and quickly.

"Illius!" He shouted the officer's name, as if calling across a vast space, but when he turned around, the Master was standing right behind him.

"Commander!" The officer looked like he was on parade, utterly unaffected by all that had happened. Chronos knew that was bullshit, that Illius was almost certainly as concerned as he was, but it was an impressive display of self-control.

The megaron was a brilliant officer, one Chronos even admitted to himself could lead the fleet as well as he could.

At least as well…

"Report to the spaceport at once, Megaron. You are to shuttle to *Hegemony's Glory* and take command of the fleet." A pause. "The enemy seems to be coming on more directly than usual, but that may be some kind of deception. I leave decisions on tactics and deployments to you. Understood?"

"Understood, sir!" Illius turned on a dime and moved from the room at a pace that could only be described as a jog. As soon as he was gone, Chronos turned back toward Akella.

"Hectoron Fesurus…you are to assemble an elite company of Kriegeri and escort Number One to the underground bunker. You will remain with her, and guard against any incursions."

"Yes, Commander!"

Chronos turned back to Akella again. "Go with him, Akella…please." The last word had been a final addition, the verbal manifestation of Chronos's realization that he was speaking to the only person on Megara not subject to his commands. "We cannot risk you being hurt or…worse…by this random enemy activity."

How random could it be, after the comm center fiasco?

She looked back at him, and for a moment, he thought she was going to refuse his request. Akella was many things, but she was no coward. But then, she just nodded. He was not sure if it was the realization that she was the supreme leader of the Hegemony, or if it was some maternal instinct to protect the child she carried…and he did not care. Either reason was sufficient to get her to the safest place possible, and he felt a wave of relief when she turned and walked out of the room, the Hectoron and the dozen of his Kriegeri who had been there already, forming a defensive cordon all around her.

Chronos took a deep breath. Now he could focus on the battle. He had no idea what the enemy planned to do, but his stomach told him it was going to be one hell of a fight.

Chapter Thirty-Four

450,000,000 Kilometers from CFS Dauntless
Olyus System
Year 320 AC

The Second Battle of Megara – "Fight...fight as you have never fought before!"

Stockton's eyes dropped down to his screen. He was still stunned every time he saw the vast array of ships lined up around him. The first strike had been large, well over two thousand bombers, but now he had the fleet's entire strike force together. They were still over five thousand strong, even after the losses his people had already suffered.

There were stone cold veterans in the mix, and raw rookies. Highly advanced Confederation Lightnings, and rusted old tubs from the Far Rim he suspected had been flying since before he'd been born. His own veteran Confederation pilots were disciplined, motivated...in every respect, the killing machines which he had forged them into. The Palatians, too. They had served alongside their Confed allies for years now, and they'd more than held their own, despite the moderate technological inferiority of their ships. Stockton had almost suggested giving the Palatians Lightnings—something he knew would be complex in terms of military balance, diplomacy, and classified systems—but he'd held back. The Confederation ships were better, no doubt, but the Palatians had been flying their own fighters since their first days in training, and the relentless Hegemony advance had offered little prospect of an adjustment period to get used to new craft. An abrupt change was as likely to harm as to help.

But experienced or raw, flying leading-edge craft or old rustbuckets, over five thousand bombers were tearing through space toward the Hegemony main fleet. The enemy force was vast, and Stockton knew the hundreds of escorts forming up in front of the Hegemony battle line would exact a terrible toll from his wings. But it wouldn't stop them. He'd already issued the orders…ignore the escorts, fly past them as quickly as possible, and hit the enemy's battleships with all the fury they could muster. Stockton knew how important this fight was, and what the consequences of failure would be, and his pilots did, too.

He flipped a series of switches, engaging the AI-controlled evasive maneuvers. He wasn't quite in range of the enemy escort line, but his engaging the sequence was the signal for the rest of the strike force to do the same. And he wanted them erring on the side of readiness.

The canned routines weren't enough to make a run through the level of fire Stockton knew awaited his people. He would be adding his instincts, his reflexes, increasing the randomness of the small vector changes intended to confuse the Hegemony's gunners and targeting computers. It was one of the areas where experienced pilots had a massive advantage over their raw comrades, and he knew he would lose a large number of green fighter jocks over the next minutes. But there was nothing more he could do about that. He'd trained them, lectured them, harassed them…done everything he could do to beat the realities of combat into their heads. The rest was up to them.

He stared at the screen, at the enemy formation just

ahead. The escorts weren't quite as tightly organized as usual, and the battleships them behind were even more disordered. Stockton was one of the few officers who'd known about the plan for the Marines on the ground to interdict Hegemony communications. It had seemed pretty far-fetched to him, but now he wondered. Perhaps it had been successful after all...

He was still looking at the screen when it lit up with enemy fire. The escorts were opening up, and again, there was a ragged look to it, almost as though individual squadron commanders were taking action on their own. It was a departure from the usually incredibly precise operation of the enemy's vessels.

It wouldn't make *that* much difference. Hegemony gunners and targeting computers were highly capable, and any lack of higher direction wasn't likely to seriously degrade their performance. But Stockton would take anything he could get.

His hand moved to the controls, and he shifted the throttle lightly back and forth, supplementing the actions initiated by the AI. Proper evasive maneuvering was a difficult skill to master. It was easy enough to fly a wild and unpredictable course, but far more challenging to do it while maintaining the same overall vector. Stockton's pilots needed to do what they could to avoid getting hit, to stay alive, but they also had to reach their targets on schedule.

His eyes caught the small gauge on the side of his screen. It had read zero for most of the time since the strike force had launched, but now it showed a small red "3." Stockton knew three casualties was statistically almost the same as none, at least with a force as large as his. He could have lost that many to malfunctions on a bad day. But it was still three of his people, and every one of them hurt.

They weren't necessarily dead, of course. It was possible they'd just gotten knocked off the net, and the AI had classified their ships as destroyed, but his many years of service had given him a good idea most of them had been hit.

He jerked his hand hard to the starboard, and then back again to port. He was closing on the line of escorts, and the defensive fire was getting thicker by the second. The "3" on his readout had changed to a "17," almost in an instant, as his squadrons closed directly into the withering fire of the Hegemony escort line.

Disorder or no, the enemy frigates and small cruisers were mostly in position, and they were blasting away as the bomber wings closed. Stockton had seen it all before—too many times—but it still hit him every time. He was scared, he supposed, somewhere in the depths of his mind, but he was mostly numb regarding the possibility of his own death. He'd seen too much suffering, fought in too much endless war to have the energy to worry about his own life. He had a strong self-preservation instinct, of course, as did anyone who'd survived the years in the fighter wings that he had. But recently, he'd thought more than once that death might actually be an escape. Living, pushing through each fight on the increasingly unreliable promise that one day there would be peace and a life without constant death and ruin, had started to feel like a trap.

A shot streaked by his ship, about half a kilometer away. That was close by the standards of space combat, but he'd had nearer calls than that. He knew it would only get worse. He'd positioned himself in the center of the strike force, and he was bearing down on the heaviest concentration of enemy ships. He was getting closer every second, his ship moving at almost half a percent of lightspeed as it raced forward.

He was running a gauntlet, as all his people were, driving through the escorts without even taking time to return fire. His resolve almost weakened, and the thought of coming back through those same untouched ships almost compelled him to send a few of his wings to fire on the vessels that were extracting such a toll on his people. But he remained focused on what was most important…winning the battle. And that meant hitting those battleships as hard as he could. Every bomb or torpedo loosed against an enemy frigate was one unavailable to blast through the hulls of the Hegemony battleships.

Stockton knew the attack he was leading was, in many ways, the most important of them all. The battleships of the fleet were coming on hard right behind his squadrons. They weren't holding back, they weren't playing complex games to try to avoid the deadly Hegemony railguns. They were a wall of force, ready to match enhanced primaries against the enemy's main guns in a showdown with everything on the line.

His people, their skill and courage over the next hour, would determine how many railguns were still online, how much of an advantage would remain with the Hegemony's larger fleet.

He was flying through laser fire so thick, it seemed like he could almost reach out of his cockpit and touch a pulse as it went by. That was nonsense, of course, and as heavy as the enemy barrage was, still, no shot had come closer than that initial half kilometer.

Then, the fire lessened considerably, and he knew he was passing by the enemy line of ships. It was harder for the Hegemony vessels to target his people when their own ships were intermixed along the lines of fire. If he'd been sending his people against the escorts, he'd have ordered them to advance to these coordinates, and try to stay in the dead zone while they completed their attack runs.

But they were just passing through, and a minute later, perhaps even forty seconds, the intensity of fire picked up again, this time coming from behind him. Technically, he knew it was no harder to evade fire coming from behind, but human psychology played a role that went beyond pure analysis, and it was impossible to argue with the statistics compiled from a hundred battles. Interdictive fire from behind had a higher kill rate.

Over two hundred of his bombers had been knocked out already, and the loss numbers continued to mount, the number on the display rising by several dozen with each hurried glance.

He'd given his people a speech right after they'd launched, but now he flipped on the comm again. He detested delivering motivational words, but he was too old a warrior not to realize just how profoundly they could bolster morale.

"All wings, listen up. We're on our final approach, moving toward the enemy battle line. I know those escorts were tough, and they hurt us, but now we're through…and we're going to do what we came to do. We're going to strike a blow to help win this damned war once and for all. I could remind you what's expected of you, speak endlessly about the Confederation, or Palatia, or the Far Rim…but you know all that already. So, I'll say just one thing, and then I look to you all to do what you're here to do." Stockton paused for a second, and then he said, "Fight…fight as you have never fought before."

He cut the comm, and he breathed deeply, centering himself, preparing for the trial that lay ahead.

He continued his evasive maneuvers, as he had during his speech, and his eyes scanned the massive formation following him in. The enemy battleships lay ahead, the greatest and most intimidating armada Stockton had ever seen. It was a fitting matchup for history's largest bomber attack, and in just a moment, he was going to see what happened when the proverbial irresistible force met the immovable object. He wasn't sure which side would get the better of it, but he was sure of one thing.

A lot of warriors were going to die on both sides.

*　*　*

"Get the datanet up and operating at full power, Kiloron. And I want damage control parties on all ships standing by the railgun systems. We've seen it enough times...those small craft are looking to take out our main guns before their battleships move into range. All railguns are to be cut off from the power grids until they have targets. If those bombers want to knock them out, they're going to have to do it the hard way, pounding them to scrap. We're not giving them any avoidable power feedback kills." Illius had just stepped off the shuttle, and he was snapping orders into a small handheld comm. He was angry. Part of that was frustration and surprise at the enemy attack, but even more was focused at what he perceived as sloppy—and entirely unacceptable—conduct on the part of the fleet's senior officers. They were doing what had to be done, but far too slowly.

"Yes, sir...as you command." The Red Kriegeri on the comm was a high-ranking officer, but he sounded like a freshly graduated cadet replying to the acting fleet commander.

Just wait until I get to the control center...

Illius moved swiftly across the shuttle bay toward the main bank of lifts. A pair of Kriegeri guards followed him, as did his two senior aides, but he hardly noticed. He had seen the wall of enemy bombers approaching the battle line, and he was utterly dissatisfied with the three hundred or so that the escort line had managed to destroy. That was a lot of ships, but not compared to what was still coming. He suspected the casualty rate could have been doubled if the interdiction had been better coordinated.

A door opened, and he stepped inside the car, followed by his small entourage. He snapped out a hasty command to the lift's AI, "control room," and then he stood quietly, his mind racing from one thought to another.

The battleships had their own defensive armament, of course, and there were almost as many escorts clustered around them as there had been in the forward line. But no matter how he looked at it, the fleet's heavy ships were going to take a hard pounding.

It was his job to see that they came through it strong enough to defeat the Rim battle line approaching just behind their bombers. He was concerned about that—a little—but d his forces were strong enough, and he believed there was a good chance a total victory in the battle would lead to a greatly shortened conflict and total Hegemony victory. The enemy was taking a massive risk with almost all their available forces, and if that ended poorly, Illius knew they were in deep trouble. The prospects of a war far longer than previously imagined had weighed heavily on the Hegemony command over the past year. Now he had a chance to turn that around, to crush the enemy's ability to fight in one climactic confrontation.

The doors slid open, and he walked out onto the floor of the massive control center. *Hegemony's Glory* was an immense ship, and it had been purpose-built as a fleet command vessel. There were over a hundred officers at workstations and, in the center, the fleet commander's suite—a massive chair, surrounded by half a dozen positions for aides.

Illius walked right toward the setup, and he started snapping out orders halfway there.

"Order those escorts to break formation and scatter. They are to re-form just behind the main battle line." His voice was heavy with disgust. No one had issued direction to the escort line, and it was simply waiting where it had been to hit the Rim bombers as they returned to their launch platforms.

Not a damned officer on this ship realized the enemy battle line is going to get there first…

The Rim dwellers had never pushed an attack so aggressively forward, but that was no excuse for an ineffective response. Not in Illius's point of view.

"Yes, Commander. At once."

He reached the chair and sat down hard, letting out a deep breath born of frustration. It had been a careless error to rely on comm lines to connect with the fleet, for the senior officers to remain in the more comfortable ground-based facilities. Perhaps Chronos had been distracted by his personal matters, or maybe they had all just become weary with a conflict that had lasted far longer than anyone had anticipated. He could blame it on Chronos, on himself to a degree, or on some of the others, but the truth was, the enemy attack had been a total surprise to all of them. That did not excuse carelessness, but Illius had to admit, the last thing he had expected was for the enemy to take the offensive. It was a bold move…and for the moment, it was on him to make sure the gamble did not pay off.

He looked up at the display, realizing as he did that a good part of the escort line was going to fail to pull out in time. The Rim battleships were moving in-system at a significant velocity, and they were still accelerating. The enemy vessels were not a one-on-one match for the Hegemony heavies, but they would tear into the light escorts savagely. Normally, Illius would have been less concerned about the lighter ships, but the enemy's bomber strike force was the largest he had ever seen. The fleet was going to need every defensive gun it had to counter those wings, and to stave off the demon pilot who had led them throughout the war.

Raptor.

Intercepts of comm chatter had given his people the nickname the bomber commander used, and with that, it had been relatively easy to come up with a real name.

Jake Stockton.

He had likely done more than any other single Confederation officer to resist the Hegemony invasion.

"I said I want those escorts moving, and that means immediately!" He knew it was not the comm officer's fault, but he was angry and impatient. Distance slowed communications, and the ships themselves had been almost at a dead stop. They were fast, but they were just about out of time.

Illius watched for a few seconds, trying to calculate how many of the escorts might escape. But then he turned his attention elsewhere. He did not have time to worry about the escorts just then.

Not with thousands of bombers bearing down on the main battle line.

Chapter Thirty-Five

650,000,000 Kilometers from CFS Dauntless
Olyus System
Year 320 AC

The Second Battle of Megara – "The Angel of Death"

Fifteen…

Olya Federov was a cool customer, as stone cold as they came. But even she could feel a slight shake in her arms and her hands. She was coming in close, her ship screaming toward the enemy at an almost insane velocity. Worse, she had over three hundred fighters behind her, trying to emulate what she was doing.

Ten…

She was counting down in her head, ready to drop her cluster bombs and pull the hell out of her desperate and deadly dive toward the Hegemony battleship. She knew her approach was reckless, but she was doing it anyway. The cluster bombs were a useful new weapon, and they allowed a Lightning to significantly increase its payload, but they lacked one advantage of the plasma torpedoes. The older weapons lost the ability to maneuver when they were triggered and converted to plasma, but once they'd become pure energy, they defied all attempts to intercept them. The bombs were different. They remained physical constructs until impact and detonation, and that meant the targets' defensive arrays could shoot them down right up to that point. She'd seen bombs picked off a few kilometers and fractions of a second from impact, and she was going to do everything possible to make sure her warheads made it home.

Federov and Stockton had come up with a simple solution to that problem, a way to minimize interceptions of bombs after launch. Pushing the already insane attack runs even closer, cutting out whatever safety margins remained, and, almost literally, taking their Lightnings down the enemy's throat.

Five...

It was dangerous enough a tactic for veteran aces, but, unsurprisingly, even without orders, the pilots in the wings copied the actions of their heroes and leaders. Losses from collisions had gone up sharply, but so had hit rates. And every pilot who missed the pull out, who slammed into an enemy ship at such staggering speeds, only inflicted greater damage on the target.

Federov hated herself for thinking that way, for equating the deaths of her pilots with hitting the enemy harder, but she knew it was true. She would do all she could to help her people fly their ships as well as possible, to guide them to become skilled enough to avoid such disastrous errors...but she wouldn't forbid them from pushing too hard. They were fighting the most desperate war in Confederation history, and the numbers killed were astronomical. However bad it made her feel about herself, she knew on some level that a green pilot could likely do no more to serve the cause than to slam into an enemy battleship at half a percent of light speed.

Three...

Her hand was wrapped around the controls, and her eyes were locked on the targeting display. The vast gray bulk of her target filled her viewscreen as her ship raced directly toward it.

Two...

She drew a deep breath and held it, as she always did when firing.

One...

Her finger tightened, and her ship shook half a dozen times as the bomb bay ejected her six bombs in rapid succession. The cluster munitions had some maneuver capability, but at such speed and with the range so short, it almost didn't matter. Intrinsic velocity alone almost ensured all the warheads would hit before they could be shot down.

What was far less certain was whether she would be able to pull away in time.

She'd already slammed the throttle back so hard, her arm and shoulder ached. Her fighter was blasting every watt of power into the engines, and she could feel the immense impact of acceleration. She was still holding her breath, waiting for open space to appear before her, the sign that she had made it.

Or for her ship to slam into the enemy vessel. *That would be quite the example to set...*

She was on the verge of giving up hope when blackness and stars moved into her view in place of gray steel, and her ship zipped past the hulk of the great battleship, now being wracked by the six hits she'd just scored.

She leaned back in her seat and breathed again, deeply. She was ready enough to die if that was her fate, but she was just as happy to live another day.

And, perhaps even more, not to become the inspiration for hundreds of suicide attacks...

*   *   *

"Initial bombing results coming in, Admiral. The first wave has completed its attack run."

Barron listened to Atara's report, his eyes fixed on the display, waiting for the incoming data to appear. The first wave of Stockton's attack included over a thousand ships, with a heavy proportion of veteran Confed and Palatian veterans. He expected good news from their attacks, but he'd long ago learned never to assume anything like that. Not in battle.

But this time there was something else. Every hit scored by Stockton's people was a step closer to winning the battle, but now, they were each droplets toward quenching Barron's bottomless thirst for blood. A million Masters and Kriegeri dead wouldn't bring back Andi, nor a billion. But he wanted them dead, all of them.

He could feel the tension of the bridge crew, and he knew it would only be worse elsewhere in the fleet. His people on *Dauntless* were veterans who'd served with him for a long time, even if few of them could boast pedigrees dating back to the early days when he commanded the old *Dauntless*. Many of those officers and spacers were gone, killed in the battles Barron had fought, and others had gone on to higher positions, to their own ship commands. Barron liked to think he remembered them all, but there had been so many over the years since he'd ascended to command rank—names, faces, deeds…and for all his reputation and responsibility, he was only a man.

"Sir, Admiral Stockton has sent a flash communique. 'First wave assault complete. Significant damage to enemy battle line. Estimate four battleships destroyed outright, and eighteen with significant damage. Bomber casualties heavy.'" Atara's report was professional, almost clinical, but Barron knew her perhaps better than anyone else, and he caught a hint of her own malice toward the enemy.

The last part of the report wasn't a surprise. Barron might have winced at the thought of hundreds of bombers shot down, but just then, all he could think of was Hegemony blood. After the nightmares into which Jake

Stockton had led his fighters over the years, he had no doubt that when the pilot said, "heavy," he meant just that. *Heavy.* But Barron's usual compassion for his people was stunted, pushed back to the depths of his mind by his own ravening grief...and his need for revenge.

"Advise Admiral Stockton he is to send his squadrons back by the shortest possible course." He wanted those squadrons rearmed and relaunched as quickly as possible, and there was no time for roundabout routes back.

Barron knew that meant he'd be sending his bombers right back through the Hegemony's line of escorts. The fatigued pilots and depleted ships would suffer even worse than they had on their first pass...save for one thing.

Barron was about to do something about those escorts.

"The battle line is to prepare to open fire. Full power to all primary batteries." Barron's eyes were fixed on the enemy frigates and cruisers just about to come into range. Someone in the Hegemony command structure had apparently realized—finally—just how exposed their lighter ships were.

But it was too late. Especially with the increased range of his forward battleships. He'd used the enhanced primaries on the forward line of battleships, but he was betting that the chaos in the enemy formation had kept the Hegemony command from noticing.

And not one of the forward-deployed battleships had survived to bring back the word.

The escorts were firing up their engines, blasting away from the Confederation battleships at full thrust. But they were beginning at a standing stop, and the ships of Barron's battle line had been accelerating since they had transited. They'd have gotten off a good number of broadsides even without the new primaries, but Barron was about to give those cruisers and frigates a surprise they would never forget.

Assuming any of them escaped from him to remember.

"All ships report batteries ready to fire on your command, Admiral." There was a familiar sound in Atara's voice, one he hadn't heard in some time. It wasn't the determination, nor the overpowering stress of battle. It was the dark and deadly sound of a predator. Barron didn't know what the final result would be when the two battle lines finally clashed, but he had a good idea what was going to happen to those escorts in just a few seconds.

He imagined a whole pack of Argellian deathcats, converging on a watering hole surrounded by herd animals. The primaries, especially the enhanced ones, could target those light Hegemony ships from well outside of their own range. It was time for turnabout, for the enemy to experience what Confed and Alliance fleets had dealt with since the war began.

And every kill would reduce the hell Stockton's fighters would face on their way back.

"Entering range now, Admiral."

A thin smile crept onto Barron's lip. There was no joy in it, just a need to feed the yawning pit inside him that craved the blood of the enemy. His eyes were locked on the display, waiting.

He didn't turn, didn't look away...he hardly moved at all. He just issued an order, one he'd been impatient to utter, sitting in his chair, the moments passing with agonizing slowness. He'd gained satisfaction watching Stockton's bombers hitting the enemy, but now, at last, it was his time.

"Captain Travis...all ships are to open fire."

* * *

Movement.

He was being dragged over the ground. He winced as his back struck a jagged stone or something else hard and sharp, and he looked up at the sky.

Blackness.

No, not complete darkness. There was a glow of lights in the distance. His memories were jumbled, incongruous. Where was he? What was he doing here?

"It's okay, sir…we're almost to safety."

He wasn't sure who was talking or what he meant, but he was pretty sure from the tone, the last thing they were was "almost to safety."

Bryan Rogan…I am Bryan Rogan.

He tried to turn his head, to look up at whoever was dragging him along, but couldn't. Then he felt the pain, and he remembered. His chest throbbed, his leg hurt like fire.

He'd been wounded.

He'd thought he was dead.

"What…where…" The words barely came out of his parched mouth, but his companion, whoever was dragging him along the ground—painfully and with great difficulty from the sound of it—heard him.

"General…it's Taylor, sir. I know this hurts, sir, but I had to get you out of there."

Taylor? Rogan tried to focus. His memory was hazy. Yes, Taylor…Private Taylor, one of his Marines.

"Taylor…what…happened?"

"The explosion, General…you were too close. You took concrete fragments from the building, in your side near your chest, and your thigh. I tried to pack the wounds the best I could, but we didn't have time. There were Kriegeri coming from every direction." A short pause. "I carried you as far as I could, sir…but I just couldn't manage it anymore. I'm sorry I've had to drag you the rest of the way."

Rogan jerked his head up, and for the first time he got a good look at the man who, it seemed, had saved him…at least for the time being.

The Marine was tall, his uniform torn in half a dozen places, and stained with blood. Some of the blood was deep red and fresh. "You're wounded, Taylor."

"It's nothing, sir…but we've got to keep going. I think I

can carry you for a bit more."

Rogan took a deep, and painful, breath, and he pulled himself up slowly. He stopped, sitting now instead of lying, and he marshaled all the strength he had left. "No, Taylor…help me up. I think I can walk."

"Sir, you're wounded…"

"So are you, Taylor. If you could carry me out of there and get me past the Kriegeri, I can walk." That sounded good, but Rogan wasn't entirely sure he could. He damned sure was going to try, though. "Now, come over here and help me."

He turned toward the side, holding back a cry as pain lanced through his body. The wound near his chest was still bleeding…he could feel it all down his side. The thigh wound was in better shape. The strip of ragged cloth Taylor had tied around it was still in place, but it was tight, and it throbbed.

Taylor looked hesitant, but he obeyed the order. He reached down and grabbed Rogan's shoulder, pulling gently, helping the general rise slowly to his feet.

Rogan stood, struggling to maintain his weakened balance. Taylor's hand was still on his shoulder, helping to stabilize him. He took a few breaths and struggled to regain his equilibrium. With some success.

A little, at least.

"Okay, let's go, Taylor."

The private stood, still holding on to Rogan's arm. "Just a little farther, General. I think we're in some kind of warehouse district on the outskirts of the city. It seems pretty deserted."

Rogan looked around, moving his head slowly. He got a bit dizzy, but he was getting a better hold on himself. His wounds hurt like hell, and he doubted he could do more than hobble slowly, but Taylor was right. There was no one in sight. He wasn't sure if that was because it was late at night, or because the Hegemony occupation forces had closed down the business operating there. He wondered how long things would stay quiet, but just then, he couldn't think more than a few minutes ahead. With luck, they might find a refuge until morning.

"Let's try that building up ahead." He was concerned about Kriegeri patrols, but mostly, he just wanted to find someplace he could sit. And Taylor didn't look much better than he felt.

"Okay, General." The Marine gripped Rogan's shoulder, and they moved slowly toward what looked like a single-story storage facility of some kind.

"Taylor?"

"Yes, General?"

"The comm center. Did we...did we..."

"It's gone, sir. Completely gone. Nothing left there but a hole in the ground...and I'd guess the explosion took out at least fifty Kriegeri."

Rogan felt a burst of excitement. His people had completed their mission, and done their part for the fleet. He tried not to think about the Kriegeri the blast had taken out, or more specifically, the Marines he knew must have been killed along with their enemies. He'd pressed the button to detonate without regard for whether his people had cleared the blast area. He tried to tell himself they had all gotten away, but he knew they hadn't. He had no idea how many Marines had made it out, who were even then sneaking around Troyus City and its environs, hiding from the Kriegeri, but in his heart, he knew most of his people were dead.

The pain of that would sink in fully later—if there was a later—but at least those who had died had been killed doing their duty. They might have saved thousands of lives among the spacers in the fleet.

He looked up, a pointless glance at the sky, and he wondered what was happening just then, millions of kilometers from Megara, where the battle for the system was raging.

*   *   *

"Commander Chronos, we have restored minimal connection to the orbital scanner feeds. We have confirmed that Master Illius's shuttle has docked with *Hegemony's Glory*. We can assume he has taken operational command of the fleet."

Chronos scowled. The report that Illius's shuttle had reached its destination was relevant—and welcome—but he was less than enthused about his people *assuming* anything. They had all *assumed* the Confederation and their allies could never launch an assault on Megara.

"What is the status on the emergency comm relays?"

"The teams are still working, Commander. No update yet on timing to restore communications."

"Well, Kiloron…then you go out there yourself and tell them I need an update. I need a specific time frame, and that had better be a short one." Chronos paused. "No, forget that. Get my shuttle ready. I am going to Orbital Fortress One." He had been hesitant to leave the main headquarters, but now he wondered how much of that had been based on tactical considerations and how much on his desire to remain close to Akella. There was no room for personal considerations, and besides, Megara was occupied by over three million Kriegeri. Despite the enemy's recent raid, the Hegemony's Number One was as safe and protected as she could be. The only thing that could threaten her would be the defeat of the fleet, and the only way he knew that he could prevent that from happening was to get to the fortress and restore some level of control. The broken link in his comm network was orbit to ground, and once he got to the station, he should be able to communicate with Illius and the other ships of the fleet.

"Commander, what if the enemy…"

"What if they what, Kiloron? I will not cower down here when the fleet is engaged."

"Yes, of course, Commander. I meant no offense."

"Then see that my shuttle is ready. I will leave here in ten minutes."

"Yes, Commander!" The officer snapped to attention and spun around on his heels, moving off to execute Chrono's command.

The fleet commander turned toward another officer. "What is the status on ground security? We allowed a bunch of battered enemy Marines to destroy our main comm facility. I would like to ensure nothing similar happens again." Chronos had switched the focus of his anger at the stunning enemy raid back and forth between his subordinates and himself. He had finally decided all parties were at fault.

If the Hegemony failed in its mission to unite and protect all humanity, arrogance would be at the root of that defeat. He believed completely in the Hegemonic system of genetic ranking and structure, but not in the effects it had on the ego and entitled attitudes of those near its top. A Master had potential and abilities beyond those of the Kriegeri he or she led, but that was far from a blanket assessment. Knowledge, courage, attitude, effort…they all played their roles in success, and too many of the elite Masters had become lazy, more concerned with their exalted place in Hegemony society than in their duty to the nation and its sacred purpose.

"We have doubled all patrols, Commander. We have rounded up a number of enemy survivors from the raids, but there is no sign of any organized activity still ongoing."

"Triple the patrols, Kiloron."

"Yes, Commander."

"And send for Master Carmetia at once."

"Sir!"

Carmetia and her Marine prisoner might yet prove useful. At least the Master had experience with Confederation Marines. He would leave her in command on the ground in his absence. If there were any other enemy operations, she was the likeliest of his people to counter them. And, if things remained quiet, she could direct the roundup of whatever Marines were still hiding out there.

Chronos had come to respect the Confederation's soldiers, and he wasn't going to underestimate them again, even when they appeared to be scattered and nearly eradicated.

No…no underestimating adversaries. No more.

Never again.

"Kiloron…"

He shouted after the officer who had turned and walked off to carry out his commands.

"Commander?" The kiloron stopped and turned immediately.

"Double the guard around Number One as well. I want that bunker protected at all costs…is that understood?"

"Yes, Commander. Understood!"

Chapter Thirty-Six

HWS Hegemony's Glory
Olyus System
Year of Renewal 265 (320 AC)

The Second Battle of Megara – "Victory first, spoils later"

"Commander Illius, the forward line is taking heavy losses."

"I can see that, Kiloron." Illius was sullen, angry, cursing himself and every last incompetent officer on *Hegemony's Glory* and the rest of the fleet. *We let this happen. We underestimated the enemy, convinced ourselves they had no choice but to sit and wait for us to resume the offensive. But they did not play along, did not buy into our belief in our superiority.*

Worse, to Illius's mind, was the fact that neither he nor Chronos were normally prone to such arrogance.

At least we thought we were not.

But we were. We saw the enemy as beaten, our repulse from Craydon a setback, one we would reverse as soon as we could bring supplies forward. We wrote off the destruction of the supply fleet as a fluke, a desperate gamble that paid off for the enemy by stroke of luck.

We have underestimated this enemy from the start.

Illius knew he could not change the past. He could not undo mistakes, whether made by himself or those around him, and he was not about to waste time wishing he could.

But you can prevent any more from taking place. You can crush the overconfidence, the arrogance, and give this enemy the respect they have earned.

"The escorts are to scatter, Kiloron. I want a randomized dispersal pattern. All units that escape the enemy battleships will regroup behind our main line." That would strip him of almost half the fleet's escorts, at least until they could regroup and advance again, but it was the only way he could see of saving any of them. The Confederation primaries were lancing out even as he watched the scanner, and those deadly beams were no joke. They were less powerful than the fleet's railguns, but one hit would cripple most of the small escort ships…and they were under attack by the entire Rim battle line.

At least if the smaller ships took off in all directions, the Rim fleet would have to scatter to effectively pursue. *And they will not do that. They know the battle will be decided by the two main lines…*

He had considered advancing his own battleships in an effort to save the escorts, but that would serve no purpose. He would never close in time to intervene, and he did not want to move his heavies too far forward. He was confident his ships were strong enough to prevail, but he was very deliberately guarding against arrogance. This enemy was dangerous, resourceful, and his gut told him he had not seen all of their surprises yet. He was going to keep the battleships within support distance of the—admittedly incomplete—orbital fortresses, and nothing short of Chronos's direct order was going to change that.

"Scatter order transmitted, Commander." A pause. "Updated loss figures on the display, sir."

Illius did not even look. There was no way to change any of it, beyond what he had just done. And it would be eighteen minutes before the escorts even received the command to scatter, much less execute it.

And those loss figures are eighteen minutes old now, too.

There was something else. The enemy ships…they had opened fire from well beyond their range.

Their former range…

He rechecked the scans, reconfirmed the readings himself. At least some of the Confederation battleships had opened fire from just under maximum railgun range.

Was it some kind of deception, a scanner ruse? His mind raced to consider possibilities, even as his insides tightened.

"Commander Illius, Number Eight is on the comm."

Illius turned toward the communications officer. "On my headset, Hectoron." He scooped the set from its harness next to his chair and pulled it over his head, just as Chronos's voice came through.

"What do you think they are up to, Illius?" There was no greeting, no formalities, just a no-nonsense question. Illius and Chronos were of like minds on most things. The acting fleet commander deeply respected Number Eight, and he dared to believe that the expedition commander felt some admiration for him as well.

"I do not know, Commander, but I am concerned. These Rim dwellers are courageous, and sometimes aggressive— bordering on reckless…but I have not seen them do something for no discernible reason." A second's pause. "Also, we are getting some readings that are…confusing."

"Confusing?"

"Yes, sir…it appears the enemy is firing their particle accelerators from considerably beyond our previously-noted range for the systems." Illius hesitated a few seconds, and then he added, "We are uncertain if this is factual, or if it is some kind of electronic countermeasure designed to confuse our scans."

"What is your gut feeling, Illius?"

The Megaron wanted to reply that it had to be some kind of trick, that the fleet had extensive records on Confederation primary beam ranges…but then his promise to avoid arrogance came back into his mind.

"I really do not know, Commander...but I do not think we can take the chance. If they have somehow increased the range of their weapons, we need to be ready for it."

"I agree, Illius. Adjust your formation to assume the enemy will open fire at the indicated ranges. We have seen enough careless assumptions backfire today."

"Agreed, sir." A short pause. "Have you been able to repair the comm system?" He had been surprised to hear from Chronos, especially since he had reviewed the damage on the surface himself, and he had been sure it would be a day at least before even limited communications were restored.

"No...the ground comm is still down. I am on Orbital Platform One." There were perhaps ten seconds of silence, then: "Illius...the enemy's change in tactics, their direct approach. They have increased their weapons range. That is why they're coming straight for us."

Illius had already turned toward the display by the time Chronos had finished. His eyes darted from one cluster of enemy ships to another, and he began some range calculations in his head.

"Commander, I agree. If the enemy decelerates just before entering range, they will have time to get in at least a partial bombing strike...and then their battleships will come into range."

"You see, Illius, again this enemy shows us their mettle. They do have a plan, and one that makes perfect sense. Just because we did not know about it did not mean it was not there. Tyler Barron is no fool, and he would not throw his fleet away unless he was sure there was some way to prevail."

"Still, we have the advantage in tonnage and guns."

"But will we still have a gunnery advantage after another wave of bombers hits us?"

Even with Chronos on board the orbital platform, the

comm signal had a two-second delay in each direction. The two men continued speaking, determined to develop a course of action to reclaim the initiative.

In the end, they came down to two choices. Accept the fact that the enemy would get another bomber strike launched, and pull back right under the guns of the orbital platforms, the ones that were operational, at least.

Or accelerate hard, push forward and try to close the distance before the enemy battleships could launch their bombers again.

Both options had their risks, and their advantages. Finally, Illius took a breath and said, "So, Commander, what will it be? It is your decision, but whatever it is, it must be made now. Do we advance? Or do we pull back under the guns?"

* * *

"You are insane if you think I'm going to help you hunt down Marines…here on Megara, or on the fifteenth moon of Evelon Zed." Steven Blanth had been a prisoner of the Hegemony for years now, and he'd made the best of it, at least as far as engaging civilly with his captors. But he'd never forgotten they were the enemy, and he had never turned coat and betrayed his comrades. He'd find a way to kill himself before he'd do that. Most likely, that would be death by Kriegeri. The Hegemony soldiers were under orders not to harm him, but he figured if he pushed one hard enough…

"Steven, have I lied to you in the time we've spent together? I promise you, on my word as a Master of the Hegemony, we are not seeking to kill your Marines, simply to move them to a secure area where they can be monitored and properly supervised.

"Prison…you want to put them in prison."

"How many do you think are wounded now? We found

more than fifty of them dead at the comm station, and that does not take into account how many were inside when the explosives detonated, and left only ashes. Or even the casualties at the sites of the other terrorist attacks."

Blanth held back a smile at a reminder of the series of raids his comrades had somehow managed to execute. He felt a moment of Marine pride, like nothing he'd experienced since his comrades on Dannith had launched their own attack on the command center there.

Carmetia was right, of course. The Marines who'd launched the raid, if any of them had actually escaped, were on the run, hungry, cold, and tired. Half of them were probably wounded. Many of them would die on their own. And his Hegemony captors *had* treated him humanely.

But given a choice, he would be out there with those Marines, clad in tattered fatigues, carrying a battered rifle with a handful of fresh rounds, with every Kriegeri in Troyus City hunting him down. He'd bristled at captivity, even while, in some ways, he'd adapted to it as well. But in his heart, he was still a Marine, as he would be until the day he died.

"Marines ignore wounds, Master Carmetia. Haven't you figured that out by now?" He could see she was frustrated. He wasn't exactly in the loop, but it appeared she'd been given the responsibility for rounding up the renegades, and certainly for making sure they didn't do any more damage.

"Steven, you are killing them by not helping me. They are out there, and over a hundred thousand Kriegeri are hunting them down. They have already found twenty-two of them, and sixteen of those ended up dead. If you help me bring them in, I will guarantee they will be treated as you have been. Help me save them, Steven. Help me save them before they are all killed."

Blanth had to admit one thing. Carmetia was convincing, all the more so because he believed she was telling him the truth. And she was right, the Marines still out there, at least any who could not get back to their previous hiding places, would most likely end up dead.

It made sense for him to help her, at least from her perspective, and he was sure his refusal frustrated her intensely. But there was one thing she didn't comprehend, one fact he'd never been able to make her understand.

Death wasn't at the bottom of a Marine's list of options, and wherever it stood, it was damned sure north of surrender.

* * *

"It is good to hear from you, my brother. Once again, we go forward together to battle." Vian Tulus sat in the center of *Invictus*'s great bridge. He was in his glory, leading his people into a great battle, advancing alongside trusted friends and allies. It was the Palatian ideal, and if Tulus had pushed beyond the tight constraints of Alliance protocols and ways of thinking, he had not strayed so far that the call to battle didn't fill him with energy, the blood of the warrior pumping through his arteries with every beat of his heart.

"You know what to do, Brother. I didn't call with orders, nor to waste time on idle chat, but simply to wish you fortune and honor in the coming fight. It is time to win the peace that will allow us to prosper."

Tulus's emotions stirred with each of Barron's words. He knew the loss his friend had suffered. His Palatian sensibilities filled him with grim satisfaction that Andi Lafarge had died an honorable death. A warrior's death. But he knew it was different for Barron, and that his friend's grief was without bounds.

"And to you, Tyler my brother. Victory, fortune, glory. Go forth to the fight, and know I am at your side, now and always." *Spoils later…and grief, too. After the fight. After the enemy feels our fire.*

Tulus heard a short click as the comm line severed.

Barron's words had fanned the flames of his courage and determination.

"Engineering is to monitor the new primaries closely. We had little enough time to test them out, and if they fail, I swear to the Old Gods, I will space whoever is responsible." The short range of the Palatian weaponry had been a source of continual frustration to Tulus, and it had kept his ships from the battle line on a number of occasions. That shame was now a thing of the past. Four of the newest and strongest ships had taken their place in the forward formations, next to *Dauntless* and the Confederation's center division.

"Status of bomber refit?" He had a pretty good idea, but he knew getting the next strike launched before the fleet entered primary range was going to be tight. He wanted up to date projections, and he wanted them now. Tyler would get his squadrons launched in time, he didn't have the slightest doubt about that. And he'd be damned if he was going to see his own people lag behind their allies.

"Launch operations projected to commence in thirty-eight minutes."

That was close, too close. "I want that schedule shaved down, Sub-Commander. Thirty-two minutes maximum. Thirty, preferably." He knew his orders were almost impossible. The Palatian ships weren't a technological match for those of their Confederation allies, even if they now carried enhanced primaries. The landing bays on *Invictus* and her sister ships were far less streamlined and automated than their Confederation counterparts.

But the flight crews on those decks were Palatians, and Tulus defied them to fail the direct command of their Imperator.

"Flight control acknowledges, your Supremacy. Launch to commence in thirty-two minutes."

Tulus leaned back in his chair, considering for a few seconds about pushing for the thirty. But he held back.

Thirty-two would be difficult enough.

There was an artform in threading the needle between almost impossible and outright impossible. And his gut told him his people would manage that maneuver perfectly.

Chapter Thirty-Seven

CFS Constitution
Olyus System
Year 320 AC

The Second Battle of Megara – "All batteries...open fire!"

"The bombers are commencing their attack runs, sir. Admiral Stockton is at the front of the formation."

As always...

Clint Winters had been a hard-driving officer since the day he'd graduated from the Academy, but it had been as a senior commander that he'd picked up his nickname, "the Sledgehammer." He was relentless, stubborn, courageous to a fault, and he demanded total commitment from his spacers. By all normal standards of human conduct, he'd always expected them to hate him for it...but they loved him instead. They followed him with unmatched fervor, and they adored him with an intensity second only to the near worship they reserved for Tyler Barron.

But as tough as Winters was, as unstoppably aggressive, he bowed his head in silent respect to the focused insanity of Jake Stockton. Without a doubt, the pilot had done more than any other single human being, Winters and Barron included, to keep the war going against the Hegemony. His fighter strikes would go down in every history of the war, and his tactics would be taught at the Academy for a century or more.

Assuming we win, and there is *an Academy…*

Winters didn't respond to the aide's report. There was no need, nothing to say. Everyone on the bridge knew the bombers were attacking. Hell, Winters would have bet everyone on the *fleet* knew. The battle lines would engage soon, and while the enhanced primaries weren't a surprise to the enemy anymore, they were still a crucial difference in the matchup. The railguns hit harder, and they retained a slight range advantage—and, of course, not all the Grand Alliance's ships were equipped with the new primaries—but the clash of the battle lines would be closer to an even match than any the forces of the Rim had yet seen.

Still, the end result of that slugging match almost certainly depended on just how hard Stockton's people could hit those Hegemony battleships, how many railguns they were able to knock out.

The savaging and scattering of the enemy's advance line had been a big plus for Stockton's wings, but Winters could see more frigates and cruisers deployed in clusters around the capital ships. There were plenty of point defense assets still out there, even beyond the massive suites on the battleships themselves. The bombing wings would pay a terrible price for driving their attacks home. The first wave had already completed its assault, and the casualty totals were grim.

Winters knew it didn't matter, and he was even more certain Stockton knew that. Jake Stockton was well aware that any chance the battle line—and the fleet as a whole—had for victory in Megara relied on his squadrons hitting the enemy *hard*.

There was no one Winters would have trusted more with that job, but it was still hard to sit and watch, knowing his own fate, and that of the crews of his ships, relied so heavily on the actions—and the sacrifice—of others.

The rest of the strike force was arrayed in three successive lines, each about three minutes apart. That was cutting it close. The battle line would move into the enemy's railgun range in about seven minutes, while the Hegemony ships were hopefully still distracted by the last bomber assault. There would be about two minutes from the moment the enemy railguns could open fire to the point when the enhanced primaries moved into range. Anything that pulled the enemy's focus from the approaching line of battleships for that short stretch was vital to the Rim fleet's chance of victory.

It was tight, well-planned, but far from guaranteed to execute properly. A hundred things could go wrong, and blow up the precise schedule. Winters's mind had meticulously listed all the problems, all the unexpected developments and combinations of factors that could upset the delicate balance.

In the end, it only took one. Winters was watching as the readings began to come in, and he realized it immediately. Engine output, all along the Hegemony line.

Are they pulling out already? Running?

Winters knew *that* was wrong the instant it popped into his mind.

No, he realized. *They're pulling back into support range of the orbital bases.*

Winters didn't know how much work the Hegemony had managed to complete on the rebuilt forts. He knew the ones at Craydon were half-done, at best, but it was dangerous to assume just what the enemy had managed to do. He'd hoped the forts lacked operational weapons systems, but now he realized those hopes had been dashed.

That's more guns against us during the main fight...

That wasn't good, especially if there were railguns on those forts. And there almost certainly were. The question was, were they completed and operational. And the answer was yes. *Why else would they be pulling back toward the forts?*

A cold thought ripped through his mind. *How should we respond?*

Nothing made "the Sledgehammer" more uncomfortable than not knowing what to do. And just then, he had no idea.

"Get me Admiral Barron." Winters snapped out the command almost instinctively. He knew he didn't have to report what was going on. He was one hundred percent sure Barron was watching too.

But they had to decide what to do, and they had to decide immediately.

* * *

"Second wave, attack!" Stockton sat in his cockpit, throttle pulled to the side, bringing his ship around after his attack run. He'd gone in with the first wave, and he'd been one of the first to deliver his deadly payload, right into the guts of one of the biggest Hegemony behemoths.

He was planning to hang back, to go in again with the last wave. He wouldn't have more ordnance to deliver, but the final wave of bombers would be the ones tasked with distracting the enemy as their railguns came into range. That would be a vital two minutes, and that short period of time could decide the entire battle.

Then the Hegemony ships began firing their engines, pulling back from the direction of his attack, and from the approaching battleships of the Confederation and its allies.

It made sense to him almost immediately. Pulling back would delay the moment when the two fleets came into range, and that meant the bombing strike would be over by the time the battle lines engaged. That would leave the Hegemony ships still possessing operational railguns to take full advantage of the brief window they'd have before the new primaries came into range.

Then he remembered the fortresses orbiting Megara, and he truly understood.

If those forts have operational railguns…

No doubt, the enemy expected a larger advantage from their advanced weaponry, one the enhanced primaries would cut by almost eighty percent. That still left the Hegemony with two minutes before the fight became a truly two-sided affair, but if they were supported by heavy orbital batteries, that seemingly short time could be long indeed. And maybe decisive.

Stockton had planned to keep the enemy focused on his bombers, a major reason he'd stayed back to make another run alongside the final wave. He'd figured he just might manage to strip away some of that advantage, giving the enemy something to worry about besides shooting at advancing Rim battleships.

That's shot to shit now. Nothing left to do now but hit them as hard as possible.

He thought for a moment about decelerating the last wave, trying to delay the engagement and reconfiguring it to the precise moment the battle lines would come into range. But that was almost impossible, an infernally complex calculation with enough variables to make his eyes bleed. Even if he had exact data on the enemy fleet's planned course and velocity—which he didn't—he had almost no real chance of pulling it off on the fly. He had no idea how Admiral Barron would react, and no time to find out, and besides, nothing his people did would do a thing about the fortresses.

Staying with the original plan would at least ensure getting his last wave in before the enemy was able to pull back too far. That was the best he could do. The rest would be up to Barron and the battleships.

"Where do you want us, Raptor?" It was "Lynx" Federov. She had commanded the first wave, despite his own presence with the wings, and she'd done a brilliant job.

Over a thousand bombers had gone in, utterly ignoring the dense defensive fire, and they'd hit the enemy *hard*. The escorts mixed in along the line added their defensive fire to that of the battleships, and they gunned down two hundred of the approaching bombers. But the ones who got through followed Federov's lead, closing to point blank range and pouring their cluster bombs into the guts of dozens of Hegemony battleships.

"Get your people back, Lynx." Stockton had sent fighters with expended bombs back into the fight more than once, throwing them at the massive enemy battleships with nothing but their lasers. But that was a waste in this case. Federov's wings wouldn't get back until the battle lines had engaged, and that would make landings a difficult undertaking, and any subsequent launches even more so. But any ships she managed to get into the bays at least had a chance of refitting in time to launch again. That offered a chance for some last-minute support for the battleships, a chance the admiral might desperately need.

"Land as well as you can, and get Stara on the refit. Tell her we need your ships ready to launch, and we need it done in record time, regardless of what else is going on." He knew just what he was asking of Stara. Those battleships would be wracked by enemy fire, their systems would be gutted, their landing bays set aflame, their crews killed, and conditions would only get worse as the lines continued to exchange deadly broadsides. It would be about as far from optimal conditions as possible, a nightmare for flight crews trying to do their work, but if anyone could see it done, it was Stara.

"Yes, Admiral." Stockton could hear in her tone that she didn't like heading back without him, leaving while two-thirds of the strike force was still engaged. But he knew she understood, and he had no doubt she would do what he commanded.

"Go, Lynx…get those birds back. Admiral Barron's

most likely going to need them. And if I'm not back yet, you take them out as soon as any number of them are ready to go, you understand me?"

"Yes, Raptor. Understood."

He watched her ship coming about, her thrusters blasting at full and, a moment later, he saw the rest of the first wave, the whole formation turning about to follow, still ragged from finishing their attack, but coming together even as he watched.

He turned back, confident his people were in the best possible hands.

The second wave was going in, with Dirk Timmons in the lead. His ego wanted to believe they needed his attention, but he knew that wasn't really true. Not with "Warrior" Timmons in the lead.

He just stayed where he was.

Waiting for the last wave.

* * *

"It is clear the enemy has developed a longer-ranged version of their particle accelerators. That is unfortunate, yet it appears that we retain an advantage in hitting power and a slight advantage in range. We are going to maximize this in the coming exchange." Illius sat in his position on *Hegemony's Glory*, looking out over the vessel's senior officers and his cluster of aides. They were all well-trained, perfectly genetically suited to their roles, yet Illius was nervous, and he had repeated the same directives several times. He had seen too many errors committed so far, and there was no more room for confusion, nor for lackluster performance. The fleet had been caught by surprise. That was a credit to the enemy's initiative, but it was one that would not have been possible without carelessness on the part of the Hegemony forces.

Arrogance…Chronos is correct. If we fail, our assurance of our own superiority will be the culprit.

There was no more time for that kind of foolishness. Illius had ordered the fleet to pull back, to take a carefully-chosen position that would allow the heavy railguns on the platforms—fully operational, despite the incomplete state of the forts themselves—to support the fleet's battered broadsides. The enemy bombers had already knocked out close to half of the fleet's railgun batteries. Some of those were blasted to wreckage, others taken offline by minor damage or cut power transmission lines. Damage control teams were working feverishly, trying to bring anything repairable back online. But the bombers had hurt the fleet's combat strength. Again.

This time, the forts will help fill that gap. Those guns are heavier and deadlier than anything we have deployed yet.

"Our timing must be exact. Every ship must follow orders with unrelenting precision." *Hegemony's Glory* shook as he was speaking. Another hit. The last squadrons of the enemy's final wave were completing their attacks. The enemy bombers had struck hard, but Illius believed the Hegemony forces still held the advantage. The fight would be a toe to toe slugging match now, a bloodbath, the losses vastly higher than anything his people had imagined before they'd commenced the war against the Rim dwellers.

We are past that now. We are in too deep to pull back, to give up on the Rim. We have to win, at all costs…

"The enemy fleet is here. When we destroy it, the war will be all but won." He turned toward the display, watching the small symbols positioned around the circle that represented Megara. Chronos was *on* one of the stations, and that troubled him. None of the fortresses were fully complete, and when the enemy realized the power of the weapons positioned there, they would find a way to hit back. They would try, at least. He had fought them long enough to understand that.

He did not like the idea of the invasion's supreme

commander being off the planet, in an exposed position. He did not like it one bit.

But there was nothing he could do about it. There was only one thing that mattered just then.

He watched as the range counted down, his ships moving into their assigned positions. The last of the enemy bombers had finished their attacks. They had savaged the fleet, but they had paid a heavy price for it. Now it was down to the battle lines, a desperate, vicious brawl…for control of the Olyus system.

And possibly for the entire Rim.

A small light flashed on his comm control, and he tapped the button on the side. "Yes, Commander…" It was not a question. He knew why Chronos was on the line.

"It is almost time, Illius."

"Yes, Commander. All units are prepared. The fleet is synchronized with fortress command."

"Very good." There was a short silence. "Good luck to you, Illius."

"And to you, Commander." Illius cut the line and stared straight ahead, battling the tension that struggled to divert his attention. He watched as the enemy battleships moved forward, as their waves of small craft pulled back. As the range display counted down, each second bringing the approaching enemy forces closer and closer.

Then, it was time.

"All batteries…open fire!"

Chapter Thirty-Eight

CFS Dauntless
Olyus System
Year 320 AC

The Second Battle of Megara – "Kill them. Kill them all."

"All batteries, prepare to open fire." Barron's voice was cold, a sound almost like steel striking steel. He had spoken the words without thought, almost on pure instinct. The fleet was entering the enemy's range. His ships had a two-minute gauntlet to run, one hundred twenty seconds before they could return fire, and bring death to the enemy.

Death. That was Barron's purpose, and all he cared about. The Confederation, the entire Rim, billions of civilians...their futures all hung on what happened next, but Tyler Barron, so long the noble leader, the warrior who fought to protect his people, was gone. All that remained was fury, rage, and an aching hurt that could only be salved by oceans of enemy blood.

Dauntless rocked hard, then again, the battleship's engines driving it forward on an irregular course toward the enemy, doing everything possible to upset the Hegemony target locks.

The flagship pushed forward, unscathed by the chunks of super-heavy metals whipping by at hypersonic velocities. The Hegemony railguns were a deadly weapon, even to the largest ships. Barron and his people knew that, but it wasn't long before they got a pointed reminder.

Vincennes wasn't one of the newest battleships, nor one of the largest, but the vessel was certainly powerful, and she was equipped with the enhanced primaries. She was firmly in her place on the line, guns ready to fire. Then the symbol on the display expanded, a shimmering halo hovering around it for a few seconds.

A hit.

Barron barely noticed the reports coming in on his own screen, the words and figures scrolling along in his peripheral vision. His eyes had always been glued to the damage and casualty reports in past battles, but now he barely paid attention.

He knew many of his people were going to die in the next hours, perhaps all of them. But there was little point spending time watching it happen one ship at a time. There were no decisions to make, no point in reacting to losses. The fleet was going in, no matter what. When it was over, he would know who had lived and who had died, assuming, of course, he was still there to see. Until then, nothing mattered but killing the enemy.

Vincennes wasn't gone, but even his casual observation told him the battleship was just about out of the fight. At least until she'd closed enough to open fire with whatever remained of her secondaries. That was a helpful thought, the kind of thing Barron had used to sustain his morale in a hundred battles.

But *Vincennes* had almost no chance of closing to firing range. The vessel had lost almost half her power, and Barron couldn't imagine the hell raging in her engineering spaces just then. Her people would endure as long as they could, they would battle the fires, the radiation, the vacuum of space tearing through damaged compartments. But their ship was half crippled, and in a fight as ferocious as the one Barron knew they all faced, those who stumbled were very likely to fall.

And never rise again.

"Fritzie…" His hands moved almost without mental bidding, connecting his direct line to the fleet's chief engineer.

"Admiral?"

"We need more power to the primaries, all ships. We need maximum rate of fire once we enter range."

"Admiral…the enhanced primaries are already on the verge of failure, that's how they function. The whole system's basically just an overload already. If we push that any harder…"

"What, Fritzie? We'll lose ships?" Barron's voice was caustic, but then he went silent. His eye caught *Vincennes* again on the monitor. The ship's engines had failed, long enough, at least, to shut down her evasive maneuvers. The enemy had already targeted her, and it was almost effortless for her assailants to deliver another railgun shot right into her guts. The chunk of super-heavy metal tore through the armor and the steel of her decks, obliterating one system after another, and delivering a staggering amount of kinetic energy to the target.

The battleship hung where she was for a few seconds, as thousands watched on their screens and scanners…and then she vanished in the hell of thermonuclear fury.

"Admiral…yes, sir. I will do what I can." *Vincennes*'s destruction had made the admiral's point with a grim eloquence words could never have matched.

Barron turned as he closed the comm line, his eyes moving back to the display. Within a minute, eight of his ships were hit…and two destroyed. *Formidable* was the second vessel lost, and the report confirmed what Barron had already suspected from watching *Vincennes* demise.

The enemy forts did indeed have operational railguns. And the monster weapons were larger and more powerful even than those on the Hegemony battleships. Such a realization might have unnerved him in another time, another place. But he'd led his people to the Olyus system to win or die, and there was no turning back. If the Hegemony wanted to stop his fleet, to hold Megara, they were going to have to destroy every single ship he had.

Because there would be no retreat order.

"Commander, put me on fleet-wide comm." *Dauntless* was in the lead, the first ship in the fleet, and the display showed less than thirty seconds to firing range.

"Yes, Admiral." An instant later: "On your line." Atara's voice was almost as cold and hard as Barron's. It was determination, courage…and, he suspected, also her way of telling him she was with him.

To the end.

"Attention, all ships of the battle line. All ships of the fleet. We are about to begin the final stage of the battle. There can be but two outcomes to this fight. The enemy flees, and we retake Megara. Or we die, every one of us. There will be no retreat. Forward now, to victory. The battle plan is simple, and clear, and all that remains is for us to execute it."

Barron paused, just for a moment. Then he added a few words, the ones he'd heard in his head, a relentless, unstoppable scream.

"Kill them. Kill them all."

He turned once again toward Atara's station. He held her gaze, for perhaps two seconds, a final instant of humanity between two friends. Then, he spoke again, one more command.

"All ships…open fire."

* * *

"Stara, we're coming in now. We're matching the fleet's course and velocity, but we're going to have to tie into the defense nets for final approach." Olya Federov had made combat landings before, though perhaps never under quite the circumstances the battle line was facing just then. The fleet's battleships were getting hammered by the enemy's railguns, and they'd just opened up with their own fire. *Dauntless* had shot first, and scored a direct hit. That was a strong start, especially at such long range, and she decided to take it as a positive omen.

She needed everything she could get just then.

"Olya, we're on maximum evasive maneuvers. Even if you're plugged into the datanet, your people are going to have a hell of a time syncing up. If you pull back, take position behind the…"

"No, Stara. Admiral Stockton wants us to land and refit. Immediately." Federov had agreed with Stockton when he'd given her the order. She still did, at least with the rationale. But now, she wasn't sure if she could pull it off. If her people could.

There was a long pause. She wasn't sure if Stara was thinking, or if the flight control commander had called up to *Dauntless*'s bridge for guidance or permission. Security was always tight around a warship's evasive routines. If an enemy could sync into a datanet like the one her people would, they could tear even a monster like *Dauntless* apart in seconds.

"All right, Olya…but you need to bring your best pilots in first. The bays are already damaged, and with the combat maneuvers…" Another pause. "If one of your people loses it…"

"Understood, Stara." She was about to ask Stara to get the other nearby battleships ready when the flight control officer beat her to it.

"I've got *Dauntless, Constitution, Remorseless, Standard, Exeter, Repulse,* and *Avenger* locked into one net for your landings. Bring as many ships as you can in...but hurry. Things are only going to get worse as we close."

"We're on the way, Stara." A pause. "And, thanks..."

"*Invictus* just acknowledged, too. Advise your Palatian squadrons they should connect with their own datanet. Imperator Tulus has commanded all of their battleships to prepare to land and refit their bombers."

"Thank you again, Stara. We'll be landing in about four minutes."

Federov glanced down at her screen, highlighting the locations of the ships Stara had specified. They were mostly close to *Dauntless*, though *Constitution* was Admiral Winters's flagship, and fairly far out on the port flank. Which was fine. Her returning wing was stretched out over a hundred thousand kilometers, and she'd already instructed the AI to issue approach orders. She wasn't worried about squadron integrity, not then. Her pilots would land wherever they could.

She wasn't going to get them all landed, not while the battle lines were so heavily engaged. But she'd get some of them in...and, she promised herself, she'd get them back out again too.

Whatever it took.

The nightmare unfolding on her screen, the desperate maneuvers, the shattered hulks of savaged battleships, the death and destruction all around...it was all screaming a single message to her, one that had started with Stockton's orders.

The fleet still needs your people...as many as you can lead back out.

* * *

"Please, General...drink." Taylor was leaning over Rogan, holding the small, metal canteen to the general's lips.

"This is your water, Taylor." Rogan turned his head away

as he spoke, but the private moved his hands as well, keeping the small canister just in front of the general's mouth.

"I've had enough, General." A lie, Rogan knew. "And we can get more once we leave here." Another lie, or at least something close to it. It seemed reasonable enough that they could find some water relatively nearby. The problem was the fact that, as soon as they stepped out of the crumbling building sheltering them, they'd most likely run into Kriegeri. It was a certainty the Hegemony soldiers were out looking for his survivors. Hundreds of them. *No, thousands.*

Of course, the other problem was, Rogan was far from sure he could even get up, much less walk. And one look at Taylor told him the Marine wasn't going to be carrying him much farther.

We're finished. It's just a matter of waiting for the Kriegeri to find us...

He'd almost spoken the words, but something had stopped him, kept him quiet. *Taylor...he deserves better than hopelessness.*

But does he deserve lies?

Rogan sucked in a deep breath, and he turned his head again, at least as much as he could manage. He didn't have much left, but he had enough to be sure of one thing. He wasn't going to drink any more of Taylor's water. It was a waste to pour such a precious resource into his dying body.

He stopped, his body tensing.

He heard something!

Steps...the sounds of boots on the rough gravel.

He tapped Taylor on the shoulder, but the Marine had heard it all himself. He had his rifle in his hands, even as Rogan pulled his own pistol from its holster. If the Kriegeri *had* found them, it was over.

Almost over.

The enemy would finish the two of them, there was no doubt about that. But Rogan and his comrade weren't going down without a fight.

No way…

He held the pistol up, pointing toward the meter-high hole in the wall that served as a door. He was silent, holding his breath as much as he could.

Waiting for one last chance to strike at the enemy before death came for him.

His eyes caught a shadow, just outside the entrance to the room, and a muffled sound. Voices?

He'd been ready for death since he'd pressed the detonator switch, but now he felt something. Was it fear, a wish that he could somehow survive? That was a normal human reaction, one not even Marines were immune from.

He wasn't sure, but it didn't matter. The only chance at survival was to surrender, to beg the enemy for his life.

And that wasn't going to happen. Some things were worse than death.

His hand tightened on the pistol as he heard someone moving forward, coming through the break in the wall…

* * *

"All power to primary batteries. We will maintain fire at maximum possible speed, Commander." Vian Tulus was the Imperator of the Palatian Alliance, the supreme leader of his people…but at the current moment, he had a more important role. The commander of a warship engaged in a desperate battle, one that could only be fought to the bitter end.

The Palatian spirit that still lived inside him waxed greatly, romantic notions of glorious combat and the pursuit of total victory feeding the fire that drove him forward. He would follow Tyler Barron and his people to the depths of hell if need be, but he would never stop. Not until the enemy was crushed…or he and his people were dead.

Still, despite an upbringing immersed in the ideals of

Palatian warrior culture, Tulus had become somewhat of a modern figure among his people, and he'd learned much from his Confederation allies. He'd dared to think of a future for his nation based on something besides endless war and conquest.

That part of him had now receded, fallen back to the deepest darks of his mind. This war had not been a choice, it was not the result of Palatian aggression. The enemy had come to the Rim, invaded the space of his allies. This deadly struggle, a nightmare of endless conflict and death, was utterly just. It was everything his Palatian brethren had been born to face, and now they stood, the warrior might of his world, gathered together, standing beside their allies.

It he was destined to die, he could hardly think of a more fitting place.

But first, before the prospect of death, there was duty. There was a battle to win.

"We have bomber squadrons coming in, too…make sure they're linked. There is to be no reduction in evasive maneuvers during landing operations."

"Yes, your Supremacy."

Tulus leaned forward, shifting in his seat, the energy of battle making it almost impossible for him to remain still. He regretted that he'd had to send Cilian Globus back to Palatian. He knew his friend would always feel shame for missing the titanic struggle. But there had been more to his motivations than his stated purpose of increasing production of ships and arms. Globus carried secret orders with him, a communique that bade the Council to name him Imperator, should Tulus fall in battle. He would never know what he carried, not unless Tulus died in the fight, but it was the reason he had sent his friend away.

If the fleet lost the battle, Tulus knew the war was over. But he also knew the mantra of his people. *Never again.*

The Palatians had lived as slaves, once, and as a race, they had vowed they would die before they did so again.

Men and women, adults and children, young and old…they would fight the enemy to the death, in space, on the streets of their worlds, in the ruins of their homes. They would battle with lasers, bombs…sticks, if need be. If his people were to die, he would have them do so standing as warriors, and he wanted them to have a leader with the courage to make the final stand. A hopeless stand, perhaps, but at least something worthy of a song.

Tulus turned, even as the bridge lights dimmed with another shot from the primaries. "Come, Warder…take your seat next to me." He gestured toward the young Rigellus. The officer had been seated at a workstation along the periphery of the bridge, but now he stood up and made his way toward Tulus, grabbing hold of a rail as *Invictus* shook hard again.

"I am honored, your Supremacy." The young man looked strong and defiant. He was scared, Tulus was almost certain of that, but there was no visible trace of it.

"Your mother's memory gives us all pride, Warder. Let us fight this battle together, in her honor. Let us ride forth now to victory."

Tulus was far from sure the Grand Alliance fleet could win the fight, but there was enough old Palatian left in him to make himself believe it.

Chapter Thirty-Nine

CFS Constitution
Olyus System
Year 320 AC

The Second Battle of Megara – "I will destroy the first ship that runs!"

Dammit...we're so close, so damned close. And yet...

Clint Winters sat on *Constitution*'s bridge, trying to hide his waning hope from his spacers.

The attack had been the right call, he was still certain of that. Perpetually yielding the initiative, waiting for the stronger, more advanced enemy to come at them had been a recipe for certain defeat. The fleet had come close to driving the Hegemony forces back. He was sure of that. He could feel it.

It's those fortresses, those damned fortresses...

The orbital stations had exacted a terrible toll on the fleet.

The enemy battle line had fought viciously, too, but the bombers had battered those vessels, and taken dozens of them out of the line, at least at long range. By the time the two fleets had closed and opened up with their secondary broadsides, the fight had been almost dead even.

Except for the fire from the forts.

Hegemony railguns had become the fear of every Rim spacer, but the weapons housed in those partially-finished orbital platforms were something else again. Their projectiles were almost double the size of those fired by Hegemony battleships, and the damage they inflicted, even on the largest targets, was nothing short of catastrophic.

Winters had wondered, as the fleet moved forward, if the enemy had managed to complete the orbital defenses around Megara. He'd thought the likelihood was something like one chance in three, maybe even four. Until he'd seen the enemy battle line pulling back.

He'd known the instant he saw the Hegemony thrusters firing up across the line, and he'd had his hands on the comm immediately, ready to tell Barron the fleet had to pull back, to abort the attack.

But there had been no point. A retreat would have been difficult, and if the enemy pursued, it might have become a disaster. And the original rationale for the attack still remained. Standing on the defensive was a losing proposition.

But now so is advancing.

The forts were just too powerful. They would be the difference, the weight that brought the scale down on the Hegemony's side. The enemy would be battered, their losses immense, but they would win the fight.

"Admiral, flight control has one makeshift squadron refit and ready to go. They request permission to launch."

One squadron? He appreciated the motivation of his people, but what was one squadron going to do?

"Negative, Commander." He wasn't even sure *Constitution*'s battered bays could manage launch operations. "Let's focus on keeping the broadside firing." His ship's primaries were long gone, but at the current range, it hardly mattered. The larger array of laser cannon dished out as much damage as the more powerful, longer ranged guns.

Then, his mind drifted back, and he wondered for a few seconds if he should let the pilots launch, if he should allow them to die in their cockpits, and not on the bays, engulfed in flames.

* * *

"I need to speak to Admiral Barron...right now!" Olya Federov banged her hand hard on the hull of her Lightning. She was frustrated as hell, angry at the confusion and chaos that was taking hold across the fleet. It was understandable, of course. The battleships were engaged in a desperate fight, and there was massive damage everywhere. But she had one hundred eighty-two bombers ready to go, situated on more than a dozen ships. They were set to take off, and she was prepared to lead them. But there were no launch orders.

The size of her force was easy to disregard, perhaps, in terms of the bloated sensibilities of a fleet that had become accustomed to strike forces numbered in the thousands, but Barron needed everything he could get, and Federov knew that well. Still, she was getting nothing but confusion and bullshit from the fleet's flight crews, and claims that launch bays were out of operation.

Stara had *Dauntless's* people in line, but even the fleet's semi-formal flight operations director was having trouble getting the other crews to *move*.

"Olya...what is it? What can I do for you?" Barron's voice sounded dead, almost as though the fleet's commander, and the Confederation's greatest hero, had already given up. Federov knew that wasn't true, not exactly. At least, she knew the warrior inside him would never yield.

She wasn't as sure about the man, whom she counted among her small number of friends. She'd heard about *Hermes*, and she knew how close Barron had been to Andi

Lafarge. She could hear and feel that he had fallen into a deep black pit of despair, but Tyler Barron, the admiral, would be at his post, leading his spacers, until the enemy put him down. There was nothing she was more certain about than that.

And as much as she cared about the *man*, she needed the warrior-admiral just then.

"I've got almost two hundred bombers ready to launch, Admiral, veteran pilots in all of them, but there's chaos on most of the ships. You have to give a fleet order for us to launch."

"Olya…in this firefight? You must be crazy. It was enough of a miracle that so many of your people managed to land. You can't…"

"Admiral, please. Raptor sent me back, told me to get as many ships ready as I could. We can help, sir. I know it's not a lot of ships in a fight like this one…but I think we can hit those forts. They managed to get those heavy railguns operational, but my gut tells me they couldn't have finished everything in the time they had. There's a good bet they're low on anti-fighter weaponry…and the damned escorts are all lined up with their main fleet. Let me go, Admiral…let my people launch. I'll get them there, somehow. I'll take those forts down, whatever it takes."

There was silence on the line. She knew it was only a few seconds, but as she waited, it felt like hours. Finally, Barron's voice returned, and in it, she heard the slightest emotion, respect for her and her pilots. "Go, Lynx, lead your people. All ships are instructed to commence launch operations at your command."

"Thank you, sir." She could tell he didn't think her people had much of a chance, that two hundred fighters were nowhere near enough to reach those forts and take them out. That was true enough, by conventional standards. But there was nothing conventional about the current fight. Federov was convinced she could do what had to be done.

"Stara…" She flipped the channel back to the main flight control line. "Admiral Barron gave us the go ahead. Let's get these birds launched, and I do mean ten minutes ago!"

She reached above her head, pulling herself up the ladder two rungs at a time and hopping into the cockpit. She had a job to do, and by God, she was going to see it done.

* * *

Rogan's finger tightened on the trigger. He was finished, he knew that. The Kriegeri had hunted the two of them, caught them in their last refuge. He and Taylor were as good as dead. There was no time for anything, not remembrances, nor even final thoughts of any significance. But there was one thing he could do. Die fighting, and take out at least one of his killers.

He could feel the presence pushing through, into the room. It was time to fire. But something held him back.

He was never sure, then or later, what it was. The shape of the shadow, the sound of the boots on the gravel…something just wasn't right.

Then the figure burst into the room, bringing an assault rifle to bear.

A *Marine* assault rifle.

The man crouched just inside was filthy, his uniform torn to shreds and stained with dried blood in half a dozen places. But through the mess and the mire, Rogan knew one thing immediately.

He was looking at a Confederation Marine. One of his.

"General…we'd almost given up hope of finding you!" The man moved forward, even as three more Marines came through in rapid succession. "Corporal Wickers, sir! Captain Klevon sent us. We've been looking for you for hours."

"Captain Klevon?" Rogan was still half in shock, but his mind was chewing on what he was being told. Klevon had been with Prentice's group.

"You were with Colonel Prentice?" Rogan nodded as the corporal managed a salute, a good effort considering he was still half crouched down, rifle in hand.

"Yes, sir." Rogan knew, the instant he heard the man's tone. "The colonel didn't make it, General."

Rogan felt as though he'd just taken a punch to the gut. It was no real surprise. After all, *most* of his Marines were probably dead. But Prentice had served at his side for the past year and a half, and helped him hold the remnants of his battered force together. He ached for the loss of his friend.

"Where is Captain Klevon?" There wasn't much point in going on about Prentice. Not just then.

"He set up a temporary HQ in the transit tubes just outside the city. We've been trying to gather up as many survivors as we can find."

"And how many is that, Corporal?"

"There were just over eighty there when I left, sir, including the search teams."

Rogan was surprised. That was more than he'd expected. Not that eighty Marines were about to defeat three million Kriegeri, but it was still about eighty more than he'd expected to find.

He pulled himself up, painfully, to his feet, reaching out and grabbing the corporal's offered arm. "Well, we'd better get going. Captain Klevon and his people won't be able to stay so close to the city for long."

"No, sir. My orders are to bring any survivors back immediately."

"Then lead on, Corporal."

"Yes, General." A pause. "Perhaps I should go first, sir, and scout outside the building. There are Kriegeri everywhere."

Rogan just nodded. He was too tired, too battered to argue.

* * *

"Grand Admiral Epheseus is on the comm, Admiral."
Atara's tone told anyone listening exactly what she thought
of the commander of the contingent from the Far Rim's
Sultanate.

Barron wasn't in the mood for humoring pointless
nonsense from his officers, and especially not from those
from the small Far Rim nations. He appreciated the aid the
conglomeration of allies had provided, and he knew the
Confederation forces alone could not have turned the
Hegemony back at Craydon, nor launched the current
offensive. But he didn't have time to waste on some fool
with the absurd title of "grand admiral," commanding a fleet
of thirty odd rustbuckets, half of which would have been
more at home in his grandfather's day.

"Tell the admiral I have no time right now. He is to
continue according to the battle plan."

"Yes, Admiral."

Barron sat, staring ahead. For a few seconds, he'd almost
forgotten about Epheseus, but then he realized Atara was
still exchanging words with the officer. She was attempting
to remain respectful and diplomatic—and he knew that was
no easier for her than it was for him—but it was clear the
Sultanate admiral was refusing to accept his "no" for an
answer.

"Commander Travis, put me on fleet-wide
comm…now!" He snapped out the orders, his words tinged
with barely controlled rage. It wasn't directed at Atara, of
course, and he was sure she knew that. But he was going to
make things clear to the pack of petty officers and lordlings
out there in the fleet, most of whom greatly overstated their
importance and their usefulness. They had seen Tyler
Barron, the celebrated admiral, the appreciative ally, grateful
for aid and assistance.

Now they were going to see something darker, the
essence of what would win the fight, if anything would. The
darkness that lived within Barron, the living nightmare,
inflamed by the stress of battle and painful personal loss.

They think they're afraid of the enemy...

"Attention all contingent and ship commanders, all
officers and spacers of the fleet. We are engaged in a
desperate fight now. Whatever discussions there might have
been on strategy and tactics...the time for all of that is past.
The next hours will determine victory or defeat, survival or
death, not just for us, but perhaps for all the people in our
nations. There is no time for anything now but absolute and
unerring obedience. There will be no change of plans, no
retreat, no reorganization. Fight now, all of you. Fight as
you've never fought before. All our lives depend on it."

He paused, just for a second, and when he continued, his
tone was even darker, more malevolent than it had been.
"We have all suffered losses, made sacrifices, and no doubt
more are to come. But I say this now, and any who doubt
me for an instant do so at their own grave peril. If it comes
down to a choice between killing an enemy, or a black
traitor whose hands are still wet with blood from the knife
shoved into my back, have no doubt what I will choose. *No
doubt.* This fleet will fight to the end, and make no
mistake...I will destroy the first ship that runs! Even if such
action hands the Rim to the Hegemony!"

Barron ripped the headset off and tossed it aside.
Dauntless's bridge was silent, no sounds save the whining of
the batteries firing. For an instant, Barron wasn't sure if he'd
gone too far, if the darkness he'd unleashed had unnerved
even his most loyal officers and spacers.

Then, it began. He didn't know who had started it, but it
was soft at first, almost inaudible. Then it grew in volume as
more voices joined in. It rose and rose, until it was almost
deafening, the sounds of voices pushed as hard as possible,

and then also booted feet slamming on the polished metal floor.

It was a chant, one that left no doubt where his people stood, at least on *Dauntless*.

"Barron…Barron…Barron…Barron!"

Chapter Forty

Platform Aryantis
Orbiting Megara, Olyus III
Year of Renewal 265 (320 AC)

The Second Battle of Megara – "It's those forts or us…only one survives"

"All fortress batteries are to maintain maximum fire, Kiloron. Engineering teams are to monitor reactors and energy transmission systems constantly. There are to be no interruptions in the frequency of attacks. Is that understood?" Chronos could see the officer almost cowering under the onslaught of his words. The Kriegeri was not a coward. He had seen to it himself, that only the very best had been assigned to the fortresses. But taking combat orders directly from Number Eight of the Hegemony was simply more than the officer was equipped to handle.

"Yes, Number Eight, as you command." The Kriegeri saluted, and he turned and hurried off to relay the orders.

Chronos turned and looked out over the control room. The orbital platform was a mess, entire sections unfinished, cluttered with construction materials, long cables laying along the floor, serving as temporary connections between systems.

These platforms are wrecks, not even close to ready for action.
And they might very well be the fulcrum of victory.

Chronos had ordered the railguns and their supporting power systems to be made operational almost immediately after the basic structures of the fortresses had been completed. Even then, as he stood in the center of the partially functional control room, almost half the station's enclosed space remained vacuum, vast stores of supplies and electronic equipment sat piled on landing bays, and virtually none of the enormous proposed command and control systems were operational. Fire control for the main guns was almost the single exception to that, and Chronos understood by just how slim a margin the forts were maintaining the deadly barrage.

He might have claimed credit for detailed foresight, for his wisdom in ensuring that the stations were ready to support the fleet in repelling an enemy attack. But the past several years had been full of humbling experiences, and whatever proclivities Chronos had ever had for unrestrained self-congratulation were long gone.

He did not even know why he'd insisted on beginning with the railguns. The size of them, perhaps, the concern that installation of such vast systems would be difficult once other sections of the stations had been completed. Or even just a whim. But he knew it would be a lie to say, even to himself, that he had anticipated the need to defend Megara from a full-scale enemy attack would have arisen so soon.

In truth, the appearance of the Confederation fleet and its allies had stunned him. He had not seriously considered it as a possibility. He had underestimated his adversaries yet again, and he had allowed them to take him by surprise.

Only to be bailed out by the gut instinct, or whatever it had been, that had given him thirty massive railguns, each half again the size of the largest shipborne units, and every one of them operational and ready to fire.

Those guns have been the difference. Without them, the enemy's audacity might have paid off.

Very probably would have…

"Commander, the scanners are detecting incoming small craft."

Chronos turned abruptly, his eyes moving toward the small screen, the only one in the control center that was operational, beyond the railgun targeting systems. There was a faint cloud, a cluster of tiny dots. They had been moving on a course that appeared to be toward the fleet's battle line, just one more wave of the hated enemy bombers moving on the line of battleships.

The station's skeletal crew had barely paid attention. Even the temporary AI operating the fort's systems had not identified the ships as a threat to any of the forts.

Then, they changed course.

Their thrust vectors had been indeterminate at first, but now it was completely clear. They were heading toward Megara. Toward the fortresses.

Of course…the only heavy guns out of range of their battleships…

The guns that are really gutting their forces.

Chronos felt a wave of frustration he could barely contain. He was the eighth most genetically perfect human being in existence, a genius by every definable measure of mental ability. He had excelled at every endeavor in his life…until he had come to the Rim.

The Rim dwellers were violent, and resourceful. They had fought each other almost without pause for over a century. Their genetics might lag his and those of his top commanders—with their chaotic breeding rituals, they almost certainly did—but they were masters of war. No matter how carefully he planned operations, how meticulously he organized his forces, they found a way to survive, if not to prevail.

Now they were coming toward the fortresses, and he knew immediately, they were there to take out the heavy guns.

Chronos did not respond to the report. He just watched, his mind racing, his eyes focused on the approaching strike force.

It was small, fewer than two hundred of the attack craft. Nowhere close to enough to take out the fortresses, if they had any of their defense grids up.

Which they did not.

Not one of the fortresses had an active point defense network. The anti-assault batteries were just one of the things that had been postponed to allow the ship-killing railguns to be made operational.

"Kiloron, send a communique to Commander Illius immediately. He is to detach two divisions of escorts at once to intercept the bombers moving on the fortresses." But even as the words came out of his mouth, he knew his actions were too late.

"Yes, Commander." The Kriegeri turned, but before he could carry out Chronos's orders, the Master spoke again.

"How many escorts are in position in and around Megara orbit?"

There was a pause, as the officer turned and leaned over one of the workstations. "Twenty-three, Commander. Nine currently in orbit, and fourteen close enough to be in position before the enemy strike arrives."

Chronos could feel his fists clench. For all the massive forces locked in battle in the system, he realized it could all very well come down to those twenty-three escorts fighting to blunt the attack of a dozen enemy squadrons.

* * *

"On me, all of you. Ignore those escorts. Ignore any defensive fire. We're here for one purpose, and one purpose only. To take down those fortresses." Olya Federov looked down at her scanner. There were almost two hundred enemy frigates and cruisers coming up behind her strike force, but they weren't going to make it in time. She'd kept her people driving their ships hard, blasting at full thrust without regard to safety margins or fuel status. Only one thing mattered. Hitting those fortresses, taking those massive railguns out of the battle. It was what the fleet needed. If her people could do it, there was a chance that the desperate attack on Megara could actually succeed.

Her eyes moved slightly, from the hundreds of escorts that could not prevent her attack, to the twenty-odd that could. The enemy ships formed a line less than fifty thousand kilometers from the planet, waiting for her people to move into range.

She thought about accelerating, increasing her ships' velocities as much as possible to reduce the time they would have the endure the enemy's fire, but she held back. Her strike force wasn't attacking a group of ships in deep space. They were hitting fortresses in Megara orbit. They had to come in and engage those stations, and that meant keeping velocities low…and taking all the fire the enemy could give.

She could see the escorts' point defense guns firing already, flashes on her display all around her formation. The pilots following her were mostly veterans, and she had more than two dozen aces in the group. That was helpful, and the skill of her pilots would certainly reduce the effectiveness of the incoming fire. But there was an element of luck there, too. She'd known some incredible pilots, men and women who were killed when their luck ran out, when their intuition failed them at the wrong moment.

She saw one of her ships vanish, followed almost immediately by another. Enemy fire lanced out, great pulses of concentrated laser energy ripping by her bombers. The ships themselves were conducting wild evasive maneuvers, at least as much as possible, but with their targets in tight orbit around Megara, they were forced to exercise more restraint than they would have in open space.

That would increase the death total, too.

Her own hand moved, executing a seemingly random sequence of changes. It was smaller and of shorter duration that she might have tried in a conventional fight, but so far, she'd managed to keep herself out of trouble. A dozen of her people had been hit, and at least eight of those destroyed outright, but the force continued on, unbroken and unbowed.

She stared ahead, seeing the large circle on her screen, a blue disk growing larger with each passing second. Megara.

Her ships were close to the enemy escorts now, and the fire was growing heavier. But it wasn't enough to stop the strike force. Her people would make it past the escorts, at least.

Enough of them to get the job done.

That was a guess…or a hope. She wasn't sure which. She hadn't even been convinced the entire strike force was enough. The answer would depend on the status of those forts. If their defense grids were fully online, and as powerful as she imagined they would be after five years of bombers ravaging Hegemony ships, her people had no chance.

They had to close to point blank range. The gravitational effects of the planet, and even traces of the upper atmosphere added massively to the difficulty of targeting. Her people were flying in at low velocity, and that meant they could come within a hundred kilometers or less of the targets.

At that range, a strong point defense network would blast her ships to atoms.

There was no way to know, no point in speculating. The fleet *needed* those forts silenced, and her strike force, now down to fewer than one hundred sixty ships, was the only chance of that happening.

They were past the escorts, but still in their range. The fire from behind was heavy, but all Federov could think of was how grateful she was they'd only had to face a thin line of enemy frigates. Hundreds of ships were racing back from the battle line's position, and they would have eradicated her entire formation if they had been in position.

It was a difference of fifteen minutes, maybe twenty. But she knew it could decide the battle.

She watched a flash on the scanner, the first enemy shot that had really threatened her. It had been close enough to make the hair on her neck stand up.

But she had more important things to think about than enemy fire. The forts were visible now on her display, and the readout showed the range dropping rapidly. It was time.

She flipped on the comm, opening the channel to all her people. "We're here. It's time. It's those forts or us...only one survives."

She angled her ship, setting up for her attack run. The fire from the escorts had dropped off. She knew the frigates were coming about, looking to enter orbit and close again, but it gave her people the time they needed. She was still nervous about fire from the platforms themselves, but the strike force was well within range, and there hadn't been a shot fired.

Was it possible? Were the unfinished stations truly devoid of any operational point defense networks?

Her eyes fixed on the biggest fort. It was straight ahead, less than a thousand kilometers from her position. That was insanely close by the standards of most space combat, but she going to come in a lot *closer* than that.

She was decelerating hard as she made the approach, slowing her ship almost to a standstill. Her hand gripped the throttle, her finger on the firing stud as her ship roared in, dropping below five hundred kilometers.

Four hundred...three hundred...

* * *

Chronos stood and stared at the display, watching in horror as the enemy bomber flew right toward the station. The ship was less than two hundred kilometers out, and two dozen others were following right behind. His thin line of escorts had done what they could, and he had enough force on the way to obliterate every bomber out there, at least five times over.

But it was going to be too late. Battles were decided by numbers, tactics…and by time. The stations were large, but their armor plating was incomplete, their defense nets non-existent. He knew he was going to lose them to the enemy attack, most likely by a margin of fifteen minutes.

He was standing there right in the center of the biggest target on the enemy scanners. Chronos was not afraid. He was no coward. Even the thought of never meeting his new child failed to break him down. But he worried about his fleet, about the battle and what would happen if the stations were destroyed.

And he was worried about who would see to getting Akella out of the system, if need be.

He almost despaired, but he knew, if he did not survive, Illius would see it done. His second-in-command was highly capable…and a friend.

He will make sure Akella is safe…and our child too.

That thought was still on his mind when the station shook wildly, as one plasma torpedo after another slammed into its massive hull. Chronos spun around, staring at the display, and shouting across the room for damage reports.

But before he got an answer, an explosion rocked the control center. A wall of flame ripped across the deck, and slammed into him.

Pain, unimaginable pain, and then something else, a cool feeling, the searing heat gone.

The fire suppression system, his mind told him…*it is one of the active systems.*

But the lucidity lasted only a few seconds, and then it was gone. The fire was gone, but the pain endured, even increased. He cried out, the sound of his own voice seeming somehow distant.

Then he fell, and as he did there was relief, numbness.

Darkness.

Chapter Forty-One

CFS Dauntless
Olyus System
Year 320 AC

The Second Battle of Megara – "The time for victory is here!"

"*Resplendent* has been destroyed, Admiral. And *Commitment*. The Palatian contingent has lost *Varianus*, as well, and...*Invictus* is severely damaged."

Barron had been half-listening to Atara's casualty reports. He knew it was her job as his aide, and miraculously, she'd not only managed it flawlessly, but none of her duties as the head of his staff seemed to reduce her effectiveness as *Dauntless*'s captain. But as much as he knew she had no choice but to sound off as each ship went down, he really didn't want to hear it. He'd led them all to Megara, and he'd already accepted that whatever fate befell them all, it was his fault.

But, for the first time, none of that mattered He was already morose, teetering on the edge of a pit of black despair, held out only by the iron bands of duty. Duty to the Confederation, to stand at his post until the very end, to bring every bit of fight that remained in him to the enemy.

And duty to those spacers he'd led into the very maw of hell's fire. He didn't care if he survived the battle, not anymore, but he owed every spacer in the fleet, sweating and bleeding and fighting with the last of their strength, his very best to bring them back home.

Through his hazy comprehension of the casualty reports, though, the name *Invictus* struck him hard. The Palatian flagship carried Vian Tulus, the Imperator and a man he trusted completely.

He turned toward Atara, and he almost ordered her to set up a line to *Invictus*. But he held back. Telling Vian Tulus to pull back at the height of the battle, in the moment when victory or defeat would be decided, would be utterly pointless…and he wouldn't shame his brother with even the suggestion that the Imperator might retreat. There was no point.

Take care of yourself, Vian. We need you. The fight needs you.

He leaned back and closed his eyes, just for a second, when Atara spoke again.

"Admiral…we're picking up new transits." A pause. "It's Captain Eaton's ships, sir…at least some of them." Another delay, perhaps ten seconds. "And Hegemony battleships coming in right behind her, Admiral. Six so far…no, seven…"

Barron turned and looked at the display, watching as the eighth, and then the ninth enemy monster transited. It was enough force to turn the tide, to give the Hegemony the victory, even if Federov's bombers managed to knock out the orbital platforms.

But was it too late? Could his people finish the fight before the enemy reinforcements could close and turn the tide?

Had Eaton delayed them for just enough time?

Or not quite long enough?

* * *

"Admiral Barron, we're breaking off. All torpedoes launched. Our scans indicate all platforms are disabled, all railguns destroyed." Federov was energized. Her report to the admiral would take about four minutes to reach *Dauntless*, and any response just as long to return, but she didn't need to hear Barron's voice to know she and her people had done their duty. They had taken out the greatest threat to the Grand Alliance's battle line, and preserved a real chance for victory in the desperate fight still raging.

Her people had paid a terrible cost for that accomplishment, however. Almost one third of their number was gone. But their victory had been total, and they'd obliterated the Hegemony fortresses. There hadn't been a single point defense turret operational on one of the giant constructs, and her ships had pushed their attack to the limit, launching from fifty kilometers, and even closer.

The plasma torpedoes had torn the partially-armored stations apart. It was a victory for her small strike force, one beyond what she'd hoped for.

But now her people faced the trip back to their landing platforms…straight through the escorts that had failed to hit them before their attack. Her squadrons had suffered terribly already, but the realization that their torment wasn't over quickly dampened the joy at their success.

"We've got to get past these escorts. Our torpedoes are gone, we've got no mission left, no duty save to get back home. We're flying for ourselves now, so keep up on those evasive maneuvers, and follow me."

She swung her own ship around, blasting hard, trying to make for the extreme flank of the enemy formation. There was no way to escape running the gauntlet back past the escorts, at least none the fuel status of her squadrons would allow, but she could at least minimize the number of enemy vessels that could maintain a fire arc.

She stared at her display as she pushed forward, watching as her pilots formed up behind her. The entire strike force would plow through the escort line in one long column, driving as hard as they could for their mother ships.

Her velocity wasn't what she would have liked. The need to come to almost a stop for the orbital attack had left her people building up thrust from nothing. It was going to take several minutes to clear the line of escorts, and even more if the Hegemony ships responded and pursue her formation.

It was going to cost.

Her people were on their own now. There was no tactic, no formation she could devise to further deflect the enemy attacks. Evasive maneuvers would help, the wilder the better, but beyond that there was a cold and simple fact.

The lucky ones would get through, and the unlucky ones…

She was startled as a shot ripped by, seeming like it was just outside her cockpit. A quick look at the display told her it had been nearly half a kilometer away—close, but not as close as it had seemed.

She'd become used to battles where she never got the slightest glance at an enemy, nor saw any signs of the fire coming her way. Distances in space combat were vast, and laser pulses were often invisible. Seeing a shot, a near miss, depended on a series of random factors…distance, sufficient particulate matter to make a laser burst visible, looking at just the right instant and at the precise, required angle. It was unnerving to actually *see* a laser pulse, but in the end, a miss was a miss.

She dodged another half dozen close shots, but then one of them got her.

Her first realization was that it hadn't been a direct hit. She knew that mostly because she was still there. Her ship was in bad shape, though, and the cockpit reeked of burned machinery. Her eyes teared from the caustic vapors in the air, though it seemed her life support was still operational.

Her thrusters were badly damaged, and she could feel almost constant variation as the battered ship's engines ranged in output. The throttle shook, and she struggled to maintain control as she worked her dying ship into a course toward *Dauntless*.

She was sure her inability to effectively control evasive maneuvers would be the end of her, and she waited, expecting the killing shot to come at any moment. But she made it through, and a quick glance at her display told her just under a hundred of her people had as well. They were heading back, making their final approaches toward the fleet. The landings would be difficult, the battleships still heavily engaged with their Hegemony counterparts, but she was confident her people could manage it.

She gripped the throttle harder, trying to keep her ship on course. The variation in her engines was getting worse. She'd make it back to *Dauntless*, or at least she had a good chance of getting that far, but she had no idea how she was going to get her shimmying, barely functioning bomber back into the landing bay.

One step at a time. First, you've got to hold this thing together and get there…

* * *

"Commander…we are receiving scanning reports from the edge of the system." The officer's voice was silent for a moment before continuing. "We are picking up enemy craft, mostly the small, unarmed carriers…but there are also larger contacts."

"Positive identification?" An instant later. "Now, Kiloron! I need to know what those ships are." Illius had been sitting silently, trying to decide what to do. He had sent three comm signals to the main orbital station, seeking orders from Chronos. But the commander had not responded.

No one had responded.

By all accounts, the fortresses were in ruins, torn to

pieces by the enemy bomber attack. Illius did not dare imagine the worst…and yet, Chronos *had* been on the main platform, and he had not responded to any of Illius's comm attempts.

Illius could not ignore the possibility that the decision of what to do—to hold and fight to the end, or to retreat from the system while there was still a chance to escape—would be his to make.

He had wanted to stay, to invoke his warrior's mantra and dig in for the final fight. But the choice was not so simple. If he risked the rest of the fleet, if he allowed his surviving ships to be trapped and defeated, the damage to the Hegemony would be disastrous. It would be years, even decades before such losses—not only in ships, but also in experienced personnel—could be replaced.

Perhaps most crucially, Akella was on Megara. If the fleet became trapped, so too would Number One. Illius lacked Chronos's personal relationship with Akella, of course, but his loyalty to Number One was without limit. He could not allow her to be captured, not matter what else happened.

He would not allow it.

He had been about to issue orders for the retreat, when the new contacts emerged.

"They're ours, Commander. Energy profiles indicate *Calphazon* and *Philoran* class battleships. It looks like the scheduled relief column."

Illius felt relief, and a short flash of excitement. There were sixteen of the contacts, enough strength to make the difference in the desperate fight between the two exhausted battle lines.

The feeling did not last, though. The new ships were powerful, but they were too far out in the system to intervene in time, and the concerns about Akella's presence remained. He might gamble ships on victory, or even his own life.

He could not risk Number One.

The new battleships could help with the retreat, though. They could hold the route to the secondary transit point long enough to evacuate the fleet...and to get Akella off Megara. It would be a longer route back to the base at Dannith, but the shorter primary course would require fighting through the entire Confederation fleet.

"Commander, we are receiving a report from Platform Aryantis. They are down to battery power. All weapons are offline." A pause. "Megaron! Number Eight is there. He is gravely wounded, but still alive."

Any thoughts of remaining that Illius had been nursing were gone. He *had* to extricate the fleet, and he had to do it now.

"Send a fast transport to Megara. They are to pick up Number One and bring her to *Hegemony's Glory* at all possible speed. They are not to advise launch control or any ground personnel of their purpose or their plans. Maximum possible security is to be maintained."

He was about to leave three million Kriegeri behind, as well as thousands of other officers and personnel. The Hegemony forces were disciplined and trained to obey without question. But he was not going to take any chances. "And send a medical shuttle to Aryantis Station to pick up Commander Chronos."

Chronos was his superior, and his mentor. He did not know if there was any chance Number Eight would survive, but he knew he could not leave him behind. Not if there was any chance of getting him out.

"All fleet units, prepare to receive nav orders and to execute on my command."

Illius sat silently for a moment. He was stunned, as he knew Chronos had been. He found it difficult to believe he was ordering the second major retreat in as many battles. Craydon had been a setback, a delay...but he knew, after this battle, the enemy's councils of war would be heavy with talk of turning points and victory.

If those battleships had gotten here even a few hours sooner…

But ifs were of no value, and neither was self-recrimination or doubt. Not then. He had a fleet to extricate, and two leaders to save.

And, notwithstanding enemy self-congratulation, there *would* be another fight, another day…and the chances of success in that conflict would rest largely on how much force he managed to extricate from the Olyus system in the next hours.

*   *   *

"The time for victory is here, Palatians! Forward, with whatever power remains to your battered ships. Forward, with whatever endurance you have in your exhausted bones. Show your ancestors, those who sired you, who raised you, who prepared you with stories of battle and glory, of just what you are made. Forward now, all of you, with me, to our destiny."

Tulus stood in the center of *Invictus*'s bridge. The battleship was battered, and there was debris scattered everywhere. Half the workstations, at least, were dark, knocked out by power failures or fried by internal fires. There were casualties, too, three dead on the bridge, still lying there where they'd fallen—and at least two hundred on the ship as a whole. The weapons arrays were shattered messes, the broadside down to three functional turrets. The Palatian Imperator knew his flagship was on its last legs, that any hit from the enemy battle line could be the one to cut through its crumbling armor and blast its reactors to scrap. A nanosecond's failure in any of the power units would be enough for the fusion reactions to turn the vessel into a miniature sun.

But Tulus didn't even consider withdrawal. Not then. Not when the battle was being decided.

Every gun was needed, every shot could be the one that

pushed one side or the other to victory. It was *that* close. Tulus's heart was that of the warrior. Even if his honor had allowed him to consider falling back—and it didn't—he could never have left his brother's side. Tyler Barron and *Dauntless* were still in the fight, and *Invictus* would remain there too. Allies, fighting together to the end, to victory…or to death.

Tulus only had one regret. His eyes moved briefly to Warder Rigellus. The young officer had moved across the bridge, sitting at one of the tactical stations next to the body of the officer who had previously occupied it. Katrine Rigellus's son had conducted himself with courage, and he had behaved in exemplary fashion.

Palatian custom was to celebrate a warrior's death, not to mourn it, to think well of one who had fallen in noble combat. But the thought of Katrine's son dying during his first battle, on the namesake of her last ship, the one she had died on, found a weak spot in his Palatian armor. He'd have sent the young officer away, if that had been remotely feasible.

Or if he'd been able to do it without disgracing the youthful sub-commander.

Invictus shook again, and he could hear the creaking deep in the vessel as her main structural supports began to give out. He turned and looked again at the display, even as he began to believe he would not survive the battle. He could accept that. Surely, death in such a climactic fight would be honorable. He could die without shame, even in the eyes of his heroic ancestors.

Then he saw it.

The display was damaged, like almost everything else on *Invictus*, but even through the wavy image and dim symbols, it was clear.

They were pulling back.

The Hegemony fleet was retreating!

Renewed strength flooded into his arms, his legs, and he

raised his hand into the air. "The enemy is retreating! Forward, with whatever thrust we can generate. All weapons, maintain fire. It is time for the final measure. Onward to victory!"

Chapter Forty-Two

Free Trader Pegasus
Olyus System
Year 320 AC

The Second Battle of Megara – "It's over, my God, it's over."

Andi Lafarge sat and watched the small screen on *Pegasus*'s bridge. The tiny room was crowded, especially since she'd let half a dozen of the *Hermes* crew come forward. She'd done all she could to make her rescued spacers as comfortable as possible, but she had six or seven times *Pegasus*'s maximum complement on board, and everything was on critical overload. Life support, sanitary facilities, even food and water. But *Pegasus* wasn't a warship. It couldn't survive even minutes in a battle like the one raging across the system. Her only chance had been to stay hidden, to rely on the stealth device holding out for just a bit longer.

She was still stunned at their nearly miraculous escape from *Hermes*. Whatever Hegemony commander had been hunting the doomed cruiser, he had been relentless, and highly skilled. She'd been hesitant to believe her trick of sliding *Pegasus* out of the cruiser's hull could actually work, that it might fool the seemingly unstoppable Hegemony commander.

But it had. She'd never know, she suspected, how much of that she owed to the fleet's arrival, and to the diversion the resulting systemwide alert had to have had on the ships that had chased down and destroyed *Hermes*. Would her hunter have continued searching, would he have detected some emission or anomaly that might have given him a scent of *Pegasus*? She would never know.

She wondered if that Hegemony officer was still alive. The losses on both sides had been beyond horrifying, and the dead numbered in the tens of thousands, if not hundreds of thousands. She'd managed to keep an eye on a single Confederation ship she was almost sure was *Dauntless*. It was badly damaged, but still there, and that gave her hope that Tyler had survived.

She was still looking at the screen when she saw the Hegemony battle line shudder, almost as one. It took her a few seconds to realize what was happening...and a few more to convince herself it really was true.

They're withdrawing. The Hegemony forces are withdrawing.

She felt her eyes becoming watery, her hands almost shaking at her sides. She'd known intellectually that the fleet had a chance in the fight, but she realized in that moment, she had never truly believed it.

Now, she looked out at the symbols on the display, and she watched as the Hegemony ships blasted their thrusters. Yes, her first thought was correct. They were breaking off from the fight.

She leaned back in her chair as she heard the chatter spreading around her, as everyone present began to realize just what they were watching. She stared at the display again, confirming that *Pegasus* was alone, that there were no enemy ships in range or heading her way.

She'd managed to make it better than halfway back toward the fleet. That was close enough. It was time.

"Lex…" She leaned over the comm unit, taking another breath before she continued. "…you've done a magnificent job keeping that stealth unit operational. But I think it's done its job for us, my friend. Cut it off…now."

She leaned back again, holding the small microphone in her hand as her fingers moved over the controls, switching to the fleetcom channel. It was time to let the fleet know they were there.

Time to let Tyler know. God only knew what had been going through his mind.

She wasn't sure what to say, what kind of message to send. As she sat there, a single thought was moving through her mind, again and again, the same thing.

The battle is over. My God, it's over…

*   *   *

"Tyler!" Atara Travis's voice was a high-pitched screech, as unlike his longtime comrade as anything he'd ever heard. His insides tensed, wondering what kind of new crisis she could have found, what would have so unnerved the stone-cold veteran.

"What is it, Atara?" Barron had begun to allow himself to believe his people had won the victory, and the thought of some new disaster was more than he thought he could take.

"A new contact…it just appeared on the display. The stealth unit…they must have shut down the stealth unit." She was excited, he realized, not panicked. Happy.

"What are you talking about, Atara?"

"*Pegasus*, Admiral. We're picking up *Pegasus* on the scanners."

The words hit Barron like a brick. It wasn't possible, was it? She was dead. He hadn't even begun to figure out how he was going to move past her death, but he hadn't doubted it, not since he'd watched with his own eyes as *Hermes* was destroyed.

But he could see the contact, too, a small blue circle in the display, where no ship had been seconds before.

Can it be? He struggled to maintain his composure, as a flood of hope and despair and rage and vengeance swirled around inside him, like some titanic storm.

Then, Atara spoke again, and his doubts poured away, like water flowing from holes in the bottom of a container.

"Tyler, we have an incoming communique. It's Captain Lafarge, Admiral...for you."

* * *

Olya Federov pulled her hand back abruptly as a shower of sparks flew up around her fighter's controls. The ship was on its last legs, coming in far too fast to even attempt a landing. She was frantically trying to get the ship's systems operational enough to get back to *Dauntless*, but she was losing hope with each passing second.

She was wounded. She hadn't even noticed as she'd struggled to get her battered ship back on course toward the fleet. She'd felt the warm wetness first, blood she'd quickly realized, and then the pain began to register.

Now her arm was numb, and she could see the electrical burns on her fingers, her hand. Her lungs were like fire, the mix of caustic chemicals leaking from her ship's systems poisoning what remained of her air. She wasn't the sort to give up...ever. But she realized she wasn't going to be able to land. She doubted she could get her ship to *Dauntless*, and even if she did, she couldn't risk closing the sole open landing bay on the battered warship. There were still fifty of her people coming in, and they were all low on fuel.

I'll have to eject...hope for the best.

She was far from *Dauntless*, from any of the fleet's battleships. Too far. It would take incredible luck for a retrieval boat to find her in time, especially with the Hegemony fleet still in the system. The two forces had ceased fire, and they were warily eyeing each other, the Hegemony ships seemingly content to withdraw if they were allowed to do so unmolested, and the exhausted Grand Alliance fleet happy to watch them go if they were of a mind to do so.

Still, the situation was far from ideal. Perhaps if she tried again, even a few bursts of well-aimed thrust could get her closer…

Then she felt heat. And more pain, searing agony. The air in the cockpit was now thick with brown smoke, and she could feel the fire raging just behind her, consuming what remained of her ship's oxygen. She pulled the visor of helmet down and buttoned up her survival gear, wincing in pain with almost every move. Then she hit the eject controls.

Nothing.

She did it again, and a third time.

Still nothing.

Damn!

She reached down, pulled the cover off the control panel, and shoved her fingers down, clawing at the mechanism. The cockpit was an inferno, and she knew her survival suit was the only thing keeping her alive in the blazing heat. She'd switched to bottled air when she pulled on the helmet, and that, at least, was fresh and cool.

But if she didn't get out of her ship in the next few seconds, she knew she never would.

She yanked at the controls again, almost frantically…and then, she felt something.

Her seat jerked hard, and she was pushed up, and then new pain, the feeling of bones breaking.

She was floating, out of her ship, drifting through space. She wasn't sure what had happened. Her best guess was the cockpit hadn't entirely broken away, and her right shoulder and leg had slammed hard into it as she ejected.

The pain from her injuries was almost unbearable, and she remained as still as she could, floating in the void—grateful, at least, for the lack of gravity pushing down on shattered bones and ravaged tissue. Whatever rationality remained to her focused at first on the unlikely stroke of luck that her survival suit had remained spaceworthy. That would buy her another few hours, if she didn't die from her wounds.

But she realized a rescue was a terrific long shot. A quick glance at one of the readouts inside her helmet told her all she needed to know.

The shock of the ejection, of the crash against the cockpit, had damaged her transponder.

Without that signal, whatever small chance she had of being found had plunged exponentially. She'd made it out of her ship…barely.

But that was as far as she was going to go.

At least we won the battle. She tried to gain solace from that, to keep her last thoughts on victory rather than despair.

The last casualty…she'd come all this way, fought hard, brought her people back, and was probably going to die right here.

At least we won. She repeated the thought, the only one she had that wasn't dark and grim.

It was a bright side, after all. If she had to die, far better to do it in victory.

Olya Federov had always hated losing.

She grew faint, felt her clarity fading away, wondering with what strength remained to her if she would go down in the history texts as the last casualty of the Second Battle of Megara.

Epilogue

Sickbay
CFS Dauntless

"She's been fighting at my side for so long, I can't remember launching without her...out there somewhere." Jake Stockton stood over the medpod that held Olya Federov. The pilot was critically injured. She'd been almost the last casualty of the battle, and she'd been given up for dead until Stockton took his fighter out with the rescue boats. He refused to give up on her, and somehow, he'd managed to pick up the faint signal of her badly damaged transponder. She'd been close to dead when they'd gotten her back. In fact, she probably had *been* dead, though not so far gone that the med team hadn't been able to resuscitate her.

Stockton had been a fixture at her bedside ever since. He'd haunted the doctors and the med techs, but he still hadn't been able to get a straight answer to a simple question. "Is she going to make it?"

He was harassing them for an answer he knew they didn't have. None of them knew. It was *that* close.

He'd seen comrades recover from grievous wounds before...and he'd watched others die. Federov was one hell of a fighter, he knew that much. If anybody was going to hang on and find the way back, it was her.

Stara Sinclair nestled closer to him, her arm wrapped around his back, looking down silently at his side. Sinclair had known Federov as long as Stockton had, and the two had been close friends for years. Federov had always been somewhat of a loner, but all those select few who'd come into her small circle of friends thought only the best of her. That group included Stockton and Sinclair, of course, but also Tyler Barron and Atara Travis. And Dirk Timmons, who'd struggled back a few years before from his own almost-fatal wounds. They had all been in sickbay, passing through in a kind of ongoing vigil, as though they believed their thoughts and support could bring her back. Perhaps they could.

"She's strong, Jake. You know that. She'll make it."

Stockton wasn't sure if he thought Stara was being sincere, and even if she was, if she'd simply let her emotions take over and control her judgment. No one had seen more pilots die than Stara. She'd sat in flight control, trying to talk damaged ships back in, listening to the final, terrified words of more doomed pilots than he could easily count. She was tough, he knew that. But everybody had their limit.

Even you, Jake. You have a limit too, no matter what nonsense you tell yourself…

He closed his eyes, just for a few seconds. The warmth of Stara standing next to him was a source of comfort, something that had become a rarity in his life. He was devastated at the thought of losing another old friend, but he was greedy for the feelings Stara gave him. He'd driven himself like a machine during the battle, fighting constantly and without rest for days. He hadn't even realized how close he'd come to breaking until he'd stopped…and the fatigue and heartache hit him all at once.

There was good news, though. The battle had been a victory, the second in a row won against the enemy. The

Hegemony fleet hadn't been destroyed, and it hadn't been sent fleeing back to its distant home far across the Badlands. But it *had* been pushed back from Megara. Even if the planet itself was still held by three million entrenched Kriegeri.

He didn't know what was next. He had an idea of the losses the fleet had suffered, and one thing he could read from those grim figures was the reality that there would be no more offensives, no operations of any kind…for a long while. The fleet had to repair itself and rebuild, and that would take time.

Enough time for Federov to recover, to be ready for the war's next phase. If she recovered at all.

He looked down at her one more time. "Come on, Olya. You can make it. I know you can."

He said the words, but he wasn't sure he believed them. He hoped she would survive, that she would return to duty…but he just didn't know what he really expected.

Just like he didn't know what was next for the fleet, or for the Confederation.

For any of them.

Hegemony's Glory
Orbiting Dannith

"The enemy's recapture of Megara, or at least of the system itself, was unfortunate. Perhaps, though, it was not as disastrous a loss as we may have believed. Our logistics are greatly simplified by the pullback of the main fleet to Dannith, and the enemy was so badly damaged in their victory, they have been unable even to attempt the recovery of any of the other occupied systems. We were only at Olyus because we had hoped a quick capture of their capital would lead to a widespread capitulation, but we already knew that was a failure even before the enemy retook the system."

Akella sat next to the medical unit, talking softly to Chronos. Her military commander, her friend—and at the current time, her mate—lay there, listening to her words, but rarely offering any of his own. His wounds were severe, nearly fatal, but Hegemony medical science was highly advanced, and he was already recovering. Physically, at least. His spirit and his morale were proving to be more obstinate problems, which was so unlike Chronos, it had her very concerned.

"You must shake this melancholy, Chronos. There is no time for it. We still have work to do, and there is no one else I would trust with it. I should have returned to the capital weeks ago…but I could not leave until I knew you would recover. Fully…physically, mentally, emotionally. Your body has begun to heal, and now it is time to drive away whatever ill feelings have taken hold of you."

"Number One, I am perfectly fine." Chronos's words were hollow, devoid of emotion and commitment. More than anything, he sounded exhausted. "I still have some pain, and it will be several more weeks before I am up and around fully, but I can assure you that when I am, my mental state will be no impediment to my continued efforts to subjugate the Rim."

She hesitated. The words were good, close at least to what she wanted to hear…but she did not believe any of it. Chronos was hurting, and the supreme confidence that had always been such a part of who he was gone.

But she had news she thought might help.

"The Rim dwellers have proven to be far more difficult adversaries than we had imagined, but that is no fault of yours, Chronos. I am as much to blame, for providing too little force to crush them quickly. I would correct that now, but I need you to return to your old form, to be the commander I need on this front."

She paused for a few seconds. "To be the commander we need to implement Project Zed, and to finish this war once and for all."

"Project Zed? It is ready?" She could hear a spark of renewed spirit in Chronos's voice. They had discussed deploying Zed to the Rim front a number of times, but she had been hesitant to agree, and the project had not been ready when they had last discussed it.

"It is not only ready, it is on its way to Dannith now."

Chronos was still weak, and his voice was soft, forced. But there was some sign, at least, of hope…or something struggling to become hope. "If it is all we have hoped, we truly will be able to finish this troublesome war…and finally bring these frustrating, gifted Rim dwellers into the Hegemony, for the good of all humanity."

"For the good of all humanity," she repeated. It was the mantra of the Hegemony, the very reason the great power existed. Too many of its people, she knew, Masters included, forgot that sacred duty.

Akella had been reluctant to throw Zed and the last of the reserves into the fight on the Rim, but her own extended visit had changed her mind. Chronos was right, the Rim dwellers were extraordinary. Their strength *had* to become part of the Hegemony…whatever the cost.

"There is something else, Chronos, another development effort I prioritized, and one that is also ready to implement, at least on a test basis. Red Storm."

She looked down as Chronos's eyes widened with surprise. Red Storm had been in development for some time, but he had been unaware of its recent status.

"This will all come as quite a surprise to our enemies. I have no doubt that, armed with Project Zed and Red Storm, you bring the Rim dwellers into the Hegemony where they belong. Where they must be."

Admiral's Quarters
CFS Dauntless

Tyler Barron sat quietly on the sofa, a stack of reports piled high on the table next to him, and Andi Lafarge's head on his leg. She was sleeping soundly, stretched out on the long couch, and he was both happy watching her rest, and a little jealous, too. Sleep had become a difficult thing for him, even more so than he'd let on to her. An hour or two a night had become the norm.

Than you think you've let on. Andi was always harder to fool than he expected. *For all you know, she's got detailed files on the whole thing. "Subject slipped into a light, proto-sleeplike state for forty-seven minutes, then woke up, screaming at a nightmare, and spent the next three hours, fifteen minutes working on fleet manifests."*

He wouldn't put it past her. He knew she loved him, that she would have harassed him about getting more sleep if she thought it would do any good. But she knew very well how little he liked being told what to do and, perhaps more to the point, she understood that he desperately wished he *could* sleep more. His sleeplessness was no choice of his own. The insomnia was a symptom of the war, and put against the millions who'd died, it didn't seem like that terrible a price to pay.

It did help him catch up on the workload. Hours passed slowly in the middle of the night with nothing to do, but it had been a very long time since he'd had nothing to do.

There was something else troubling him, too. He was still shaken about how close he'd come to losing Andi, how surely he'd believed he had. His feelings and his pain had given him a true glimpse at what Andi's death would feel like, and it haunted him like some unshakable spirit, invading his thoughts, rendering sleep that had been difficult, almost impossible.

His and Andi's relationship had been tumultuous, and one both of them had tried to keep at arm's length time and time again. He was a naval officer, sworn to a life of duty. She was a hardened adventurer, a fighter, a woman who had made her way through desperate frontiers and deadly conflicts since she'd been a teenager. She was hardly the type to fit into a role as "the admiral's wife" and, he was "the admiral," a designation as inescapable as the deepest, darkest prison.

But those were excuses. They'd struggled to stay apart, faced endless dangers, fought, argued, screamed at each other like the warriors they both were. None of it had driven them away from each other. Instead, every crisis, every danger, every stolen moment they shared, had only pushed them closer together.

He'd told himself a hundred times...*when the war is over, when there is peace, when things are less desperate...maybe then.* But he didn't believe that would ever happen, not anymore. He'd come to accept that his life would be one of war and strife, unending, for as long as he lasted, as many times as he managed to survive some deadly fight and press on.

It wasn't ideal in terms of hearth and home, far from it, but he'd decided one thing, finally. He would have whatever life he could have with Andi, whatever moments they could share...because he knew either one of them could lose the other at any time.

Besides...who decided what "the admiral's wife" should be...or what weapons she might pack under her magnificent gown at whatever interminable political reception they were compelled to attend.

Andi always looked comfortable in worn leather pants and a faded tunic, but she cleaned up awfully well, too.

Barron sighed softly. His people had won a great battle...but he knew the war had not ended, that no conclusion was in sight. He was tired of waiting, tired of pushing away the one thing that still brought him joy.

He figured it was about fifty-fifty she'd tell him he was crazy, but he'd faced worse odds than that and lived to tell about it.

He reached into his pocket, feeling around for the ring. The thing was nearly an artifact—it had been in his family for at least five generations, last gracing his mother's hand.

He wasn't going to disturb her sleep—he was far too practical for that, and he respected the value of a few hours rest.

But when she woke up, he was going to hand her the ring. He was going to ask her to marry him.

Blood on the Stars will Continue with

The Colossus
Book 12

Appendix

Strata of the Hegemony

The Hegemony is an interstellar polity located far closer to the center of what had once been the old empire than Rimward nations such as the Confederation. The Rim nations and the Hegemony were unaware of each other's existence until the White Fleet arrived at Planet Zero and established contact.

Relatively little is known of the Hegemony, save that their technology appears to be significantly more advanced than the Confederation's in most areas, though still behind that of the old empire.

The culture of the Hegemony is based almost exclusively on genetics, with an individual's status being entirely dependent on an established method of evaluating genetic "quality." Generations of selective breeding have produced a caste of "Masters," who occupy an elite position above all others. There are several descending tiers below the Master class, all of which are categorized as "Inferiors."

The Hegemony's culture likely developed as a result of its location much closer to the center of hostilities during the Cataclysm. Many surviving inhabitants of the inward systems suffered from horrific mutations and damage to genetic materials, placing a premium on any bloodlines lacking such effects.

The Rimward nations find the Hegemony's society to be almost alien in nature, while its rulers consider the inhabitants of the Confederation and other nations to be just another strain of Inferiors, fit only to obey their commands without question.

Masters

The Masters are the descendants of those few humans spared genetic damage from the nuclear, chemical, and biological warfare that destroyed the old empire during the series of events known as the Cataclysm. The Masters sit at the top of the Hegemony's societal structure and, in a sense, are its only true full members or citizens.

The Masters' culture is based almost entirely on what they call "genetic purity and quality," and even their leadership and ranking structure is structured solely on genetic rankings. Every master is assigned a number based on his or her place in a population-wide chromosomal analysis. An individual's designation is thus subject to change once per year, to adjust for masters dying and for new adults being added into the database. The top ten thousand individuals in each year's ratings are referred to as "High Masters," and they are paired for breeding matchups far more frequently than the larger number of lower-rated Masters.

Masters reproduce by natural means, through strict genetic pairings based on an extensive study of ideal matches. The central goal of Master society is to steadily improve the human race by breeding the most perfect specimens available and relegating all others to a subservient status. The Masters consider any genetic manipulation or artificial processes like cloning to be grievously sinful, and all such practices are banned in the Hegemony on pain of death to all involved. This belief structure traces from the experiences of the Cataclysm, and the terrible damage inflicted on the populations of imperial worlds by genetically-engineered pathogens and cloned and genetically-engineered soldiers.

All humans not designated as Masters are referred to as Inferiors, and they serve the Masters in various capacities. All Masters have the power of life and death over Inferiors. It is not a crime for a Master to kill an Inferior who has injured or offended that Master in any way.

Kriegeri

The Kriegeri are the Hegemony's soldiers. They are drawn from the strongest and most physically capable specimens of the populations of Inferiors on Hegemony worlds. Kriegeri are not genetically-modified, though in most cases, Master supervisors enforce specific breeding arrangements in selected population groups to increase the quality of future generations of Kriegeri stock.

The Kriegeri are trained from infancy to serve as the Hegemony's soldiers and spaceship crews, and are divided in two categories, red and gray, named for the colors of their uniforms. The "red" Kriegeri serve aboard the Hegemony's ships, under the command of a small number of Master officers. They are surgically modified to increase their resistance to radiation and zero gravity.

The "gray" Kriegeri are the Hegemony's ground soldiers. They are selected from large and physically powerful specimens and are subject to extensive surgical enhancements to increase strength, endurance, and dexterity. They also receive significant artificial implants, including many components of their armor, which becomes a permanent partial exoskeleton of sorts. They are trained and conditioned from childhood to obey orders and to fight. The top several percent of Kriegeri surviving twenty years of service are retired to breeding colonies. Their offspring are Krieger-Edel, a pool of elite specimens serving as mid-level officers and filling a command role between the ruling Masters and the rank and file Kriegeri.

Arbeiter

Arbeiter are the workers and laborers of the Hegemony. They are drawn from populations on the Hegemony's many worlds, and typically either exhibit some level of genetic damage inherited from the original survivors or simply lack genetic ratings sufficient for Master status. Arbeiter are from the same general group as the Kriegeri, though the soldier class includes the very best candidates, and the Arbeiter pool consists of the remnants.

Arbeiter are assigned roles in the Hegemony based on rigid assessments of their genetic status and ability. These positions range from supervisory posts in production facilities and similar establishments to pure physical labor, often working in difficult and hazardous conditions.

Defekts

Defekts are individuals—often populations of entire worlds—exhibiting severe genetic damage. They are typically found on planets that suffered the most extensive bombardments and bacteriological attacks during the Cataclysm.

Defekts have no legal standing in the Hegemony, and they are considered completely expendable. On worlds inhabited by populations of Masters, Kriegeri, and Arbeiters, Defekts are typically assigned to the lowest level, most dangerous labor, and any excess populations are exterminated.

The largest number of Defekts exist on planets on the fringes of Hegemony space, where they are often used for such purposes as mining radioactives and other similarly dangerous operations. Often, the Defekts themselves have no knowledge at all of the Hegemony and regard the Masters as gods or demigods descending from the heavens. On such planets, the Masters often demand ores and other raw materials as offerings, and severely punish any failures or shortfalls. Pliant and obedient populations are provided with rough clothing and low-quality manufactured foodstuffs, enabling them to devote nearly all labor to the gathering of whatever material the Masters demand. Resistant population groups are exterminated, as, frequently, are Defekt populations on worlds without useful resources to exploit.

Hegemony Military Ranks

Commander

Not a permanent rank, but a designation for a high-level officer in command of a large ship or a ground operation.

Decaron

A non-commissioned officer rank, the term defines a trooper commanding ten soldiers, including or not including himself. Decarons are almost always chosen from the best of the base level legionaries, pulled from combat units and put through extensive supplemental training before being returned to take their command positions.

Quinquaron

The lowest rank truly considered an officer. A quinquaron officially commands fifty troopers, though such officers are often assigned as few as twenty and as many as one hundred. Quinquarons can also be posted to executive officer positions, serving as the second-in-command to Hectorons. Such postings are common with officers on the fast track for promotion to Hectoron level themselves.

Hectoron

The commander of approximately one hundred soldiers, or a force equivalence of armored combat vehicles or other assets. As with other ranks, there is considerable latitude in the field, and Hectorons can command larger or smaller forces. The Hectoron is considered, in many ways, the backbone of the Hegemony armed forces.

Quingeneron

An officer commanding a combat force of five hundred soldiers or a comparable-strength force of heavy combat or support assets. In recent decades, the Quingeneron rank has been used more as a stepping stone to Kiloron status. Quingenerons also frequently serve as executive officers under Kilorons.

Kiloron

The commander of one thousand soldiers, or a posting of comparable responsibility. Despite the defined command responsibility, Kilorons often command significant larger forces, with senior officers of the rank sometimes directing combat units as large as twenty to fifty thousand. Kiloron is usually the highest level available to Kriegeri, though a small number have managed to reach Megaron status.

Megaron

The title suggests the command of one million combat soldiers or the equivalent power in tanks and other assets, however, in practice, Megarons exercise overall commands in combat theaters, with force sizes ranging from a few hundred thousand to many millions. Megarons are almost always of the Master class.

Blood on the Stars will Continue with

The Colossus
Book 12

41538171R00228

Printed in Poland
by Amazon Fulfillment
Poland Sp. z o.o., Wrocław